Michael E. Lloyd

OBSERVATION ONE

Singing of Promises

Published by Bewildering Press
The imprint of Bewildering Stories
Moses Lake, WA 98837

An initial version of this first novel in the *Observation* series appeared in the online magazine *Bewildering Stories* (www.bewilderingstories.com) in 2004-5.

Layout completed by John-Dan Key.

Published by
Bewildering Press
10075 Rd H N.E.
Moses Lake, WA 98837
www.bewilderingpress.com
www.bewilderingstories.com

ISBN 0-9787443-3-0

First BwP Edition: July 2007

Printed in the United States of America

Acknowledgements

With thanks to my trusty first readers in Europe and the USA, and to Jerry Wright and Don Webb of *Bewildering Stories* for their early faith and continued confidence in the *Observation* series.

MEL
Cambridge, England

To Michael & Alexandra, with my very best wishes.

Michael E. Lloyd

Lyrics from some very special songs illuminate this story:

For Susan, Janis, and my friends

... singing her siren song
luring you far from the harbor
and into the gales
she must be beautiful ... so beautiful
to have stolen the wind from my sails ...

Bilbao, Spain

The quiet, unassuming music student looked up abruptly from the textbook he was devouring, and found himself at once entranced by the sight of a smart young woman crossing the street towards the café and smiling broadly in his direction.

She selected the table farthest from him, but still quite close by, at the front corner of the patio next to the flower tub, and sat down facing back the way she had come.

'Yes,' he was rather ashamed to be thinking, 'a very elegant profile, too.' And unable to take his eyes off her for even a moment, he closed the book and returned it to his briefcase.

From the top of her shoulder bag she took a large denim jacket, draping it roughly over the chair on her left, and then pulled out a pocket camera, which she set down carefully on the small round table, again to her left.

The waiter appeared beside her.

'*Una cerveza y un agua.*' Her Spanish was rudimentary but, she persuaded herself, adequate for the task in hand.

She relaxed for two, perhaps three minutes, absorbing the late morning sun, adjusting her crimson scarf, occasionally closing her eyes as if composing herself. Then, as the waiter re-emerged, she delved into her own jacket, taking out what looked like an ultra-compact mobile phone. She paused, then pressed a single button.

The circuit must have been closed instantly.

She spoke clearly and rapidly in another tongue, leaning forward, looking down, never once putting the device to her ear. Then, after one more touch of a button, she slipped it back into her jacket pocket.

The waiter had, meanwhile, placed a small glass of beer beside the camera, and a half-filled goblet of water and its bottle directly in front of her. He had then moved off to serve another table. But both he, and the fascinated student who was now ordering an unplanned second beer for himself, then spotted her extracting a ten-euro note from a tiny purse and positioning it on top of the unexamined bill.

She sat fully back again, now looking suddenly drained. Once the waiter had retreated into the cool of the café's interior, she placed the camera and the denim jacket back in the bag, turned in her chair, and cast another irresistible smile in the direction of the café doors. Then she rose smartly and strolled off up the Gran Vía Don Diego López de Haro, leaving the beer and the water spoiling nicely in the sunshine.

The young man stood up unwittingly from his own table next to the doors, leaving a few more coins in payment for his second drink — this one also untouched and still inside on the waiter's tray. Puzzled, as he hurried past the woman's table, to see that the banknote had disappeared, despite the lack of any breeze, he began to follow her at a respectful distance.

* * *

The high-frequency signals routed from mobile phones to telecommunications satellites in geostationary orbit are ordinarily relayed straight back down to an appropriate ground station on the surface of the Earth, for onward transmission to the called party.

The extraordinary signal sent that Monday morning from a fashionable Bilbao café was, however, acted upon fully within the orbiting equipment which received it, with no need for further onward routing. And other eyes continued to follow the woman's movements, from a somewhat greater distance, but with considerably less risk of losing her.

* * *

Oh, the frustration! If only she could have picked up the water glass and discreetly poured its contents into that flower tub! It would have maintained the pretence so much better — and, from what she had seen so far, would have been so much more human ...

* * *

It took the authorities just over thirty minutes to get there — in three waves.

First at the scene, after a slow start which luckily would not need to be explained to their superiors, was the closest available *Policía Municipal* patrol car. Their orders were straightforward: to cruise up quietly, wait outside for the arrival of the special branch, and discourage the departure of anyone hoping to leave the premises.

The second car, coming across the city centre but arriving only four minutes later, had no such need for discretion, its driver desperate to keep his contribution to the speed of their response free from any subsequent reproach. He took the final junction on three wheels, veered across the path of an oncoming scooter with little care for the safety of its terrified rider, and screeched to an ugly halt on the pavement only inches from the front of the patrol car and a small corner table and low flower tub.

The uniforms-in-waiting had not previously met the lady and two gentlemen who now piled out of this unmarked car, but they were quick on the uptake and out of their own vehicle and following the newcomers towards the café doors without any demand for their IDs. But they were stopped halfway across the patio by the still-buzzing driver, who ordered them to stay with him and detain the dozen people sitting at the outdoor tables.

Nor did his superiors stand on much ceremony with the owner inside.

'Listen, *hombre*. How many people used a mobile phone here in the last ten minutes?'

The owner, who had been behind the bar for most of the morning, pleaded total ignorance and began praying for the survival of his licence and his teeth. He was saved from such fears by his waiter's rapid intervention.

'I didn't see one being used either. But there was a young guy out there, not long ago, with a phone in his shirt pocket. He paid up and left suddenly while I was inside, without even waiting for his second beer. I saw him walking off towards the square, as if he'd suddenly been told to go somewhere fast. And I think he stole some money from one of the tables ...'

While the woman extracted from the trembling waiter a brief but usable description, her colleague borrowed her phone, made a staccato call passing his situation report and demanding a large search force, told the control room to stand-by, handed back the phone and hurried out to brief the others. She proceeded to relay, calmly and very precisely, a jargon-rich summary of what she had learned from the waiter. Then, shouting at her partner and the bemused policemen to watch over the bar, its staff and its present clientele until told otherwise, she raced back out to their car and would have taken it over herself if the driver had not anticipated her intentions perfectly. His two-point reversing turn to get back into the downtown lane was executed blind, with the few words of caution muttered by his senior officer totally ignored, and only another miracle of timing avoiding a huge pile-up.

The military had been a good deal farther away, but their scrambles were more practised. Less than twenty minutes after the manhunt had been set in train, a helicopter approached the nearby Parque de Doña Casilda de Iturrizar. Its pilot realised quickly that his initial plan to land in the park itself was flawed; no touchdown was possible on that sharp and tree-clad incline. With the remonstrations of his high-ranking payload ringing in his headset, he descended instead onto a huge river-level building site just south of the Guggenheim Museum. The two officers who emerged had no choice but to zoom-in their GPS handhelds, find a way back up to street level, and literally run down the reported co-ordinates of the café across five or six blocks.

* * *

She walked for a minute or two. Then, once she was certain the young man was following her, she turned at the next corner, moved quickly into a shady doorway ... and un-made.

When he appeared, only moments later, a deep impression of loss showed suddenly on his face. She smiled to herself in satisfaction.

Five or six minutes passed, as he scanned the street up and down, hurried to the next block and peered both ways, retraced his steps to the corner, and searched around and around for her in vain. Finally, with a bitter sadness clearly overwhelming him, he crossed the road and languidly continued his interrupted walk back from his lecture. Now, unseen and unseeable, it was she who followed him.

They were taking a roundabout route. He was clearly still hopeful of stumbling across her again — or perhaps he just did not want to go wherever he had planned. They passed the Plaza de Bizkaia; he paused to watch the children laughing and shouting in the play area. She imagined again the sadness in his face.

They turned into Calle Ercilla. She sensed they were close to his home. She was ready to make her move.

Then the police car passed her, passed him, and stopped. And they took him.

Her surprise was great, but her resolve was undiminished. As the car sped off, she made her decision. Still observed by no human, she joined up with it in close outrider formation, and pursued it back towards the café.

* * *

The officers' plan, concocted in haste during the short helicopter flight, had anyway been to set up their initial base at the café, rather than get embroiled in the police dragnet. But as they turned the final corner, breathless and sweating, their radios informed them that the suspect had just been caught and was on his way back to the café to make their acquaintance.

* * *

'Name?'

They filled his vision — intimidating, violating, leeches on his soul.

'T ... Toni ... Antonio Felipe Murano,' he stammered.

'Age?'

'Twenty.'

'Address?'

He gave it.

'Your own place?'

'No — it's my parents' apartment.'

They checked his mobile phone first. It looked perfectly normal. The anti-terrorist officer who had been speaking seemed somehow deflated. His colleague was more impatient. He opened up the phone, expertly took it to pieces in seconds, found nothing extraordinary. They looked again at the well-dressed and trembling young man. There was already little doubt of the mistake.

'So why did you leave here so fast?'

'I was following the woman.' It felt like an admission of guilt.

'What woman?'

Toni took a deep breath. They seemed a little less aggressive now.

'She walked across the road about ten minutes after I'd sat down. She seemed to be heading straight towards me, and she was smiling right at me. It was almost unreal — the sort of thing you'd see in your dreams ...'

'OK, OK, Romeo — but what did she look like, what did she do?'

'She was smart. In her twenties, long dark hair, red silk scarf. I thought she might be coming over to my table. But she sat down at the corner and ordered drinks — two drinks. Then I realised she must have been holding on to the jacket and the camera for a friend — probably a man. I was a bit disappointed ...'

'What camera?'

'She took it out of her bag with a jacket, and put it on the table. But her friend never arrived. After a while she put the things back in the bag, then she suddenly turned round quite deliberately and smiled straight at me again. Then she just walked away without even touching the drinks ...'

Toni was abruptly aware of two photo flashes somewhere ahead of him.

'So why did you follow her?'

'I don't know. I really don't. I just couldn't stop myself. I've never done anything like that before!'

'What do you do for a living, Toni?'

'I'm a student — at the Conservatorio. Piano and History of Music ...'

'And your parents?'

'My father's an architect, and an evangelist preacher at the Santutxu church. And my mother's a freelance fashion writer. She's Italian.'

'Any Basque connections in the family? And don't mess us about — we'll be checking.'

'No — for God's sake!' He was scared again. They were watching his reaction like hawks.

'Stay there, Toni.'

They searched his briefcase. They found textbooks, classical sheet music, lecture notes, a modern songbook, a magazine. He watched them muttering to each other.

They were being forced to accept that this timorous boy had simply been fascinated by the woman for the obvious reasons, and nothing else. One of them went a little further. 'That kid looks like he's never been near a real woman in his life.'

But there was no time for further debate. So now they quizzed the special branch inspector, who had only just returned and had been waiting uncomfortably at a suitable distance, seemingly outranked and reluctant to intervene. And they discovered it was the waiter who had given the false lead. So it was his turn next. He confirmed everything the student had just told them, and then he mentioned a dictation machine ...

'I guessed she was a foreign journalist.' ... 'No, I've never heard that language before.' ... 'No, it can't have been a mobile phone — she was just talking straight into it, like this.' ... 'Yes, right next to that camera.'

Then a new false penny dropped for this new set of agents. The camera was obviously part of the transmitting equipment. Somewhere around the city a major terrorist incident should by now have been triggered! Why on earth hadn't they heard about it yet?

They pressed Toni and the waiter for fuller descriptions, and then issued an urgent demand to the special branch inspector for a second intensive search: this time, for the elegant young woman with the captivating smile.

Their new target had been observing all of this at very close quarters. She now began to recognise in broad terms just what had happened, and she was feeling frustration and considerable sympathy for the young man's plight.

She watched while the officers consulted, re-interviewed, worried, radioed, argued, and consulted again. She watched Toni standing there alone and scared; saw him finally sitting down at the table she had earlier used, looking around for some explanation, finding none. And they both just waited.

* * *

At last the officer who had examined the mobile phone came over to Toni and crouched down beside him.

'Did you steal the money she left on the table?'

'There was no money left on her table! It must have blown away!'
He was feeling angry now, and something inside him wanted to fight.

It was exactly the reaction the officer had expected. He knew the
boy was telling the truth. He looked over to his partner and shook his
head.

'All right, Toni. Looks as if you just got caught in the crossfire.
Here's your briefcase, and your phone — it's switched off, but it's
still working. The patrol car will drive you home now.'

With that he was gone, back inside the café.

* * *

Still unseen, she followed the car back to where Toni had been picked
up. She watched it drive off round the first corner, as they both crossed
the street towards a large residential building. Pursuing him
effortlessly through the main entrance, and then into the lift, she
finally re-made a few feet behind him, as he unlocked and opened the
door of his parents' apartment.

'*Hola,*' she ventured.

Toni started, turned round, and saw that smile once again.
Dumbfounded, but now smiling shyly himself, he stood to one side
and ushered her in, then followed, closing the door gently behind him.

She was irresistible; but it did not seem sexual. She commanded his
attention in a quite unknown but delicious way.

He felt an urge, impossible to ignore, to hear music playing.
Forgetting all courtesies, he made a clumsy bee-line for his parents'
sound system and selected his favourite Janis Ian CD.

> *Would you like to learn to sing?*
> *Would you like to sing my song?*
> *Would you like to learn to love me best of all?*

Then he turned back towards her, looked her fully in the eyes, and
spoke, in his native Spanish, which he had now heard her use twice.
'What is your name, *señorita*?'

She clearly did not understand, though she clearly wanted to. So he
pointed to himself. 'Toni. My name is Toni.'

She smiled in recollection and recognition.

He tried again. 'But who are you?'

Once more her face was blank. He nervously pointed towards her, afraid to offend, desperate to touch, desperate not to. 'And you?'

Now she understood. Now she felt ready to exercise the little Spanish she had absorbed in the last few hours. But she had an able and willing partner for conversation. She could proffer, at this stage, only a few simple nouns, verbs and adjectives, but Toni, with surprising ease, would find himself supplying all the grammar needed to turn her efforts into perfectly understandable Spanish.

'Choose a name for me, Toni.'

He searched around in his mind for a moment or two, and then, without knowing why, said simply 'Carla.'

She smiled in appreciation. 'Carla. Yes. I shall be Carla.'

Toni felt his knees suddenly weaken, and he sank into the sofa, motioning his guest to sit down beside him.

'Do you live here alone, Toni?'

'No. It's my parents' place. But they're away for a few days in Barcelona.'

'So nobody else will be visiting you today?'

'No. Well, maybe ... no.'

'Are you sure?'

'Yes, Carla.'

'Are you happy to be here with me, Toni?'

'Oh, yes. I can't explain the feeling — but yes, I am ...'

Carla smiled again, her smile as warm and deep as the lagoons of her homeland. Slipping smoothly off the sofa and down onto her knees immediately in front of him, she slowly raised her arms and extended her hands towards his face.

Any moment now she would be holding his head in those beautiful hands. Any moment now ...

> *And when my party's over*
> *You can fall in love with me ...*

Transferral Sphere

Toni had been confidently anticipating a kiss.

He had of course done nothing to encourage one — that was certainly not in his nature. Despite often picking up hints that he was considered "cute" by many of the girls at school, and now by those at the Conservatorio, he had always been terrified of getting a bad and noisy reaction from an unwilling object of affection. Which was why he had actually kissed very few young ladies in his first twenty years. In fact, leaving Paula aside ...

But he had not tried to discourage one, either. A kiss had just seemed pleasantly inevitable.

Instead, he slowly sensed (no, he was quite certain) that he was in two places at once.

He was undoubtedly still in his parents' living room, with his soothing music still playing. But Carla, so close only seconds before (or so it seemed), had disappeared.

And he was also in a quiet and gently-lit space, intimate but with no clear boundaries. It felt very natural. Or perhaps just comforting: definitely not threatening, thank goodness. He hated confrontation.

But the clock on the wall was telling him that over an hour had passed since he had walked through the door. How could that possibly be? And he knew that the song now playing began nearly halfway through the album ...

He turned and said 'I set you free' ...

And though nobody had taken Carla's place, there was a new voice speaking to him now. At least, his common sense and his brain both told him it was speaking — and in his mother tongue of Spanish. But before he had digested even the first few words, he knew there were no sounds in that other space; nothing to disturb his music ...

This must feel a little strange for you, Toni.

Relax. You will enjoy what is to come. It will enrich you,
as does your music.

Are you feeling comfortable?

'Well, yes I am, as it happens. But I'm also very confused! What
am I doing here? I don't understand this other place inside my room ...
and the woman has gone again!'

He was definitely speaking aloud, he knew it — and it did feel
strange to be addressing that space so empty of objects and sounds.

Toni, your present state is a little like what you appear to
call "hypnosis" — and it is also, I think, rather more than
that suggests. But you need have no fear. Carla is still with
you. She is also here with me. We are all together.

'Ah!' He was smiling widely again.

Carla has chosen to work with you, Toni. She feels great
affinity with you. Do you feel this too?

'Yes, I do. Oh, yes. But I still think you ought to ...'

That is good. Carla is very pleased. She is smiling too.

'Well, you both seem very kind — and polite. More polite than
those policemen ...'

Ah, yes. That was most unfortunate.

You too are very polite, Toni. We have been rapidly
learning all about you. Carla needs to understand you
extremely well, you see. And since we promise, in return,
to tell you much about ourselves, we hope that you will
not object to this too strongly. Are we right?

'Well yes, I suppose so. I don't understand why, but I *do* want to
get to know Carla, to share with her. But on the other hand ...'

Then all is well. And I am happy to report that we have
completed our learning of all there is to know of you —
indeed, of everything you know.

Toni, you have opened your soul to Carla. You can now begin to help her, and she, in turn, can enrich you.

> *He said 'Come unto me*
> *I am beauty*
> *I am the light*
> *Come unto me ...'*

'In what ways?'

That will soon become clear.

In sharing yourself with Carla, you have quickly provided a fascinating picture for us. Because, you see, it is the only detailed insight into your world that we have at this time.

We have already seen much from a distance, and also in close-up — and we have heard much noise, but it still means little to us.

It is Carla's task to reveal what we cannot yet observe or understand. But to do this, Toni, she needs an interpreter, and a guide, and a friend.

In short, she needs an Illuminator. And this will be your role.

'Look, I admit I'm fascinated by Carla, but I'm not at all sure about any of this. You can't just come in here and start telling me what to do ...'

Toni, I had hoped you would not argue so hard and so soon. If you will only hear me out, you will quickly become much more comfortable with the situation. Please allow me to explain things properly.

'Well ...'

Toni, you are a musician. That is how Carla located you. But since you are dedicating yourself to the arts and you are still young, you may not yet be especially rich in other areas of knowledge. Do you have a good understanding of the physical sciences?

'No — I was never very interested in science at school. Music, and poetry, and art, and history ... oh, and beer — they're the things I care about. But look, I really ...'

> Yes, we are well aware of all this. I simply wanted you to acknowledge it to yourself. You will now be quite open to understanding what I need to tell you. Are you ready to learn?

Toni felt a sudden drop in his level of resistance, and he knew it had not been of his own doing.

'Well, yes, I suppose I am ... oh, wait a minute, I don't even know your name yet!'

> Ah, I have already broken with protocol. I have failed in what I believed had been so well rehearsed. As Carla herself has already done. To err is clearly not just human! I apologise sincerely.

> We now know the importance which names hold for you. So, perhaps you will think of me as "Quo". I feel this may carry some meaning for you ...

> The woman you know as Carla is not of your world. You have already concluded this for yourself. Carla's world, at this time, is here with me and our other colleagues.

> We are explorers, Toni; we are discovering New Worlds. We know you will understand this. We see, from knowing you, that your own country once sent men on great travels to new worlds on your Earth ...

'You mean the voyages of Columbus?'

> Just so. We come to your world as Columbus came to his new lands.

> > *There's never much to read between*
> > *the lines of what we need*
> > *and what we'll take ...*

'Well, that's not particularly reassuring, Quo! Columbus was not just a peaceful explorer, you know — especially on his later voyages! But how can you know of him anyway, if the Earth is not your world?'

> Because we now know you, Toni. We knew nothing of Columbus until a few brief minutes of your time ago. But now we know everything you know of him — and everything you know of your world's other great explorers. Do you understand this?

'I don't think so. I am trying hard to — and I'm not fighting you just for the sake of it ...'

> We know that, Toni. You would, in any case, find fighting very difficult — and fruitless. But you are already proving a great support to Carla.

'Oh ... thank you.' Toni was abruptly smiling again. Grinning from ear to ear.

> And I shall try harder to help you understand.

> > *We live beyond our means*
> > *on other people's dreams ...*

> Carla is close to you still, although you cannot see her. You *will* see her again very soon. She has helped us to learn your knowledge and your memories. To learn your thoughts, your pleasures and your fears. So that she can later share with you, and enrich you; so that we can know your world, and enrich us all.

> May I now share a little more about ourselves?

'Yes, I think I would like you to do that. But, you know, I really should be practising at the piano right now, and I'm worried I'll be late for my meeting with ... wait a minute, I can't remember her name ... oh, this is crazy ... ah, yes, with Paula.'

> > *... and no-one's looking on to say*
> > *'You're mine' ...*

Toni, can you imagine the challenges that faced your Columbus, or any other explorer, when he approached those unknown shores? Different landscapes, different peoples, different languages, different outlooks, and great potential for hostility directed against him and his crews. Can you imagine how he felt?

'Of course.'

And the natives: what is their reaction to the sight of these strangers? It can only be fear and an instinct for self-defence, can it not? Particularly since, merely because they have been able to travel there, the explorers will be assumed to have greater powers and more sophisticated technologies than those they are visiting ...

'Again, I can't argue with you. I wrote such things in my history essays at school.'

Of course you did. But how deeply did the challenges of true exploration strike you? How could a Captain, despatched by his monarchs on a mission of exploration, be sure of persuading the natives of the new world that he came only with the goal of simple discovery? How could he come to understand their languages and their ways, their knowledge and their beliefs? How could he safely chart their lands?

With so much potential fear and distrust, the slightest error of judgement could be fatal. Would he be well advised to simply wade ashore with a smile on his face and his hands raised in a gesture of peace? How many such approaches probably ended with an arrow in the heart?

'He'd need to arrive in secret, Quo, if he possibly could. He'd want to minimise the taking of risks, and find a way of gaining trust and keeping it, and slowly establish the information he sought.'

Precisely, Toni. You are a good student of all history, not just that of music!

'It's simply good political theory. The persuading couldn't be achieved with any certainty by shouting to the masses from the hilltops, or these days by using radio or television. Some sort of infiltration would be the only way; to earn the trust of individuals, and gradually build a picture ...

'But maybe persuading shouldn't be in the plan at all, Quo. Just fact-finding. That *was*, after all, your explorer's objective, wasn't it? Assuming of course that discovery really *was* the only goal of his patrons ...'

> Toni, you continue to prove to us that your insight is truly great.

'Hmmm. But anyway, why should those individual natives choose to co-operate?'

> Because they would quickly perceive that there *was* no threat, and that mutual understanding was a goodness in its own right. The explorer might also offer to help them in some way. As we have already agreed, he would probably have more sophisticated tools and techniques to share with them, for their own personal benefit and for the broader good ...

'Yes, I do feel that's how it could be — and I suspect that what we're discussing is closely related to what's happening to me here and now.'

> You are absolutely right.

'Let me think about this for a moment.'

> *Sometimes I feel like*
> *I haven't learned anything ...*

'Quo, I've realised I have an awful lot of questions on my mind.'

> I know this, Toni. And I want you to ask them all. I do not wish to simply give you lots of uninvited answers, even though I could. That would not serve our purpose well.

'I don't know where to begin. So much has happened in the last few hours ...'

> Begin at the beginning.

'Well — if Carla has come here exploring with you, and has made contact with me, then she's obviously your infiltrator. But how could she have waded ashore? How is it that she looks so perfectly human? And why Bilbao? Why me? Why has she gone away again? Where are the rest of you? And ...'

> *It's a sacrificial altar*
> *and I'm laying down my head*
> *and I'm telling you up front*
> *that I haven't much to give ...*

Be patient, Toni. I shall help you to understand much of this immediately. For it is essential that you do understand. And Carla, as you have named her, will later tell you more ...

Carla is a member of our crew. She is a Handler — and a Finder. Her role is indeed to infiltrate, although I can see that this word has worrying implications for you. Remember our earlier conversation, and think of her instead as the brave and honest missionary who secretly paddles to shore, and befriends the natives, and develops the insights of the explorers.

> *Every body has its price*
> *Mine is yours for free*
> *if you'll be in love with me ...*

Our Carla plays her part in the mission from her Handler's Studio here on our craft. She cannot physically travel to the surface of your planet and operate there. There are countless reasons for this, as I can see you appreciate.

The other Carla, the Carla you have met and embraced so happily, is ... let me try to make a label from your language heritage — I know how important labels are for you ... your Carla is a "Radimote".

'Quo, this is getting a little difficult again!'

Not really, Toni. Just allow your wondrous mind to relax for a moment and work its magic for you ...

Santander, Spain

The Commander, Anti-Terrorism (North) of CeSID, the Spanish Intelligence Agency, barred his phone and closed the door of his office with a firmness which made it clear to everyone outside that it would stay closed until he chose to re-open it. He needed to clear his head again, and think harder.

Things had started to go crazy at seven o'clock the previous evening. That had been the end of his Sunday with the family. He couldn't have had more than an hour's sleep since then, and it was still far from over.

Two huge concurrent bursts of radio energy, the alerts had trumpeted; coming from somewhere on high, very close to each other, and directed at the northern coast of Spain.

The Spanish army, air force, navy and internal security forces had been on joint anti-terrorist rapid-reaction stand-by for many years, of course, with helicopters stationed near the high-risk areas. Bilbao was certainly one of those. His biggest headache.

So, *he* owned the problem within CeSID. And his phone had scarcely stopped ringing. Every imaginable defence and policing agency in and around Europe, and some others that very few people could ever imagine, had gone secretly onto their highest levels of security alert. And they all wanted answers and action.

Sure, it had been feared for some time that subversive elements might try to re-programme an existing communications satellite, for terrorist purposes. But he could offer no explanations to those who were hounding him. No, there were *not* two malfunctioning satellites in that area of the sky at that time — no, not even one! They knew that anyway. How was he supposed to know what had caused the signals? That's what he expected someone to tell *him*.

And it had gone on like that; round and round the same argument, with countless "extremely important" callers (extremely impotent, he had started to call them now), throughout the night and most of the morning.

Then, just when things had begun to calm down, when those callers were probably at last starting to focus on what, if anything, they should tell their minor politicians and the press, there had been that abrupt, very strong signal from the centre of Bilbao itself. That really *had* worried him; it was probably the precursor to some terrible attack. His people had reacted fast — they had been airborne within five minutes. Then it had all gone badly wrong, with that stupid false lead ...

And there had been no incident, anyway.

What *was* that signal from Bilbao? It must have generated a strong sympathetic transmission on a particular mobile phone frequency, because the initial reaction of the first monitoring station to jump on it was that a "doctored" phone was being used for something special.

This conclusion was then obviously just simplified down, at the Bilbao HQ, to an abrupt order to the local special branch: "Find a mobile phone at these co-ordinates." All the Bilbao police forces were on continuous alert for terrorist activity, anyway. Rapid over-reaction this time, perhaps — because the reports were *now* suggesting it had not been a phone call, but something more sophisticated ...

Well, whatever the reasons, they had lost those precious early moments — and with every minute that passed now, the chances of picking up that woman grew slimmer. She sounded like the sort of operator who would have an extremely good escape plan. But why do it all in public? Was she a separatist? What sort of signal had she sent? Where to? Who to? Why? And what had been done with the message?

Nobody had come back to him with any answers — not even something on the type of signal. That was what bothered him most. Why couldn't all those techies crack it? It seemed to be as big a mystery as yesterday's. So, were they related? They *had* to be — the coincidence was too great. But then again — it was certain that no known satellites were misbehaving. And no newly-rich power had tossed up two rockets in the last few days to deploy two new ones! The very idea of that was laughable, of course. No, yesterday's events must just have been some strange sort of cosmic radiation, something for the eggheads to puzzle over for months to come. Just because the rays happened to strike the Earth near Bilbao, everyone assumed the worst ...

If they *did* strike the Earth, that is ...

He had been trying to sort this one out in his mind for hours now. Why had there been no reports stating exactly *where* the rays had ended up? Surely that mattered? Why had the monitoring agencies only discussed the sources of the bursts of energy, and not mentioned their targets? Didn't he need to know this, to be able to deliver the goods they were demanding? Without such clues, they were just searching for a needle in a haystack; and that needle wearing the red scarf had made her clever escape, many hours earlier ...

But he could not conjure up the answers. He had to work with what they had been given, and the precious little his team had since discovered.

He picked up the phone and issued two new sets of orders.

To his agents in Bilbao: 'Get more men. Widen the search. Stay with it till 1700 hours. Then drop it. Debrief at 0800 tomorrow, my office — I want some sleep tonight!'

And to his personal assistant: 'Another pot of coffee — and find me a sandwich!'

Briefing Sphere

Are you feeling a little more comfortable now, Toni?

'I think so, Quo ...'

Then may I continue?

'Well, I'm not at all sure! I know there are lots of other things I really ought to be doing this afternoon ...'

They can wait, Toni. They can all wait ...

> *How do you do*
> *would you like*
> *to be friends?*

Now, as you know very well, your Columbus made his voyages to the New World in sea-going flotillas of various shapes and sizes.

We, on the other hand, have come to your shores from our own world — let us call it "Dome" ... that should help you — in a single, very large craft. I have just been searching your languages again for an appropriate name for our temporary home. The *"Mater"* seems to suit its several roles quite nicely.

'Well, I can see the obvious meanings ...' said Toni, cautiously. His Latin and English were sound; however, he was already a little concerned at the less desirable allusions for a Spanish speaker. But he said no more, preferring to hold on to the new and attractive images of himself and Carla which had just appeared uncontrollably to his mind's eye.

Ah, Toni, that is much better — I see you really are entering into the spirit of things now!

We arrived in the vicinity of your Earth quite recently. The mode and duration of our voyage here need not concern you; from what we have observed so far, even your finest scientists would not comprehend it. Natives and explorers again — which I hope will not offend you.

'I'm not offended, Quo. But I did think it was quite impossible for people to travel those huge distances between the stars!'

Toni, if you can accept that our entire crew greatly looks forward to being back at Dome in the not-too-distant future, you will perhaps believe that we can indeed cover such distances well within our own long lifespans ...

'Well, I don't understand it. But I suppose I must accept it.'

Excellent!

Light a light, light a light for me ...

As we approached your Earth, Toni, we were easily able to measure its dimensions and analyse its atmosphere. It is a core aim of our mission to conduct such geographical observations and fact-finding.

But you will appreciate that this has to be an exclusively one-way observation. We now see much evidence of the Earth's own technological eyes and ears and defence mechanisms — and naturally, we do not wish to alert those systems any more than is absolutely necessary.

So we have arrived veiled in a cloak that prevents them from detecting the *Mater* in any way; just as your armed forces, as we now recognise, have similar but more basic techniques for rendering their own aircraft apparently invisible.

However, we need to come much closer still, both to achieve the accuracy we require in our physical data collection, and then to move on to our next great aim: to understand the ways in which your peoples live and think and act in this world.

Lover, am I coming home again ...

Are you following me so far, Toni?

'Oh, yes. It's quite clear — I think! I'm just trying to juggle all the questions that keep coming into my mind ...'

They will all be answered.

'I hope so, Quo ...'

So, Toni, we have entered an orbit above the Equator. We are slightly farther away from you than the many small satellites you have placed in a very special circle around your planet. Their height above the Earth allows each of them to fall towards you forever, yet always be the same distance from you, and always above a particular point.

And although we are a little beyond them — it is very crowded in that ring of gleaming metal, and we are a large craft compared with those fragile birds — we too can maintain such a fixed position, by making continuous minor adjustments to our velocity.

So now we hover over your Africa, and we see all of your Europe spread out before us (it is good to know their names at last, and to use them with you) — and we can see in close-up and high-resolution, when we so choose.

'And that's good enough for what you're trying to discover?'

Ah no, Toni. It is a bird's-eye view only — which has many weaknesses. Columbus could only make very limited observations from the safe vantage point of his ship. A rather two-dimensional view. We must also have the surface view; we must come among you.

And this is Carla's role.

Carla, with me up on the *Mater*, is the Handler. Carla, down there with you, is the Finder.

'I'm trying very hard here, Quo. But I think you'll need to explain it more clearly for me.'

Of course, Toni ...

Carla the Finder is a radimote.

We create her using many technologies, including some which we see you have already learned to exploit in very basic ways on Earth: laser beams for the powerful focusing of uniform light, radio waves for vision and sound, radar for detecting and measuring distances, capacitors for storing energy, and much, much more.

But simply and essentially ... the Carla you have met and embraced in spirit, Toni, is a many-dimensioned, opaque, mobile hologram.

...for my true love is gone.

'But wait — surely that means ...?'

Please allow me to finish, Toni.

To produce her for you, we generated a laser beam of immense power. That beam was then split in two, and each half was passed through many different systems on the way to its own transceiver. There is one of those sited at each extreme of our craft — a separation of many kilometres in your terms!

Each of the beams then travelled the long distance to your Earth — and the two of them finally came together again at a very particular point ...

It's a long, long time 'til morning
plays wasted on the dawn ...

Before we could begin this process, Toni, the Handler needed to be comfortably installed in her special studio on the *Mater*. She had a very demanding task ahead of her, for which she has rehearsed long and hard.

Only when she was fully ready did she give the command. Then the laser fired — and the radimote was born, in its little image sphere, just a few feet wide.

It will never reflect Carla's own person: it will instead always present whatever image she chooses for it. At that time, of course, we had no proper images to copy. But we did not yet need any. We did not wish the people of Earth to believe they were seeing the first ever flying human, as it glided to land before their very eyes!

'You have a good sense of humour, Quo.'

I have learned much of it from you, Toni.

So Carla's first real task as Handler was then to locate a suitable initial image for Carla the Finder to adopt. Once this was done, and fully remembered, the radimote was ready at last to become visible — to be "made" — whenever the Handler wished.

Of course, when several images have been learned in this way, the one presented by the radimote can be changed by the Handler at any time — and elements of each can be readily combined. And whenever necessary, there may be no image visible at all; the one currently presented can be instantly "un-made" at the Handler's will. As you have discovered, Toni, your Carla can disappear.

> *And now I lay me down to sleep*
> *forever by your side.*

Now, positioning the radimote for the first time required a major release of energy from the *Mater*. This was impossible to disguise, and it must have been highly noticeable on Earth. This is one of those few risks we are forced to take.

Many great minds must now be puzzling over the cause of those recently observed radio bursts, from two close but invisible sources — as well as the very different burst produced on the surface earlier today, with those rather unexpected side-effects ...

'You know, Quo, I think Carla is the White Rabbit.'

I beg your pardon?

'I think I must be dreaming. I sit in the sun, I drink a glass of beer, then along comes Carla. She makes a bit of a show, I follow her, and then she disappears down a rabbit-hole. I have all those problems with the police, then Carla pops up again, and now here I am in a wonderland of Cheshire cats and disembodied voices. It's obvious. I'm Alice, and I'm dreaming her story.'

> Toni, I do apologise: I was slow to register the connection you had already made with a story you have recently re-read. I see now the logic in all you have said. You really have a finely suggestible mind! Carla is very lucky to have found you.

> But I can assure you that you are not dreaming. And since you have nothing to lose by continuing to learn, may we proceed?

'Well, if you insist; it *is* all quite fascinating. But, you know, I'll definitely be late for Paula at this rate, and I'm worried about that! She's going to be so annoyed ...'

> *This is a lover's lullabye ...*

> Now, that first positioning locates the radimote well above the surface of the Earth (or whatever world we are exploring). It is very important to avoid the beams' hitting the ground on the initial firing — all those different types of reflection would cause many unwanted effects, believe me!

> So, the two beams come together at a carefully planned height. In the case of your Earth, this is somewhere between a kilometre and a mile above the surface.

With good luck we can position the radimote within a hundred metres of the intended level. And that low altitude of about 4000 feet allows the Handler to conduct a rapid and well-informed final descent.

'All these numbers are a bit too much for me, Quo!'

I am sorry, Toni. You said you were no scientist. It is rather hard to get the balance right on one's first real engagement, you know. No more numbers — I promise you!

'Thank you.'

But after the initial positioning, and the procedure of "gliding to land" (Carla will tell you later of her own glide to Earth; she is very proud of that story — things did not go precisely to plan: your weather turns out to be very unpredictable), the energy level required to sustain the radimote, and to move it around in its new world, is extremely low. Indeed, you would call it merely "noise level", and it is not readily detectable on Earth.

So all the subsequent movements of the Finder are done in complete radio stealth.

> *Softly now — close your eyes*
> *Lightly will you fade ...*

From the moment the radimote is born, Toni, it is under the Handler's full control. The beams transmit exactly what the Handler continuously thinks about doing next. She has no need to physically move around in her studio.

Whenever the radimote is actually presenting an image, its physical posture and movements and locomotion will actively follow the Handler's exact train of thought. And its body language will reflect the Handler's emotions.

'That's just what I keep worrying about ...'

So, Toni, the radimote becomes the vehicle for the Handler to travel freely and participate fully in the world under survey. And "freely" means exactly that — the radimote is not constrained to the speed of unassisted humans. Its image sphere can move as fast as the Handler chooses. It can follow fire engines — or even trains and aeroplanes.

And not just in open spaces, but also inside buildings — because the beams, and all the radio waves they carry, pass harmlessly through most solid materials, such as those used for normal roofs or walls. Of course, we had to hope this would apply to the building materials used on Earth; fortunately, that has proved to be the case, so far ...

But the power of the beams can be degraded if the material is too dense, or if there are too many layers. We tested the procedures for recovering from this as fully as time allowed, back at Dome. We do not want to lose our radimote! That would mean starting all over again, with another big radio disturbance ...

Is this still all quite clear to you, Toni?

'Yes, I think so, Quo. You're a good teacher. I've just been amusing myself by thinking about the risks of your radimote bumping into a plane as they both come in to land!'

Your sense of humour will serve you well, Toni! Do not worry: there is a lot of sky around your aeroplanes and the radimote; and anyway, if there were a "collision", the pilot would know nothing of it — and the Handler would merely observe the plane's passage. The radimote has no substance — it is purely waves of energy.

'Yes, of course it is! But that means that Carla ...'

Toni, you and Carla will share much in the days to come. Be calm, and I shall paint the final part of this picture for you ...

'No, hold on, Quo! How can the radimote see those things all around it? You said the bird's-eye view was no good for that. How can it hear me talking? And how can it speak to me? In Spanish, for God's sake ...'

Ah, you are running ahead of me once more. So many questions!

As you clearly appreciate, Toni, the radimote — well, the Handler in truth — naturally needs to become quickly familiar with some key elements of its new environment.

And yes, the familiarisation process must include visually observing local native behaviour, and listening in to their conversations to establish a basic vocabulary, primarily of nouns and verbs — the sophistications of grammar are, at least at this early stage, something of a luxury for the radimote! And it also needs to be able to communicate actively, as soon as it can.

Any one can learn the words
and the melody's so plain ...

So those intensive beams from the *Mater*, which are focused in the radimote, support many other important functions, including those of "sight, hearing and speech" which you are so keen to understand.

'Yes, I am!'

But Carla and I would like to leave an explanation of this until a little later. We need to move ahead right now ...

'All right, Quo — if you really insist ...'

Toni, we have heard this song before, have we not?

'Oh, yes. The system is set on continuous repeat. You are very attentive.'

Ah, music is part of our life-blood ...

There is just one more very important thing to tell you right now, Toni.

The radimote's appearance and movements can be so accurate, and can seem perfectly natural for the world in which it is operating (for example, subject to your normal gravity), because the Handler sees very well, and learns rapidly, and has the ability to copy what she sees with great precision.

This copying includes not only the physical appearance of any selected persona, but also all its clothing and accessories. Those can be moved around at will by the radimote. They can even be positioned physically separated from it by a small distance, within the small image sphere generated by the focused beams. And they can subsequently be retrieved.

But when the radimote moves on, it is the image sphere that is moving, and any accessories that are "left behind" just fade from view, for ever.

And, naturally, the radimote cannot in any way exert a physical force on an object that is not part of its own transmitted image.

So, as you observed, Carla the Finder could remove a jacket and a camera from a bag she had been carrying, and place them on a chair, and later retrieve them and put them back in the bag. But she could not pick up a real glass of water that had been placed on the table by an occupant of the Earth possessing muscles made for lifting and pushing and pulling. And you spotted that the banknote had vanished, didn't you? A radimote's act is not an easy one, Toni — and it needs a very good supporting actor, as you will surely be.

> *We sound so good together*
> *and so poorly sung alone ...*

So there we have it. The radimote looks like a human. It can move around just like a human. As Carla has demonstrated, it can see, it can hear, and it can speak — and we shall later explain exactly how, as I have promised. It can learn very fast. But it has no senses of taste or smell, nor does it stimulate with a scent of its own — and of course, it does not eat or drink.

Being out and about with Carla will pose some challenges for both of you, Toni! She has spent much time learning that she must not apparently bump into people, or walk through solid walls or panes of glass within the public gaze. The image would come to no harm — but the illusion would be compromised.

And finally — Carla cannot touch things. She cannot touch you. And you must not try to touch her. It would destroy so much. I hope that is clear to you.

'Yes, Quo, it is clear, though it saddens me to hear it. But I really think I need to be leaving now ...'

Ah, Toni, it is clearly time for us to take a short break. Maybe a little walk around the room? And then I shall tell you of the very special role that you are to play with Carla, in the days to come ...

Not Together Now

A tall, slim teenager with long fair hair emerged from the cool interior of the Bilbao Conservatorio into the heat and brilliance of a beautiful spring afternoon. She turned at the first corner and, encumbered as always by her bulky cello case and a large canvas bag, she made her halting way down Colón de Larreategui like a pretty flamingo with a wooden leg.

Arriving at last at Bar La Masia, she gratefully took the weight of the case off her shoulder, trundled it inside, and flopped down at the nearest table.

She forced a breathless smile, and as usual her green eyes flashed. '*Hola, Alberto!*'

She's meeting that boy again, the owner thought, as he returned her greeting and immediately began to prime the espresso machine.

'And some olives please — I'm starving!'

'Don't you ever eat anything else, Paula? Look — we've just made a beautiful cherry tart ...'

'Stop it, Alberto! You know I hardly eat during the day! Anyway,' she intoned gravely, 'my body is a temple ...'

'It will end up a very meagre temple if you carry on like this!'

'Albi ...' she cautioned.

'Well, I don't know! Where do you get the energy to do all those aerobics every evening?'

'Maybe you should try it yourself, *hombre*,' she countered, staring pointedly at his ample belly. 'Anyway, where's that coffee? I'm parched. You'd better make sure there's a beer in the cooler, too ...'

* * *

She had gone very quiet. Alberto had never seen her like that. But the boy had still not arrived, and that was unusual too. There was another plate of olives ready and waiting for them, and he had made sure the beer was nice and cold ...

He busied himself behind the quiet bar, surprised at the growing concern he was feeling for her. It was the look on her face; it suggested far more than mere annoyance or disappointment at her friend's lateness.

She had finally stopped pretending to read her lecture notes and was presumably trying to phone him. An immediate look of disgust. Obviously: "The mobile phone you are calling is switched off". She was trying another number now. Ah, this time it must be ringing for her — and ringing, and ringing. Nobody at home. He felt compelled to sympathise.

'Is everything OK, *señorita*?'

'Yes, Alberto ... yes, thank you, I'm fine.'

A bad liar.

'Some more olives?'

'No, thank you. I must go. I have a lot to do. If Toni turns up ...'

'Yes ...'

'No, it doesn't matter. I'm sure he'll call me soon. *Hasta luego, Alberto.*'

'Hasta luego, señorita.'

Missioning Sphere

Lay down and slumber
Mama's boy is torn asunder
All the fields have gone grey
All the leaves are gone brown ...

Are you rested now, Toni?

'I do feel much more alert, thank you, Quo. And I think Paula may have been trying to phone me ...'

Do not worry about Paula, Toni. Paula is fine, I am sure.

'Oh, that's good. And Carla?'

Carla is still here with us. You know that, don't you?

'Yes, of course.'

And your music is still playing.

'It sustains me, Quo ...'

Toni, I am going to reveal the first great role you can play in our exploration of your world, and tell you how you can meet up with Carla again and come to know her better. Are you ready for this now?

'I think so, Quo. But it's so hard to be sure ...'

All is well. Relax and listen carefully.

Once was a magician ...

Firstly, Toni, the surveyors on the *Mater* have a very specific mission. They need to conduct, remotely, a high-precision mapping and modelling of your Earth.

But they begin this project with a complete lack of knowledge of your technologies and your scientific rules and standards. And they were not able to learn very much by listening in to your planet's inscrutable radio emissions as we approached!

> *He promised us three favors*
> *Said he was a savior ...*

So, to get them started — and for one other important reason — we have to take some very accurate "position fixes" on the surface of the Earth.

However, we cannot achieve the precision we require just by monitoring the feedback from the radimote. No, Toni, we need you to help us establish those fixes.

'But how can I possibly do that?'

Well, once we have taken a fix ourselves — and you do not realise it, but you have already seen us do this in Bilbao — we have then "learned" about one specific point on the Earth, in our own terms. We know its exact distance from us, its position between your North and South Poles, and its distance around the Earth (we can base this on some point on your Equator that we choose at random at the start of the survey).

But we need to be able to calibrate this data against whatever scheme you use here on Earth. *That* is how you will be helping us, Toni. You will be taking your own corresponding fix for us. And to ensure the accuracy of our model, we shall need to do this not just once, but three times, in well-separated locations.

Meanwhile, in your role as our Illuminator, you can help us to seek out, in records that must be held on Earth, complete details of the precise locations of many thousands of places of interest to us.

Then, after taking just those three sets of matching fixes, we shall be able to confidently make an initial model of the entire Earth within our own systems!

'That sounds very neat, Quo! You make it seem easy and obvious. But I'm no scientist. Is that the simplest way to do it?'

It is, when we know nothing to begin with, and we are thousands of kilometres away! It is like lighting a fire with the spark from a stone. You are that spark, Toni.

By knowing you, we already know a little of your main system of world co-ordinates: lines of Latitude, based on your Equator of course, and circles of Longitude. You have at least recalled that from your schooling!

'I thought I'd forgotten all about it, Quo. I've never done anything with that particular bit of learning!'

You have now.

And we shall soon establish the precise position used to define your own arbitrary reference point. It is "somewhere in London, England" in your recollection. That sets the base on your Equator for the longitude co-ordinates you use to identify any point around the Earth.

As for recording the heights of individual places, we are assuming you use the overall level of your oceans as your reference base — but I can see that you are not clear on this either. History, as you said, but not Geography!

It does not matter; we shall both soon discover if we are right.

'Give me another moment to think, Quo ...'

Certainly, Toni.

This is a lullabye ...

'I wish I could take in everything you're telling me. It's all a bit of a mystery ...'

> It is not really, Toni. You just suspect that it is. It is like your belief that you cannot draw or paint. That is what you believe, isn't it?

'Yes. I've never been able to draw. I wish I could. I adore great paintings.'

> How do you know you cannot?

'Because I tried over and over again when I was a child, and I always produced really stupid pictures. People made fun of them. It was very embarrassing.'

> So you stopped trying. And nobody showed you how you could really draw well and with ease, did they?

'No — and I've steered clear of it ever since, thank you, Quo!'

> Be calm, Toni. If humans are in any way like ourselves, I suspect that some day you will discover how beautifully you can draw, simply by learning how to take control of the insensitive, over-clever part of your brain! Perhaps Carla will be able to teach you ...

> But enough of that for now. What I want you to realise is that you really can absorb all that I am about to tell you, with ease, if you will only admit to yourself that you have the capacity to do so. Will you try — for me and for Carla?

'Quo, you have a way with words. You are very persuasive. I don't think I would trust you if I met you in a bar and you invited me to join a poker game!

'But we're not in a bar, are we? We're in my living room — and the album has started over again — and we're also still somewhere else ...'

> Toni, you are the perfect mate for Carla in this world. Now listen again ...

> *Would you like to learn to tango?*

The first fix, which Carla the Handler took when your Carla was pretending to finish a phone call, tells us exactly where that table in that Bilbao café is situated on the surface of the Earth, from our point of view and using our measuring tools.

Very soon, we shall ask you to establish for us the location of that particular point, in terms of your own system of latitude and longitude co-ordinates. That will then allow us to calculate where your base longitude line is located: "somewhere in London", as you have revealed.

'How can I do that?'

Your harmony's an open breeze
into my sheltered home ...

Ah, you are still ignoring the knowledge you hold inside and have shared with us!

Your Global Positioning System uses many satellites which have been placed in orbit around the Earth for the purpose of providing that information. And you, Toni, can use a simple device to establish your position via those satellites, precisely as we need you to.

You actually know all this already — you have read of it in newspapers, and some of your friends possess such items. If you did not know of this, then we could not know it too. But you are simply not exploiting that knowledge actively.

'All right, Quo — I give in. You obviously know me better than I know myself!'

Well, Toni, that is probably correct, but it is no triumph for me to acknowledge it. Everything you will do with Carla in the days to come will serve to open up your own self-knowledge, and resurrect much that you have learned but temporarily forgotten.

'That is an attractive prospect, Quo.'

It is indeed.

So, after you supply us with that first specific position, we shall in principle be able to locate any other place in the world whose co-ordinates we later come to know.

But, as I have said, it is not enough to make just one measurement. There will be minor errors in the accuracy of our own fixes and what you will capture. So, in places distant from Bilbao, we shall both need to measure again. As it happens, Toni, the next place will be Rome. In a few moments, I shall tell you why.

When you arrive there, we shall already be able to predict roughly where you and Carla are located. But then we shall receive further specific fixes from both of you. These will allow us to tune our systems much more finely.

Later, you will both travel again (though we know not where, at this time), and once you have provided us with your final GPS co-ordinates, we shall attempt to predict your position with great accuracy. Then, when Carla confirms this with her final fix, we shall have an extremely high level of confidence in our data, particularly if the three locations form a good wide-angled triangle. Our model and your system will be completely co-ordinated. And your initial task will be complete.

'But how does Carla transmit these fixes, if she is nothing but ...?' Toni's voice trailed off at his recurring realisation of Carla's virtuality.

Ah, you are alert again; you are back to asking good questions!

I shall need to explain this carefully for you. But before I start, are you perhaps a little thirsty? There *are* some bottles of beer in your parents' refrigerator, you know ...

'No, thank you, Quo.'

At the invisible core of the radimote's image sphere, Toni, there is a great energy store. This is fully charged during that initial downward transmission. It is then kept continuously topped-up via the low-power radio beam coming from the *Mater*. Any excess energy is normally allowed to leak out of the radimote, completely unnoticed.

When Carla the Handler, in her studio, identifies the correct moment to take a fix, she simply reduces the level of that top-up feed to the radimote. This stops the energy drain from the image sphere, and it also causes an immediate switching of the internal flow, releasing much of the energy stored in the capacitor onto the *Mater's* input beam in a fraction of a second.

The very high strength of this signal allows us to identify the exact position of the radimote at that instant in time. We see its precise distance from your Poles and from our own selected reference point on the Equator, and we record the time it takes to reach us, which gives us the exact distance to that surface elevation.

'But doesn't something like that affect the radimote itself?'

Yes, Toni. Very good thinking.

Each time we trigger a fix, Carla will appear quite exhausted for a short while, until the capacitor's energy level is back to normal.

But fortunately this is the only situation in which the radimote needs to "generate" a signal of its own. All the other energy flows passing through the radimote — either received directly by it, or reflected back through it — originate from the low-power, disguisable sources on the *Mater* ...

Incidentally, Toni — both Carla and I think the song playing right now is particularly beautiful.

'It's called *At Seventeen*, Quo. It's peerless. It gives you dreams for free.'

Now, that very high-powered burst of energy from the surface is, as we expected, easily recognised by detection equipment on Earth.

'So this is another of the risks you have to take ...?'

Exactly, Toni. But we have a strategy to deal with it. A pretence will always be made that the radimote is using some sort of Earth-based signalling equipment. And this needs to be done in full public view, so that there will be witnesses.

This will cause any local investigation to consider it to have been some sort of suspicious human activity, but human activity nonetheless, rather than something "paranormal", which could be the case if it simply happened out of the blue with no obvious explanation. We do not want to advertise our presence any more than necessary!

So, Toni, we decided yesterday that the radimote should always appear to be talking on a mobile phone, just before each fix transmission takes place.

Unfortunately, in her first attempt at that pretence today, Carla forgot to place the phone to her ear! After so many rehearsals last night! So the waiter thought it was a dictation machine — and then you were dragged into a police hunt which should have been focused from the start on an invisible woman.

'I didn't enjoy that at all, Quo.'

I can only apologise again.

That first fixing burst was commanded to be sent at great magnitude, because we could not know how strong it would need to be, to reach us through your atmosphere. We have now been able to carefully measure the signal we received, and we are sure that the energy release was much greater than we actually needed.

So, the next two bursts — in Rome and some other place — can both be at a much lower level than today's. But they may still be quite noticeable — with the unavoidable risks which that entails.

I'm leaving by night
I'm leaving alone
Leaving it lie
When you waken I'll be gone ...

'OK, Quo. But you said there were two reasons for taking these fixes. I think I now understand how your surveyors can use them to start mapping the Earth. What's the other reason?'

Well, Toni, a radimote can move, or rather can be moved, with great accuracy once this "triangulation of fixes" is completed. Carla the Handler will be using powerful systems which can exploit our developing model of the Earth, and the data we collect from your records, to send your Carla precisely where she wishes her to go. To put it more bluntly, Carla will become less and less dependent on following the sherpa.

'And I am the sherpa?'

Exactly. We are all heavily reliant upon you in these early days. We know you will not disappoint us. But Carla's increasing self-sufficiency will liberate you both — for the good of your missions, and your knowledge of each other.

'You have an answer for everything, Quo.'

I am doing my best for you. And I know you have two more big questions.

'Yes, I do. First of all, how do you know so much about me?'

It is very straightforward, Toni. We have simply read all of your memory. This is another use of the *Mater's* beams.

When Carla knelt before you and reached out to you, apparently to take your head in her hands, she was in reality on the point of embracing your human mind and absorbing it into our own on-board systems.

> *And they'll do their best*
> *to keep you from the light ...*

We can read your memory using a separate transferral circuit, which we establish just for that purpose, using specialised light sources.

The currents of light are sent down the *Mater's* left beam and through the left hand of the radimote. They pass directly through your brain, then into the right hand of the radimote, and back up the other beam. Despite the immense complexity of your mind, it does not take us many of your minutes to read and analyse all that it holds stored.

And when we desire later to update or add to your memory, then the reverse direction is used. Information is sent from the *Mater* down the right-hand beam, and is stored into your brain. It then emerges through the left-hand beam, and passes back up to the *Mater*, confirming that the writing of all the new information has taken place successfully ...

'Something tells me I shouldn't like what I've just heard, Quo!' Toni interrupted. He was frowning for the first time in hours.

That is a very natural reaction, Toni. But I think you already understand the great benefits that we can all reap from this. In particular, the enrichment that Carla can bring to you ...

'Yes. I think that's why I don't feel particularly concerned — even though I know I should! But there's still this business of the radimote only being made of light ...'

Toni, I give you my word that your fears will soon prove groundless.

Bright lights and promises
A pocket full of dreams ...

'I have to believe you, Quo.' Toni was briefly aware again of the sound of his own voice, and was not fully convinced of his own words.

> Finally, Toni, reading and writing a subject's memory uses up a very large amount of the energy in the radimote's radio beams. So while this is happening, the Handler's "vision" and "hearing" can be maintained, but no speech is attempted. And most importantly, the radimote often needs to be un-made for the duration of such an engagement. So the whole exercise should normally be done in private, to avoid the shocks to the surrounding population that would be caused by its sudden disappearance!

'All right, Quo. You have very neatly led me to my final question. Carla cannot speak to me at the moment, as you have just pointed out. So how on earth are you able to?'

> On earth indeed! You even make bad jokes with style!

> I am not speaking, Toni. I do not need to bend the waves of your air. And you know this. You can hear no sound, save that of your treasured music, which will play forever in your heart. You absorb my thoughts directly into your mind, as I pass this knowledge on to you.

> *Everywhere I hear*
> *a ringing in my ears ...*

'Quo, I think there's someone trying to phone me again.'

> Do not worry. I am certain they will call back soon ...

'Very well, Quo. I know I must accept all you have told me. But I have not forgotten my original questions — and you have so far ignored two of them ...'

> I know this, Toni. You asked: "Why Bilbao?" and "Why me?"

'That's right.'

If you will again be patient, and wait until you soon meet up with Carla once more, she will answer those questions for you as well. The second of them, in particular, is very personal for her — very personal indeed.

'If this is what you wish, Quo.'

Thank you, Toni.

Now, to be able to take on your mission, you need to see the world as much from our point of view as from yours.

So we have revealed to you today, Toni, far more than we shall tell the others. To play your part, you have a need to know all of this; but you will never divulge to anybody the information we have flagged as "secret" in your mind. And you will remember it only for as long as we wish, though most of it will now remain in your subconscious mind.

> *Overused and much-abused*
> *promises of delight ...*

In particular, when you begin your travels, with Carla at your side, you will not recall that she is merely a radimote. You will think of her instead as a *maestra* of disguise and illusion, who nonetheless needs the regular attentions of her charming assistant. She is and always will be, for you, the beautiful woman you chose to follow from that café.

Carla lives, Toni.

The anxiety and tension that had been steadily rising throughout Toni's body evaporated in an instant. He grinned again at last.
'Ah, Quo, that is wonderful news!'

Beyond the Spheres

The special branch inspector was feeling extremely frustrated.

She and her colleagues had done their best to try to recover the situation. Nobody was quite sure who was most to blame for the mess-ups, so for once in their lives they were all keeping their mouths firmly shut.

The Santander squad had given them a hard time, of course, and her in particular; but you didn't make it to inspector by having it easy. No, the spooks would fly off home soon and be forgotten; she didn't give a damn about them. It was her colleagues she feared much more, and the sly remarks that would be just loud enough to overhear in the canteen the next day ...

It was approaching four o'clock. They'd been searching for their "smiler" for well over three hours now. The all-ports alert had gone out at once, of course, but that was not her concern. She was expected to work the *local* miracle!

And they'd really thought they'd cracked it at two o'clock.

A young woman matching that description perfectly had been spotted coming out of a beauty salon, just off Plaza Moyúa. They'd rushed her back to the café, and the boys from Santander had gone though the whole procedure again.

And she'd claimed to have been in the salon continuously since ten o'clock, most of the time under a hair dryer — which four members of staff had then proceeded to confirm. Oh, and she just happened to be the wife of a young head of department at a city school, and chairwoman of two local charities. Wonderful.

Really weird, though, the inspector thought for the umpteenth time, brushing aside her frustrations and her self-criticism; it was really weird that their "fine lady" had matched so perfectly the description given by that timid Antonio Murano ...

Her own boss had just told her to give it another hour. She knew it was fruitless now. At five o'clock, once the helicopter was gone, she would stand the team down, keep out of everyone's way for a while back at the station, then head straight home and try and forget it all with a very long bath.

What a shambles. Her notes could wait until the morning. She had real work to get on with ...

Benign Machines

And so at last, Toni, to your primary mission.

You are to be Carla's constant companion and guide. She will come to be more independent as time passes, but she will often need you to interpret and illuminate what she sees and hears.

'But what are we trying to do, once we've taken those fixes?'

Toni, we wish to learn the truth in people's minds.

Over time, we shall readily be able to discover everything that is patent in your world, by simple observation of its contours and its public statements and records and images.

But we are just as interested in what is hidden or disguised; in what well-intentioned men and women may truly believe, but perhaps do not always say. And we wish to understand how widespread and deep-rooted such dissimulation might be.

To reveal this, with the help of you and Carla, we shall seek out individuals with knowledge, insight, understanding, and strong views on issues of importance.

We have begun the building of our great model of human integrity with our analysis and assessment of no less a person than yourself. We already have immense respect for you, Toni. And we shall be constantly refining that model, with our regular observation of your thoughts and deeds, and through the transferral and continuing observation of our future subjects ...

Bright lights and promises
That's all it's for ...
... Honey, can you show me more?

'And you believe you can understand our world just like that? — by finding out what a few smart people really think of things?'

Toni, we know that we shall only need to study a quite small sample of such people in order to draw some very valid initial conclusions.

'I'm no statistician, Quo. I'm still not convinced — about any of it!'

You must trust us. We know, from our own long history, that there can indeed be great and easily observed differences between public posture and private thoughts. But we need you to help us in our search to discover just what, in your world, is truly happening between the lines. Your music is speaking to you, Toni. Follow its lead.

'How can I do that?'

We shall direct you. And now you are ready.

We have studied your memories to find the ideal place to start — and we have discovered that you have a relative who turns out to be of particular interest to us ...

'Which one is that, Quo? Everyone has lots of relatives!'

He is an uncle of your mother. You have scant knowledge of him. You *are* aware that he is involved in the administration of government. Not in Spain, but in Italy, your mother's homeland. You remember his name, do you not?

'Is it Great-uncle Giuseppe? I've never met him. I think he lives in Rome ...'

Well, Toni, your subconscious recalls a little more than that. His full name is Giuseppe Marco Terleone. Your mother has mentioned him to you on several occasions.

She is very proud of her "illustrious young uncle", as she called him once. He is still in his fifties — "in his prime", she told you — and he is a senior civil servant in the central government offices in Rome. Indeed, when she last spoke to him, he was the principal advisor to a Junior Government Minister ...

'Well, Quo, I'll believe you. It rings a few bells — but I've never been very interested in modern politics, and you won't find many kids these days who know much about their great-uncles!'

You know enough. It is a most promising place for you to begin. Your mother has told you where she proudly noted down the details of Don Giuseppe's present place of work. We have high hopes of gaining, through him, some early insights into the way your world really ticks ...

I am wiser now, you know
and still as big a fool
concerning you ...

When you find yourself back in your apartment as normal, you will not see Carla there. Do not fear. The Handler needs to rest — these have already been the most demanding exertions of her life. You will meet up with your Carla again very soon, in Rome — and from that time on, you will often be very close.

And you will immediately have much to do, Toni — so please do not allow yourself to be disturbed at home, as you prepare to leave.

You must arrange to travel by air to Rome, as soon as possible tomorrow morning. It will be surprisingly easy for you to do all that is necessary for this — you will find your plans are already firmly established in your mind.

In particular, you will visit a city store at once, and purchase a simple pocket GPS unit, just like the one your friend Rodrigo recently showed you. But do be careful to avoid being spotted by anybody who knows you, while you are outdoors.

Then, very early in the morning, to avoid being seen and arousing suspicions again, you must go to the corner table of the café where you first saw Carla, and record its latitude and longitude on your new GPS unit. You should practice this carefully beforehand, Toni. And please capture the information twice, for good measure. Then write the results large and clear on a sheet of paper — we shall need to calibrate our reading abilities too!

And then you must leave for the airport.

> *You are with her now, I know*
> *I'll live alone forever*
> *Not together now.*

When you have arrived safely in the centre of Rome, you should find your way to another pavement café. I suspect you can manage that with ease! Carla will then join you — and you can welcome her at your table this time! She will help you to transfer to us the co-ordinates of the Bilbao café.

'How will Carla get to Rome, Quo?'

Toni, I have already told you — Carla can follow fire engines.

'Of course. How could I have forgotten!'

You and Carla must then immediately organise another position fix for us — and as I have said, this one can be at a much lower power, which hopefully will avoid the problems you experienced earlier today. Carla will help you with this as well. And she will make sure that you and she are not seen together this time.

> *He turned and said 'You ask much of me' ...*

We need you and Carla to take those fixes in Rome as soon as possible, so that we can continue the detailed planning of our survey work, and to allow her to start engaging others to help us with those tasks.

We wish the fixes to be captured *before* you meet your great-uncle, while you and Carla are still unknown to anyone in the city. We also do not want to delay taking them until after you have met him, because Carla needs to be heavily involved in the process of engaging him in our work, and she will then need to relax once more.

So once you have captured those fixes, Toni, you must go to a pavement telephone booth — we do not want you using your present mobile phone, now that the police are aware of it — and call your great-uncle. Tell him the story that has already been built in your mind, and arrange to meet up with him as soon as possible. After that you will be able to follow the script that has been written for you ...

Go on, be a hero, I set you free ...

'And what happens when Carla has finished her work with Signor Terleone?'

Well, perhaps you and she can take some time together to discover the sights of Rome — I can see you have always wanted to!

Until the next time, Toni ...

And now those heady combinations of light and shade were slowly melting away, and Toni was simply back in the familiar setting of his living room. Carla was indeed nowhere to be seen, although he still sensed her aftertones. And his music played on.

He was hungry and exhausted. He checked that his mobile phone was still off, switched the sound system to "mute" and the house phone ring volume to "low", and set the alarm on his wristwatch for six o'clock. He made a rough sandwich and hurriedly ate it, leaning against the kitchen sink, before flopping onto the sofa and falling sound asleep.

He was not disturbed by the feeble ringing of the phone, repeated every ten or fifteen minutes. Nor did he hear, because he knew he must not, the gentle beckoning of the door buzzer or the young woman calling his name.

* * *

He awoke twenty seconds before the alarm sounded.

Taking out his credit card and the yellow pages, he phoned a travel agent and booked a seat on the early morning airbus to Madrid, connecting one hour later with the next airbus to Rome. He would be in the city centre soon after midday. With one more call, his taxi to the airport was arranged: Plaza de Moyúa, five-thirty.

He adjusted the volume on the sound system so that it was just audible again.

... and broken dreams that somehow slipped away ...

He quickly packed a light rucksack. Then he consulted his mother's address book. He found only a crossed-out telephone number for his great-uncle; but alongside it were some notes that she had indeed proudly written: "... and he even has an office now at the Chamber of Deputies!"

Sitting at the living-room table, he scribbled a short note to his parents, and placed it against the empty vase in front of him. He then picked up his pen again ...

Bye, my love — sleep tight, my love,
and softly fade away ...

As soon as he had finished his second letter, he walked slowly across the room. He finally stopped the music that had been playing over and over throughout the long afternoon, put the CD back into its case, and stored it carefully in his rucksack. Then he took his reserve of spare cash from his bedroom drawer and put it all in his wallet.

Reminding himself to check carefully at every corner that he was not being observed, he left the building, posted his letter to Paula, and used his bank card and credit card to draw two large lumps of extra cash from a dispenser. Then he sought out the nearest open-all-hours electronics store ...

* * *

Feeling reasonably confident in his grasp of the "Mark" function of his shiny new GPS unit, Antonio Murano was in bed, exhausted again, by eight-thirty, with his alarm now set for half-past four. Undisturbed by the further insistent but muted callings of the phone, and the door-buzzer, and his Paula, he slept deeply once more.

* * *

He was up with the alarm, and closed the front door behind him soon after five — knowing that he must make no attempt to contact either Paula or his parents while he was away.

At the deserted café corner, in the deserted street, he took his GPS fixes as instructed, then walked briskly in the cool morning air up to the main square. The taxi was already waiting for him. Once he was settled in the back seat, he pulled a large sheet of paper and a thick black marker pen from his rucksack, and carefully transcribed the co-ordinates of the café that were displayed on his GPS unit. He even checked his written version against the second "mark" he had captured — yes, it was precisely the same as the first: N43°15'49.1" W002°56'16.9". He folded the paper and stored it, with the marker pen, in his inside jacket pocket.

He checked in for his flight to Madrid Barajas just before six o'clock.

* * *

Two hours later, as Toni's plane taxied in to the terminal at Madrid, the CeSID team assembled in Santander.

The Commander listened carefully to his officers' reports, read through the written descriptions of Toni and Carla, and glanced at the two rather over-exposed photographs of the student of music. Concluding that no more action could sensibly be taken, at least for the time being, he ordered his men to file their reports and the photos on their internal system, at the highest security level, until he had received guidance on whether and how the incident should be further publicised.

* * *

At the same time, in a small office in the Bilbao police headquarters, the special branch inspector finished typing up her notes, including her own versions of the descriptions of Carla and Toni. Relieved to be ready to move on to something less frustrating, she quickly ran the spelling checker, then stored the report on her "Incidents" database. It was immediately and automatically copied across to the InterSB "World Alerts" system and, over the next few minutes and hours, it would be spotted by police intelligence co-ordinators in cities throughout Europe and beyond, and studied as an interesting but not immediately relevant item ...

Rome, Italy

With no arrival delay, the transfer at Madrid went smoothly. Toni even had time to seek out a pocket guide to Rome, complete with street plan. The tired-looking student, moving through on his own into international departures, merited no more than a quick glance from the passport officer. But the student's close attendant, still exhilarated from her recently completed first solo cross-country flight, could command none of the official's attention at all.

The second Iberia flight also arrived on time at Rome Fiumicino at eleven-fifteen. After a long wait to clear customs, Toni made his way to the airport station, and soon afterwards he was boarding the train for Centrale Termini. He passed the short journey by studying his street map of Rome, and deciding to aim vaguely towards the city centre and some of the obvious tourist spots he had read about on the plane. And he was now wishing he'd taken up his mother's repeated offers to expand the small amount of Italian she had taught him as a child.

Emerging from the front entrance of Termini Station into fine early spring weather, he turned left and made his way along the street to the Piazza dell'Esquilino, pausing briefly to admire the huge magnificence of the church of Santa Maria Maggiore. He then crossed the busy Via Cavour and, looking straight along the Via Depretis, he took in the gentle contours of the famous seven hills of Rome, as the long streets extending ahead of him dipped and rose and dipped and rose again, reminding him of the backs of the sea-snakes presaging the sack of Troy ...

Setting off down the first of those streets, he soon came to an unassuming square, the Piazza del Viminale, with a likely looking bar on the corner. This would be perfect for his long-anticipated rendezvous. He took off his rucksack, sat down in the warm sunshine, ordered a beer and a small pizza, and waited for Carla to appear.

And a few moments later, she walked round the corner. She was wearing exactly the same clothes as in Bilbao. Toni was a little surprised — but at the same time, immensely relieved. And then, having dabbled once in potted psychology, he realised that surprises were the last thing he needed right now. And he understood.

She smiled, and sat down at the chair which he had unconsciously readied for her. They exchanged a few slightly embarrassed words. That is, Toni felt embarrassed. Then Carla got straight back down to business. Once again, he was automatically resolving all the missing syntax in his mind ...

'Toni — please show me the paper with the co-ordinates of the Bilbao café.'

He held it up directly ahead of her. She smiled once more, then nodded in confirmation that the data had been successfully read and interpreted back on the *Mater*.

He plucked up the courage to speak again.

'Carla — Quo promised you would explain how you can see and hear and talk ...'

'Ah, Toni — please be patient. We shall tell you all you need to know, very soon. But right now, we have work to do.'

The arrival of his pizza conveniently prevented any further argument. Carla waited patiently for him to finish it. But he could see she was very keen to proceed ...

'I must move away now. Please wait for five minutes, to give me time to un-make in seclusion and then get you back in my sights — remember, I don't want to frighten you or the natives, or alert the authorities! Then continue your walk along the hilly streets. I shall be following you. Stop by the first busy pavement café you come to, consult your map, just like the tourist that you are, and discreetly capture two GPS marks. Then just walk on — we don't want you to be linked to that spot. Stop at the next corner and wait for me to join you later. I will make an appearance at the same café and pretend to place another phone call. Don't look back, Toni; look anywhere but back. You wouldn't recognise me anyway. Your Carla is not going to be associated with that spot either!'

She strolled casually away and around the nearest corner. After five minutes, Toni stood up and moved off down the hill. Arriving soon at another major junction, with a large café-restaurant on his right, he stopped, studied his map, and then pulled out his GPS. The screen was blank. Where was the command menu? He pressed every button in turn — nothing! Then he noticed the tiny power switch, and realised he had not turned the device off after copying out the co-ordinates in the taxi. In fact, he hadn't switched it off once, ever since he had experimented with it at home in the evening — eighteen hours ago. Flat batteries! How stupid. He must have been so tired last night — and he'd never even thought about it today. His mobile phone was always running down, as well ...

He shuffled uncomfortably on the spot, worrying that people would start to take some notice of him, well aware that Carla would be watching him intently. Then he pulled himself together, made a decision (he was not used to doing that), sat down at the nearest empty table facing the direction from which he had come, planted a huge and unmissable smile on his face, and vigorously waved his arm. He converted the wave into a grand gesture of distant beckoning, then sat back and prayed.

It was a full minute before Carla turned the corner and, smiling sweetly, walked up to his table. But her eyes reflected her feelings — puzzlement, not annoyance; frustration, but a genuine appreciation that something else had gone wrong.

He explained.

'Well, you'll have to buy more batteries, or another unit,' said Carla's limited nouns and verbs; she was trying to come to terms with such an unreliable technology, and failing completely. 'But we don't know how long it will take you to sort that out. We'd better try and make contact with Giuseppe first. Because there's no knowing how long that might take either. And we have to reach him during the day — you only know his place of work, not his home address or phone number. When you do reach him, you'll just have to try and delay the meeting as long as possible, to allow us to capture the fixes first ...'

They left the table before the arrival of any waiter. Carla walked alongside Toni, keeping clear of passers-by, as he sought and located a telephone booth — no easy task in the era of the all-pervasive mobile phone. Then, after several attempts at finding a sympathetic operator who could understand his request, first attempted in Spanish, and then in English, for a phone number for the Parliament office buildings, he finally got through to a reception desk which recognised the name Terleone at once; and suddenly, without fully realising it, he was talking to his great-uncle's personal secretary.

He identified himself again, and made a simple plea to talk to his relative; it was very important, he begged. She must have believed him; only seconds after her request for him to hold the line, she put him straight through.

'*Terleone. Chi parla?*'

'Ah ... hello, sir. Good afternoon, Great-uncle Giuseppe. Pardon me. I am the son of your niece. Anna. My name is Antonio. And ... sir ... I really need you to help me, if you will ...'

'*Ma cosa vuoi?*'

So, with an enforced combination of Spanish, some old school Latin, a few words remembered from his mother's early teaching and a smattering of holiday Italian from a week spent in Viareggio, Toni managed to blurt out to the urbane and rarely-hoodwinked civil servant, who had pretended a complete ignorance of English in response to Toni's initial efforts, that he was in Rome on vacation, and that he had lost his wallet, and that he was suffering from a nasty upset stomach, and that he really didn't know what to do, and that his parents, who were themselves away on a touring holiday, had given him their honoured Roman relative's contact details, "just in case" ...

Don Giuseppe listened to this multilingual tirade with no small irritation, at first, at being disturbed by someone he had never met. He had received plenty of calls from cranks in the past, despite his secretary's efficiency! But as he took in the crucial points of the garbled message, he too came to accept that the caller really was his great-nephew; and then of course he could not argue. Nor did he want to. Family was special. Family was everything.

'It's all right, Antonio. You can relax. I understand completely. And yes, I will of course do all I can to help you.'

The suave arranger was back in full control. And Toni was very relieved to hear the perfectly spoken English language which earlier he had dared not pursue further.

'Where are you?' asked Giuseppe. 'All right, I can be with you in thirty minutes from now. At two-fifteen — understood? We'll sort something out, for the afternoon at least.' ... 'No, I have an important meeting at three o'clock, which I cannot miss. You will need to get a taxi.' ... 'Yes, it's near the Spanish Steps.'

So Toni was forced to agree an immediate rendezvous inside an elegant little café in the Via Frattina, only a short stroll from the place where Giuseppe Terleone was working that day: his office within the Chamber of Deputies in the Palazzo Montecitorio.

'How will I recognise you, *signore*?'

Terleone did not hesitate. 'A yellow rose.'

Toni summarised the challenge to Carla. She seemed to understand, and, as before, appeared resigned to such adversity. She took charge again.

'You must get some new batteries at once. Test them in the taxi. Take the fix as soon as you reach the café, and copy it down, and keep the sheet of paper in your hand. I will follow you, and meet you both inside.'

Toni suddenly felt he had experienced more "happenings" in the past thirty hours than in the whole of his previous twenty years. He wasn't sure he could handle all this action ...

'Come on, Toni — wake up! Give me three minutes to un-make, then get on with it!'

That was enough to kick him back into life. Embarrassment again, unfortunately, he thought ruefully to himself.

Carla had already walked away. He spotted a tobacconist's shop on the opposite corner. After the obligatory short wait, he hurried over to it, emptied the batteries onto the counter, put on his most helpless look, and prayed for good luck for the second time in the past half-hour. And they had dozens of the commonplace things. He bought three sets — he was beginning to learn some real-life lessons at last.

He then spent several minutes wandering around the busy road junction, seeking out a taxi in every direction. Finally he spotted one, waved at it furiously, and luckily was able to grab it before anybody else could. He dived into the back seat. *'Via Frattina, per favore!'*

The Rome traffic was on his side at that hour of the day. In the short time available, he rapidly installed a new set of batteries, prayed once more, and switched the GPS back on. "Initialising ... Ready". Perfect! He pressed "Mark" and checked that it was all working just as before. OK. He deleted that mark. It still looked right. He was really getting the hang of this! He was ready again. He would leave the unit switched on for now, but he definitely *would* remember to turn it off after taking the next fix ...

* * *

The taxi pulled up outside the café only five minutes before the appointed time. Toni peered through the plate glass windows, past the people queuing for the wonderful-looking ice creams. No yellow roses. Holding the door open for a little longer than necessary (he knew that Carla could pass through without his help, but he had been well brought up), he walked in as casually as he could and sat down in the corner chair of the table nearest the back stairs, which afforded him a clear view of the front door and the street outside. He placed his rucksack on the chair next to his, reserving it for Carla's arrival.

He pulled out his GPS, checked it was all still looking as it should, then pressed the "Mark" button, waited a few seconds, and pressed it a second time. He confirmed to his satisfaction that both fixes had worked correctly, and without wasting a moment, used the marker pen to copy the co-ordinates clearly onto his sheet of paper, and cross-checked them carefully. Then he switched the unit off, then on again, and finally off. Done! This was easy, now! But where was Carla? Giuseppe would be here at any moment ...

Instead, the waiter had appeared.

'Ohi ... sì ... una birra, per favore.'

As the waiter moved off, a woman in her early fifties — short, rather overweight, and wearing a loud red anorak and beige check trousers — emerged puffing from the top of the stairs to Toni's left. Clearly relishing this latest, highly convincing manifestation, Carla glanced across to his table. She showed no sign of recognising him, but was very relieved to see the folded sheet of paper ready in his hand.

She moved forward a little, to stand by the wall between the end of the counter and the top of the stairs. Taking out her mobile phone, remembering this time to place it to her ear, and then furtively turning sideways to face the bar staff, with her right hand cupped to her other ear, she pretended once more to be making a call — but this time talking so quietly that the language she used was discernible by nobody.

On the *Mater*, the Handler dropped the radimote's energy capacitor feed level to 50% for less than one second, and its low-magnitude fix transmission was instantly received.

Low-magnitude it may have been, but it was still, by Earth's normal standards, another immense and unmissable burst of radio energy from a single, highly locatable, unaccredited, and probably mobile source. And none of the agencies who rapidly received the news of this transmission could fail to notice the great similarities with the previous day's alert ...

Carla the Finder recovered quickly from what was a far less draining experience than that of the previous day. By the time the elegant man wearing a yellow rose in his lapel approached the café door and hovered outside, looking rather ill at ease, she was ready to descend the stairs again and, in the fortunately still-empty toilet lobby, to become Toni's Carla once more.

Toni stood up, walked in pretended discomfort to the door, pulled it open, and smiled a silent welcome to his great-uncle, who was clearly keen to be rescued from this position of unaccustomed limbo. Then he turned and hobbled straight back to the table, with his illustrious relative trailing behind.

The waiter had just put a small glass of beer on the mat at Toni's place, and with an enthusiastic '*Benvenuto, signore!*' he helpfully drew back the empty chair opposite, ready for this impressive new arrival. So Terleone sat down facing the rear wall and stairs, rather discomforted by these enforced arrangements (he never liked to have his back to the action), and very surprised to see a beer being delivered to a purportedly upset stomach. He waved the waiter away, and smiled as sympathetically as he could at his unlucky great-nephew.

Taking a deep breath, Toni attempted to strike up a conversation. Terleone at once raised his hands in a calming gesture and attempted a gentle "hushing" sound, readying himself to regain control of the situation. But before he could speak, his eyes moved away from the young man and towards the top of the stairs.

Toni looked to his left. A familiar figure had emerged from the lower floor. At least the face and the figure were reassuringly and delightfully familiar — but there was no red scarf now, and the crisp, pale blue suit was brand new, and unmistakably Italian. Toni's mother would have been most impressed with Carla's taste.

With a curiously disarming smile on her face, she sat down opposite her target, on the chair from which Toni had now removed his rucksack.

And Terleone was indeed immediately and utterly disarmed. He even started to hum a little tune. But he still retained some grasp of the situation as he had previously understood it.

'You didn't tell me there was somebody with you ...' he complained meekly to his great-nephew, his eyes however fixed firmly on Carla's.

Toni began, in his very best English, to introduce her as his travelling companion, and to explain that she had been downstairs because she too was suffering from the same stomach bug as he was. But Carla was growing impatient with the distraction that he was unwittingly creating. She was keen to involve Giuseppe more fully than she had so far managed; then they could all move off quickly to somewhere much more secluded.

Her hopes of a smooth and straightforward continuation of her latest seduction were, however, to be dashed for a second time. The police forces of Rome are large in number, and are always ready and waiting for action, especially in the city centre. And while the duties of the *Carabinieri*, and the *Polizia Municipale*, and the Special Branch are all officially well-demarcated, there is nothing like a top priority call to bring out the spirit of competition in each of them.

No fewer than five cars and vans, one of them unmarked save for a hastily-positioned blue lamp, converged noisily on Via Frattina within four minutes of Carla's transmission, and only two minutes after receiving the broadcast alert. Even the driver of a passing Prison Police car toyed briefly with the idea of joining the party, but resisted the temptation admirably.

The approaching sirens gave Carla the few seconds' warning she needed. She had heard these sounds before. Grasping her stomach and grimacing dramatically to indicate a sudden return of her virtual gastro-enteritis, she broke off her involvement of Giuseppe in mid-flow, and fled back down the stairs. Relieved to find there was still nobody around in the lobby outside the toilets, she un-made in an instant, then moved rapidly back up the stairs and began another unplanned observation ...

Carabinieri and city police barred the café entrance, and two special branch officers entered and ordered everybody to sit still and quiet. But instead, everybody jumped up and started protesting loudly.

Don Giuseppe Marco Terleone, in his immaculate suit and with a golden cashmere overcoat draped across his broad shoulders despite the heat of the afternoon, chose merely to look round and observe these events in stony silence. He then calmly turned back to Toni.

'Do you have a mobile phone, my boy?'

'Yes, but ...'

'Good — then your friend can meet up with you later.'

He rose and walked across to the two officers, the jostle of bodies seeming to part like the waves before him. The interrogation of the barman was under way. Terleone touched the more senior-looking officer lightly on the shoulder and spoke a few quiet words, briefly turning at one point to indicate Toni.

Within seconds, the two of them were escorted down the back stairs to the staff entrance. The officer opened the door just a few inches and peeked out. No uniforms deployed there yet! Not very good, he thought, but very fortunate. Terleone and the boy were allowed to leave.

Carla, not needing to employ the same discretion, simply descended the stairs once more and made her own exit through the wall beside the staff door, again obliged to take up an unplanned and unseen close pursuit of her latest quarry.

The other officer, meanwhile, had hit the jackpot with the barman ('Yes, red jacket ... mobile phone ... back down the stairs ...'). The inspector got the shouted message as he hurried back up. Down he went again. Nobody there. He ordered his sergeant to demand an immediate city-wide hunt for the woman in the red jacket. She too must have simply strolled out of the back door. She had nearly ten minutes on them. A very cool customer; she was not going to be easy to catch ...

* * *

Toni's newly-found relative ushered him firmly but calmly out of the rear yard of the café, turning right into the Via de Fiori and then crossing several of the city's most fashionable shopping streets, but keeping them well clear of the crowds and the policemen who were always stationed at the Spanish Steps. Rounding another corner shortly afterwards, they emerged into the quieter north side of the Piazza di Spagna, which boasted a few modest benches beneath the occasional shade of five tall palm trees, just a hundred metres away from the steps. No one was watching — the crowds were all in front of them, looking away up towards the steps.

Giuseppe Marco Terleone sat down facing those crowds; he was not going to have his back to the action again! Toni silently followed suit. No words had been spoken since they'd left the café, he felt utterly out of his depth, and he had no idea what to do or say next.

Terleone paused for a minute or more, actively working to recover from the very slight loss of composure he had suffered during the recent events. He then decided he must attempt to re-start his acquaintance with his great-nephew and establish how he could best help him in the immediate future. He must forget about that indescribable brief encounter with the boy's lovely companion. Yet his concentration was lapsing as fast as he tried to maintain it; he was inexplicably keen to hear the eventual ringing of Antonio's phone.

But Carla could never make it ring. Instead, she suddenly appeared from behind their bench, smiling as usual, before Giuseppe had uttered a single word.

He was extremely surprised. He would never have expected her, or anyone else, to have been allowed to leave the café so soon after the raid, whatever it was all about — he hadn't bothered to ask. And how could she have been lucky enough, even then, to stumble on them like this, so very quickly? But at the same time, it did not seem necessary for him to understand the answers to these questions; and this, in itself, was a blessed relief.

Then, glued to that bench in the heat of a Rome afternoon, Giuseppe Marco Terleone found himself again humming his favourite aria, and allowing himself to become completely engrossed in the woman in the pale blue suit who had sat down between Antonio and himself, and was now turning to face him.

* * *

There had been hurried consultations back on the *Mater* about how Carla should now proceed. It was out of the question to allow the Finder to vanish, at a stroke, as the engagement began — there were too many people around for them to take that risk. But they could not countenance another promenade around the streets of Rome; they had Terleone by the scruff of his neck now, and they must hang on to him.

So ... Carla would have to carry out the engagement without disappearing. But that would bring several undesirable side effects. The whole affair would look rather strange to any observer, so it might have to be cut short at any time — and it would have to be conducted at low engagement energy levels. For both those reasons, they would probably not be able to take a full memory reading, nor plant their seeds in Terleone's mind as deeply as they wished to.

But they had made their decision.

* * *

Toni Murano, unhappily embarrassed yet again, sat and fidgeted quite naturally as his great-uncle and their new shared girlfriend billed and cooed at each other. Then, as Giuseppe's face went blank and his eyes glazed over, Carla took his head in her hands and seemed to kiss him fully on the lips. And again, and again. Terleone just took it all with a balmy smile. But not one of the Italian passers-by batted an eyelid. This was Rome, after all ...

Quo rapidly engaged with their very first Collector, moved him through a partial transferral (they knew the human brain structures now, and could be quite selective), bypassed briefing completely, and gave him some simple missioning. They would re-engage him later. Right now, it was essential to get the ball rolling.

Not surprisingly, the strong-willed Giuseppe raised occasional muted objections to all of this — but Quo's powers of persuasion were more than a match for the man. And the whole process took no more than seven Earth minutes.

Carla sat back in her space on the bench, took out her mirror, adjusted her hair and her lipstick, and would have lit up a cigarette if only the laws of radimotics had allowed it. Meanwhile, Don Giuseppe came slowly back down to earth, and Toni wondered just what might happen next ...

Terleone was fully alert again, and the romance had left his face. He had completely forgotten Toni's story about sickness and a lost wallet. Or rather, he had been told to forget it. The boy would be able to cope without any special help from him. So the man with the new mission now looked down the bench to where Toni was still sitting, with barely a smile for Carla as his gaze passed her by ...

He gave Toni some clear and simple instructions, in English: to switch on his mobile phone and leave it on (Carla frowned; that did not feel right); to dictate its number for Terleone to write down; and to wait for him to call them during the next twenty-four hours. By then, he assured him, he would have worked out where the pair of them should be moving on to next. Toni did what he was told. Carla frowned again.

Finally, Giuseppe took the street plan that was still in Toni's hands, carefully wrote a few letters and numbers in the margin, drew a circle in the map area itself, and handed it back. Then, without another word, he walked swiftly away.

Quickly calling his office at the Parliament building and making his excuses for the afternoon meeting that was just about to begin, he hailed the first free taxi he could find and directed the driver to his other, less ornate place of work. His mission for Quo was set quite clearly in his mind. He made straight for his private office and placed three phone calls in quick succession.

The first was to an Italian Member of the European Parliament, a gentleman who was well aware that Terleone possessed some interesting knowledge of his business affairs, which he was very keen should remain concealed. It was not the first time he had been politely asked for information in exchange for Terleone's silence.

'Yes, *signore*, I have a rather unusual request. Please take a little time to identify and provide me with the name of a colleague MEP possessing, in your considered opinion, an extremely high level of political and moral integrity, and an untarnished reputation. Perhaps you would like to work on this for an hour or two this afternoon, to ensure an excellent result, and call me on the usual number at eight o'clock? *Bene. Molte grazie, signore.*'

The second call was to the head of the research group within his own department.

The final call was to the personal extension of a bishop in the Vatican City.

He then unlocked a drawer of his desk, selected the first of six brand new mobile phones which were stored neatly alongside one another, and re-locked the drawer. Strolling casually out into the afternoon sunshine and onto a busy street, he proceeded to place several very private calls, putting out feelers and discreet inquiries as to why exactly that particular café had been raided so soon after his arrival ...

* * *

Carla and Toni sat silently together under the palms for quite some time, each happy with the other's company, but each preoccupied with very different thoughts. Finally, Toni remembered to hold up his sheet of paper again, and the co-ordinates of the café were promptly sent to the *Mater*.

Then, at Carla's gentle insistence, he consulted his map, and worked out an indirect route to the address of the town apartment which, in response to Quo's direct order, Terleone had written in the margin. Taking great pains to keep Carla clear of all passers-by, which forced a laboriously slow pace, they made their way along many side-streets until, after nearly an hour, they finally reached the impressive apartment block halfway up the hill of the Via Veneto. Pausing for a moment, apparently for a further map consultation, Toni switched on his GPS again, reassured himself it was fully operational, and took two more fixes.

* * *

At three twenty-five, a woman wearing beige check trousers, carrying a bright red anorak, and consuming a double cheeseburger and fries was detained outside a fast-food restaurant not far from Via Frattina.

Despite the protestations of her husband and two other married couples travelling with them, she was destined to spend the night in a police cell while the various interested authorities ignored diplomatic protests and decided what charges, if any, they could press. The investigating officer would finally be forced to acknowledge that displaying bad taste (multiple counts) was not actually a criminal offence, even in Rome, and she would be released late the following morning, given a small amount of Poor Fund cash in compensation, and provided with clear directions to a nearby fashion house and a good restaurant for lunch.

* * *

With the special fix taken, Toni and Carla sat down again, this time at another pavement café. At her request, Toni took out his sheet of paper, copied down the co-ordinates of Terleone's apartment, and then held the paper up for her, allowing them to be safely read by the *Mater*.

Then he ordered a beer, and Carla allowed him to gather his thoughts once more.

'Quo suggested we should see the sights,' he finally offered. 'We haven't had much time for that yet! Shall we make our way down to the Trevi Fountain? It's really beautiful in the photographs. But I suppose it could be very crowded. Or there's the Colosseum — there should be more space for you there, and it looks incredible! And we must look for a hotel room. And we — sorry, I mean, I could think about an early dinner. I'm absolutely famished.'

Carla was pensive. 'Yes, Toni, I am happy to take another walk. But I feel that things are still not under proper control, and I do not see a clear path into the future. This is not how it should be. I truly wish to enjoy the beauty of Rome with you — the pleasure will fulfil me more than you can know. But something is not right. We have not been able to engage with your great-uncle in the way that we wished — and there have been so many disturbances since we met. I feel the need to re-gather my strength and be ready to take the initiative again, if necessary ...'

Toni did not understand very much of this. The words sounded more like Quo's than Carla's. But he heard the honesty in her voice, and saw it on her face. 'That's fine, Carla. It's still a lovely afternoon. No plans, then! Let's just stroll and enjoy it, and see what the evening brings ...'

'Thank you, Toni. You are very understanding. I promise to share my thoughts with you again as soon as I am ready.'

* * *

The InterSB co-ordinator in the Rome special branch HQ had become fascinated by the increasingly striking parallels between the Bilbao and Rome alerts. Both now included different mystery women (and they were still searching for theirs, despite the arrest of that tourist!). Then, at four-fifteen, the co-ordinator was alerted to the appearance of a new item that had just been just filed in the database by the Spanish Intelligence Agency. It described the events of the day before, in much the same terms as the earlier report from the Bilbao special branch officer, and announced the formal downgrading of the incident to "top secret". But in addition to the largely similar descriptions, it included a photograph of the young music student, labelled "released, no charge". She instantly printed the complete item and, in the absence of her sergeant, hand-delivered it to the inspector himself.

That was the last thing he needed! So that dandy bureaucrat was even involved with an international terrorist suspect! For the student Murano was obviously not an innocent bystander after all. And right now, he and the sergeant were the only ones who knew it! But the muted warnings given to him quite clearly, earlier that afternoon, as he was persuaded to allow the smooth operator and his boyfriend to leave the bar at once, were weighing heavily upon him. He told the waiting co-ordinator to leave it with him for a few moments. 'Something rings a bell here — let me think about it ...'

* * *

Giuseppe Terleone's contacts had not let him down. He had been shown that latest intelligence report, including the photograph of his own great-nephew, a full six minutes before it was picked up by the Rome special branch. It had been hard to control his shock as he dismissed the messenger ...

He was now a very worried man. This was close to getting out of hand. He knew exactly how he would normally handle this sort of public threat to his carefully orchestrated private world. But Antonio was family. He had no choice. And there was this other new business that he was somehow being forced to pursue. He must continue to pay attention to that. He suspected that Antonio was linked in with it, though he couldn't work out why he had come to that conclusion.

So his instincts were telling him he must do all he could to help his young relative and that amazing sister-in-arms.

What had he done to deserve this? Well, that inspector had better remember the warning he had received ...

He needed to clear the decks, to give himself some breathing space, to plan his way out of this, without these urgent pressures. Yes — he would have to spirit the boy away from the police hunt in Rome, and then somehow get him out of the country. That would be expensive in time and money. Calling Antonio's mobile phone would be a big risk now. But ... no, there was no other way, with all those influences bearing down on him, and no time to lose — they had probably started the manhunt already ...

He made his decision.

* * *

The police inspector had made his decision, too. He closed his office door and phoned his sergeant, who had been out for the past half-hour and would not yet have had the challenge of discussing the latest news with his colleagues. He reminded him, very firmly once again, to forget that the boy and the smartly-dressed man were ever seen in the café, and told him that he was about to report that he now remembered spotting the newly-revealed suspect, Murano, walking down the street away from the scene, just as they had arrived. Another manhunt would begin immediately. And he would order the full monitoring of the student's famous mobile phone, and his bank and credit cards. But, he stressed to his uncomfortable subordinate, absolutely no mention would ever be made of the man in the cashmere coat.

The barman and the waiter had already been given the same sound advice, as the inspector left the café. And, because none of the staff had spotted the fleeting appearance of a woman in a pale blue suit, the police officers would never even learn of her virtual existence.

* * *

Terleone selected a second pristine mobile phone from his drawer, hurried out of the rear of the building and into another busy street, and called Toni's number.

'Antonio? This is your new friend. Do not say anything yet. Listen carefully and do exactly as I say.

'The police are searching for you. They have a photograph.

'You must leave Rome at once. Do not ask why — just trust me. You must not use your present mobile phone again after this — do you understand?' ... 'Nor your passport, nor your identity card. Is that clear?' ... 'Now — are you near any shops?' ... 'Have you got plenty of cash?' ... 'Good. Buy a large pair of sunglasses, a large baseball cap, and something to go on top of the clothes you're wearing. Pay cash. Put them all on straight away. Make sure you tuck all that hair under the cap! Then you must both take a taxi straight to Termini station, and go to Venice. Pay cash for everything. Find somewhere to stay — somewhere private. As soon as you are settled in, call me from a street phone. Write this down ...'

And he read out the number of yet another mobile phone.

'Read that back.' ... 'Right. Nobody else knows that number, Antonio. When it rings, I shall know it is you calling. Then I shall tell you what to do next. Meanwhile, keep the sunglasses and the cap on at all times. And stop shaving. Is that all clear?' ... 'Good — now switch off your phone and go, my boy!'

Terleone rang straight off, praying that the call had not been monitored, praying that his regular confessions were appreciated. His prayers would, as usual, be answered, with eight minutes to spare.

Then, using his regular mobile phone, he spoke briefly again to his Head of Research, and modified his earlier request. 'No problem,' he was assured; the new information he sought would be provided to him within half an hour.

* * *

Toni switched off his phone, sighed deeply, and was again obliged to explain to Carla about yet more problems.

Her continuing concerns were therefore proving quite justified. Although Terleone probably *was* actively pursuing the mission which he had been rather hurriedly given, he was obviously working to a very different agenda as well.

But resigning herself in her turn to the situation, and deciding that this level of confusion must, after all, be closer to the norm on Earth than she and her colleagues had expected, she nodded her acceptance of Toni's enforced new plans.

So she waited outside a nearby drugstore until he emerged wearing a baseball cap, a pair of less than fashionable sunglasses and a navy-blue cagoule. Then she pointed out that a taxi was luckily dropping off its previous fare only a few metres away. Without ceremony, Toni rushed straight for it, pulled the rear door open, jumped in and moved over. Carla slid elegantly alongside him. Then he reached back across her and slammed the door.

The traffic was moving much more slowly at this hour of the day. Neither of them was speaking. They were both too bemused by the ever-changing situation. There would be quiet time for proper conversation soon, they both hoped ...

Then Toni suddenly had a thought. 'Are you going to join me on the train?'

'Will it be crowded?'

'I don't know. Yes, probably — it's the rush hour now.'

'Then I must not, Toni. We don't want any hysterics from the other passengers. I will leave the taxi soon, and follow you in the usual way. If you do get the chance to find a quiet corner, I might be able to join you for a while. That would be nice. But whatever happens, I will watch you as you leave the train. I must see where you are spending the night. Then I have more work to do, while you sleep. I will meet up with you again in the morning, I promise ...'

The traffic had halted. Carla spotted a suitable doorway, Toni opened the nearside door, for appearance's sake, and she slid out. Nobody was watching as she simply evaporated in the shadows ...

* * *

Toni studied the railway timetables, suddenly realising how exhausted he was again. He had been up since four-thirty, he had only eaten some crisps and a small pizza, and his brain hadn't stopped buzzing all day. Yes, plenty of trains to Venice — but it would be hours before he got there, and then he'd need to find somewhere to stay, very late in the evening. But the trains stopped at Florence — and that was only about an hour and a half away. He would break the journey there. Carla would cope.

He stood in line for some time to buy his ticket, and paid in cash. Yes, Terleone had said he must pay for everything in cash. He still had plenty of euros left but, with ten minutes to spare before the next departure, he hurried over to a dispenser to draw some more. He always felt happier anyway with plenty of real notes in his pocket, as well as plastic. He inserted his bank debit card.

This transaction cannot be completed. Please try later.

But the card was returned to him. Strange. There was always plenty of money in his account: his parents saw to that. So he tried with his credit card instead. The same result. Must be a faulty machine. But there were no others immediately visible, and the next train was due to leave in four minutes. He would get more cash at the other end — in the morning.

Then, in their different ways, Toni and Carla boarded the 1830 express to Florence.

* * *

The police cars, invoked by a string of alerts initiated by the computer systems of two separate banks, converged on Rome Termini six minutes after the train departed. For over an hour, the officers scoured the station for Antonio Felipe Murano.

* * *

As the train slowed down and stopped, ninety minutes after its departure, Toni stood up, and Carla, who was tracking him carefully from outside, prepared to follow him. She spotted the station sign: Firenze S.M Novella. This was presumably not Venice. But once again she had to tag along, still not back in the metaphorical driver's seat ...

A single policeman languidly watched the station entrance from behind the wheel of his patrol car. Trying to get cash, they had radioed. So he probably hadn't bought a ticket at that stage, anyway. Could have got on any number of trains since then. And this one had left Rome only five minutes after he'd tried to use the machine. Not likely to be on this one, then. More likely the one arriving at half-past eight. If he was actually getting off here in Florence. If he was going north. If he was planning to catch a train in the first place. Probably still in Rome.

And seeing, in the rush hour crowd, nobody obviously matching that vague broadcast description of a smartly-dressed student with long flopping dark hair and a shiny face, he resigned himself to another twenty-five minutes of tedium before the arrival of the next train, which held more promise. Then he would be able to drive back and go off-shift ...

* * *

Toni separated himself from the large group of commuters who had unknowingly helped to conceal him from those less-than-eagle eyes, and began his search for a small hotel. He soon spotted one, and yes, they had vacancies.

'*Passaporto, per favore.*'

'Ah, I'm sorry ...', he mumbled in his broken Italian, putting on his little-dog-lost face again. 'It was stolen this afternoon in Rome. I've reported it to the police. And my embassy says they will sort it all out tomorrow. But I have an important interview here early in the morning, so I had to come. I'm very sorry ...'

The owner hesitated for a few moments. He then consulted his list, offering Toni his most expensive room, after adding 25% to the official rate. 'Cash in advance. Take it or leave it. Out of the place before seven o'clock. If anyone asks, you did not stay here. OK?'

'OK,' said Toni gratefully, and handed over a lot of money.

He climbed the stairs with all his energy sapped, unlocked the door of his room, shuffled inside, and dumped his rucksack on the king-size bed.

Carla, following close behind, noted the position of the room and then left him to rest at last.

Retracing the route she had just followed, she was back in the centre of Rome within seconds, readying herself to appear unannounced at the now-known and adequately-calibrated co-ordinates of the city home of Don Giuseppe Marco Terleone.

Collection Sphere

Giuseppe Marco Terleone, Quo had earlier established, was the youngest of five brothers and sisters. Born in late 1945, he recalled a childhood spent in a climate of post-war austerity; but his parents had been rich compared with most families for miles around. For his father had taken advantage of the excellent business opportunities offered by the light munitions industry that had flourished in the wooded hills of Umbria for the previous five years, and those opportunities were readily adaptable with the coming of the peace.

So, after a simple but very comfortable childhood, and a sound basic education at the local town schools, where he demonstrated great promise, Giuseppe was sent at the age of ten to an expensive private institution in Rome. Payment of his fees was transacted by his father in both cash and kind.

Doors continued to open smoothly for him with the passing years, and in his early twenties he emerged from the Paris Sorbonne ready to exploit an excellent degree in Economics and Administration, a year before the rest of its students emerged onto the streets of Paris with different intent.

Three years later he married into rich and influential Rome society, and would be well looked after by the dons of that family for as long as he retained their respect and their confidence.

A generation later, his daughter and his son were similarly embraced by notable Roman families. Don Giuseppe now proudly possessed three young grandchildren, who were his greatest simple pleasure in his very complex life.

The urbane Terleone was in excellent health. He ate the finest food Rome could offer, but always chose carefully, with great regard for his regular exercise regime. His clothes were from the best Italian fashion houses. His occasional evenings out were typically spent at the Opera (he favoured the Italian composers, with only rare concessions to others). He had little real interest in the other arts, but ensured that he was a lauded patron of several of Rome's smaller museums.

And, busy man that he was, he always conducted his confessions by telephone, and at the appropriate level.

The call which Terleone had most recently received at his town apartment was however in response to the very first of his earlier enquiries. The result seemed very satisfactory, well deserving of a further gracious thank-you to the MEP who had frantically devoted the past five hours to achieving it. Giuseppe's demand for that gentleman's services had been honoured. Until the next time.

So he now had both the names he was after. Yet he still did not really understand why he needed them. Or for whom. In fact, he had never in his well-ordered life felt so uncertain; almost insecure ...

* * *

Carla found herself safely back and unobservable at the co-ordinates of the front entrance to Terleone's apartment block.

She moved through into the lobby and consulted the incomplete lists of names and floors on the interior wall. No sign of a Terleone. But then she deduced a pattern in the apartment numbering system, and passed quickly up the lift shaft to the fourth floor.

She soon found herself outside a door with a number corresponding exactly to the one Terleone had written on Toni's map. But still no name was displayed. A private individual indeed, she thought. Without pausing for breath, since she needed none, she passed through the door and onwards into the living room, and discovered Don Giuseppe standing at his front window, gazing pensively out over the hills of Rome.

She re-made at once, behind him, then whispered engagingly '*Ciao, Giuseppe.*'

He turned around, saw her unforgettable smile, and returned it in great surprise — she ought to be on her way to Venice! Then, for no special reason he could think of, he moved straight over to his vintage Linn turntable, selected his favourite recording of *La Bohème*, and set it playing.

He then turned back to Carla and opened his arms wide to welcome her ...

She did not lose the moment. Although his left brain set off warning bells as his arms passed straight through her, his right brain had already taken over, as previously arranged, and he was quickly and fully engaged. And then Quo was with him again, speaking soundlessly in Italian.

Good evening, Giuseppe ...

The first thing Terleone revealed, in response to Quo's polite demand, was the single name and personal profile which he had finally received from his primary source.

After much searching, he said, his contacts had come up with a surprisingly short list of names of European MPs whose records were both completely untarnished by any hints, accusations or actual reports of wrongdoing or misdemeanours, and also characterised by a history of willingness to speak out, even when their views conflicted with accepted or encouraged party wisdom.

'And among that small cluster of stars,' Terleone was pleased to announce, 'a certain Mevr. Hilde van Wostraap, native of Amsterdam, Dutch MEP, citizen of Europe, appears to shine out as the brightest by far.'

Then, in answer to Quo's request for the results of the second part of his mission, he was indeed able to supply the name, home address, and description of a very capable, computer-skilled research assistant.

'You told me, Quo, that Carla would need to work with the person I found. Well, after I decided to send Antonio away from here, I realised that it would be unhelpful to identify a researcher based in Rome. So I then located one for you in Venice ...'

Giuseppe, we are most grateful to you for your efforts. You have collected the information we requested smoothly, ingeniously and effectively. We shall put it to very good use, you may be sure.

'Thank you, Quo.'

Now, as we implied to you this afternoon, we had intended to recruit you solidly to our ranks of Empowered Collectors, so that you might serve our cause, both directly and indirectly, in the days to come. That cause being, as we informed you, the continuous improvement of our developing model of the hearts and minds of the human race.

'I feel I have an inadequate grasp of what you are saying ...'

Precisely, Giuseppe. And there is the rub. Your young relative Toni provided us with our initial profile of the human condition. Limited perhaps in depth and experience, but high in quality. We had then hoped to make a major enhancement to our model with a full understanding of your own mind, and to make contact, through you, with many other persons of note.

But, unfortunately, that aim has been hindered by the difficulties encountered during your engagement. I can now see clearly that the inadequacy of our transferral and missioning, and your very strong instincts for self-preservation, have left you in a state of highly confused loyalties. I suspect it would be difficult to achieve the purity of engagement we require, without considerable further effort and risk to us all.

'I am very sorry, Quo.'

However, we are well aware that Toni is somewhat imperilled by recent events, and that you are strongly motivated to assist him and Carla. For this, we are most grateful.

'Thank you, Quo. Yes, indeed — in the past half-hour I have in fact been worrying that Antonio might try to draw more cash using his plastic cards. I regret that I failed to warn him specifically not to do so ...'

It is most helpful of you to alert me to this, Giuseppe. You may rest assured that I will attend to your concerns at once.

But in summary, we fear that it is far too dangerous to continue to use you as an agent for our evolving model. We know that you, more than most, will appreciate our need for great confidence in our level of control! So, from this point onwards, we shall cease to regard you as a Collector. But we encourage you to continue your planned support for Toni, so that he and Carla may successfully pursue their missions. Can we rely on you, Giuseppe?

'Of course. You have no need to ask for this. Antonio is family. There is no question ...'

Thank you, Giuseppe. In which case — you will immediately lose all recollection of Carla, and of the tasks you have just completed. You will focus much effort, as you already intend, on securing the passage of Toni to a place of safety. Once that is achieved, you will forget that he was ever here. And, despite your natural inclinations, you will not involve yourself in any dialogue about this with the rest of Toni's family.

'As you wish, Quo. I understand very well the benefits of co-operating when encouraged to do so.'

* * *

By the time Terleone became clearly aware that he was once again in his own living room, and nowhere else at the same time, Carla had gone, and was forgotten.

She was, in fact, thanks to the now much-improved accuracy of the *Mater's* world co-ordinates, already back in Florence and outside the door of Toni's hotel room. Entering silently and unseen, she found that he was already sound asleep.

Only then, as in Bilbao on the previous evening, could Carla the Handler pass the watch over to one of her studio assistants, and at last retire gratefully to rest in her own particular Doman way.

* * *

Don Giuseppe sat down purposefully at his desk and thought hard for nearly half an hour, putting the finishing touches to the major rescue plan that he had been building since late afternoon. Finally, he unlocked a drawer, removed yet another brand-new mobile phone, and made the first in a further series of very special requests.

Between the Lines

Toni woke with his alarm at five-thirty. He felt surprisingly refreshed after his long deep sleep, and he was now very hungry, but he had a grand plan! He was in the heart of the city, so he was determined to take a quick look at Florence, and then get some breakfast, before catching an early train to Venice.

Soon after six o'clock he was ready to don his sunglasses, cap and waterproof. He picked up his rucksack, crept down the stairs, and left the sleeping hotel.

Then he was able to spend two almost perfect hours seeing the most celebrated sights of the magnificent city, with hardly another tourist in view, and only the build-up of rush-hour traffic to disturb him towards the end of his tour.

He wandered around each of the three great piazzas. He gazed in awe at the campanile and the dome of the cathedral. He was sad that he could not visit the treasures of the Uffizi Gallery at that early hour. He strolled across the Ponte Vecchio, then back again, marvelling at the details of its construction. And then he felt he must cross over and back once more, this time to absorb the glorious views it offered of the River Arno and the beautiful city.

Finally, accepting that he needed two weeks in Florence but was lucky to have had his two hours, he grabbed a coffee and a large pastry for breakfast, and was back at the station in time for the 0838 departure to Venice Santa Lucia, stopping at Bologna and Ferrara. There was not a policeman in sight.

* * *

Carla had been accompanying Toni, unseen, ever since he left his room. And she now continued to follow his tracks, just as before.

But she had decided to develop a technique for maintaining the same speed as the train at all times — by setting herself at a precise distance from a close part of it, and then commanding the *Mater's* systems to maintain that distance exactly. Once that virtual tow-bar was perfected (and it shouldn't take long), she would be able to set her speed to be precisely that of Toni, and perhaps then re-join him ...

The first leg of the journey took them to Bologna. Carla had already completed her trials, and the *Mater* was fully programmed. But Toni had been in a very full carriage for the previous hour, and there had been no question of joining him.

At Bologna, a large number of people disembarked, and only a few boarded the train — the rush hour had passed. Toni stood up as it pulled out of the station, and spent the next few minutes reconnoitring. At last he found some empty seats at the front of the very first carriage, with nobody else in the adjacent block or the one immediately behind. He took up a position by the window, facing forwards and hidden from the rest of the carriage, and crossed his fingers ...

Carla had been travelling alongside and watching his efforts through the windows. She was satisfied with the results — this looked safe enough, at least until the next station. Still unseen, she passed into the front carriage, hovered in the vicinity of the seat next to him, and set her velocity to track Toni's absolutely. Then, when her speed was stable, and he was looking away through the window, she re-made and quietly said, as she had in Bilbao, '*Hola.*'

'Oh, hello Carla,' Toni whispered. 'It's good to see you again.'

Carla smiled. 'It's good to hear your jokes again! But there's no need to whisper — I could have been sitting here all the time, as far as anyone else in the carriage knows.'

'Of course you could.'

'Now — I met up with Giuseppe again last night. We at last have some promising contacts to pursue.'

'Oh, good,' said Toni, not sure what else to say.

Carla rescued him from his familiar discomfort. 'So we have a little free time together at last. I am very happy to try and answer all your remaining questions.'

'Ah, that's great, Carla.'

'But since we are not overlooked at the moment, and my Spanish is still rather thin, and we know you need and expect proper answers, I might have to invite Quo to help me. So if we need to engage with you at any point (don't worry, I shan't disappear — it will only be a gentle briefing), you will not object, will you?'

'Of course not!'

'Then go ahead with whatever questions you like ...'

'All right — let's take it from the top. Remind me: what happens immediately after the radimote has been created by those beams?'

'Ah, a technical subject straight away! Just a moment ...' And Carla reached over and took his head in her hands ...

Good morning, Toni.

'Good morning, Quo.'

Well, Toni, once the radimote is generated by our laser systems, it then has to make a controlled glide to land. It cannot simply descend from its point of birth — because we cannot "hit" that point with perfect accuracy.

Of course, we aim at a location which visually interests us. But initial positioning errors are inevitable: they are caused by atmospheric conditions that we cannot fully predict. This means there will normally be a small variation, in longitude and latitude, between where the radimote is created and where we later bring it to ground.

All our previous tests of this procedure worked well — we proved the technology on Dome itself and, with simulated atmospheres, on several satellites and on two of our moons. The radimote always appeared within a few kilometres of our target point — perfectly acceptable for the glide which then followed in each case.

'OK, Quo. So why did you come to Spain?'

We positioned the *Mater* over the west coast of Africa, Toni, because we could see many cities to the north (in your Europe). There were several other possibilities, of course, far across the oceans to the west and the east, but we simply had to select one, with little further information to guide us.

We then chose the north coast of Spain as our target for the radimote, because it is almost exactly halfway between the Equator and the North Pole. We guessed that the climate there should be moderate by Earth's standards, compared with the planet's extremes — which should make the area conducive to relatively comfortable living for the inhabitants. And, because it is a sea coast, we hoped it would be a fairly active example of a trading civilisation.

'Explorers and natives, again, eh?'

Perhaps, Toni. Anyway, we finally targeted a large city and port located further along the coast from Bilbao.

'Probably Santander.'

Yes, it was indeed Santander. We aimed a little to the south-east of the city, so that the radimote would not have to travel over a very large area of water. It is much better to glide over land while selecting a final touchdown point!

'So how did you end up in Bilbao? It's seventy kilometres away!'

Well, do you remember a short, windy downpour, with some lightning, in Bilbao late last Sunday afternoon? That bad weather had been over Santander two hours earlier, but we did not recognise it as such. We could see the area we were targeting quite clearly (and we can see through all types of cloud), and there were no obvious warning signs. But our initial transmission was dramatically affected by the electrical storm over to the west. We are sure the wind had some effect too, but we don't know how. Anyway, the result was that the radimote ended up being generated many kilometres to the east of Santander, and some way south of the coast — and was still being "pushed" eastwards by the weather.

'So it was heading for Bilbao ...'

Exactly. We made a decision quite quickly to abandon the plan to land in Santander. The weather ahead to the east looked fine, at least for the time being, and we knew the other city was not too far away — so we set off on a low level glide, and the radimote came to earth on its western outskirts.

'So I only met Carla and got involved in your missions because of an accident of the weather!'

Everything is an accident, Toni.

'I won't try to resurrect my religion essays on free will and predestination, Quo!'

A good decision.

Then, after the storm had passed over Bilbao, the weather improved quickly during the evening, and it was calm and very warm the next morning — as you will recall.

'It certainly was.'

Now, I know Carla wishes to take up the story herself ...

Carla moved her hands away from Toni's head.

'Yes, I do,' she broke in quietly, in her usual limited but totally understandable own words. 'I was very busy that Sunday evening, Toni, and all through the night and early the next morning! I was doing several things in parallel ...

'My main task was to find an image to adopt, at least for the first few hours. I soon worked out the main differences between men and women, though I'm sure it's more complex than that under the surface! Then it seemed quite natural to take on the guise of a female, for the purposes of the first involvement, as least. So I located several women who seemed to be very popular in the company they were keeping, and I learned and stored the image of one of them, and then moved off to the other side of the city ...

'But when I eventually made myself visible in that image, and sat down at an outdoor café to practice my techniques and listen in to some of your language, I was repeatedly accosted by some rather undesirable characters! Fortunately, none of them tried to touch me. After the third of these approaches, since I was unable to say very much (I had learned hardly any Spanish by then), I just had to stand up and walk away. I tried it again a little later, after I had picked up a few more words, but the same thing happened. So I gave up practising — but I had learned something. That's why, when you met me, I played those games with the camera and the jacket. I wanted everyone to believe I was already accompanied.'

'You're very smart, Carla.'

'A girl soon learns, Toni! And I also decided that perhaps I had not chosen an ideal image for the purpose of attracting someone like you. So I un-made, and spent most of the next few hours working on that challenge.

'Lots of observation of individuals and couples was needed, in many places around the city — with some learning of vocabulary on the side (but not much!). Finally, on Monday morning, I discovered a young woman who seemed to fit the bill perfectly. I watched her as she shopped, and I followed her until she went into a beauty salon ...

'And then I was ready to find you.'

'But how did you know where to look?'

'Music is really important to us, Toni. It is almost as important as your food and drink, and the air that you breathe. That is why we seek out those who love music — we know that our involvement of them should go very smoothly, and that they will probably prove to be great supporters and Illuminators ...

'So while I'd been seeking a suitable image, and learning some Spanish, I was also in search of music. I did not hear very much, in fact — perhaps Bilbao is not the ideal place for it on a Sunday night. Although I did come across the sounds of several beautiful church organs in the early evening — and some rather raucous noises in the bars of the old city!

'But in the morning, after I had found my ideal image, but was still un-made, I also discovered the music I was looking for — in the Bilbao Conservatorio. I wandered in and out of the practice rooms and the halls, and listened to many young people making glorious music, alone and in concert. This was perfect! Then I spotted a young man, in a space of his own, at a piano. I know now that it was the music of Beethoven that you were playing at that moment, Toni. I was very moved. Then, when you had finished that sonata, you went quickly into a slow, slinky piece of modern blues, and I could hear you singing quietly along with it! Incidentally, I heard that very song again a few hours later, in your living room ...

'So I resolved to make you my companion. I knew at once that our souls would entwine. When you left the building soon afterwards, and wandered down towards the square, I followed you — all the way to the café.'

'Yes, I would normally have gone straight home after my lecture and a bit of practice on the grand piano — but I was thirsty, and the weather was perfect again after that storm.'

'And you ordered your beer, and then I came to you, Toni.'

'But what did you do to make me follow you? That wasn't like me at all ...'

'I smiled. Twice.'

'I know you did! But why?'

'Toni, we are able to smile a very special sort of smile. It sets off an automatic response in the subject we wish to involve. He or she immediately wants to hear or sing their favourite music, and places all their confidence in the Finder, and becomes extremely malleable. We can then proceed with whatever engagement we desire.'

'It sounds utterly supernatural to me, Carla.'

'Really, Toni? For human males, are there no corresponding mental or physical reactions to the sight of another human who strongly attracts them?'

Toni went bright red, and had no answer. And then he saw Carla's hands coming to embrace him once more, and heard Quo's "voice" taking over again ...

> But the music alone is not enough, Toni. The subject needs to feel extremely comfortable with the situation in general, or needs to be strongly motivated to be there. Otherwise there will be all sorts of unpredictable reactions. That is why it was necessary to begin your involvement when you were relaxing with your beer. And to complete it in the seclusion of your home, with the wonderful music that you chose ...

And the Finders are not mind-readers, in the way that real Domans are. They reflect the minds of their Handlers, no more, no less, and a Handler's mission is to seek and select, to involve and engage, and to support the subject's transferral and missioning.

The Handlers' great learning ability allows them to rapidly appreciate the rich characteristics of an organism's behaviour. But they remain observers and students; they cannot see directly into human minds. The process of transferral, and all that then needs to follow, can only be conducted using the specialised equipment held ready in the *Mater*.

But this does not prevent Handlers from having a fair degree of intuition. They can readily spot another smart student, and those, such as Carla, who possess a particular talent for music can often, unconsciously, be quite dramatically selective ...

'So, Quo, back to my old questions. How can Carla see me?'

Well, by understanding you, Toni, we now know that our own faculty of vision uses a range of light frequencies that is not very different from yours. Fortunately, it allows us to see all that you can, and rather more. Incidentally, our colleagues presently exploring other new worlds may encounter bigger challenges in that area — there are so many unknowns when you plan a voyage like this!

So, we can send a low-energy spectrum of our visible light down one of those beams from the *Mater*. Those light waves spread out from the radimote in all directions, and bounce off all the objects they encounter. Some of the rays reflect immediately back to the radimote, and are transmitted onwards up the other beam to the *Mater*. This provides the visual input (or "sight", as you call it), which is used by Carla the Handler for her continuous operations.

'I see! And how can she hear me?'

In a similar way. The light waves that come in to the radimote, from all around, are accompanied by concurrent sound waves. Those are also transmitted up to the *Mater*; so, to use your terms, the radimote serves as a powerful microphone. And since we "hear" the sounds in the context of the visually observed activity which accompanies them, our processing systems can learn quickly, though only in a rudimentary fashion, the meanings of words and phrases spoken by nearby local inhabitants. The Handler learns this in parallel, of course.

'All right. But what about Carla's ability to speak?'

All the sounds that have been learned, Toni, can be reproduced at will down the other beam from the *Mater*, resulting in an audio output at the radimote. Since this mimics the words and phrases that have been heard, with the same level of fidelity as the copying techniques used to present the radimote visually, it can appear to be speaking quite clearly and accurately, in the local language, and in a voice appropriate to the person whose image is being portrayed. You are correctly thinking of it as rather like ventriloquism.

Carla's first real attempt at this, when she ordered those drinks at the café, went rather well, we feel; she had picked up that little Spanish phrase very nicely, a few hours before meeting you. She is learning quickly to speak much more fully with you, Toni, in all your languages. And her voice will no doubt soon become coloured by her emotions, just as her body language has already ...

'Thank you, Quo,' interrupted Carla, as politely as she could. Then she gently took her hands away from Toni's head, and spoke once more to her precious companion.

'I think you now have all your answers, Toni.

'And I want to add a personal thank-you for all you have done for us already — and an apology. As you probably realise, these are Dome's first voyages of discovery, and the first real use of the *Mater* and our new technologies. So we are all feeling rather nervous, and we have made several small mistakes. We're sorry this has made things difficult for you. It's all quite stressful for us too, and, believe me, it's very tiring ...'

'I believe you, Carla. I really do.'

They had stopped at Ferrara station. There were many people waiting on the platform outside their carriage. As several of them boarded and made their way down the aisle towards her, Carla sighed and said quickly 'Close your eyes, Toni. I'll see you in Venice.'

As soon as he had done what she asked, she un-made, moved out onto the platform, and waited for the train to depart.

Venice, Italy

Toni arrived at Santa Lucia station just before eleven-thirty, still wearing his sunglasses and his baseball cap. It was too warm for the cagoule, and he was looking forward to taking the cap off again and washing his sticky hair. But that would have to wait. At least the weather was still good, and he wouldn't look too much out of place.

Trusting that Carla was still with him in spirit, he bought a street plan of Venice from the station bookstall, and turned left out of the main entrance. He was immediately stunned by the magnificent facade of the church of Santa Maria di Nazareth degli Scalzi. The temptation to go inside was great, but he decided that to do so in sunglasses would be pushing the bounds of credibility too far. Anyway, he would probably end up walking straight into a stone column ...

So he checked his new map, and chose not to take the wide bridge crossing the Grand Canal and leading off towards the popular tourist spots. Instead, he continued north-east past the shops of the Lista di Spagna.

'Strange,' he mused. 'I'm still in Italy, but again I find myself in a Spanish place.'

Crossing the next canal via the Ponte delle Guglie, he spotted just ahead, on the Fondamenta di Cannareggio, an ideal place for a beer, a lunch and a rendezvous — the Trattoria Bar Pontini.

The routine was familiar now. Find a quite corner table on the pavement. Pull back another chair. 'Yes, a beer, please, and a lasagna. *Grazie.*' And before even the beer had arrived, there was Carla strolling towards him and sitting down and smiling.

For the very first time since all of this had begun, he felt they might at last have a little breathing space.

* * *

They chatted casually as he ate his lunch. He looked at the street plan
and identified some sights they could later visit together. Carla
supported all his suggestions — with a reminder about the need to
avoid the crowds. Nobody disturbed them. No phone calls. No crises.
They stopped talking and gazed out at the city spreading ahead of
them. Toni was thinking about another beer and a short nap, and was
again secretly admiring the profile which had entranced him back in
Bilbao ...

His tranquillity was destroyed by the call of a different siren. A
water ambulance, on its urgent way to the city hospital, was bearing
down towards them from the right, doing at least 20 knots. It careered
under the Guglie Bridge and then made a very fast left turn into the
Grand Canal, throwing up a large side wave which heavily rocked the
passing gondolas, and everything else moored nearby, for the next
three minutes.

* * *

Their reveries had been broken, and they both realised that it was once
again time for some practicalities. Toni would need somewhere to
sleep. His cash reserves were reducing fast, so he would have to be
careful ('… until when?' he wondered.). But Giuseppe had told him
to find somewhere private, and he also now clearly recognised
(though he did not know how) that he must not try to use his plastic
cards again. So hotels were out of the question.

Carla came up with the idea. 'Toni — why not try and find some
students like yourself, and ask if you can sleep in one of their rooms
for a little while?'

Toni did the rest. He couldn't just march up to people in the street.
Well, maybe some could, but he couldn't. No, he would need to meet
the students on common ground. With common interests. Music! Yes,
there was a very famous Conservatorio here, the Benedetto Marcello
— and there were bound to be other schools. He must find a music
bar, or something similar. The sort of place where students could
afford to go in the evenings.

He looked at his map again. Surely not in the centre of Venice, near
St. Mark's Square — that would be full of expensive restaurants and

classical recitals; very inviting, but not what was required today. No, the bars and clubs he needed would have to be more out-of-the-way, perhaps hidden in the rabbit warren of side-streets and small canals lying north of the Rialto Bridge. In fact, between here and the centre! So their plan was made; they might see some real sights later that day, but they would make their way towards them through the quieter backwaters of the city ...

They strolled back to the Ponte degli Scalzi, and then for over an hour they wandered southwards, several times getting slightly lost in the maze of narrow streets and alleys, whose fading names were invariably inscribed in old Italian languages and often corresponded poorly to the map's modern abbreviations.

As usual, their progress was slowed by the need to keep Carla away from physical contact with others. Of course, it would have been safest for her simply to un-make — but neither of them wanted this today, and the idea had not even been raised. Their bravado nearly caused a stir. In one of the narrowest passages, a single hurrying tourist brushed carelessly against her — or, rather, straight through her elbow. His surprise was great; but, as he turned and watched the pair of them strolling blithely on, apparently taking no further account of him, he blinked, gulped, decided he must have imagined it, and walked away without a word.

Carla made a mental note that this lucky result would not always be achieved: and probably never, if more than one person were involved. Toni happily knew nothing of the incident at all.

And then suddenly, in the tranquil and much wider Calle Raspi dei Sansoni, just south of a tiny bridge of the same name, they found just what they were looking for:

The 900 Jazz Club — Live jazz every Wednesday evening

'And it's a Wednesday today, Carla!' The place was shut up tight in the heat of the spring afternoon, but he wrote down the details posted outside. 'I'll be back by nine!'

Toni's deep pleasure at the success of his first real initiative was very apparent to both Carla and Quo. But they did not allow him to rest long on his laurels.

'Toni, you now need to help *us* for a little while.' And Carla played back, loud and clear and with a perfect Italian accent, the name and home address of the government researcher which Terleone had read out the previous evening. 'He's going to collect some of that geographical data Quo told you we are so keen to acquire.'

Toni had written the details down carefully on his trusty sheet of paper. The street plan was consulted again. 'It's not too far,' he said brightly. 'Over the Rialto, then down towards the Arsenale. Let's go!'

'I think I should un-make for this particular walk. You said we would start meeting lots of tourists as we reach the Rialto ...'

'Of course — and that will let me move along much faster. Good thinking, Carla!'

'It is only a matter of experience, *carísimo.*'

Toni's face went bright red in an instant.

* * *

He gave Carla the customary five minutes to wander away, disappear, and get him back into view. Then he hurried off south and soon reached the Grand Canal once more, as it straightened out after its majestic sweep round to the right. He crossed the busy bridge without taking much notice of its architectural delights (there will be time for that later, he promised himself), then, to avoid the worst of the anticipated crowds, he bore left and pursued a zigzag route to the east.

He found the street with no difficulty, and soon located the correct building. There was a stack of bell-pushes by the front door, with names scribbled against most of them. He took a quick glance. "11. S. Pirone". Yes! A perfect match with the number and the name on his piece of paper.

He looked back the way he had come, and, as casually as he could manage, waved vaguely into the distance. Then, hands in pockets, he meandered on down the street, turned at the end, and meandered back. Good — Carla was coming towards him, and at the perfect rate to ensure a meeting right in front of the apartment building.

He was ahead of the game now, or so he thought. 'This is it, Carla. Shall I take the co-ordinates?'

'No, Toni. It is no longer necessary. Since we took the unplanned GPS fix at Terleone's home, which matched quite well with the

Mater's estimate of our position, I can now revisit anywhere I have been on Earth, with more than enough accuracy. That's how I returned to your hotel room in Florence! So I can come back here whenever I wish, and I can be outside the jazz club by nine o'clock to watch you arrive, and then follow you when you leave ...'

'Oh.' Toni was deflated again, and for two reasons. 'You mean you're going to vanish again, right now?'

'Not yet,' Carla chuckled. 'You're going to take me for a nice stroll along the waterfront of St. Mark's Canal, and then we're going to find a quiet little park where we really can sit and relax for the rest of the afternoon. I promise I shan't go off again till it's time for your evening meal!'

Toni was all smiles once more. So they took the walk that Carla had suggested, and they found the pretty Giardini ex Reali between the waterfront and St Mark's Square, and they sat down on a bench together — and Toni dozed straight off to sleep.

When the sun got lower, and the office workers could be seen walking down to the waterbuses, Carla woke him up again. 'Toni, I must now try and find our Signor Pirone. Have a good dinner. Remember, I shall watch you arrive at the club, and I shall see you again tomorrow. Good luck with your house-hunting!' Then she all but pecked him on the cheek, and walked away.

Toni felt suddenly very alone.

He didn't fancy another hot meal. So he toured the small streets and beautiful buildings surrounding St. Mark's Square for over an hour, then stopped at a café and chose a chicken baguette and a large cappuccino. Then he found a bench in a quiet canal complex to the west of the square, set his wristwatch alarm for eight-fifteen, and had another little nap.

* * *

As Salvatore Pirone, matching well the description supplied by Don Giuseppe, walked the last few yards to his apartment block, he could not fail to notice the petite blonde approaching from the other direction in a bright orange blouse and an above-the-knee skirt. As he reached the front door, she slowed down, stopped and smiled broadly.

He paused, appeared to think very hard for a moment, then opened the door and stood back to let her enter.

When they were both inside, he made straight for the radio and tuned in his favourite jazz music station. Then he turned back to face his new acquaintance. She smiled again, and took his head in her hands ...

The missioning was short and sweet. Two minutes later, Pirone had switched on his personal computer, and shortly afterwards his browser was connected to the Internet.

He then searched expertly for web sites containing comprehensive databases of the precise co-ordinates and elevations of places throughout the world. He searched the public Internet, and he searched the secure networks to which he had privileged access. And he soon found the ideal site.

Then, with three or four customising clicks, he was ready to request a continuously scrolling display of hundreds of thousands of cities, towns, and villages, airports, mountain peaks and modest hills (enough to get them started, the Chief Surveyor had thought. More sophisticated coast and lake outlines another day ...). And once the large, crisp display was clearly visible to the systems on the *Mater*, he was given the go-ahead, he clicked again, and the scrolling began.

Carla and the onboard computers could have handled a much higher data rate. But the modest dial-up modem speed was fast enough to allow them to reach the end of the huge table of data within ninety Earth minutes.

So she would not be late for her next appointment.

'Thank you, Salvatore. You can disconnect now.'

While the young researcher's brain responded smoothly to this pre-arranged signal, which would bring him properly back home and remove from his memory all knowledge of the previous two hours, Carla moved behind him to avoid undue shock and swiftly un-made. Then, with no need for make-up, she went straight out to a club.

* * *

Toni's alarm brought him back to life. Now he could make his way back to the 900 Club, not needing to rush, but taking care to arrive at exactly five to nine and hover around for ten minutes. He wanted to get the feel of the place from outside, and also to be sure that Carla would see him, so that neither of them would fear that she had missed him.

* * *

He could hear the music had already started, and it sounded good. When he finally dived in, it was very dark. Then he remembered he was still wearing the sunglasses. 'Damn it,' he said to himself, 'I don't need them in here.' And off they came, along with the cap. He stuffed them both into his rucksack.

Now he could see there were lots of people already there, sitting at tables or milling around up near the five-piece band. He made for the bar.

He had guessed that English would be the lingua franca in this place. Overheard snippets of conversation confirmed it. That was fine — he could handle jazz club English ...

'A large beer, please!'

'No problem!'

Good — the young American barman seemed friendly, and not too busy right now.

When the beer arrived, Toni leaned across and aimed his voice at the barman's right ear. 'Do you happen to know if any students from the Conservatorio are in here tonight?' The man looked at him a little incredulously, then remembered this was a new kid in town.

'Take your pick! Those three over there, and the girls up near the band. And that table of six near the stairs. Our best customers, those students. Sometimes do cheap shows for us too. Hey, what do they call you?' ... 'Toni? Good to have you here, Toni!'

He stretched out his arm and shook Toni's hand as if he were a visiting celebrity. 'What do you play?'

'Oh, just a little piano. But I don't have it with me tonight.'

'Ha ha ha! Never heard that one before!'

'Really? Well, anyway, thanks for your help.'

'Sure! Have a good time!'

* * *

So Toni found his students, and they welcomed him to their table, and they listened to some great music together. And when there was a suitable break, he told them he was very short of cash for a couple of days, and he needed somewhere to sleep, and there really was money on the way, and he wouldn't stay long, and he would pay them something as soon as he could ...

And the three of them, who all lived together in the same lodgings, laughed at his daring, and decided to believe him, and said 'Of course you can sleep on the couch!' and 'Who's buying the next round, then?' And naturally, it was Toni.

The friendly barman placed the four fresh beers on the counter in front of Toni, then tapped the shoulder of the man sitting on the bar stool next to him.

'Hey, Salvatore, meet Toni — he's a great pianist!'

The solitary young researcher turned round, nodded, and shook Toni's hand politely, then turned away again and went back to wondering why he had fallen asleep for such a long time earlier that evening.

* * *

At about half-past twelve the four of them piled out of the club, all having had a little too much to drink, but with none of the lads regretting the offer of hospitality to their interesting new friend (they had persuaded him to give them a twenty-second burst on the band's keyboards during the interval — and he had passed the test).

Toni had remembered to pick up his rucksack, and they hadn't forgotten their short cuts, and they all were soon back at their rooms, not far at all from where Toni had eaten his lunch, twelve long hours earlier. But he had no idea of this. He just knew he was at last about to get some more sleep. And this time, with no alarm set on his watch! His new house-mates left him on the couch with a spare blanket, and stumbled noisily upstairs.

Carla followed them all home, unseen. She noted the location, summoned another guardian angel, and went off-duty herself.

* * *

Toni awoke with bright sunshine streaming in through the window and onto his face. He looked at his watch: nine-fifteen. Well, he'd deserved a lie-in after the last three days. But he knew there were things to do, and he dragged himself up and called out 'Anyone about?' Nothing. He scrabbled around in the rucksack for his toilet bag, located the bathroom and had a long shower. His hair was clean again at last!

He looked in the mirror for the first time, growled at the sight of his untidy stubble, then spotted a key taped in the centre of the glass. Good guys! Now he was free! He could go out, and phone Giuseppe, and get things moving. He didn't know or care what things, as long as they involved not having to wear a stupid cap and sunglasses every minute of the day ...

He pulled out a change of clothes (he must organise some washing soon, he remembered, but straight away managed to forget again) and dressed quickly, finally donning the detested sunglasses and cap. He spotted a telephone handset on a small table: that could be useful. He wrote down its number, but decided not to use it just yet. Then he opened the front door onto another bright morning. He was enjoying this excellent weather, so early in the spring. The key fitted; the lock turned. He closed the door behind him, then unlocked it again to double-check that all was well. Perfect. Peace of mind.

He took out a piece of paper and wrote down the number inscribed on the front door, then walked to the end of the street, and wrote its name down too. Then he located it on his map, and pointed himself back towards the railway station.

Ten o'clock: a reasonable hour to phone his great-uncle. After that, he could think about some breakfast. And then meet up with Carla? Wait a minute: they hadn't arranged anything! What if she had lost him?

'Think, man, think ... yes, she said she would follow me back from the club ... so she knows where I'm living. So she's probably following me now ... but if not, she can always look for me back there ...'

He had convinced himself that everything was under control. He walked into the station, found a vacant payphone, and dialled Terleone's secret number.

The message passed to him was polite, but terse.

'Antonio, you must leave Italy. The police are still hunting you. I am not concerned with what you may or may not have done. I simply want to help you. I am organising everything. You must trust me. I am sure you will be able to return home soon, once things have been sorted out.'

'But, *signore* ...'

'No, Antonio, there can be no arguments. Have you found somewhere to live?' ... 'Students? Good. Tell me the address.' ... 'Is there a telephone number?' ... '*Bene*. I shall only use it in an emergency. Now, write down this address and read it back to me.' ... 'Good. Do you have a map?' ... 'Can you see it in the list of streets?' ... 'Good. You will go there at exactly twelve noon today. You will be expected. The gentleman who will receive you will explain everything. You must follow his instructions precisely. Is that clear?'

Terleone's powers of persuasion were more than enough to ensure Toni's compliance.

'Yes, sir.'

'Good. We shall talk again soon, Antonio.'

And he was gone.

Toni put the receiver down and stared into space. He knew he should be resisting all this — but he knew he couldn't. So he would just have to carry on.

Right ... Calle della Regina — yes, another little street, back down near the jazz club. Only a few minutes' walk. Everything was a few minutes' walk in Venice!

He crossed the Grand Canal, found an outdoor café, and ordered a coffee and pastry. And suddenly, there was Carla again. He pulled back a chair for her.

'Carla, I have to leave Italy. I have to meet somebody at noon. They'll be organising it all. I really don't know what's happening. Do you?'

'No, Toni: we are all still being driven by events. But we are learning much, and we are hopeful that things will calm down soon. Do you know where you will be going?'

'No — they haven't told me yet.'

'Well, let us hope it will not take too long. We wish to use the rest of the information Giuseppe supplied to us as soon as we can. But you are still in his hands at the moment ...'

'So will you just be following me until things are sorted out?'
'I will, Toni.'

* * *

His expectation of a "little street", Toni discovered, was rather an over-estimate. Back-alley was a better description. And in its dingiest and narrowest stretch, he found the number he was after, chalked onto an otherwise anonymous old wooden door. He tapped on it very politely.

It was opened by a small elderly man, who let him in with a cautious '*Buongiorno,*' immediately removed Toni's sunglasses and smelly cap, tut-tutted at the state of his clothes, and spent the next three minutes simply staring intently at his face. He made a few notes, then picked up a tape, took several measurements of Toni's head, and proceeded to his neck, shoulders, arms, chest, waist, hips, legs and feet. All noted down. Then Toni had to stand against the wall. Several light pencil marks were made. Finally, it was the bathroom scales.

At one point in this ritual, Toni felt he must speak.

'What are you doing this for, sir?'

'Sshhhh ...' was the only reply. It did not seem much like "explaining everything". But Toni waited.

When the measuring was finished, the old man looked him in the face again.

'Your age, *signore*?'

'I'm twenty.'

'And ...'

'And eight months.'

'*Va bene.*' It was noted.

'Do you have money?'

'I have very little cash left — and I have been told not to use my plastic cards.'

His host pulled open a drawer, counted out three hundred euros, and handed them over. He then took a small piece of paper, wrote briefly, and passed it to Toni.

'You will go to this address at two o'clock this afternoon. It is just around the corner. Do you have a map?'

'Yes.'

'*Va bene.*'

He handed back the cap and sunglasses. Motioning Toni to put them on once more, he opened the front door just a few inches, peeked out, ushered him through, and closed it without ceremony. He then returned to his notes and picked up the telephone.

* * *

Well, at least they were organising his schedule nicely around meal times ...

Toni decided to get himself a proper lunch. He had a nasty feeling he might be travelling again soon. He wouldn't worry about being near crowds — Carla could look after herself: that at least was clear. She probably wouldn't join him this time.

He strolled back down to the Rialto Bridge and found a long row of restaurants spread along the north bank: the Riva del Vin. And there were outdoor tables, so he could maintain his disguise. He chose the Ristorante Canal Grande, no less, and for the next hour enjoyed some sights and sounds of tourist Venice, an excellent pizza and two glasses of fine house red wine.

* * *

At two o'clock he was back in the rabbit-warren; in Calle del Ravano this time, just beyond Ponte del Ravano — and knocking at another nondescript old wooden door.

This one was opened by a well-dressed woman in her forties. She smiled a welcome. Toni felt more comfortable this time. But she said little as she went to work.

She sat him down in front of a large sink. On went a plastic cape. First she attacked his hair. The long, thick brown waves were soon lying all over the stone floor. Then a thorough wash and rinse. Then a darker brown dye. Then another long rinse, and a proper cut. '*Bene*,' she said to herself. No mirror for him to monitor progress. Probably just as well.

Then she turned her attention to his stubble — well, it was nearly three days' growth by now. She tidied, looked dissatisfied ('Not enough there yet, sir ...'), delved into a box, and carefully applied something all over his developing beard and moustache.

Finally she selected a pair of small and very fashionable spectacles ('Plain plastic lenses, sir — very lightweight') and adjusted them till they fitted him perfectly. An identical pair, with dark lenses, was then prepared in the same way, placed in a soft case, and pressed into his hands.

When she had finished, she took off his plastic cape, stood back, smiled in satisfaction, then dramatically rotated his chair. Toni gasped. He did not recognise the face he suddenly saw in the wall mirror in front of him. Instead of a carelessly-combed young student, he saw a sophisticated, sharply-coiffured young blade. His reaction was exactly what she had hoped for.

'Sit over there now, please.' She indicated a simple upright chair by the wall. For the first time he noticed the camera and the lights. When she was satisfied with his position, she took six exposures, carefully examining each result in the digital display, and encouraging him to relax again between each one.

Finally she led him back to the sink, the cape was deployed once again, and the "extras" she had applied to his face and chin were washed away.

'It should look like the photographs by tomorrow evening, sir. That will be fine.'

'Fine for what?'

'Now, listen carefully,' she said, ignoring his question and handing back his old sunglasses and cap. 'You may move freely around the city, while you are waiting, but you must not get into any trouble. Is that clear?'

'Yes, of course. And ... can I leave the cap off now?'

'While you are out and about, yes. That is one reason for our speed! But you will need to put it on whenever you return to your room. Your student friends should not be allowed to see your new look. Keep away from them if you possibly can. Do not worry, it is only for another day ...'

'*Grazie, signora!*'

'But tomorrow you must be back in your room by three o'clock in the afternoon, wearing your old sunglasses and the cap, and you must not leave until a delivery has been made to you. It will be addressed to "Toni Farello". That will be your name, tomorrow, for that delivery only. OK?'

'Yes ...'

'And when you sign the courier's document, with some scribble that looks like "Farello", you must add the name "Anna" underneath.'

'That's my mother's name!'

'So you are unlikely to forget it, sir.'

'That's true.'

'As soon as you have fully studied the contents of the delivery, which will be of great benefit to you, you will call your contact in Rome again. Understood?'

'Understood.'

'*Benissimo.*'

She took the same precautions as his previous host, as she opened the front door.

'It is clear, sir. Go now. Goodbye, and good luck.'

She closed the door and turned her attention to her camera and her personal computer. The short e-mail and its precious attachments were sent off ten minutes later.

* * *

Carla soon joined up with Toni again, and smiled her approval of his makeover. Then he told her of the enforced wait. She executed an almost perfect shrug of the shoulders.

So for the next twenty-four hours they toured the beautiful city. They visited the Square and the Basilica, the Campanile and the Doge's Palace. They splashed out on a gondola ride (Toni was counting on something turning up), they marvelled at the Rialto, and they took a waterbus around the whole lagoon. In short, they did almost everything that two lovers would do on their first trip to Venice ...

Toni crept in very late that evening, after his student friends had finally switched off the house lights and gone to bed. And with a great effort of will, and a lot of help from his wristwatch alarm, he was up and straight out again before seven o'clock, for the rest of his free time with Carla.

So when he returned to the empty lodgings at two-thirty that afternoon, to await the arrival of the messenger, he had managed to avoid all contact with his generous new house-mates since that boozy Wednesday night.

* * *

An unremarkable man stepped off the train from Rome, pulled a large wheeled suitcase down from behind him, and walked with several dozen tourists along the platform and out of the station entrance. He passed the Scalzi Bridge and entered the Lista di Spagna. Then, deviating from the route that Toni had taken two days earlier, he turned right and soon penetrated the gloom of a small local delivery agent's office, in a basement room close to the Grand Canal.

He negotiated the immediate delivery of the suitcase to Sr. Toni Farello, and paid cash in advance, with the promise of a further large cash bonus on production of the signed receipt exactly thirty minutes later.

He then tailed the courier expertly. He observed the bell being rung, the door being opened by the young man in the sunglasses and cap, and the form being signed without incident. And he followed as the courier hurried straight back to the office with a close eye on the time and the bonus. He was glad there was no need for any corrective action, on such a pleasant day. Five minutes later, he presented himself at the office as arranged, checked and pocketed the receipt with its code word written precisely as expected, and handed over a further cash sum that was twice what he had promised. The courier looked up in surprise. His customer put a single finger to his lips, and looked the man straight in the eyes. The message was clearly received.

* * *

Toni opened the suitcase. It was full of clothes — shirts, trousers, pullovers, jackets, socks, shoes, underwear — and everything else you would pack for a long holiday. He had no doubt it would all fit perfectly. Then, near the bottom, he found a bulky, unmarked brown envelope. He shivered. Then he tore it open.

A passport, with his own sharp new photo — but in the name of Rafael Luis Barola. A bank card in the same name, with its PIN hand-written on a little sticky yellow label. But no credit card. An extremely thick wad of used twenty-euro notes! A smaller quantity of Czech currency. A sheet of plain paper with a single line of text: *rafi@worldmailweb.com — p/w gaudi777.* A mobile phone and charger, with another yellow label: "CALL ME NOW USING THIS — G." And a smaller envelope with the words "Learn me, burn me" written on the outside. He opened this more cautiously. Another single sheet of paper.

> *Your name is Rafael Luis Barola (but if you ever forget and accidentally call yourself Toni, simply explain that it is a "pop star" nickname which you were given at school, and it stuck). You were born on 4 February 1982.*

'Five months before me,' thought Toni. 'So you are now twenty-one, Rafael!'

> *Your mother died when you were two years old. You never saw your father. You were brought up by foster parents in Barcelona.*

That was where Toni was born and had lived until he was thirteen! But of course Terleone knew that. And of course it had to be so ...

> *Practise the signature you see on your new passport. When it comes easily, sign the bank card. Memorise its PIN, then burn the label when you burn this note.*

> *Then spend a little time developing your new history further. Names for your foster parents; what you would have been doing in Barcelona since the age of thirteen; and so on. It is better for you to invent these things for yourself. You will manage.*

> *Now, telephone me at once.*

'Rafael? It is good to hear from you. Are you well?' ... 'Good. Do you understand everything you have received?' ... 'Yes, you can use the bank card anywhere, just like a credit card. There will always be adequate funds.' ... 'Yes, but you need not worry about him. He died aged fifteen.' ... 'No, fifteen days ...

'Now, Rafael — remember, you are Rafael! — you must depart as soon as you can. Make sure you dispose of all your old papers carefully. The Italian police are still very interested in you, believe me. So I have made some arrangements.

'I have a friend whose son is presently studying music in Prague. I have told them that you might be visiting the city soon, and they have agreed to assist you if you should do so. I want you to go there immediately. The young man will welcome you and help you to find your feet. Enjoy a little holiday. Relax. Listen to some good music. Meanwhile, we can both take some time to think more carefully about how you should later proceed.'

Toni's weak protests got him nowhere, but he did not really mind. Although he was increasingly experiencing nagging doubts, concerns about things that he probably should have been resolving, these were all so ill-defined that they evaporated whenever he tried to turn his thoughts towards them.

So he just breathed a deep sigh, and answered 'Very well, sir.'

'You should go by train to Prague. It will be far less risky than the airports for this journey. Once you are safely out of Italy, there should be no problems with flying elsewhere, if you wish to. Here is the name and number of the son of my friend ...'

Toni read it back, as usual.

'*Va bene.* Finally, Rafael, I suggest you should only try to contact me in a dire emergency. Will you agree?' ... 'Thank you. And now I must say goodbye and good luck, my boy.'

'Goodbye, sir — and I really must thank you ...'

But Terleone was gone.

'Are we moving on, Toni?'

He turned around. Carla was leaning against the table.

'Oh, hello,' he murmured, and was immediately ashamed at his apparent nonchalance. 'I'm sorry, Carla — yes, I think we are. My great-uncle's arranged it all. I have a new name, and a new phone, and lots of money and clothes, as you can see.

'We must go to Prague, in the Czech Republic. Uncle Giuseppe has given me the address of someone I can contact there ...'

'Very well, Toni. Perhaps we can start our mission properly again once we arrive.'

'I hope so, Carla,' he said, wondering what he meant by that mechanical response.

He turned back to Terleone's letter and carefully read it again. When he looked up, Carla had disappeared.

* * *

He practised his new signature on the back of the letter, until he was happy with it. Then he signed the bank card and memorised its PIN.

He found some matches in the kitchen, and burned the letter, its envelope, and the sticky labels in the ashtray. Then he decided he should also burn the pieces of paper with the addresses of the students' lodgings and the two mysterious little houses he had visited the day before. He put all the remains into a small plastic bag, which he tied up and dumped in the kitchen bin.

Then he changed into some brand new clothes, put on the plain-lens glasses, and checked his latest image in the mirror. OK! Smart!

He tucked his toilet bag into the brand new suitcase. He took his bunch of keys, his old passport and identity card, his old plastic cards and everything else from his wallet, and put them all in the large brown envelope. Then he added the piece of paper with the phone numbers of both Giuseppe and his friend's son in Prague. He placed the envelope at the bottom of his rucksack, alongside his old phone and all his other bits and pieces. Finally, he stuffed all his old clothes back into the rucksack. Then he stowed it at the bottom of the suitcase. He would decide what to do with it later ...

His wallet was then recharged with plenty of cash in two currencies, his new bank card and the note with his new e-mail ID. He put the rest of his new cash into another pocket of his new jacket.

Next, he sat down for a few minutes and did what the letter had instructed. He thought up some names for his "foster parents", and he tried to imagine how he might have spent the last few years in Barcelona.

Then he took several twenty-euro bills from his pocket and placed them on the table under his door key, with a very brief note: "*Grazie — Toni.*"

He opened the front door and checked for approaching students. All clear. He knew that Carla would follow, and would join him when the time was right. He slammed the door and, trundling the suitcase behind him, he set off towards Santa Lucia station.

* * *

As he passed Santa Maria di Nazareth for the last time, he thought suddenly of Paula. She would have visited her own church many times since last Monday, he was certain. Whereas he rarely went inside one, especially the Catholic ones — except as a tourist, of course. That was probably their biggest point of difference ...

He stopped in his tracks, turned to the right and entered the church, the noise from his suitcase wheels disturbing the dull and musty silence. He sat quietly for several minutes in the back row of chairs, with many layers of indefinable guilt weighing on his shoulders. Then, for no apparent reason, the weights lifted. His blithe nonchalance had returned.

He strode back out of the church, turned right and walked into the station forecourt. Antonio Murano was in hibernation. Rafael Barola was abroad ...

Behind the Tears

Just as Toni was emerging from his unplanned visit to the church in Venice, Paula Ramírez was leaving her own church in Bilbao. As Toni had surmised, it was her fifth visit that week ... and on this occasion, it was to seek forgiveness.

* * *

Five days earlier, she had attended morning Mass as usual with her parents and her younger brother, and had then attempted a normal Sunday at home — rehearsing the cello, watching TV, doing some light aerobics in her room, and looking hard at her slim young body in the mirror.

But as the evening approached, she had found herself overwhelmed by multiple emotions and deep feelings of guilt. So she had returned alone to the church — and this time, to the confessional.

She had forced herself to spend Monday morning at the Conservatorio, in her lectures and ensemble rehearsals. Then, just before three o'clock, she had gone for her rendezvous with Toni, to tell him the secret that was certain to shock him. But, for the first time in their ten months together, he had not appeared. And he had not phoned.

After waiting half an hour, she had gone home, repeatedly trying to call him. She had returned to town in the early evening, and had visited his apartment twice, both before and after her aerobics session. No answer. And she had continued to try to reach him by phone.

The next day she had gone back into town especially early, taken a detour to Toni's apartment yet again, and constantly tried his phones all morning — but with no success. She had been stuck in rehearsals all afternoon. Then, returning home in the early evening, she had found his letter waiting for her.

Paula ...

I've decided I've spent too long here in Bilbao, with my parents, in the family home. I love the Conservatorio, and my music, and I still adore you, but I need to break away. I've seen so little of the world. I want to travel, but I know that, at this time, you do not.

I'm going to discover Europe, and maybe I'll go farther afield. Please don't worry if you can't contact me. I'll be fine. I just need to be myself ... for the very first time.

With my love, Toni

In a state of great confusion, and with very mixed motives, Paula had abandoned her regular evening aerobics, compelled instead to return again to her church in search of clarity and guidance.

But the next morning she had woken with a completely clear conscience. Toni's decision to leave had taken away the opportunity to tell him to his face what he had to be told, and relieved her worries about his immediate reaction or the long-term effects.

So she had gone off to the Conservatorio for a relatively normal day.

* * *

Toni's parents had returned from their stay with the Murano family in Barcelona early that Wednesday evening. A special branch officer had watched their homecoming, then called his inspector. She had been happy to allow the couple a few minutes to settle back in. So they had read Toni's letter, but scarcely digested its surprising contents, when the doorbell rang.

Their relief, when told that the presence of the police was nothing to do with his health or safety, had been short-lived. They had been utterly stunned to hear of the events in Bilbao and Rome. Willing to accept — but not understanding why — that it *was* Toni who had been apprehended by mistake in Bilbao, they would not however believe that it was their son who had been spotted by the policeman in Rome.

They could not deny the coincidences in the two incidents, and the fact that Toni had abruptly decided to leave the country very early the previous day, and had passed through immigration at Rome airport only hours before the terrorist scare. But his father had pointed out quickly and vehemently that there seemed to be little real evidence against his son, beyond the word of a single Italian policeman on a sighting that had not been corroborated in any other way. He had insisted he would be taking the matter up with the inspector's superiors the following day.

And then the inspector had decided that there was not much more she could achieve that evening, and a lot she could lose. So she had left the Murano household in some kind of peace for the night.

Her officers would interview the parents formally in the morning, and over the coming days they would pursue investigations into the broader family, which would reveal various connections in Barcelona and elsewhere. These would all be checked out, and the interesting Roman civil servant would of course be a priority. But Signor Terleone would turn out to be singularly unavailable until late on the Friday evening, and by then he would have forgotten everything about Toni's visit, and would regrettably be unable to provide any information on the subject. And, of course, because the Rome inspector and his sergeant both valued their futures, no connection would ever be made between Giuseppe, his great-nephew, and that fashionable bar ...

And later in the week, after another very similar transmission incident with no reports of anybody matching Toni's description, there would be a significant downgrading of his status as a potential suspect — since, as his father had observed, it was only based on the verbal report of one policeman, and could just have been a bit of wishful thinking, or worse. So the all-ports alert for him across Europe would be reduced in intensity, and would effectively be shut down a few days later. Particularly since there had been no actual terrorist incidents to implicate him or anybody else in any actual plots. Just those very strange radio transmissions.

* * *

After the officer had left, Anna Murano had been adamant, and her husband had not disagreed, that until things were a great deal clearer, the whole business of the police should not be discussed with anyone else, including their families.

So, when she had telephoned Paula later that evening, she had made no mention of the inspector's visit. She had talked only of Toni's letter, which turned out to match the one Paula had received almost word for word. They had shared some mutual sympathy, but neither had gained any new insights, for the teenager gave no hint of the secret that was still preoccupying her. They had ended the conversation simply promising to contact each other as soon as they learned anything new.

Toni's mother and father continued, of course, to call his mobile phone for days and days afterwards, but every time they tried, it was reported to be switched off.

* * *

On the Thursday, Paula had lunched with a close friend to celebrate a momentous decision. She had not returned to the Conservatorio that afternoon. And in the evening she had gone to her church again: this time, simply to give thanks.

But the following evening, after writing her reply to Toni's letter and posting it to his parents' home, marked "For Toni to open when he returns", she was back at the church once more, seeking forgiveness for all the hurt that must surely now be caused.

And as she emerged from that so-familiar place, she knew that she would never again feel able to pass through its doors.

Like her lost boyfriend, Paula Mercedes Ramírez was now a new person with a fresh new life.

Night Trains

Toni reached the head of the queue for tickets. He had carefully prepared his request in Italian.

'How can I get to Prague, please?'

The booking clerk tapped her keyboard. '2043 departure. Change at Villach and Salzburg. Arrive Prague at 1051 in the morning.'

Toni paused and translated. 'That's seventeen hours from now!' he exclaimed. The woman simply raised her eyebrows.

'Are there any direct flights from Venice to Prague?' he asked, completely forgetting his great-uncle's specific instructions.

The look he received was a credit to the loyalty of this employee of the Italian Railways.

'Oh, please ...' he tried again, oblivious to the queue building up behind him.

The clerk sighed and resigned herself to the lesser of two evils. A single click took her instantly to the Marco Polo Airport web site; one more click gave her a full list of international departures.

'CSA/Alitalia. 1435 tomorrow afternoon.'

'Nothing tonight?'

'1435 tomorrow.'

'OK.' He gave up. And he had remembered Terleone's warning at last. 'I'll go by train. Can I book a couchette?'

'There are three separate trains. Do you want a couchette on each one?'

'Oh — what time does the first train arrive at ... er ... Villach?'

'0106.'

'Then I will take a couchette for the second and third trains only, please.'

'*Finalmente!*' she exclaimed. She printed the tickets.

Should he try his shiny new bank card? Giuseppe seemed to think Italy posed the biggest risks to him, whatever they were. He now recalled hearing things about those bank computers ...

He paid cash.

* * *

He had over three hours to kill. He would have loved to wander around the city again, but he realised there were risks, and anyway he now had a large and precious suitcase which he did not want to deposit anywhere. No, it would be safest to stay here, and get something to eat in the station buffet. He could have a little nap as well — he suspected he wouldn't sleep too well on those trains. And he could perhaps go back inside the church for a while.

So Rafael Luis Barola dined modestly at Santa Lucia station and then had his little nap. But he did not re-visit the church, and he finally boarded the 2043 departure for Villach.

* * *

He found a quiet corner seat in a fairly empty compartment, set his alarm for ten to one, and soon dozed off.

Carla tracked the train in her usual way, giving him an hour to rest, then settled in next to him, adjusted her velocity, and re-made.

'*Hola, Toni.*'

He woke up and rubbed his eyes. 'Oh, hello Carla. There you are again. I never know when you're going to pop up next!'

'I think you probably do, Toni.'

Carla's command of Spanish had not significantly improved, of course — she had not had much energy left, after Toni's initial transferral and missioning, to go out on the town in Bilbao and pick up lots of vocabulary in a range of interesting contexts. In fact, apart from some research at the airports, which had largely served to confuse her, since so many languages were being spoken, her only close observation of Spanish had been when listening and talking to Toni — and that had often been a little thin on context.

In fact, she had seen and heard far more Italian and English during their four days in Rome and Venice. So her fledgling vocabulary was now an amusing combination of nouns, verbs and adjectives from all three languages, strung together with some early attempts at grammar.

But her efforts to communicate in the tongues of others were already far better and more valiant than those of countless humans of many great nations.

And her precious sherpa was unconsciously still able to convert everything she uttered into perfect communication ...

'Toni, we need to plan how we will take the final pair of fixes. I suggest that when we reach Prague station, you should capture the co-ordinates as soon as you can, somewhere in the forecourt. You should then leave the station, walk some way towards the city, stop, and wait there for me. I will join you a little later, after the *Mater* has taken its final fix. No-one will recognise me, I promise!'

'I really hope there won't be any trouble this time.'

'I hope so too. And after that, we *must* try to get our other mission re-started. You know it is over three days since we had to abandon everything in Rome ...'

'Yes, Carla. Believe me, I haven't enjoyed all this cloak and dagger activity. Not my style at all! I'm really glad I can relax a little now — even though there are so many things I don't understand, hanging around somewhere in my brain.'

'Do not worry about those things, *carísimo*. Everything is for the best. We must concentrate on our work. We must cultivate our own garden ...'

Carla waited for her sherpa to relax, as he had suggested he might.

'Now, our initial study of you, Toni, revealed the potential usefulness of your great-uncle. We did indeed gain two valuable contacts from him, one of whom we have used already for our mapping work — and some information he obtained about a Dutch politician should eventually prove very useful. But, for various reasons, we have now been forced to abandon Don Giuseppe. You should not try to call him again ...

'You have already begun your journey to Prague, so we shall stay with that plan. But we do not want you to make contact with his friend's son there. That could well lead us back to Italy, which would *not* be a sensible move! And we are sure the student won't worry too much if he doesn't hear from you after all.

'And since you have not been able to provide us with any other promising leads yourself, particularly in Prague, we must initiate a completely fresh chain of contacts when we arrive.'

'OK, Carla ...' said Toni, rather hesitantly.

'But we won't try to plan this out right now. We can begin tomorrow afternoon. First, you need to rest properly on the trains; then we will take the fixes as I have proposed, and after that we must get you and your suitcase checked into a hotel — and as Rafael, don't forget!'

'You seem to have it all worked out, as usual.'

'We both play our parts, Toni ...'

'Carla?'

'Yes, Toni?'

'May I ask you something?'

'Of course.'

'I really would like to know a lot more about you. There never seems to be time to talk together quietly — we're always rushing around, or seeing the sights, or making new plans!'

'Don't worry about that, Toni. I honestly don't mind.'

'But I do! I really want to know you better. I want to know all about where you come from on Dome ... and what instruments you play ... and lots, lots more ...'

'I fear that if I tried to describe my homeland, it would make little sense to you ...'

'Oh, Carla — please! Please try, for me!'

'Very well. I will just say that I come from a region known as Arunura. It is a place of great inspiration. It is famous for its beautiful "bottomless" warm lagoons, and for the glorious colours of its sunsets. Yes, we too need a sun to warm us on Dome.'

'It sounds gorgeous, Carla. I'd love to be able to go there.'

'I fear that will never be possible, Toni. But perhaps one day I shall be able to help you to draw a picture of Arunura for yourself ...'

'Ah — now that *would* be wonderful.'

Toni fell silent for a few moments, then recovered his train of thought.

'All right — if you don't think you can say any more about your homeland, at least tell me about your musical instruments. And what else do you do when you're not rushing around on voyages of discovery?'

Carla completely missed his playful attempt at irony.

'Toni, we do not use instruments of wood or metal, fibres or plastic. Nor do we distinguish between composers and performers.

'Ours is a music of the mind.

'It is born in very special situations and places, such as Arunura. Our music makers know when the moment has come to visit one of those places. Several of us may go together, or one may go alone.

'A composition is then — how can I say it? — is then *revealed* by us, often over a substantial period of time. It may not sound like hard work, but I can assure you, from personal experience, that it is very demanding and highly satisfying. On Dome, musicians are held in the highest regard.

'And when a piece is at last complete, it is carried back to be enjoyed by those who desire to hear it. But in its glorious performance, no sounds travel through our "air". We listen to the music, or the song, in the same way that we hear each other's thoughts and voices — in our minds alone.'

Toni was again pensive for a few moments.

'So — how does your music compare with what you have heard on Earth?'

'Ah, Toni, I think comparison is fruitless.

'Our music is more complex than yours, both in its creation and its projection. It is born and it grows organically — it is, at once, both a single expression of truth, and a near infinity of tonal elements. It can never be broken down into constituent parts, nor documented in any way. And it can only be heard if the listeners give it their full attention. It is the pinnacle of artistic beauty on Dome.

'Whereas, I see that even the most sophisticated works of your greatest composers on Earth need to be made up of small groups of simple, individual notes, which are then fused together to form a perfect whole, and are often carefully captured in a written code. And this is then interpreted in performance, by the composer or by any number of different instrumentalists and singers, using humble animal, vegetable and mineral materials, and human voices, for your ears to hear in their own special, vibrating way — and often, amazingly, while also listening to countless other sounds!

'But judging by all I have heard so far, Toni, the creations of your musicians are no less beautiful than ours.'

Toni spent several minutes thinking more deeply than he had ever thought before. Finally he spoke again.

'Carla, perhaps it is your music that inspires ours here on Earth.'

'And perhaps also, Toni, it is yours that inspires ours on Dome ...'

Toni would have loved to continue this delightful conversation, particularly to pursue his interest in Carla's other pastimes. But he suddenly found himself overwhelmed by an intense tiredness, and he could not stifle a long, deep yawn.

'It is time for you to rest again now, Toni. You will see me in Prague tomorrow, as we have agreed.'

Toni was looking straight into her eyes.

'Carla, I wish I could hold you.'

For the first time, Carla's voice quivered as she replied.

'So do I, Toni. So do I.'

As soon as Toni had closed his eyes, she un-made, left him in the safe tracking hands of another of her guardian angels, and attempted some relaxation of her own, her mind filled with many strange new thoughts.

* * *

Toni's alarm woke him at ten to one, and soon afterwards the train pulled into platform two at Villach. He crossed to platform three, and had less than twenty minutes to wait for the departure to Salzburg. He climbed on board, found his way to his couchette, reset his alarm for a quarter to four, and despite his expectations was soon fast asleep again.

The alarm woke him as planned, shortly before the train arrived at Salzburg's platform one.

This time he had about forty minutes to wait for his connection. He decided it would be safest to take his suitcase for a walk around the concourse, rather than risk falling asleep in the waiting room. After a while he left the station building to try to catch a glimpse of an Austrian skyline. But it was still far too dark.

Then he had another abrupt realisation that there were many things he really should have been attending to in recent days, and many things he should have been doing differently — and many things he should not have been doing at all. But he could not put his finger on any of them. Then that awareness once again died down as quickly as it had arisen. He turned on his heels, and walked back into the station and straight onto platform three.

The third of Toni's night trains also departed right on time. He found his new couchette and reset his alarm for twenty to eleven.

He slept well for a couple of hours, then wakened with the dawn. He spent the rest of the journey simply staring out of the window, initially dozing off from time to time, but later enjoying his very first views of spring time in Bohemia.

* * *

The train arrived in a sunlit Prague just before eleven o'clock. Rafael Barola switched to his smart new shades, and towed his heavy suitcase down the platform and into the station concourse.

Prague, Czech Republic

Carla was now back on unseen duty. She watched as Toni made straight for the station bookstall, chose a city guidebook with a map, and then calmly pretended to consult it as he expertly took his final pair of GPS fixes. He then emerged from the station into yet another sunny spring day, and walked off southwards down Washingtonova, arriving a few minutes later opposite the huge bulk of the Národní Museum. He sat down on a low wall to study his guidebook, and Carla returned unseen to the station.

* * *

At eleven-thirty, a well-dressed, middle-aged businessman emerged from the shadows in a corner of the concourse, walked towards the bookstall, and spent a couple of minutes simply staring up at the covers of the magazines on display all over its interior walls. The woman behind the counter eventually approached him.

'*Čím vám mohu pomoci?*'

Ignoring this polite offer of help, he pulled out his mobile phone, and made a rapid call in a very low voice. Popping the phone back in his inside pocket, he smiled pleasantly at the assistant who had spoken to him, and swiftly departed through the main entrance. Within two minutes he had found a narrow alleyway and disappeared into it ...

Shortly afterwards, Carla emerged from behind a small brick building by the roadside and sauntered up to Toni with a bright smile on her face.

'*Hola, Toni.*'

He felt a deep sense of relief that she was back with him, but at the same time he could not dismiss his concerns about what might happen next. This fixing business now seriously unnerved him, though he had not admitted as much to her on the train. Thank goodness this was the very last one — he hoped!

He had already written the co-ordinates onto his sheet of paper. He held it up, Carla read it, and the *Mater* received it.

'Excellent, Toni. Our Chief Surveyor informs me that this data matches very accurately with the estimate which they have just made, based on the fix I sent a few moments ago. The triangulation task is complete!

'We now know exactly where your longitude reference base, at Greenwich in London, is physically situated — and as we expected, you do indeed measure your surface elevations based on mean sea levels. So our first-level model of the whole Earth, based on all the major location co-ordinates we captured in Venice, is fully in place. Our Finders can now go anywhere the Handlers may wish. We are very grateful. Thank you, Toni.'

And she very nearly kissed him again.

The grin on Toni's face lasted three seconds. Then he heard the sirens.

A tiny white Smart car with *Městská Policie* inscribed on its side came hurrying up Wenceslas Square, heading straight towards them. He froze. The car reached the end of the long square and, as it slowed to take the left turn immediately in front of them, Toni could have sworn that the driver took her eyes off the road for a split second and stared straight into his ...

And then the little car was gone, careering down Washingtonova towards the station. But other approaching sirens could be heard, further out to the north.

* * *

A large number of police officers had converged on the station concourse. But it took them some time to establish that at least eight people had been seen using mobile phones there in the previous ten minutes. The senior officer pressed his control room for the precise time of the huge burst of energy. Then they questioned again, and the bookstall assistant's report seemed the most promising.

So although the descriptions of several different individuals were included in the general search orders which were then issued and pursued for the rest of the day, the strongest suspect was a smartly-dressed businessman carrying a small attaché case.

When the detectives arrived, hoping to firm up this identification, they went straight to the station security office and demanded to view the recent videotape footage. Rewinding to a point two minutes before the logged time of the signal, they watched impatiently for the moment to arrive.

In fact, they only had to wait a few seconds before something very strange happened. A vague, blurred shape moved into view, hovering directly in front of the bookstall. It stayed there until just after the precise moment of the signal, then rapidly moved away, and the image of the bookstall behind it went back to its normal quality.

For weeks afterwards, many security agencies around the world would puzzle over how a suspected terrorist, in no way matching the description of the temporarily notorious Spaniard named Antonio Murano, but obviously part of a large Europe-wide cell which was inexplicably *not* wreaking any actual havoc despite its strange signalling habits, was able to radiate a remarkable, continuous interference pattern which prevented the camera from observing him as intended.

And the definitive timing of the signal, and the fascination of the mystery of the fuzzy man, meant that nobody ever thought to search back a further thirty minutes on the videotape. Not that a short-haired, smart young tourist buying a map and checking some sort of handheld computer would have attracted any particular attention. Especially since the driver of a local city police Smart car would probably not have been the officer doing that extended search.

* * *

Responding to Carla's reassuring smiles, Toni pulled himself together, and they set off. As they walked down the full length of Wenceslas Square, he admired out loud the expansiveness of the space and its already apparent contrasts, and she simply watched and listened carefully.

Keen to rid himself of his suitcase, but already fascinated by the charms of the city and delighted to have Carla strolling beside him, Toni wandered happily around the relatively quiet streets surrounding the Old Town Square for some time, until he eventually spotted a likely-looking hotel.

Agreeing to join him later for lunch, Carla discreetly un-made and followed him inside.

It will be English again, he thought as he approached the desk. He was right.

'Good afternoon, sir. Welcome to Prague!'

The charming receptionist confirmed that there were indeed some single rooms available — and at very reasonable rates, Toni thought.

'Yes, I'll take one. For at least two nights, please.'

'Certainly, sir. Your name, please?'

'Toni ...'

A loud noise to his right drowned out the rest of his words. The receptionist looked up from her computer screen in surprise, but decided it must have been her new guest coughing, despite the fact that the sound seemed to have come from just behind him.

'Oh, please excuse me,' said Toni quickly. 'I have a rather sore throat. And I nearly gave you my nickname! Hah! How stupid of me! Anyway ... I'm Rafael Barola.'

The receptionist smiled sympathetically, finished entering the booking details, took an imprint of Rafael's bank card, and then asked him for his passport.

'You can collect it again when you next come down, Sr. Barola. Your room is number 14, on the first floor. Enjoy your stay.'

'*Děkuji.*' Toni had memorised only three simple words of Czech so far, from his short study of the list in his new guidebook, but he was determined to make the effort at least to say 'Thank you.'

'My pleasure, sir,' came back the response, this time in perfect Spanish.

* * *

Toni was grateful for the chance to wash and change again after nearly twenty hours of travelling in the same clothes. Then, with his new passport safely back in his pocket, he was soon outside in the fresh and surprisingly warm air, and making his way the short distance to the magnificent Old Town Square.

Drawing back two chairs at one of the few vacant tables outside the Caffè Italia, and wondering at the strange pattern of place names he was continuing to encounter, he sat down, ordered his lunch, and waited for Carla.

She arrived at the same time as his beer ('... no, nothing for the lady, thank you.'). Then, while he ate his sandwich, and managed to fit in a second beer, he and Carla talked again.

'We *must* re-start our Insight Gaining mission now, Toni.'

'Yes, Carla — I do realise that.'

'OK. Now, I chose you, as you appreciate, because of your dedication to music. And that has already proved very worthwhile for you in our recent difficulties.

'We believe a love of music brings with it a level of integrity which is the key to the insights we are seeking. So, may we try to pursue that path again?'

'What do you suggest?'

'Ah, Toni, we were counting on you for some sparks of ideas here ...'

Toni went silent. He was abruptly aware that he was being firmly encouraged to get back to his role of Illuminator. He sat for some time in the sunshine, endeavouring to let the beer do its work on his brain cells. Then suddenly, he had an answer.

'The Message Board!'

'Yes ...?'

'I often log into the message board of my favourite songwriter, on the Internet — the World Wide Web. There are lots of really interesting people in that community. They all love good music, and they live all over the world. I'm sure I've spotted one or two Czechs there in the past! Maybe I could try to contact one of them!'

'Toni, you have surpassed yourself again! We suspected that some such solution would be possible. You have provided the detail and the motivation. But do you have all you need to attempt such a contact?'

'Yes — Uncle Giuseppe gave me a new e-mail ID, and lots of cash. All we need is an Internet café.'

'Then let us find one!'

So Toni's hopes of more relaxation and some early sightseeing with Carla were again confounded. He paid the bill, and together they began to search the streets around the huge square. With many people milling around, this presented the usual challenges for Carla. But they persevered, and not long after, just off the small square near the medieval astronomical clock of the Town Hall, they found exactly what they were seeking.

* * *

'Are you sure it's a good idea to use your own name?'

'Yes — in fact, that's the best thing about it. Almost everyone else on the message board uses a nickname — so even though I'm now Rafael, I can still use "Toni" as usual! That'll make me feel much more comfortable, anyway.'

'I must trust your judgement, Toni.'

So he typed his message, in his very best Internet English:

> *Hi everybody. Long time! Got a new e-mail ID, but I'm still the same Toni!*
>
> *At last I have a bit of time, while I'm travelling, to catch up with all your latest crazy postings!*
>
> *Actually, I'm in Prague! If there's anyone else on-line who's in the city centre today and fancies a beer and a real chat, please let me know straight away!*
>
> *I'll be watching the board for the next couple of hours ... Toni.*

After fifteen minutes of browsing his huge stack of unread messages and their follow-ups, Toni refreshed the main screen. It now showed there was one response to his earlier post. He clicked on it excitedly.

> *Hey Toni, good to hear from ya! Where ya been? We've missed ya!*
>
> *Anyway ... enjoy the trip! Oh yeah ... whadd'ya think of Czech ice-creams?*
>
> *Dario*

False alarm.

He carried on browsing the message stack. Carla watched, only mildly fascinated.

Ten minutes later he checked again. Another greeting from an "old friend".

The third message appeared, timed at 1444.

> *TONI — WELCOME TO PRAGUE. I'VE BEEN WATCHING THE BOARD FOR MONTHS, BUT I DON'T SAY MUCH! GOOD IDEA TO MEET UP. E-MAIL ME PRIVATELY NOW? ED.*

Carla got the message by watching Toni's reaction. Then she studied the screen.

'What shall I say, Carla?' he asked.

'Just say what comes naturally. We want to meet up with Ed as soon as possible.'

'Of course.'

Toni copied the inscrutable e-mail address from ED's profile, and then made his way across into the *Worldmailweb* site, where Rafael Barola's e-mail address had been registered. He logged in successfully with his brand new ID and password, selected "Compose", pasted ED's address into the "To" field, and then typed his text:

> *ED — it's good to meet you! There's an Internet café just off the Malé Náměstí — I'm sure you know it. Can you come over straight away? Toni.*

He hit "Send", and they waited. Three minutes later came the reply:

> *I'LL BE THERE BY 1545. YOU'LL SPOT ME. JUST WAVE.*

* * *

There was time for a long cappuccino and some more browsing. Carla sat composing herself again. She had decided there was little point in any further joint planning before Ed's arrival: things seemed to get very unpredictable whenever she began a new involvement, and she was anyway becoming a deft improviser. So, a few minutes before Ed was due, she simply moved over to the side wall and pretended to study the café's notice board ...

Toni failed completely to wave as instructed to the well-built female with cropped red hair who breezed cheerily through the door in baggy blue jeans and a large white tee-shirt. She, in turn, peered around through the lenses of her large spectacles and failed to spot the woman she was expecting to greet her.

But she did not allow this situation to drag on for very long. 'Toni?' she shouted, loud enough for everyone in the café to hear: even those in the basement.

Toni gulped and finally found his wave and his Internet English voice. 'Ah ... ah ... I'm over here!' he called out as quietly as he could, his poor brain in turmoil again.

The new arrival was equally stunned by her discovery that Toni was a young man. She cautiously approached him, extended her arm, and gingerly shook his hand.

'You're Toni? Oh ... well ... hello. I'm Eva — but everyone calls me Evita these days. Little Eva, get it? Me! Hah! Locos, all of them!' She laughed nervously at her own regularly practised rock music joke. Toni was rather too young to pick it up.

'Yes, I'm Toni,' he said, now on autopilot. 'But your nickname's Ed ...'

'Not Ed, Toni ... "ED". My initials. My name's Eva Dvořak. Simple. But your nickname's Toni — now that's a girl's name!'

'Not in Spain. It's short for ... oh, never mind. Pleased to meet you, Evita.'

Eva was looking less than pleased to meet Toni. So now it was his turn to cough pointedly and stare across at the notice board with a look that simply cried 'Help!!'

Carla, who had picked up some of this English conversation, but had not caught all the implications straight away, turned around at once and moved back towards them. Like Toni, she had been surprised to discover, as soon as their new friend arrived — for she had eyes in the back of her head — that Ed was, in fact, a woman.

Toni now mumbled an introduction, and Eva at once looked much happier. She again extended her hand in greeting. Carla, of course, had to decline to shake it, but she smiled very sweetly instead, and her target was more than satisfied.

The involvement of Eva was thus quickly and easily achieved, with no need for background music (for it was playing inside her head). And this time there were no sudden alarms to interrupt business.

Once Ms Dvořak was thoroughly entranced by Carla, they discreetly left the café (and Toni stayed with them, of course, to continue to open doors), and penetrated the surrounding back streets until they found themselves momentarily unobserved.

Then, to avoid a shock to his system, Carla quietly asked Toni to turn his back. She smiled once more, took Eva's head in her hands, and quickly disappeared as the intensive engagement began ...

It revealed a most promising line for Quo to pursue.

Eva, it turned out, was a clerical assistant in a rather uninteresting government department. But she had an old friend, known affectionately as Jo, who worked in a more central role in the civil service. Sixteen years earlier, under the old regime, he had been her first supervisor when she had started out as an office junior in a minor finance unit. They had traded favours in those days, and her career, without exactly blossoming, had at least stayed on the rails. She was sensible enough to remain grateful for that.

But Eva had not been loved by a man in quite a while, and Jo had moved on and up. They now only met from time to time, and always by chance — but they were still good friends.

However, Eva, like all around her, had found it hard to lose the habit learned at an early age in those bad old Prague days: to watch and listen to *everything* — both for your own protection, and to keep a few tricks up your sleeve. So she was quite aware, albeit rather loosely, of Jo's ongoing entrepreneurial activities, and was readily able to share those insights with Quo ...

Josef Samek had run many little rackets in the old communist days. He still continued with some of them, and at greater profit now. But he was increasingly at risk of exposure in the slowly "opening" government that was the by-product of democracy and the new Republic's recent intensive courting of the European Union.

He was a physically weak and cowardly man, nervous by natural disposition. His power was based solely on his intelligence sources and his knowledge, which had for decades allowed him to hold the threat of blackmail or violence against the hierarchy of many little people who did his grubby work for him.

And Eva was certain that he was, in his turn, manipulated at his place of work by powerful elements of the old guard ...

While Eva remained standing in an apparently idyllic reverie, and Toni looked forward to admiring some more fine architecture, Quo and the Handler formulated their plan. Which did not take very long.

Eva was then moved smoothly through an appropriately limited briefing and missioning. In the absence of any external disturbances, the whole process appeared to those on the *Mater* to be working perfectly.

Their aim, of course, was to reach Jo Samek and enable him to become involved by Carla. As usual, the subject would need to be in a highly accommodating state of mind before this could be attempted. Toni and Salvatore had both been child's play: the power of the siren's unspoken call had been enough. Terleone had been motivated by family, and Carla's smile had done the rest. Evita had come because of the music and the anticipation, and she too had then fallen for that smile.

But the nervous and probably suspicious Samek would be a very different challenge. To get him anywhere near Carla, they would have to rely on his respect for his old lover, and counter his mistrust of everyone by making him an offer he could not refuse ...

As Eva returned to a single plane of consciousness, and Carla reappeared at a conveniently quiet moment ('We're ready, Toni ...'), Quo became aware that something was not quite right. Eva had not fought against them during the process of her engagement, but now she did not seem to have come totally under their control — and she was not disguising this as effectively as the maestro Terleone had managed to.

She was already marching off towards the Old Town Square, with Toni and Carla in tow, and addressing them over her shoulder in a surprisingly businesslike way.

'I have some work to do for you. I need to get on with it at once. But Carla, I must see you again — and alone this time, eh? Will you meet me later this evening? We can take a nice walk down by the river, and then we can go to a great Jazz Club — it's just round the corner!'

Now Carla was in the hot seat. Rapid consultations, lasting only a few seconds, took place between Quo and the Handler. Eva had not been briefed or missioned to anything like the depth that Toni had been. Should they risk another attempt at engagement here and now, to give Eva some clearer operational guidelines? The Handler was already very tired. No, they would have to take the risk. The Finder should be able to look after herself. If things started to go wrong, they could always initiate another emergency engagement on the spot ...

But an unchaperoned walk was all they would entertain.

'All right,' Carla accepted — and Eva could now interpret her English words with ease. 'I guess Toni won't mind eating alone this evening, so we can go for a stroll then. But you'll want to go to the club later, won't you Toni?' ... 'Of course you will! I can't leave him alone on our first night here, now can I?'

They were back in the square, and had halted beside the Jan Hus monument. Eva thought about protesting against the compromise plan, but decided to stop while she was ahead. She proposed a rendezvous with Carla there, at the monument, at seven-thirty and, with an easily assumed reluctance, scribbled an address for Toni on a scrap of paper, agreeing they would meet him outside the club at nine ...

Leaving her rather bemused new friends standing beside the monument, Eva walked to one side of the square and found a cool corner near an Irish pub. She took out her mobile phone. She didn't remember Jo's number, and she certainly didn't have it stored. But she knew where he lived: he had been in the same house on the outskirts of the city for the past twenty years, since before the birth of his first child. The Prague directory enquiries service luckily found the number with ease.

He answered at once. With a worried and broken tone to her voice, she bluntly told him she must see him as soon as possible — otherwise, they would both be in serious trouble. She refused to elaborate.

Samek had heard enough intimidated voices to recognise another one now. Somebody had got to Eva. He had no choice. Not bothered about inventing an excuse for his family (he was always having to go out on "business" at a moment's notice — his wife was grateful that their total income allowed her to provide for their four children better than most of her neighbours could, and so she kept her mouth firmly shut), he agreed to meet his old friend in a city centre café at six-thirty.

Eva pocketed the phone and made her way back to her own modest apartment in a large, run-down old tenement block by the railway lines, west of Republic Square. She would need to dress very carefully to suit the three rather different evening engagements that were suddenly looming ahead of her ...

* * *

Toni was pleased, as usual, to be stood down from his duties as Carla's minder. He much preferred the more general job of Illuminator, especially when it involved some sightseeing in a city as glorious as Prague ...

So they did their first little tour. With only three hours to spare, they stayed in the old town area. They strolled in the main square at their leisure, admiring the huge variety of beautiful buildings surrounding them. Then, retracing their steps from earlier that day, they walked the short distance back to Wenceslas Square. Although the evening was still young, Toni was obliged several times to reject the offers of the street girls stationed all the way along Melantrichova and Na můstku. And if any of the countless currency touts had tried to touch Carla on the arm, as they did with Toni, they would have been in for a big shock.

At the corner of Wenceslas Square, Toni bought a huge, blood-red sausage from a pavement stall, took one bite, and decided to take no more. Then they took a full walk around the square: '... for the benefit of your Spanish, Carla, this is hardly a square, more a huge, long rectangle!' He marvelled again at the beauty of the buildings' façades, when viewed from a distance, and was dismayed by the contrast of their eye-level shabbiness on closer inspection — an impression deepened by the sight of a steady stream of well-dressed men rummaging deep into the roadside litter bins in search of anything of interest.

Carla looked and learned with Toni. But as the sun went down, she suggested it was time for him to sort himself out for the evening and then get some dinner, while she went off for her rather unwelcome stroll with their new friend.

'Good thinking,' said Toni. 'Have a nice time!'

'Thanks a lot, partner! See you at nine.'

* * *

Just before half-past six, Josef Samek walked across the Old Town Square, down a side street, and into U Karla IV café. He descended the stairs to the basement bar.

Eva was already waiting for him, deep in thought.

She didn't understand why she had chosen that particular bar, with Carla's name in it. Anyway, in this city, there were Karlas everywhere you looked, from the famous bridge outwards in all directions. Perhaps it wasn't her real name. Perhaps it was just a temporary nickname while she was here. Strange though: first the confusions about Toni and herself, and now a woman with a man's name ... and a king's name, an emperor's name, here in Prague!

She was brought sharply back from her daydream by the abrupt arrival at her table of a very worried man.

'What is it, Eva? Who is it? What do they want? What have they done to you?' He was talking quietly, but with an attempt at firmness and support.

'Oh, Jo, you are so sweet. Don't worry, no-one has hurt me; it's just the usual menaces.'

'Eva, don't play around! I want to know what they have said to you ...'

'Oh, you really do worry too much ...'

For a couple of minutes, she stuck to her plan to try and stretch things out for dramatic effect. But the closer she came to having to reveal the pretended "problem", the less she found herself able to concentrate on the matter in hand. She could not get that woman off her mind.

She made a valiant effort at regrouping. 'Jo, I'm feeling a little faint. Would you get me another glass of water, please?'

He hurried to the bar and brought back the water and a small glass of beer. He was already intensely frustrated at having come all this way only to be obliged to tolerate Eva's nerves and maladies, without gaining any insight so far into the real issue. He was not a naturally patient man, nor was he particularly strong on charm ...

'So — come on, Eva, pull yourself together. Tell me what it's all about!' He was becoming visibly agitated now, but he kept his voice very low, and took a nervous sip of his beer.

'Jo, they know all about you ...'

'Who? What are you talking about?'

'They want you to do something for them ...'

'Eva, for goodness' sake!'

She really could no longer handle this. Just too much to cope with at once.

'I'm sorry — I've got to go. I really am feeling quite ill now. I just need to rest. I'm sure I'll feel better in the morning. Look, can I meet you for lunch — at The Three Ostriches, say? At twelve o'clock? I'll reserve, I'll pay ...'

'Eva, this is crazy! You've got me really worried ...'

'Please, Jo — I must go now. You must be there tomorrow. It's so important!'

Then she rushed from the table, ran up the stairs, and was gone.

Josef Samek, Deputy Head of the Strategic Studies Group in the Department of European Union Relations, knew the importance of not causing scenes in public. He sat back coldly in his chair, took another sip of his beer, and tried to work out what could have so disturbed his trusted old friend ...

* * *

Half an hour later, Eva had calmed down and done her best to forget her mission for Quo, at least for the time being. Feeling it was now safe to emerge from her hiding place in the toilets of another nearby bar, she made her way back over to the main square.

Like the educated and modernising sovereign and namesake who had preceded her into the city many centuries earlier, Carla was, as ever, alert to the need to keep her subjects as contented as possible. So she was already waiting in the warm calm of the evening when Eva arrived back at the Jan Hus monument.

Quo and Carla were then very dismayed to hear that Eva's mission had been temporarily abandoned. But they realised that, once again, they had little choice but to accept the revised plans that had been made for them.

* * *

Throughout their walk, Eva played her cards carefully, and was the perfect guide and companion. She maintained a respectful distance from Carla, who was delighted that she and Quo did not have to invoke an emergency engagement as a result of any physical contact, accidental or otherwise.

They strolled from the square down to the Charles Bridge, and Eva described its history as they crossed the river. They admired the huge towers at each end, and the many historic statues positioned along the full length of both sides ('but very few of them are the originals, Carla.'). And when they reached the west bank, Eva pointed out the restaurant where she would meet Jo again the next day.

Eva rejected her companion's suggestion of what would have been for them both a breathless walk up the steep hills to the Castle, and instead she led her through a maze of small streets on the Lesser Town side of the river, until they emerged onto the attractive little Kampa Island, between the river and the Maltese Grand Prior's Palace Gardens.

'It's like a little Venice, Carla,' said Eva. 'This tiny park was really popular with the "flower children" back in the 60's. Before I was born, by the way! But the whole place was devastated by last year's terrible floods. Look, even the grass has hardly started to grow again; it's all still so very wet and muddy ...'

And as they walked around, she pointed out many buildings whose lower wall coverings had been stripped away by the rising water. Clearly only very slow progress was being made in their reparation. Then she stopped and gazed back across the river at the countless spires of the beautiful Old Town. 'We seem always destined in this country, Carla, for one step forward, then one rude step back. Perhaps joining the European Union will change that pattern. Perhaps not ...'

* * *

Toni, meanwhile, had decided to experience a traditional Czech dinner at the elegant Staroměstská on the Old Town Square.

When he was ready to order, he tried out his Czech pronunciation of the names of the dishes.

The waiter smiled and said, in perfect English, 'Very good, sir.'

Wondering what he really meant by that, Toni resolved to abandon his pursuit of this unfamiliar language, and to enjoy instead the restaurant's fascinating décor.

* * *

At nine o'clock they all met up again outside the Ungelt Jazz & Blues Club, hidden away on Týnská Ulíčka behind the ancient, towering Týn church.

Eva was back in tourist guide mode.

'You'll love this place. We go right down into the fifteenth century vaults ...'

Carla turned to Toni and whispered: 'I hope I won't fade away down there! If that happens, I'll need to get out quickly, before the *Mater* loses me forever — and I'll meet you back outside the Internet café!'

Eva was still gushing.

'... lots of different little rooms, bars, corners, balconies and so on. Super acoustics, and always great bands!'

Toni and Carla both had to admire her enthusiasm and her love of life. And Toni was really looking forward to the music.

He was not disappointed. After acting as doorman for Carla at the entrance, keeping alert to the need to shield her from any careless passers-by as they descended the stairs into the music cellar, and politely readying her chair as usual, he left her with Eva and made for the bar. Then, just as he got back to their table, carrying two very large beers for himself and Eva ('No, I'm not thirsty,' said Carla in response to Eva's raised eyebrows), the Chicken Soup Band began to play. Toni was immediately impressed, and for the next hour they all just sat and lapped up the excellent jazz fusion sounds.

Or rather, Eva lapped up the huge beer within ten minutes, and returned twice to the bar before the interval, bringing back a double vodka for herself on each occasion. And she seemed honestly disappointed that Toni insisted on sticking with his original beer and Carla just sweetly shook her head each time she was invited to 'Come on, have a drink with us!' ...

At ten-fifteen the band stopped for a break. Toni's glass had been empty for some time, and now he was very thirsty again. Eva requested another double vodka, and he went off to wait his turn at the busy bar.

Now that it was quiet for a few moments, Eva tried to strike up another conversation with the object of her new desire. Carla, already feeling ill at ease and wishing they had not had to agree to this episode in the first place, said something agreeable for the sake of politeness, and smiled sweetly again.

That did it. Now fully primed with alcohol, Eva succumbed to temptation. She reached across the table and made to stroke Carla's beautiful long hair ...

And found there was nothing there.

Toni heard the commotion and at once recognised the voice doing the shrieking — even though it was shrieking in Czech.

Within ten seconds the manager and a security guard burst into the music room, with Eva screaming at them to call the police. Carla had had enough. But she was desperate to remain fully visible. With the men still focused on trying to get the incoherent Eva to explain what was wrong, Carla squeezed past two startled couples and out through the open door. She peered into the bar where Toni stood speechlessly staring towards her, jerked her head in an unmistakable order to "Get out of the place, now!", turned two corners into an empty kitchen area, and un-made at once.

It was another minute or more before one of the security staff came looking for her, paying lip service to Eva's now slightly more lucid ravings. Failing to find her, he simply assumed she had left the place by the back stairs. 'So would I, with that crazy woman screaming at me,' he thought, as he went to report back to the management.

Nobody thought twice about the young man who had abandoned the queue for the bar and, forgetting that he had left a brand new pullover on the back of his chair, walked quietly up the main stairs and out of the front door ...

Eva Dvořak continued to demand the police, and eventually they were called. She gave a vivid description of Carla, and then proceeded to insist that the woman's head simply did not exist. Nobody believed her. The barman was consulted, and he reported that she had already drunk at least two double vodkas, probably more.

One of the police officers suggested very pointedly to Eva that she might perhaps like a lift home. She tried one last little rant, then realised she was onto a loser, and noisily stormed out.

* * *

Carla made straight for the Internet café and hovered invisibly nearby. Toni soon hurried up and waited by the entrance. When Carla rounded the corner and walked towards him a minute later, with as annoyed a look on her face as she could imagine, he silently opened the door for her and they went inside.

She took less than ten seconds to explain what had happened. Then she got down to business once more.

'We have to get her back, Toni. She hasn't done her work yet. We can't start all over again. It is your moment now. You must seize it.'

On his way across, Toni had flipped, in a mild sort of way. He could now only see the funny side of it all. 'So I stop being an Illuminator and become an Eva Retriever?'

This washed straight over Carla. 'Exactly. You must call her and agree to meet her — at once. You must try to pacify her. You must get her to agree to complete her mission tomorrow, exactly as planned. Do it now, Toni.'

Toni was stunned by the firmness of Carla's voice. He had never seen her like this. But then, she had just been through rather a lot ...

'Very well, Carla. Of course I'll do it. I'll do anything for you. You know that.'

Carla seemed to spot the effect she had unwittingly had. 'I do, Toni. I do. I'm sorry I was abrupt. And thank you, once again.'

'Wait a minute, though. I don't know her phone number!'

'I do.'

'How?'

'We know a great deal about Eva, Toni ...'

'Oh, yes.'

But he insisted on a cup of coffee before placing the call. Carla conceded. It would extend Eva's cooling-off period, and improve Toni's concentration..

Then Carla dictated the number, and he called Eva's mobile phone. She was just arriving back at her apartment.

'Evita, it's Toni.' ... 'Don't ask.' ... 'Yes.' ... 'Yes, Evita, she is sorry, we don't know what happened — perhaps she just moved at that moment?' ... 'Well, maybe you aren't feeling too well.' ... 'No, I'm sorry, I wasn't suggesting ...'

Toni presented Carla with a helpless look. She scowled and encouraged him to get on with it.

'No, Evita — look, can I come over and see you? We could have a quiet coffee, maybe play some of our favourite music, and I could explain exactly how Carla feels. I know it'll all be fine again tomorrow — she really wants to see you again ...'

Carla was smiling now in approval of his new approach.

'Please trust me, Evita ...

'Evita ... please ...

'Good — give me the address.' ... 'OK, I've got a map. How long from the Internet café?' ... 'Thirty minutes — that's fine. See you soon!'

He rang off.

'Good for you, Toni,' said Carla. 'Make any promises you need to. I can break them all. Just make sure she meets up with Samek tomorrow. I'll join you when you leave the hotel in the morning, and we can go sightseeing all day! But we'll be splitting up for lunch. I'll need to be watching them ...'

* * *

It was eleven-fifteen before Toni found Eva's apartment. She let him in without a word. She looked a mess and had not tried to improve things before he arrived. And she wasn't going to make it easy for him, he could tell. She sat back down on her sofa and glared unhappily at him, even though she knew he was blameless for ... whatever.

Once again Toni felt way out of his depth. But the force was with him ...

'Can we have some music, Evita?'

Nothing.

'Please?'

She shrugged, reached forward and touched one button of her CD remote control. Their favourite singer had already been singing, silently: but she was un-muted now. Their common ground was re-established.

'Are things any clearer now, Evita?'

'I don't know, Toni. I just can't understand. I would swear on my Bible that there was just empty space where I touched Carla's hair ...'

Then she started to weep. He could see something close to terror in her eyes. He would definitely have to abandon some principles here.

'Evita, you know it simply can't have been like that. It must just have been your imagination.' He attempted a friendly chuckle. 'Or maybe the vodkas!' The ploy seemed to work: at least she didn't blow up again this time.

'I was really scared, Toni.'

'I know. But can you imagine how Carla felt when you started screaming? She didn't understand, either. She still doesn't. She was scared, too. That's why she left. She's very sensitive. But she does like you a lot, Evita ...'

'Really?' Eva sniffed.

'Really. Now, will you see her again later tomorrow, after you and Jo have done your work?'

'Yes. I'd like that, Toni.' She was attempting a smile now.

'Good. Now, why don't you get some sleep? Good job you didn't make us any coffee after all!'

'Oh, I am sorry. Would you like one now?'

'No — I'm very tired too. I'll get straight back to my hotel. Carla wants to meet you at seven o'clock at the Internet café ... OK?'

'OK.'

He stood up and made for the door. 'And you will definitely see Jo, as arranged, tomorrow lunch-time? You know how important that is, don't you ...'

'Yes, I will. Look — thanks for making the effort to come over. It wasn't fair of me to give you a hard time. Carla's your friend, and ...'

'No problem, Evita. Get to bed. Look forward to tomorrow. I'll see you when I see you ... OK?'

'Sure.' She walked over to the door and opened it for him. 'Thanks, Toni.' She chanced a little kiss on his cheek, and was very relieved to find the flesh was real.

The night air was still warm as Toni wandered back to the hotel, in a daze from the events of the past three hours, and not sure whether to feel impressed or ashamed after his catalogue of lies. Well, it was done now, and it was what Carla wanted.

He picked up his key from the night porter just before one o'clock, and made his way wearily up to his room.

Carla had witnessed his entire stellar performance at Eva's flat, and followed him all the way back. Once she was sure he was sound asleep, she called in her deputy and went off-duty again at last.

* * *

Toni slept long and woke very late that Sunday morning. Eventually, discovering that the hotel breakfast service was now not an option, he wandered back to the old town square, sat down again at the Caffè Italia, and ordered his usual coffee and pastry.

When Carla arrived, she complimented him profusely on his success with Eva, and assured him that she and Quo would now take care of everything.

'But first, Toni, I need to listen in to her conversation with Jo. You stay right here and get some lunch. I'll be back soon — and then we can do some more sightseeing. I have some interesting things to tell you about Prague ...'

She was enjoying herself again.

* * *

Jo arrived just after twelve for his lunch engagement at U Tři Pštrosů restaurant.

If he had been anxious not to make a scene in the basement bar of the small Karla IV café, he was certainly keen to avoid any hint of trouble at this prestigious establishment nestling into the embankment at the western end of the Charles Bridge.

So he counted to ten as he walked through the door, and he greeted Eva pleasantly; indeed he gave her a fond hug, for old times' sake. He ordered the drinks, and insisted that *he* would be paying for everything. And when the waiter had retreated, he sat back and listened.

And so, unseen, did Carla.

This time Eva followed, to the letter, the script that had been written by Quo.

She told her old friend and colleague that "somebody" (she didn't know who — they hadn't identified themselves when they'd phoned — but they'd kept saying "we") claimed to know all about his "activities of the last twenty years", and had a huge dossier which they were threatening to reveal. And she had been fingered to be the messenger ("because you can convince him we mean business").

And to keep their silence (they had told her), Josef Samek must secretly obtain specific information on the internal decisions which would have been made, the previous Friday, for the letting of the major contracts for "Vixen" ('... isn't that the code name for some big urban regeneration project, Jo?'). He must memorise the names of the companies that had been chosen, and he must then meet up with the caller's contacts — a woman in a green hat and a young man with a beard. At six o'clock tonight! At the Old Town Square Restaurant. At an open-air table. Unaccompanied. Unwired. And they would be checking. Scrupulously.

If he co-operated fully, he would receive a large cash sum on the spot, and he would not be pestered again. He *would* co-operate fully, they were certain, or the consequences would be very serious for him and his family ...

Her task completed, Eva sat back with an appropriate degree of concern registered on her face. Carla held her virtual breath and waited for Jo Samek to bite.

He bit.

The first course arrived soon afterwards. For appearances' sake, he consumed it, and the course that followed, with hardly any sign of the distress he was feeling inside. For her part, Eva, now purged rather than primed, found the excellent and free meal rather more enjoyable. Part of her was feeling sympathy for Jo's plight. Most of her was focusing on her upcoming rendezvous with Carla.

Carla, meanwhile, was saying her goodbyes.

Without proposing a dessert course, Jo then paid up as quickly as he decently could, gave Eva an unconvincing thank-you kiss, and hurried away. He had just over five hours to spare. But worse, on a Sunday afternoon, he had little hope of a result.

On the way directly to his office building, he phoned his wife and, for the third time that weekend, made his apologies.

At least he would be able to work undistracted. But they knew that, of course. That was exactly *why* this was all happening at the weekend ...

* * *

By five o'clock he was really beginning to panic.

After entering the building, and then his own office area, using his magnetic ID card, he had been alert enough to cover his tracks by doing a small amount of real work at his own computer before leaving it logged on and starting his quest for the data his unknown enemies were after.

But in the three hours since then, he had located only a small amount of Vixen-relevant information from open files lying around on desks or in cupboards — and it was nothing special: he reckoned that the people who knew this much about him and about Vixen must already know far more than he had been able to discover. He had certainly not been able to establish the names of any of the selected contractors ...

And he simply could not just try to log in to the procurement system and browse the records. Even if he made it through the security controls, which was unlikely, they would then have a complete log of his activities and would be able to trace it directly back to his personal system ID.

If it had been a weekday, he could have put pressure on any one of several individuals to make some discreet enquiries. It would have been their computer IDs and their careers at risk, not his — and they, like him, would have had little choice about co-operating.

But with only half an hour to spare before he would have to leave, he knew there was only one other option left open to him. He could physically break in to his Director's office, and hope that something useful had been left in an unlocked drawer. It was still only an outside chance. The Director might possibly have been told something about which contractors had been selected, but he was very unlikely to be in possession of any of Procurement's paperwork. Of course, Security would know Jo had been in the building, but he could probably bluff his way out of that — especially if a couple of windows were found to have been carelessly left open ...

He struggled with his dilemma.

* * *

While Jo was hard at work, Toni and Carla completed their tour of Prague. Carla led him back over the Charles Bridge ('Karlův Most — my bridge, Toni!'), and this time they did make the pilgrimage up the hill to discover the magnificence of the Castle and the Cathedral.

When they returned to the eastern bank, they branched off to visit the ancient buildings of the Jewish quarter. And later, as they wandered up and down the side streets surrounding the old town square, they saw all the contrasts again. Shabby exteriors, but beautifully neat and clean interiors ('It's so often the other way round, Carla ...'). A full-time dog's mess collector, whom they spotted on at least five occasions over the whole weekend, and who seemed to be very happy in his work. Hardly a police officer to be seen — a vivid contrast with Rome. But many beggars on their knees on the pavement, or sometimes fully prostrated before them as they passed. Thousands and thousands of puppets, of every shape and form, for sale wherever they looked ('... but nobody buying any, Carla!'). Poor and ill-educated traders and waiters speaking near-perfect English with affluent foreign tourists who had never once tried to learn a word of another language.

And, again in sharp contrast to Rome, there was music, sweet music, on offer everywhere ...

* * *

Eva Dvořák had left the Three Ostriches with an afternoon to kill and in a high state of anticipation.

Quo had of course decided that there would be no further rendezvous between Eva and Carla, despite Toni's vehement promises. But Quo was not, by nature, a cruel being. So it had been arranged, from the start, that Eva's subconscious hearing of Carla's gently-whispered 'Goodbye', at the end of her lunch with Jo, should carry a very particular additional message ...

Over the next four hours, one small degree at a time, Eva's anticipation steadily diminished. Soon after five o'clock, she was the happy victim of Cupid's Hypothermia. Her ardour had cooled and died away. She had forgotten Carla completely, and all the business about Jo. She only remembered a short, pleasant meeting at the Internet café with her new message board buddy, and she knew she had some bridges to rebuild at her favourite jazz club.

Eventually, she found herself walking briskly back to her apartment to catch up with her household chores and get ready for the working week ahead.

* * *

At three minutes to six, as Jo Samek hurried past the huge bulk of the Týn church, he consulted his watch for the fifth time in as many minutes. Finally deciding that he could attempt to regain some dignity, he slowed to a brisk walking pace as he entered the Old Town Square and approached the Staroměstská restaurant.

Seated at the corner table nearest to him were a sharp young blade and an elegant young woman in a green straw hat. His heart skipped two beats — the first in deep relief, the second in abject fear.

Toni's role as Illuminator had been clearly expanded by Carla, while they had been waiting, to include that of host and gentle intimidator. Now she gave him the nod. He stood up, smiled courteously, and gestured to the sweating Samek to join him at their table.

Jo did exactly what was suggested. Then he waited for a few moments. Nothing was said. He guessed they must be expecting him to begin.

'Look, I really tried,' he blurted out. 'There was nothing worth showing you. Nothing!! I even thought about breaking into the Director's office — but that would have blown the secrecy. I can definitely get something tomorrow. You must believe me ...'

His voice trailed off as he caught Carla's smile. His face instantly lost its mask of fear and, by comparison, took on an air of utter grace.

He jumped up again and, for the first time in thirty years, broke into a little folk dance, accompanying himself in song. Then he sat back down, Carla took his head in her hands (Quo was testing to see whether this engagement could be completed without a disappearing act), and Jo and the *Mater* joined minds.

Toni was used to this routine by now. He sat back in his chair, sipped his beer, studied his guidebook, and worked again on matching the magnificent buildings all around him to the written descriptions. And he simply ignored the rather gruff stares of the older generation of Sunday promenaders who were less than amused by Jo and Carla's public display of affection ...

Quo, however, found Josef Samek to be a very interesting subject. His insights into the goings-on in the many central government ministries of the old Czechoslovakia, and the new Czech Republic, were deep and wide-ranging. He might not have ready access to the latest list of construction contractors selected by the Ministry of Works procurement section (Quo had not been interested in that red herring anyway), but he knew a vast amount about who, within government and on its peripheries, was doing what with whom, and why, and how dubious each of those relationships might be. Especially in his own area of responsibility — forward planning for the Republic's recent zealous efforts at adoption by the European Union. Which suited the visitors' aims perfectly ...

But they would need to be quite selective. Carla could not go around engaging the dozens of mildly interesting contacts that Jo had revealed. The crucial conclusion drawn by Quo was that the Czech Republic was obviously still on the sidelines of Europe: rapidly modernising, and desperate to join the club, but with one leg still stuck quite firmly in the quagmires of the past.

Studying those in power here would reveal plenty of intrigue, but everything would be coloured by the effects of this state of transition. No — Jo's greatest contribution to the visitors' goals would be the provision of one or two major contacts operating much closer to the hub of European affairs. Taking that approach should lead Quo more quickly to the hearts and minds of some real power brokers — and hopefully, towards the apparently pristine Hilde van Wostraap ...

(Dutch MEP, untarnished record, 'star of European Parliament') introduced to Quo by Terleone (Toni's Gt uncle in Rome)

So a two-pronged strategy was established.

Its first element could be resolved at once, based on the transferral that was now complete. Samek had revealed one very promising contact — a certain Monsieur Jean-Christophe Nallier, Junior Minister Delegate for European Affairs in the French Foreign Ministry. Jo had worked closely with that department for the past four years, and knew all the important telephone extensions, including that of the junior minister himself, whom he had encountered twice in the recent past.

Their first meeting had been about a year ago, in Paris, when Jo had been part of a small Czech delegation dedicated to courting the French (who were always willing to be courted — without any prejudice or commitment, of course).

The second, follow-up meeting had been here in Prague, five months later, when the minister had visited the city alone for a couple of days to avoid the July heat, had drummed up what could turn out to be some highly lucrative potential business for French infrastructure construction companies (Quo wondered for a moment, on discovering this: 'Do I really have seventh sight? — it would be fascinating to know the names on that Vixen shortlist after all!'), and had enjoyed himself in the evenings by taking advantage of some mutually beneficial tips from Jo on the city's most entertaining night spots.

Jo's ongoing insight into Nallier's European affairs even extended to the knowledge that the minister was at this very moment away from Paris again, opening up new frontiers with a business contact in a luxurious chalet in the Italian Alps. But, it seemed, he would return to Paris the following Wednesday afternoon. And, Jo was able to reveal in response to Quo's direct enquiry, the romantic Monsieur Nallier's musical preferences were the popular and mellifluous waltzes of Johann Strauss.

But the aspect of Jo's familiarity with the life of Jean-Christophe which was of greatest interest to Quo was the fact that the French politician was apparently a founding member of an organisation entitled the *Campaign for Real Truth*.

The second element of Quo's strategy would however require another active contribution from the good Mr Samek. He had shown that he was aware of a senior NATO political advisor, based in Mons,

Belgium, who could be a potentially rich source of insights for the visitors, and was believed to be somewhat compromised; he might be easily won over. But Jo had never dealt directly with NATO, and knew no more details. Those, it seemed, would need to be gleaned from his own manager in the EU strategy group ...

So Jo's first engagement, on that warm Prague spring evening, concluded with one simple, real mission (which could indeed be given to him at the lower energy level available with Carla still fully "made") — to pursue those details with vigour at his place of work, first thing in the morning, and to report back here to Carla at one o'clock precisely.

By the time Jo realised he was back in the square, his new acquaintances had departed. But he was now very clear on what he must do. His fears for his own safety and survival, indeed all his memories of the last few hours of frantic searching, had evaporated as the sun disappeared behind the Town Hall. Now there was just a straightforward piece of muck-raking to be done, for a different sort of anonymous caller. Easy.

* * *

'What shall we do tonight, Carla? We'd better not try the Ungelt again — but it was a wonderful place, and I'm really sorry I missed the rest of that band's set ...'

'Toni, you know there's lots of music to listen to in Prague. Go off and enjoy yourself. Have the night of your life! You don't want me spoiling it for you again! Just be back in your hotel room by half past twelve tomorrow afternoon, and start packing — we may need to leave at short notice.'

'OK, Carla. I like that idea. But will you be all right?'

'Oh, Toni — you are the perfect gentleman! But you must stop being silly. Of course I'll be all right. Now, just go!'

* * *

Jo Samek did indeed find it easy to complete his mission. Soon after arriving at his office the next morning, he went to his head of department, Petr Stojespal, with the usual sort of story, which in this case was perfectly true.

'Petr, my team has recently identified some very good reasons to get a lot closer to the power centres at NATO, urgently. But since we joined in to it all, four years ago, it's become much harder for us to bend the rules and get inside things — as you are well aware. But we know one of the special teams did some covert work a while back, and we've picked up a possibly interesting name from them: Raymond Martin Graves. Do you have anything positive on him? — and anything dubious?'

Co-operation with Samek was usually the best policy, both for the sake of the department and for one's own personal security, although he was kept under careful scrutiny, and was never allowed to step too far out of line. In fact, he often did the authorities great surrogate favours, without being at all aware of it.

So Stojespal told his subordinate most of what he knew.

Yes, Graves was a significant figure in the NATO machine. He worked at SHAPE — the Supreme Headquarters Allied Powers Europe. Yes, he could prove to be a valuable contact, for various reasons. Petr mentioned a few of them. And yes ('how did you guess, Jo?'), there was at least one Achilles heel. Graves had a girlfriend in Brussels, whose name was — Petr consulted his little black book, and then a bulky file taken from his huge safe — whose name was Mireille Daurant. And Mireille was known to be very amenable to inducements. Did Jo perhaps need her address and telephone number?

'Thank you, Petr. I think this will all prove very useful. I'll keep you in touch. Oh, yes, one other thing — have you heard of a Dutch MEP by the name of Hilde van Wostraap?'

Petr had not. 'Must be quite newly elected. Have you looked her up?'

'No, not yet — just thought I'd ask while I was here ...'

'Hold on.' Stojespal clicked into the EuroParl web site and quickly found the right page. 'Yes, here she is. Netherlands. Not had many dealings with them. And judging by her profile, it doesn't look as if she'd be interested in any specials deals with us!'

* * *

At one o'clock, Samek sat down again next to the attractive woman he had met at the same restaurant the evening before. She had no minder with her this time, but he did not give that a second thought, particularly when she once again presented him with that winning smile.

Carla remained in full public view, and the process of collection was carried out in a matter of seconds. Quo was satisfied. Josef had proved to be a very easy-to-manage subject, and the results were most acceptable. And since the Frenchman, Jean-Christophe Nallier, was known to be otherwise engaged for the next few days, the next destination for Toni and Carla would definitely need to be the Belgian capital.

So Jo could now be released from all his responsibilities to the visitors. He would need to remember what his boss had just told him, of course, and would maybe use that information one of these days in the normal course of his work. And obviously he would recollect that he had popped into the office the previous day, to do a bit of catching-up. But as he blinked his eyes on his return to the bright light of the midday sun, to find that Carla had once again departed in silence, everything else to do with the extraordinary events of the past forty-eight hours had been forgotten forever. Jo Samek had been demobbed.

* * *

Carla softly called '*Hola,*' and Toni looked up from his packing to see her standing beside his window.

'Ah, you're back. How did it go?'

'Very well, thank you. We learned exactly what we needed to.'

'So are we moving on, then?'

'We certainly are, Toni — straight away. You need to book a flight to Brussels ... and a hotel room.'

'Ah! Another city I've never visited! Are you coming with me?'

'Of course! I think I'll travel inside the plane this time, just for a change. But nobody will see me — it'll be a little too congested in there to make an appearance, I would imagine. So you only need to buy one ticket.'

Toni smiled at Carla's first, very reasonable attempt at humour, took out Rafael's bank card, and picked up the phone.

Council of the Regions, Dome

Long before Toni encountered Carla, the Council of the Regions had met in special session.

Their extraordinary debate on the Missions of Exploration had been conducted with passion, and was reaching its inevitable end ...

'I am certain that nobody is suggesting that the Initial Missions should not have been launched when they were,' the leader of the Utor Party was thinking with a final dramatic flourish. 'Am I correct?'

The stony silence of acceptance in every delegate's mind was more intense than the actual silence that had accompanied the entire debate.

'At least, then, we are all agreed on this. I suggest therefore that we have a simple decision to make: whether to leave the objectives of those Missions exactly as they stand, or to modify their priorities, as proposed.'

The President rose, took over control, and reasoned 'Our discussion has come full circle.'

Recognising, as could everybody else, that there was a new Consensus, but mindful of the need to allow for any last-minute changes of heart, the President then proceeded to summarise the issues before the full Assembly, mentally articulating each point with absolute clarity.

'There has always, as you are all well aware, been unanimous Council agreement on the fundamental desirability of carrying out the Missions of Exploration, following the success of the early Detector Missions and the identification of the five radio sources — the so-called New Worlds.

'One of the core objectives for the Initial Missions, the Observation Imperative, has also always had unanimous Council agreement. The three Observation Aims within this Imperative are, of course:

> To map and model, as completely as possible, the geophysical characteristics of each New World of interest.

> To collect, through observation and engagements, other categories of factual information relevant to the establishment of an initial profile of the populations of each New World (all living forms) and their behaviour patterns; and, in the case of the Controlling Species, its technologies, its overt modes of operation (especially in the area of world government), and the overall stability of its Civilisation.

> To gain further insights into the underlying true beliefs and integrity levels of carefully selected significant individuals of the Controlling Species. This to be done using standard sampling techniques, within the constraints imposed by the total time available in the environs of that New World and the inefficiencies of the insight gathering technique.

'However, this Council has not, to date, achieved full agreement on the relative priorities of these three Aims. But for as long as the Observation Imperative remained the sole active objective, this was of little consequence. The three Aims could be pursued in parallel, with the commander of each Mission dynamically deciding the most appropriate tactics as each situation developed.

'Closely allied to the Observation Imperative, of course, is the passive Moral Imperative, which again has always had unanimous Council backing. As you are all aware, this simply mandates that if any specific assistance or improvement can be readily given to any New World by the visiting crew, then it shall be given.

'Finally, a proposed extension to the objectives of the Initial Missions, the provisionally-labelled Exploitation Imperative, has already been debated at length. Even in its most conservative forms, this Imperative has always been rejected by a significant majority vote. Only a small number of Parties has ever proactively supported it. However, it remains a technically feasible Imperative, and draft proposals representing further reductions in its scope, along with revised cost estimates, are under development and will be presented, as planned, at the next scheduled meeting of this Council.

'In conclusion: at the time of the Mission Launches, the priorities of the Observation Aims had not been resolved, and the question of a possible extension to the Initial Missions' scope had not been properly considered.

'I must remind you all, in addition, that the time-limited experimental projects and launches, using prototypes of the star-craft and the radimote technologies, had identified many minor weaknesses and a number of significant technical shortcomings — and costs were continuing to spiral.

'Despite all these issues, at our last full meeting it was unanimously agreed that the launch of the five Initial Missions should proceed immediately, to the originally proposed schedule.

'Pragmatic analysis of this situation had concluded, in any case, that the outstanding technical shortcomings could only be properly resolved "in the field". Most significantly, however, the abandonment of the launch schedule would have precipitated huge delays for reasons of expected unfavourable atmospheric conditions, and might well have encouraged further, more stringent financial reviews by the Independent Treasurer.

'This, then,' the President pondered, 'was the position at the time of the five Mission Launches.

'However, the newly-wealthy Utor Party has recently achieved a significant increase in its voting power, as a result of its peremptory negotiations with the Council on other matters, which relate principally to the continued security of the Ovanavo Region.

'This increased power has enabled that Party to exercise its constitutional right to force this extraordinary debate on the Imperatives of the Initial Missions, so soon after the departure of the first five craft.

'As a result, and after due deliberation, I recognise that the latest Consensus is that the three Observation Aims should now be adapted and explicitly prioritised, as follows:

> The Mapping and Modelling Aim should be modified and extended, to include a full study of the sites of all mineral resources on each New World, and this Aim should be given a higher priority than the other two Aims.

> The Fact Gathering Aim should be sustained, and be given a higher priority than the Insight Gaining Aim. Special attention should be given to the actual and forecast usage of all natural resources on each New World, with a focus on those of greatest abundance and those of which there appear to be particular shortages.

> The Insight Gaining Aim should be continued, but at a lower priority. This should not present any serious exposures to our objectives, since the benefit of understanding the political integrity of New World populations is now judged by a Council majority to be somewhat lower than originally conceived; and by the time each Initial Mission receives its revised orders, a sufficiently large sample of insights should have already been achieved. Any shortfall in results can either be made up in background mode, or can simply be considered as statistically insignificant. In addition, the focus of Insight Gaining will be changed. The true thoughts and views of the New Worlds' principal geophysicists, rather than their leaders and thinkers, should now be actively pursued within this Aim.'

Having thought all of this through very clearly, and recognising that every delegate was fully understanding that thinking; being acutely aware that the 70% vote required for a change in Initial Mission priorities had now been over-achieved; appreciating that this position could not be overridden despite the weighting of the rarely-needed casting vote; and knowing that every delegate perfectly understood all of this too, the President then definitively concluded that the motion proposed by the Utor Party had been carried.

Full financial analysis of the effects of these changes would proceed in post-facto mode, and the results would be presented to the Council at the next timetabled plenary session, along with the already scheduled and far more contentious latest proposals for the future addition of a limited Exploitation Imperative.

With the debate at its end, the President of the Council of the Regions issued the formal order for new Mission Instructions to be prepared at once.

Communication I

The carrier pigeon glided silently through the blackness.

Like the other identical quins, it had been travelling for a very long time. But its energy levels were still high, and would remain so.

It had departed in precisely the same direction taken by those for whom its particular message was intended. It was made of the same stuff as its larger target, and with no winds or weather to disrupt its flight, it had been able to track them to perfection, and at an identical speed.

And now it had come at last within reach of the place where they were moored. So it sang its simple song, received their confirmatory reply, and then continued on its fixed trajectory for all eternity.

Conference Room, *Mater*

Quo, Carla and the Chief Surveyor had been summoned to the Conference Room for an impromptu progress review. Only Quo had some inkling of the possible reason.

At the Captain's request, the Chief Surveyor's report was considered first, and the others absorbed it with an appropriate level of decorum and interest.

'Our initial Mapping and Modelling activities have been extremely successful. We obtained three fine corroborated fixes in Bilbao, Rome and Prague, forming an excellent wide-angled triangle. Remarkably, London, the reference point for zero degrees longitude, makes an almost perfect parallelogram with the other three cities.'

Quo and Carla were easily able to contain their excitement.

'Our access to the database of co-ordinates of all major cities, towns, mountains and so on was a very good start, and our surveyors have already made great extrapolations from this and from our direct visual observations of coastlines and lake shores.

'I have no problems to report. We are in a very positive position from which to continue this excellent progress. Our forward plan, when the time is right, is to acquire the next level of surface cartographic data by further engagement of expert geographers and the accessing of more specialised databases.

'Finally, I have a special comment. The subject Toni, despite his lack of familiarity with the principles of surveying and the technology of positioning systems, and in the face of considerable adversity, has performed his role with diligence and to great effect.'

The Captain nodded in approval.

'Thank you, Chief. A very good start.'

Carla's set of thoughts was more concise.

'In the area of general Fact Gathering, we have made reasonable progress. Toni has provided us with an excellent initial set of data, and this has been refined by the knowledge and broader experience of four additional subjects, and by our continuous observation of several different environments. The limited quantity of fact-gathering which we have achieved by transferral is more than compensated by the first-hand evidence we have gained of the population's capacity for misunderstanding, miscalculation, distrust and deviousness.'

'We clearly have certain things in common with them,' the Captain pondered wryly to all those present. 'Thank you, Handler. Keep up the good work.'

'Now, Number Two ... what are your thoughts?'

'It is, of course,' mused Quo, unhurried and all-inclusive as usual, 'the Aim of Insight Gaining which has seen hardly any progress of substance. The immediate link to Terleone promised much. But the technical difficulties which we encountered forced us to curtail that potential chain of contact. Subsequent events, all beyond our control, impossible to predict, and indeed well outside the range of our natural assumptions of risk and our associated contingency strategies, then caused major delays in the establishment of a new contact chain.

'The limited social and political insights gained from Giuseppe are of some value, of course, and we do have two promising leads to pursue immediately, with a good longer-term target in Ms van Wostraap. But in terms of significant insights actually gained, we essentially find ourselves almost back at the point where we first engaged with Toni. We are, therefore, substantially behind expectations in terms of timetable and results.'

'Thank you, Number Two,' reflected the Captain. 'I appreciate your honest assessment of the facts of which we are all aware, although from a personal viewpoint I feel rather less concerned at our overall lack of results. I am confident that the procedural problems will not recur; that we have all, including Toni, gained much experience in this first phase; and that we shall make rapid progress as we come closer to the heart of European government and opinion.

'For a quite separate reason, however, I do share your concerns. And I apologise for the apparent melodrama of this meeting, and of what I now have to reveal.

'I have called this progress review at short notice because I have just received and read a Special Communication.'

Carla and the Surveyor looked at each other in considerable surprise.

'Yes, it is a surprise to you, because I have read its contents in a privileged mode, which is only available for use by the Mission Captain, and whose existence has been concealed within my mind and has not been revealed to any other crew member, save for Number Two in a similarly privileged way ...'

Quo did not attempt to pretend any apologies for this — being fully briefed and programmed to be able to invoke that mode in the event of the Captain's indisposition — but still had no idea of the contents of this special message itself.

'This mode is reserved for the handling of special new orders only. It permits me to consider those orders without immediately sharing my reactions to them with the rest of the crew. So it allows you to present your situation reports, untainted by those new orders — precisely as you have just done. I thank you all for your forbearance and for your continued trust.

'I can see you have concerns that this special mode may have opened up an opportunity for secrecy within the team, which I know would be utterly unacceptable to us all. Let me reassure you: its key characteristic is that the new orders remain unshared in my mind for a very short period only. After that, they are automatically revealed to you, as usual. I cannot tamper with this highly sophisticated, ultra-secure process. So you will soon all see exactly what the orders were, and you will be able to judge my present actions in our normal open way.

'But before that moment arrives, I intend to reveal the main features of our new orders to you directly.

'As we all know, a complete policy for the Initial Missions had not been established at the time of our launch. We anticipated some clarification on priorities at a somewhat later stage. However, there has been a significant change in political influence back at home, and the Council has been obliged to agree immediate and major revisions to the scope of our work.

'The Aims of Mapping and Modelling, and of Fact Gathering, have been increased in priority. Both of them are now, for us, focused on the natural resources of the Earth. I am well aware that we have, thus far, been unable to make much headway on this aspect of those Aims. I therefore expect you, Chief, to devote considerable planning attention to this new emphasis with immediate effect. I must point out, however, that the motivation for the changes is not articulated in the new orders.

'The Aim of Insight Gaining has been proportionately downgraded, and is to be re-focused on the true thoughts of individuals possessing certain specialised geophysical knowledge.

'However ...' — the Captain paused, to ensure the undivided attention of each member of the team — '... because of the serious delays which we have suffered to date, I do not intend to implement this particular instruction at this time.

'I believe we need to continue our pursuit of the contacts which we have recently established. We must use them to achieve a dramatic and exponential increase in the total number of samples taken and associated insights gained into the population's overall integrity. And we must do all this with renewed speed and vigour.

'When a minimum statistically valid set of such samples has been obtained, I shall review the situation and consider the adoption of the orders revising the scope and priority of this Aim.

'Our controllers will, of course, remain unaware of this particular delaying decision — the one-way communication enforced by our technology at least holds the merit of allowing me a small amount of commander's discretion!'

Quo, the Chief Surveyor and Carla the Handler all smiled, both out of politeness at their senior officer's joke, and in sincere approval of the chosen tactics.

'Very well,' the Captain cogitated in conclusion. 'I am delighted to see that you are all in complete agreement with my decision. In a few moments you will find yourselves able to digest the full details of the new orders. Please now act with great expedition, to allow us to make substantial progress, on all fronts, in the immediate future.'

Brussels, Belgium

Toni had still been on the phone when Carla had made her apologies and gone off to the Captain's meeting, leaving a guardian angel watching over him for those few minutes.

She appeared again as he was closing his suitcase. But she did not reveal any changes of plan.

'Everything fixed, Toni?'

'Yes. I'm on the five o'clock flight to Brussels — and the travel agent has booked me a hotel room very close to the Grand Place. That's a magnificent square, Carla — the heart of the city. I'm really looking forward to seeing it!'

'That's great. OK — time for a snack?'

'How did you guess?' Toni smiled.

He called the receptionist to arrange a taxi, then had a relaxed lunch on his own in the hotel bar. Just before three, Carla rejoined him in the lobby, and they slid into the spacious interior of an expensive private hire car.

Carla was back in briefing mode, giving him some general information about Raymond Martin Graves. Then she issued her latest orders.

'While you're waiting for the plane, will you please try to call Mireille Daurant's home number, from a public phone? Hopefully she will still be out at work. Then we shall later be able to pretend that Graves tried to call her this afternoon and got no reply. And that he also first tried her mobile, but there were "network problems". But listen — if she does answer, just put the phone down at once, and we'll think again ...'

'Whatever you say. You're the boss.'

'Toni — was that what you call sarcasm?'

'No, Carla, I promise you it wasn't. You are the boss. I don't do sarcasm. But I'm glad you're on the lookout for it now. You must try and pick up on my jokes and my ironies instead — there are lots of them, I'm afraid!'

* * *

Toni checked in for his flight with time to spare. Then, as Carla had requested, he found a phone booth and called Mireille's number. It kept ringing out, and fortunately no answering machine kicked in — so she obviously was not at home and monitoring it before answering. He replaced the handset, and the trap was sprung.

Then, before he passed though the departures channel, Carla explained the first stage of their plan for Raymond's engagement ...

* * *

Carla's sense of humour certainly was improving. She amused herself on the flight to Brussels, unseen of course, by walking up and down the aisle and passing gaily straight through the flight attendants and their drinks trolleys, while everyone else had to wait for them to pass. At one point she bent down and whispered sweet nothings in Toni's ear. He was really taken by surprise and nearly spilled his beer. Then he looked forward to some more such nothings, and was not disappointed.

* * *

The queue for taxis at Brussels airport was long, but they were plentiful and the rush hour had passed, so Toni soon arrived at his hotel, with Carla in virtual tow as usual.

'How long will you be with us, Sr. Barola?' smiled the receptionist, unconsciously smoothing her hair back behind one ear.

'I don't know. At least two nights, I expect ...'

'I hope you enjoy your time in Brussels, *señor*. Here is a street plan of our beautiful city. And if there is anything else I can do ...'

But Toni had barely noticed the pretty young woman or her very personalised welcome.

* * *

Carla materialised in the bathroom as he was unpacking.

'*Hola.*'

'Hi, Carla. I enjoyed your little game on the plane! It's a pity you couldn't have moved on to blowing in my ear ...'

She laughed out loud for the first time. He loved it.

'Now, Toni,' she said, easily able to switch back to business, 'I think we should set up an emergency rendezvous plan, in case anything goes wrong and we lose each other or have to separate quickly, as we did in Prague.'

'Fair enough.'

'So, I suggest that, if it's ever necessary, we each come back and stand outside the front entrance to your hotel, on the hour throughout the daytime if we can manage it, and wait for five minutes, until we manage to meet up again. We should also make this the rule for any other city we visit. OK?'

'That's a good plan.'

'Well, Toni, maybe you can be learning some better planning while I'm picking up your sense of humour!'

'Ouch!'

* * *

Just before eight o'clock, Toni pulled out his mobile phone and called Mireille.

'*Allô?*'

'*Bonsoir, Mlle Daurant. Parlez-vous anglais?*'

'Yes, I do. Who is this, please?'

'Ah — please just call me Toni. I have an important message for you from a mutual friend — Monsieur Graves.'

'From Rayo? Is he sick? Or ...?'

'Oh, no, no, *mademoiselle*, he's fine. Please don't worry. Raymond has simply been called away at very short notice, and cannot see you for several days.'

'Oh! Where has he gone?'

'I'm sorry, but I do not know. It's top secret, I understand. Raymond tried to call you this afternoon on your mobile, but he could not get through. And he tried you at home, in case you were there. He could not risk calling you at work, for security reasons. That's when he asked me to help. He's not permitted to use telephones for the next few days. He wanted me to let you know this — and also, to tell you that yesterday morning he bought a very special present for you, which he was going to surprise you with this evening. It's extremely fragile, and it will not last long without tender care. So he asked me to deliver it to you, by hand, tonight ...'

'This is very strange, Toni. I'm not sure. I thought nobody knew about Rayo and me — and he's never mentioned your name ...'

'And Raymond, *mademoiselle*, whom I have known for more than three years, had never mentioned yours before asking me to help him this afternoon.'

Mlle Daurant, who always avoided worrying if she could instead be enjoying herself, plumbed the depths of this remark for a few moments and concluded it was mysterious enough to prove that the caller was genuine.

'Oh, Toni, *pardonnez-moi*. I am sorry to have doubted you. As long as Rayo is safe. Thank you so much for your kindness. And please — you must call me Mireille.'

'That's fine, Mireille. You are wise to be cautious. So — may we meet up briefly in the centre of Brussels, as soon as possible? I need to travel south later tonight ...'

'Yes, of course. But I'm afraid I can't come out at once,' she giggled. 'I was in the shower when you rang ...'

'No problem. I have to drive in from Mons.'

'Then can we meet in the Grand Place, at nine-thirty — perhaps inside the Chaloupe d'Or?'

Toni decided he had better not demonstrate his ignorance of an obviously famous meeting place. He would have plenty of time to find it ...

'Yes, certainly, Mireille.'

'Sit as close as you can to the entrance. How will I recognise you?'

Toni had to think quickly.

'Er ... OK, I shall be reading a music magazine. I shall make it obvious!'

'Ah, you like music! That's great, Toni. See you soon!'

* * *

Toni bought his magazine in the hotel shop, then ambled down to the Grand Place with an hour to spare. He located the Chaloupe d'Or café straight away, then resisted the temptation to wander around the beautiful square and succumbed to a stronger force. He followed the natural flow of evening strollers down a bustling side street and into the busy Rue des Bouchers, where he found an abundance of fine restaurants and was able to enjoy some excellent Belgian cuisine.

By nine-fifteen he was walking purposefully back to the café. Ignoring Mireille's request, he followed the instructions that Carla had given him just before he left the hotel, and made his way up the wide staircase at the back to the more private tables on the upper floor. He found a quiet one next to the wall, sat down facing the stairs, and bravely ordered the house's special "Golden" cocktail from a passing waiter.

A few moments later, Carla emerged from the ladies' room near the foot of the stairs and smiled at the attendant seated outside. Receiving no tip from this customer as she walked past, the elderly lady scowled in a well-practised way — and then suddenly wondered why she had not noticed the woman going in ...

As Carla approached his table, Toni smiled and stood up, and she slid along the bench seat to take up her station by the wall. He sat back down and opened up his magazine, making sure the maroon-coloured electric guitar on the cover was clearly visible to anyone walking up the stairs.

'Here we go again, Carla,' he whispered, unsure whether he was excited or anxious.

'Be brave, Toni,' joked Carla, and he smiled and was immediately relaxed again.

* * *

A beautifully groomed young woman eventually appeared at the top of the stairs. Toni was stunned by her similarity to Carla. The same dark hair — but a little longer. The same small face — no, a little narrower. But she was slightly taller and even slimmer than Carla, and her eyes were brown rather than dark blue. And she wasn't smiling ... ah yes, now she was ... she had seen his magazine!

Mireille approached their table, with some uncertainty accompanying her smile.

'Toni?'

'Yes, Mireille, I'm Toni.'

'*Mon Dieu* — there are three empty tables downstairs. I've been waiting for five minutes down there — I thought you had not yet arrived ...'

'Oh, I'm sorry — it was full when we got here!'

'Really? OK, Toni. But I did not realise you would be with somebody ...'

She smiled at his companion as sweetly as she could manage, and Toni politely introduced Carla — who proffered neither a hand nor a social kiss, but simply smiled even more sweetly in return.

Mireille's pretty head and shoulders at once jerked gently backwards, as if she had bumped into an unseen pane of glass. Then she lost her mildly affronted appearance, smiled an honest smile, slid onto the opposite bench, stared directly into Carla's eyes, and broke into a tranquil and quite respectable rendition of Madonna's *Vogue*.

Her new girlfriend gently seized the moment, and Mireille's head, without hesitation. There was then no discussion by Quo of the false pretext for their meeting — that would be immediately erased from Mireille's memory for ever. And only a light one-way transferral would be needed, with no briefing or missioning required. So despite this cosmopolitan girl's predilection for the less deadly of the species alone, her involvement by the still-visible Carla was simplicity itself ...

Quo was therefore quickly able to establish precisely where Deputy Political Advisor Raymond Martin Graves could be found, first thing the following morning (he would be at his village home, before driving as usual to the NATO SHAPE complex in nearby Mons — he called Mireille every day, so she always knew where he would be), and what time he would be leaving for work, and his very private mobile phone number. And what he had given Mireille on her last birthday. And that his favourite piece of music was George Gershwin's *Rhapsody in Blue* ...

Mireille was disengaged. No longer concerned about her Rayo, or the forgotten little present, or Toni's earlier identity, but instead regarding her table companions as very welcome (no, very attractive) new friends, she brightly suggested they should all go for a stroll around the Grand Place in the still-warm spring evening.

Toni was enthusiastic, of course.

Carla, however, quickly made her excuses (she 'had to get off home ...') — but as they stood up to leave, she engineered a private word with Toni. 'Set your alarm for seven o'clock, *amigo* — I'll join you in your room, and we'll make our next set of plans.'

Then she marched straight off down the stairs with a cheery '*Au revoir!*' giving her latest victim no chance of a friendly farewell kiss on the cheeks.

Mireille did not, anyway, seem too concerned to see her depart.

She and Toni emerged from the café into the splendour of the Grand Place, its principal buildings illuminated by a few gentle floodlights, but sadly without the full *Son et Lumière*, which would not begin until the summer. And over the next hour, Mireille expertly revealed to Toni — and, unknowingly, to Carla, who was in fact still in close attendance — the detailed history of that great square and the special and unique golden statues and images high up in the gables of every single façade.

'Each house on the square has a name, you know, Toni — the wheel-barrow, the she-wolf, the fox (and the little fox!), the golden tree, the rose, the windmill, the pewter-pot, the kite, the angel, the peacock, the ass — and many, many more.'

'But what do the names all mean, Mireille ...?'

'Well, at the end of the seventeenth century, this square was fully rebuilt by the city's guildsmen, in only four years, after it had been totally destroyed in two days by Louis XIV of France. In various ways, those names, and the statues and the carvings on the buildings, are symbols of the crafts and trades that were practised in Brussels at that time. You can't understand their messages unless you can read between the lines. For example, the narrow house in front of us is called "The Sack". Its façade is decorated with tools, and with two people — one carrying a sack, the other plunging his hands into it. It is the house of the Joiners and Coopers ...'

'How do you know all this, Mireille?'

'I was born here. It is my heritage.'

'It's a mystery to me.'

'That's possibly what they intended ...'

When Toni had learned enough, and Mireille's enthusiasm for describing the square's history was sated, the conversation turned naturally to music — and they quickly discovered that Janis Ian was a shared heroine.

'Toni — you do know she's in the middle of a European tour right now?'

'Oh, I'd completely forgotten. That's ridiculous — yes, of course I do! But she doesn't usually make it to Bilbao!'

'We're not in Bilbao, Toni — we're in Brussels. And she's playing in Amsterdam tomorrow evening. I've been toying with the idea of going to the show on my own — I'm afraid Rayo isn't interested; he prefers Gershwin and ZZ Top — but now you and I can go together!'

'Mireille, that would be wonderful. I've got every one of Janis' albums, but I've never yet seen her in concert. If only we could ...'

'Why not? What's stopping us, Toni? Oh — maybe it's Carla ...'

'Oh no, don't worry about her — I just don't know if I'll be free tomorrow.'

Mireille's dejection and Toni's uncertainty were patent to Carla, who was still very much with them in spirit. She thought for a moment, decided her plans were secure, and whispered in her Illuminator's ear.

'It's OK, *carísimo* — you must go. It is a wonderful opportunity for you. I shan't need you after lunch tomorrow ...'

Toni's surprise at her intervention was badly disguised.

'Whatever is it, Toni?' asked Mireille, concerned at his sudden facial reaction to Carla's secret message.

'It's all right. I was just thinking things through. Yes — I would love to go to the concert with you!'

Without hesitation, Mireille pulled out her mobile phone and made three rapid calls. As she neared the end of the third one, Toni realised she had taken his hand in hers.

'It's all booked. We have seats in the fourth row of the stalls — that's the best place to be for a concert like this! And I'm paying!'

'Oh no, Mireille, I must buy my own ticket, at least ...'

'No arguments, Toni — this is my treat! But listen ... I can't possibly leave work before about two-thirty. If you want to go up to Amsterdam a bit earlier, that's fine — have you ever been there before?'

'No — it would be great to do some sightseeing if I can ...'

'OK, I'll get a train at about three o'clock, and I'll meet you at six-thirty on the canal bridge directly opposite the front of the Rijksmuseum.'

Toni could see that resistance was useless.

'Now, I must go home, Toni. I shall need to start work very early tomorrow, so that I can get away for our special event ...'

As they said goodnight, Mireille did not hesitate to kiss him fully on the lips.

Toni wandered back to his hotel in something of a daze, and collected his key from the still smiling receptionist, who asked him if he had any plans for the following evening. He blurted out an enthusiastic 'Yes!' and she smiled much less encouragingly. Something nearly registered in Toni's brain.

He brushed his teeth in a trance for a long time, then snapped out of it, set his alarm for seven o'clock and tumbled into bed. But with so many attractive new prospects suddenly materialising on the horizon, he found it unusually difficult to fall asleep ...

* * *

When he awoke, Carla was already sitting in the chair near his bed, waiting to plan the morning's events.

'Oh, hello Carla. Did you sleep well?'

'In my own way, yes, thank you, Toni.'

She made no mention of the previous evening.

'Now, at eight-thirty you must call Raymond Graves and read out a message to him, in English. Please write this down ...'

Toni rubbed the sleep from his eyes and found a pen and paper.

'OK, I'm ready ...'

'Is this Raymond Graves? ...

'Good. Listen carefully. Do not speak. Do not argue.

'We have Mireille. She is wearing the pretty little silver bracelet you gave her for her birthday. She is very frightened. We are not squeamish. If you do not co-operate absolutely, she will suffer at length. You will hear her suffering, each time we telephone you ...'

'Carla — what is all this?'

'Toni, please do as I ask. This is our mission. Do not fear — I promise you that no harm will ever come to Mireille or Raymond. This is only a means to an end ...'

Toni was not comfortable, but had little will to fight.

'If you say so. OK, carry on ...'

'... and after that, your involvement with Mireille will become publicly known. And your fingerprints will be found on several of the items used to inflict her injuries ...

'So do not argue.

'We require you merely to do a small favour for us. You will follow these instructions precisely. Providing you do so, Mireille will be freed unharmed, and she will telephone you later this afternoon. And it will all be over.

'You will travel at once to Brussels, and you will purchase a bouquet of roses, for recognition. Then you will enter the City Park, by the entrance opposite the Royal Palace, at 1100 hours precisely. Your initial contact will be a woman standing nearby, who has no idea what you look like. As soon as she sees the roses, and is sure that you can see her, she will sit down on a bench, and you will approach her and receive a further message.

'You will appear cheerful and carefree throughout.

'You will inform nobody of this. If the police or any other forces appear near the Park at any time, we shall observe it, and Mireille's suffering will begin at once. If the police approach the bench, your contact will loudly claim

complete ignorance of you, and will make a formal complaint that you are propositioning her. This will not be good for your reputation with the police or your masters — and Mireille's suffering will immediately increase. You will bear the blame, and later hear the results.

'Now, do exactly as I have instructed.'

'This is preposterous, Carla!'
'No, Toni, it is just our way of encouraging him.'
Toni was revising his opinions on the desirability of visiting Dome.
'I'm still not happy.'
She left him to dress and eat his hotel breakfast in uneasy peace.

* * *

But at exactly eight-thirty, Toni Murano, retained Illuminator, telephoned Raymond Graves and slowly dictated his frightening message.

The seasoned diplomat began to apply his situational analysis experience after hearing the very first few words. He knew there would be no time to try and set up a trace on the call — and anyway, that would bring everything out into the open. And dragging it out by arguing would also be counter-productive. So to buy himself precious thinking time, and to avoid worsening the situation, once Toni had finished speaking he merely said 'All right. I'll be there ...' and put down the phone.

He soon decided to follow his first instincts, concluding that his girlfriend's young life was more precious than whatever information, influence or betrayals her captors might be seeking from him, at this time of all times — the height of the invasion operations in Iraq. He phoned his secretary and regretted that he was feeling most unwell. Leaving her to handle the effect of his absence on several very important meetings, and figuring that, for this critical journey, the railway was safer and more predictable than the roads, he drove carefully to Mons station.

Halfway through the train journey, he suddenly remembered it was April Fool's Day, and began to pray that this would turn out to be just a very sick joke ...

* * *

As he cut the phone call, Toni was absent-mindedly reflecting on Raymond's accent in the few words of English he had uttered. It didn't sound at all like that of a Frenchman or a Belgian.

Carla, already re-made and observing from the corner of the room, interrupted his thinking and politely demanded a situation report, which her aide-de-camp at once provided with surprising aplomb.

'Excellent, Toni. Thank you! Right — you must go straight out and buy a small portable CD player with speakers, and two set of batteries, and a CD of *Rhapsody in Blue*. Oh, yes — please also pick up some Strauss Waltzes while you are there! Get the Gershwin piece all ready to play. And throw away that sheet of paper with the message I dictated!

'Then you must go to the Park, using the entrance opposite the Palace (yes, I did my reconnaissance last night!), and sit down at a quarter to eleven at one end of the first empty bench you see. I shall then join you, and we'll wait for Raymond to arrive. After that, you can leave it all to me. But I'll probably need to disappear, when it's safe to do so — so please don't watch ...'

* * *

As Toni was about to leave his room, he suddenly realised he could have some music to accompany him around Brussels. He delved into his rucksack, pulled out the one and only CD he had brought from home, and tucked it into his jacket pocket.

He got directions to the nearest shops from the hotel concierge, and remembered, while he was there, to ask about the trains to Amsterdam.

On his way to the shops, he took the note he had written for Graves, tore it into several pieces, screwed them all up, and dropped each one into a separate litter bin.

He soon found and bought everything Carla had ordered. He made sure that the CD of *Rhapsody in Blue* sounded all right, then swapped in his own CD and set it playing. Now he had nearly an hour to spare. So he revisited the Grand Place, this time in daylight and with the songs of *Between the Lines* playing quietly in the background, and he tried to recall at least some of what Mireille had told him about the glorious square.

Then he strolled up the hill to the east, passing the magnificent Saint-Michel cathedral and the Parliament building, then crossed the Place de la Nation into the north entrance of the Park and walked its full length, watching the Palace façade come steadily into full view. He turned back once he had reached the square, and sat down on an empty bench, just as Carla had instructed.

A couple of minutes later, she appeared from behind a large tree.

'*Hola, Toni.*'

'Hi, Carla.'

'Toni, your own music sounds wonderful, as always, but will you *please* set up the Gershwin piece, straight away?'

'Oh, I'm sorry — I'm not thinking!'

'Well, you are, but maybe not exactly the right things for this moment.'

'Your jokes are getting good, now! Anyway — there, it's all ready ... listen ...'

Carla moved off a few yards to Toni's left and stood admiring the view of the Palace.

Just before eleven, a stocky man with a round, confident face and blond crew-cut hair lumbered through the gates, cradling a large bunch of beautiful red roses rather self-consciously in his arms.

'He's seen me, Toni,' said Carla, without moving her lips. 'Start the music. I'm coming to sit down ...'

With his internationally respected mind in an unaccustomed ferment, Raymond Graves was trying unsuccessfully to ignore the young man who was seated at the end of the bench and listening to the music he loved so much.

'Good morning, ma'am ...' he managed, rather unconvincingly.

As soon as their visitor opened his mouth, Toni's suspicions were confirmed — he was certain now that Graves was not European, but was most definitely an American! Then Carla smiled with a vengeance, and took control, and Rayo was hers.

And now, at last, Toni was thinking clearly.

'Let me take those ...' he insisted, relieving Raymond of his roses before they could be thrust upon the insubstantial Carla. Then he noticed that Carla was making faces at him. He realised there was no-one nearby, and remembered her advice. Taking an inspired cue from the military activities at the palace across the square, he turned on his heels and mounted guard duty directly in front of the blissful new couple, only seconds before Carla vanished into thin air ...

Quo's first action, upon engagement, was also to relieve the worried Mr Graves — in this case, of all his unnecessary concerns about Mireille and the awful blackmailing plot. Raymond's large frame at once relaxed visibly into the contours of the bench, where he had sat down next to Carla and been embraced by her charms.

Quo naturally established the basics straight away. And that skilful talent spotter's self-confidence, as an identifier of potential subjects for engagement, was then very quickly restored.

Raymond Martin Graves, it was revealed, was born in 1950 in Dubina, Texas.

His father, Alan, had been an air force engineer throughout the war in Europe, returning to his home town of Houston with a good command of French, and joining a large business equipment corporation in 1946. Two years later the high-flying young salesman had met and soon married the youngest daughter of a Czech émigré couple, who had followed other members of their family to Dubina in 1906 and built up a farm of their own. Milada Novák had spent the first thirty years of her life playing and then labouring on the farm, but when the demands of the war were over, she had moved to the big city in search of her man.

Just after the birth of their first son in 1949, Alan and Milada had been sent to Paris to support his firm's rapid expansion into the European market, and his steady rise through the company ranks had then continued at an increasing pace. But they were able to return regularly to Texas, and especially to the farm, now run by Milada's brothers, which Alan had adopted as his tranquil second home. Their second son Raymond had been born there during one of those happy family vacations.

And the pattern was thus set for the rest of Raymond's life. Most of his childhood and teenage years were spent in and around Paris. From the age of seven onwards, he was despatched to a series of good international boarding schools. He correctly did not interpret these early, long separations from his family as rejection, but took the changes in his stride and continued to develop into a very well-balanced young man. From the start, his academic results were excellent across the board. And despite his bulk, he performed well in many different sports — except, to his eternal regret, his secret favourite, basketball: there were many other strapping young Americans in his teenage schools, but he was a mere 5'10" in height and rather too cumbersome ... so when sides were chosen, his name was never called.

His family continued to return to the Texas farm at least once every year, and so he gained from his grandparents, aunts and uncles a deep and direct understanding of the history of Bohemia and Moravia, and a good command of the Czechoslovakian languages, to supplement his ever-increasing knowledge of European history and his fluency in French.

At the age of nineteen, Graves easily won a place at the London School of Economics, gaining, over the next five years, an excellent BSc and then an MSc in International Relations. He returned to Paris in 1974 to join an international strategy consultancy, and three years later he married Mlle Claire-Louise Carnac, a long-standing family friend and a highly acceptable career accoutrement. He then proceeded to move easily on to ever greater responsibilities over the following twenty-five years.

Inspired by his father's war record, he initially focused his sights and his continuing studies on politico-military strategy, and rapidly became a sought-after junior member of some highly influential teams, judged by colleagues and clients alike as a provider of consistently sound and complete analyses and conclusions.

After eight years of learning the ropes from the outside, he left the consultancy and joined the U.S. diplomatic service, subsequently being posted to embassies in many countries throughout Europe and beyond, and rising to the position of Consul. Seconded later to various government agencies as a senior security advisor, he was soon recognised as a highly skilled negotiator, and proceeded to enhance his reputation in his handling of several high-profile international situations.

And in early 2000, he accepted the position of Deputy Political Advisor in the NATO SHAPE Command Group. The Supreme Allied Commander Europe (SACEUR), and his Deputy, relied on their team of political advisors as their primary liaison with NATO's political authorities and with all the member and partner governments.

He had now been three years in post. His team's mission embraced continuous information collection and analysis; the briefing and influencing of NATO governments; the maintenance of ongoing dialogues with countless security agencies, academic bodies, embassies, and the foreign ministries of both NATO and non-NATO countries; the exploitation of informal channels to oil the wheels of subsequent negotiations; the co-ordination of high-level visits to and from SHAPE; and of course, based on all the insights thus gained, the provision of invaluable strategic advice to their commanders.

And Raymond was aware that he was tipped to take over from the head of his team in the not too distant future, and become *the* next NATO SHAPE Political Advisor.

('Yes,' thought Quo privately, happily finding the perfect American expression. 'You will do nicely ...').

Raymond and Claire-Louise Graves had only one child, born in 1983 and named Alan after his grandfather. Towards the end of 2002, he too had opted for a career in the United States Air Force.

And Raymond had known Mireille Daurant for nearly eighteen months.

Quo was most grateful, though rather surprised, that this guru of international security had chosen the path of quiet diplomacy, rather than vocal force, in his strategy for saving Mireille from apparently great danger. In fact, Quo would never be able to decide whether Raymond's necessarily rapid analysis of the degree of exposure to himself, and to countless other important personalities and situations, had been very sound or seriously flawed.

The man himself would, of course, never consider the question again.

One other item of interest to Quo emerged from this initial transferral. Graves was familiar with the name of Hilde van Wostraap. She had, it seemed, been only recently elected to the European Parliament. Graves had never met her or investigated her particular agenda, and was not aware of any significant intelligence held on her within his group. His knowledge of Ms van Wostraap extended only to her general reputation as a woman of high moral ideals.

Quo could now see that this would need to be a relatively complex engagement, conducted in several waves; but it could then culminate, with one broad sweep, in the netting of a loose shoal of very big fish, and get the *Mater's* unofficially sustained Insight Gaining programme nicely back under control ...

This initial transferral, about to be completed, would establish Raymond's own public and private views on some key issues of the day. That would give Quo a starting point, a baseline for understanding how far the secret opinions of such a well-informed and influential man might actually differ from his official posture.

Graves could then be sent off to do some direct collecting of the apparent views of his immediate team of professionals, on one or more of those issues, and report back with the results. That would provide a further set of baselines.

But the key to the success of the overall engagement would then be the full Empowerment of Raymond himself.

The systems on the *Mater* had by now had more than enough time to analyse the workings of the human brain and to generate the appropriate empowerment procedures. Quo was thus already in a position to recruit Raymond, during their next encounter, as a fully-fledged Sub-Engager. Then, Quo confidently predicted, the political advisor's extensive world would be their oyster.

So now the game plan was built, and they could move on to the first real business ...

At the forefront of Raymond's mind was the ongoing invasion of Iraq. Quo could see that the Deputy Advisor had been obliged to put a delicate but definite spin on the sum of the intelligence he had received over the previous year, allowing his team's daily pre-conflict recommendations to SACEUR to match sufficiently with the strong pro-invasion urges of the U.S. and British governments. Behind the scenes, however, it was clear that Graves was extremely dubious that the military action would have a beneficial net effect, and indeed he feared a precipitate and significant political vacuum and a drawn-out local backlash.

But the man clearly had a very different personal attitude towards the broader "war on terror" that had been semi-formalised in September 2001. With a few minor exceptions, he strongly supported the proactive line that had initially been taken, by a rough consortium of western governments, for immediate action in Afghanistan and elsewhere. Indeed, he was disappointed that the international foxhunt for those at the heart of the many plots and actions executed in the years up till "9-11" had so quickly slipped down the interest ratings and been subsumed under what he called "that phoney cause" of protecting oil supplies to the West.

Quo also observed some serious misgivings, in Graves' mind, on a subject which he obviously considered to be globally critical. The question of the adoption, or otherwise, by the various European states of a single European currency, the euro (or "dollar" in all but name), had so far been, for the different countries and peoples of the existing EU, either a singular non-issue or a reason for protests approaching the fever pitch of martyrdom. Graves knew that full monetary union made good sense from almost all the financial and commercial angles, and had taken that line in his briefings and recommendations. But secretly, it seemed, he had huge concerns about the move towards a totally unified European currency; not because it would pose a threat to the dollar or the yen or eventually the yuan, but for precisely the opposite reasons — it would place a single manifestation of what he considered to be a sub-efficient economy into the firing line of its more agile competitors. All three of them. And some day, he feared, their massed financial computers would all aim and shoot at the same millisecond, and the global results of the European economy's instant demise would be catastrophic ...

But, Quo discovered, the subject which was clearly preoccupying Raymond more than any of these was the monumental vote, due to be taken in the very near future in the European Parliament, on the substantial enlargement of the European Union. No less than ten

Eastern European and Mediterranean countries were officially hopeful, and unofficially very confident, that their long-standing applications for membership would be formally accepted within a matter of days.

Quo quickly absorbed the long list of political, economic and military factors which Graves and his colleagues had investigated over the past few years; observed the official conclusions which the Deputy Advisor had drawn on each; noted the terms in which he had communicated his recommendations to his seniors; and then looked inside the man's soul and saw a very different set of judgements.

Even more interestingly, Raymond's general insights into the private views of many of those close to the heart of the debate also suggested some significant ambivalences.

So Quo triumphantly concluded that although the Doman Mission had no particular interest in the subject of EU enlargement itself, it had now found the single Issue which it needed to investigate, in order to rapidly establish its initial Insight Gaining samples; and, in the person of Raymond Martin Graves, the perfect instrument with which to obtain them ...

Thank you, Raymond. You have been most co-operative. It almost feels as though you are already in active support of our aims.

'The ability to gain such insights holds great potential for peace, Quo.'

Indeed. As we discovered some time ago for ourselves.

Now, here are your immediate instructions.

You will return at once to your normal place of work, and advise your colleagues and staff that your health is improving but you are not properly recovered. You will ignore the rest of the day's formal appointments, which should already have been backfilled for you. You will then, under the pretext of some minor administrative topic, organise short individual meetings with each of the seven other professionals in your team. Use the telephone if they are not in the office. If necessary, work in the evening and tomorrow morning until you have finished.

In each private meeting, you should discuss some potential office layout changes for a few moments. Then, you will request that colleague to summarise his or her principal views on the main issues of European enlargement. Take care to remember the responses. You are then to ask, in an extra-friendly way, implying that you are in special need of that person's particular help: 'But, off the record, what do you really think?'

In each case, take note of any significant differences in the two sets of responses, and privately write these down after each meeting, so that you can later memorise them all thoroughly before our next engagement.

Instruct each person specifically not to discuss the contents of the meeting with their colleagues, and imply to each one that it is his or her view alone that you have sought on this issue.

And you have one other initial task, Raymond. By the time of our next meeting, here, at noon tomorrow, you will have drawn up a list of four senior NATO country politicians, four such politicians from non-NATO countries, and the heads of four agencies or academic bodies which you consider particularly relevant to the issue of European enlargement. Choose individuals whom you know personally, and who would not hesitate to grant a request from you for a special private audience at very short notice.

Ah, I see that you have one minor scheduling concern, Raymond.

'Yes, Quo. It is imperative that I attend a critical meeting in Mons between ten and twelve tomorrow morning. To abandon it would not serve your cause well, believe me! I shall do all that you have requested before that meeting begins, but I simply cannot be back here in Brussels by twelve o'clock.'

Raymond, your conscientiousness is admirable. Thank
you. You will rendezvous instead, with the same contact
as today, at twelve-thirty, immediately outside the main
entrance to Mons railway station.

'I shall be there.'

Released from Carla's tender grip, but undermined now in a fashion
far different from his earlier expectations, the Deputy Political
Advisor stood up, made a polite, almost oriental bow to his once-more
visible go-between, gave Toni and the CD player another very
quizzical glance, and strode off back towards Brussels Central station.

* * *

It was approaching eleven-thirty. As Carla had expected, she and Toni
were both now free for almost twenty-four hours. So he could go
straight off to Amsterdam ('... are you *sure* you really don't mind,
Carla?'), and they could rendezvous at ten in the morning in his hotel
room ('... you'll obviously be back from Amsterdam rather late
tonight, Toni — but we *shall* need to get going by mid-morning!').

'What shall I do with these roses, Carla?'

'Well, you tell me, Toni. Can't you think of any ladies to give them
to today?'

Toni fell silent, then realised he could indeed think of two. Carla,
however, could silently think of four.

He mumbled 'OK — *hasta mañana*,' and left her sitting in the park.
He hurried back to his hotel room, dumped the CD player on a table
along with the unopened Strauss CD, and quickly got changed. He
found a laundry bag to hold the roses, and left for the nearby Central
station at twelve-fifteen, in plenty of time to buy a ticket and catch the
1250 departure to Amsterdam.

Amsterdam, Netherlands

Carla, having little else to do, had decided to see Amsterdam for herself as well. So she would once again be with Toni every step of the way.

* * *

He bought his ticket, and had time to pick up an English paperback and a street map of Amsterdam, as well as a sandwich and a can of beer, before boarding the train. After making some rough sightseeing plans, he passed the rest of the journey enjoying the first few chapters of his new Michael Cordy novel and then just gazing out of the window at the increasingly flat countryside.

'Still only Day 8 of my travels,' he thought at one point, 'and this will be my sixth new city!'

Fifteen minutes after filling up with passengers at Schiphol Airport, the train arrived at Amsterdam Centraal at 1539 precisely. Toni had not thought of Carla once during the whole trip.

The street plan had recommended a canal tour as a good way to get to know the city. And soon after Toni crossed the busy junction outside the station and began to walk up the Damrak towards the city centre, he spotted a one-hour waterbus trip due to depart at four o'clock. He seized the moment and went aboard with only minutes to spare.

The boat took him on a smooth, clockwise journey around the heart of the city. He loved the colour and variety of all the canal-side buildings, and the sensible, multilingual recorded commentary on their histories. He felt especially moved as they cruised respectfully past the Anne Frank House. And finally, as the trip drew to a close, he chuckled at the sight of the huge multi-level bicycle park beside the station.

Carla learned a great deal, too.

But it never occurred to Toni how much more romantic that canal tour could have been with a close friend by his side ...

Then, at five o'clock, he started walking towards the Old Church. He soon stopped again for a relaxing beer at Het Karbeel bar, then moved on to take in the church, and in the narrow streets opposite he discovered his very first red light district. He wasn't sure quite which way to look, and whether to stop or to keep walking past the windows, and he quickly discovered the perils of returning the ladies' smiles. Then he was happy to move on to the New Church and the Royal Palace on Dam Square, and to stroll along and across several canals until he reached Rembrandt Square, and then to continue his walking canal tour towards the huge façade of the Rijksmuseum.

He arrived on the bridge at six twenty-five.

Mireille was already waiting for him. She had caught the 1450 train and walked single-mindedly direct from the station to meet her date for the night.

She gave him another more-than-friendly kiss, which turned out to be rather one-way, and then noticed what was in his plastic bag.

'Nice roses!'

'Yes, they're gorgeous, aren't they!'

She waited. Then she shrugged her shoulders, and they set off towards the theatre.

'There are several restaurants nearby, Toni. Are you hungry?'

'Are you kidding?'

She smiled with pleasure at Toni's increasingly relaxed mood. They chose Peppino's on Leidsekruisstraat, and they both enjoyed fine pizzas. By way of a civic apology for eating Italian on his first trip to Amsterdam, Toni selected a *calzone,* because they always reminded him of clogs.

* * *

They arrived at the Nieuwe de la Mar Theatre half an hour before show time, collected their prime-spot tickets, and chatted to a few people standing near them in the foyer. Toni wondered if any of his Dutch pals from the Message Board were now only feet away from him. But he wasn't Evita, and he wasn't about to try and find out in the way she probably would!

He had not thought about Carla for several hours now. But when Janis Ian came on stage with her guitar, to rapturous applause and then a perfect silence ... when she gently struck the chord that lives between the lines, and began singing *Watercolors* ... and when Mireille took his hand in hers, he could not contain a broad and happy smile, and the memory of that day in Bilbao came flooding back, and he smiled more broadly still.

But Carla did not see these things. For she too was captivated by the presence of the singer and the songs ...

In the interval, Toni overheard mention of the Message Board. So he did, after all, connect with two of his regular board-buddies — both women, both long-time fans, both renewed once more by the healing balm of their heroine's music. They even offered him a handful of tasty *stroopwafels*, which he devoured shamelessly. Mireille politely declined hers.

* * *

Before the concert ended, to sustained applause and successful demands for encores, Janis had reminded the audience that she would do her usual "meet and greet" after the show. She would stay until everyone who wanted to had met her and exchanged a few words. 'You're the people who support me and my work. I figure I owe you all. It's the least I can do ...'

Toni had forgotten this would happen. But, of course, he and Mireille seized the opportunity, and waited happily near the front of the line, chatting to more like-minded neighbours once again.

Suddenly, it was their turn. Mireille was clearly very nervous — which he found really surprising — and she simply murmured something bland about how great the show had been. And when Toni tried to speak, he too found himself desperately tongue-tied — but Janis smiled encouragingly, and finally he leaned forward, kissed her on the cheek, and managed to blurt out 'My name's Toni — and I've just loved your music for years and years ...'

His heroine smiled another grateful smile. 'Thank you, Toni. That's why I keep doing what I do! Do you have anything you'd like me to sign for you?'

He remembered the *Between the Lines* CD that was still in his jacket pocket. He handed it over, and the writer wrote:

> *For Toni ... one day, I hope to admire something great that you have done. You know, Stars and Fans are one and the same! Best, Janis*

He was speechless as he took back the CD. Then he remembered the roses, pulled them from their bag, and thrust them into the singer's arms. 'It's the spring time still, Janis!' And then (he could not later recall these last moments) he and Mireille must have mumbled their thankyous and their goodbyes to the artist and her jovial assistants, and, with many more people still waiting in the queue behind them, made their way back to the foyer.

* * *

By eleven o'clock they were strolling towards the station, drunk on the heady wine of the music and the meeting, and happily exchanging their own favourite memories of the wonderful evening. Then, for once, Toni had a practical thought.

'What time's the next train, Mireille?'

'Oh, there's not long to wait now,' she whispered, wrapping her arm around his waist. And when they were still several minutes' walk from the station, she stopped outside one of the many hotels on the Damrak.

'We have a double room booked here for the night, Toni.'

'Oh, I don't know about that, Mireille ...'

Cosmopolitan girl studied him carefully.

'This will be your first time, won't it?'

He said nothing, half ashamed, half bursting with anticipation.

'Don't worry, Toni. Tonight's the night!'

He wondered again about arguing, but quickly abandoned the idea.

So Toni and Mireille checked in to the hotel. Carla the observer did not need to. Then their virtual eternal triangle climbed the stairs together to the first floor room ...

* * *

The happy couple had eventually remembered to set their individual alarms for a quarter to six — she needed to be back at work in Brussels by nine-thirty at the very latest, and he had a rendezvous at ten (and Carla was closely watching him and definitely expecting him not to be late!)

They dressed in silence; but they both perked up when the fresh air hit them as they walked the short distance to the station, and they managed some light conversation. But no mention was made of the events of the previous night.

They each bought something to eat at the station café, and their train departed at 0623.

In the absence of any further conversational offerings from Toni, Mireille stared out of the window for the whole journey. Toni was happy to allow himself to drift back to sleep, and only woke when she nudged him gently as they approached Brussels. Carla, as usual, observed their journey from a measured distance.

Mireille had to rush.

'I'd like to see you again, Toni — where are you staying?' ... 'OK ... and here's my mobile number — will you call me again soon, before you leave Brussels?'

Toni didn't know what to say. So he just said 'Yes.'

* * *

But he would not call her.

Mireille would however try to contact him at his hotel that evening. But she would be told that nobody with a first name of Toni or Antonio had stayed there over the past two days. She would begin to describe him, but the receptionist, knowing when it was time to stop being helpful and time to start protecting the privacy of her clients, would make no reference at all to that nice young Sr. Rafael Barola who fitted the description perfectly (and who, she thought, really might have paid her a bit more attention). And she would politely terminate the call.

* * *

Toni walked the short distance from Brussels Central to the hotel. Carla followed. He lay down on his bed and waited for her to appear from the bathroom, and at ten o'clock she did exactly that.

'How reliable you are, Carla,' he smiled.

'Yes,' she said, unusually unsmiling herself.

'You don't seem as bright as usual. Wrong kinds of ray today?'

'Not really, Toni. Not really.'

Her voice sounded a little sulky, he thought.

'Let us get on, Toni. We must prepare to engage again with our other new Ray ...'

'Ha, ha, ha! Your sense of humour really is improving, Carla!'

'If you say so. Now, we need to meet up with Mr Graves at half past twelve. So please find out the times of trains over to Mons. If he has done his job as we hope, we shall then have no further immediate contact with him. We shall be able to turn our attention to our other new channel, in the French government.

'Then pack your suitcase and check out. As soon as we have finished with Raymond, we can move straight on to Paris ...'

Empowerment Sphere

Toni phoned the concierge and got the information they needed. The 1129 departure from Central Station, arriving Mons at 1215, would be perfect.

When he looked up after finishing the call, Carla had disappeared.

He packed his suitcase in a strange daze of unaccustomed feelings. He was only just able to make room for the new CD player.

Then he checked out ('It's been a pleasure to have you with us, *señor*,' the pretty receptionist smiled in vain), and had a quick coffee in the hotel bar. At eleven o'clock he left the hotel and walked to the station in a pensive mood and a light drizzle.

The train was on time. It was not very busy. Carla joined him. '*Hola.*' There was no more conversation. Only a single instruction: 'Just play him the CD again, Toni, and leave the rest to me ...'

Toni was still very wrapped up in his own thoughts, but he did vaguely notice the still rather cool timbre of Carla's voice, and wondered briefly what might be wrong. Then he pressed on with unlocking his case, and pulled the CD player out again.

* * *

They got off at Mons. Carla walked into the ladies' room, re-emerged outside the station, joined up with Toni again, and found somewhere to sit and wait. There were few people about, and he had proved to be an effective sentry the day before. So a bench would once again be the stage for Carla's next brief encounter. She would just need to choose her moment to disappear.

As soon as he spotted Raymond emerging from the car park, Toni pressed the "Play" button, then moved off to one side to admire the distant scenery, as Gershwin's clarinet trilled its baneful welcome once again ...

Quo was delighted to discover that Graves had been completely true to his word.

The team leader had held five short private meetings the previous afternoon, phoned another colleague at home in the evening, and caught up with the seventh a few minutes before he disappeared into an early morning briefing.

The results, Quo could judge, were in Graves' opinion quite unremarkable.

Six of his seven highly experienced professional colleagues had initially summed up their views, on the issue of European Union enlargement, almost exactly along the lines of their team's official briefing positions. Those briefings had evolved progressively over the past few years, and presented at this particular juncture a position which was generally pro-enlargement, but with a number of significant "cautions", especially in the military arena.

When Raymond had then gently and privately pressed each one of them to take on the role of his special confidant and tell him what they really felt about the issue, they had all, with one or two tiny and insignificant variations or reservations, insisted that they did indeed feel precisely as they had already explained to him.

The seventh guinea pig, one of Graves' more senior colleagues, a Briton named Haynes, had presented a slightly different picture. His initial position, which he had explained in considerably greater depth than Raymond had expected or wanted, had proved to be rather different from the distillation of team views represented by the many briefing papers that had been produced for their commanders. This again had not surprised Graves — he knew that Haynes always took the opportunity, whenever he could, to try and persuade his colleagues and external contacts of what he considered to be the huge benefits, and the almost complete lack of disadvantages, of an ever-expanding Union.

But when Raymond had asked Haynes for '... your real views, buddy,' he had been rather taken aback by what he heard. His colleague had privately admitted that he felt almost exactly along the lines of the team's briefing positions. 'I put it about that I'm heavily in favour of enlargement, Ray, because I think people should believe there is a fair spectrum of opinion in our group. Frankly, old boy, if I didn't, we'd probably be accused of being a full house of stooges and yes-men. But in reality, I'm with the rest of you. Generally a good scheme, but lots of risks ...'

Quo digested this for a moment.

> Thank you, Raymond. Most interesting. So we have a team that basically insists to you, its group leader, that its public and private postures are one and the same. Except for one man, who claims that the differences in his two stated positions are motivated by team loyalty rather than personal aims, and that he actually takes a more balanced, rather than a more extreme position in his true thinking.

'Exactly, Quo. I don't find it as interesting as you obviously do. But there it is.'

> Ah, Raymond, this is only the baseline, the control measurement. We have yet to discover what your colleagues really *do* think about this issue. We only know, so far, what they say in public, and what they choose to say in answer to the private enquiry of the man who controls their immediate career prospects ...

'Well,' Graves joked, 'you're not planning to go and read their minds on the subject, are you?'

> No, Raymond. No. We are planning that you will do that for us ...

> And it is clear, Raymond, that you have also identified twelve highly relevant government ministers and other leaders, as I requested. Thank you. You have done extremely well. You have proved that you have the authority and the skills to complete the remainder of your mission. We are ready now to proceed to the next stage.

> I observe that the final voting on EU enlargement is scheduled to take place, in Strasbourg, exactly one week from today. I should like to improve my insights into this

issue before those votes are taken. So I require you to complete the following set of tasks within the next five days.

When you find yourself fully back in your normal world, Raymond, you will have gained a useful new skill.

You will possess the ability to engage with others in such a way that they will reveal to you their true thoughts on any topic you wish to pursue. Your chosen targets will not be aware that they are doing this, nor will they later recall it. To effect this, you will simply smile a special smile, which you have now been taught, and they will at once be at your service. This ability is a rough, humanised, local-area version of the remote transferral and collection processes which we are deploying with you at this very time. The closest parallels to this technique in your world appear to be what you term "hypnosis" and "mind-reading". But you will not be attempting to plant heavy suggestions on your subjects, let alone trying to change their minds in any way. You will simply be observing, learning the truth, and then reporting back to us ...

When you return, in a few moments, to your headquarters, you will inform your immediate superior that you have received confidential information which makes it imperative for you to hold urgent, low-profile meetings with certain key European individuals, in advance of next week's vote on enlargement. You will easily obtain his agreement to this activity, and a promise of his silence and your protection, simply by utilising the smile which comes with your new empowerment.

Then, having smiled, you will also take the opportunity, swiftly and silently, to collect his own true feelings on the plans for enlargement of the Union. You will be able to remember what you have learned without any special effort, and you can later compare and contrast your findings with his official position, which is already well known to you.

And then, as you will discover, you will be able to terminate the process of engagement automatically. No external stimulation of your subject will be required. When you are ready to return to standard interaction mode, simply decide to do so, and you may then continue your conversation as normal ...

You will subsequently take steps to directly arrange urgent personal meetings with each of your selected government ministers and heads of agencies and academic bodies. You will find an appropriate pretext for each meeting, such that all of your subjects will feel flattered that their particular views are so highly valued for this last-minute NATO policy review, prior to the voting in Strasbourg.

If it should prove absolutely impossible to set up any particular appointment, you must attempt to meet with that person's deputy, or preferably identify a different individual of the same status as all the others.

Organising and completing twelve such meetings, in person, in a little over five days will be a huge challenge, we realise. But we are convinced that you can achieve this, Raymond ... and you will.

Once all these arrangements have been made, but before you depart to pursue them, you will call a full meeting of your seven professional team colleagues. Advise them that the reason for the meeting will only be announced once it has begun. Do your utmost to achieve a full quorum, but not at the expense of prejudicing your schedule of external visits, which takes priority over any unfortunate office absences.

When your team is settled around the table, smile your new smile, and then enquire within their minds. You will find that no dialogue is required; your colleagues will all be silent, inactive, and happily unaware of anything around them or the transferrals that will, one at a time but very rapidly, be taking place.

Once you have observed the true thoughts of each of them, on the questions you recently posed (there will be no need to take notes — you will memorise everything), you will verbally inform the team of your imminent travel plans. You will tell them that your trip is classified at an extremely high level of secrecy, and that they should make no comment if asked about it. If necessary, tell your colleague Haynes to pass these instructions on to any absentees.

Remember, Raymond, you will not be corrupting their memories in any way, as you request this support, but merely taking advantage of their highly suggestible state to ensure their full co-operation with your orders.

When you decide to conclude the engagements, and proceed to close the meeting in the usual way, your colleagues will not question the instructions they have received, and they should be very pleased at the brevity of the session!

You will then conduct your urgent grand tour of consultation.

In each of your twelve private meetings, you will ask your subject if you may briefly summarise his or her position on the issue of enlargement, as you have understood it from their various public statements. Secure their agreement to what you have summarised, along with any adjustments they choose to make to your interpretation. Memorise this agreed position fully.

You must then smile your new-found smile.

Then, just as with your team of colleagues, you will learn the truth. You will discover, with no further discussion, what each leader really feels, really believes, really wishes to happen. And you will automatically remember all of this for us.

Raymond, there is something I want to stress here, and instil deeply in your mind. We are not suggesting that you will necessarily discover significant differences between public and private views in any particular meeting. We are interested in the purity of each and every result. They will all contribute to the evaluation of our Hypothesis. So you in particular, Raymond, must not bend the truths that you discover, in any way, merely to try and please us!

For if you did attempt to do this, we would, of course, very soon find out — and we would not be amused.

Finally, Raymond, if any opportunity should arise, over the next five days, for you to engage with your further superiors (that is, the Head of Command Group, or the Deputy Commander, or even SACEUR himself), either singly or together, then you should take it — simply by smiling your special smile and immediately learning, as an added bonus, the true feelings of those gentlemen on the issue we are pursuing ...

You will complete these tasks by Monday evening at the latest, and will then proceed to meet with your usual contact, at five minutes to midnight, at this very spot.

Good luck, Raymond. I know you will not let us down.

Carla was visible again by the time Graves was alert enough to notice. He gave her his customary bow, flicked a sideways glance of recognition at Toni (who was guiltily avoiding all eye contact with him), and then hurried back towards the car park.

'OK, Toni — Raymond will be back here next Monday night for his debriefing.'

'But Carla, we're just off to France, and who knows where after that! How can you be sure we can get back here for a specific rendezvous?'

'Ah, you have forgotten that I may go anywhere I have previously visited, or to any other co-ordinates which take our fancy. I shall be perfectly capable of returning without you for our final engagement with Mr Graves.'

For her to add that sort of damper to her still inexplicably cool mood struck Toni as just downright unfair. But he could think of no sensible riposte.

'So,' she continued, 'may we now please go straight on to Paris?'

'Very well, Carla,' sighed Toni.

He went to the booking office. By far the quickest route, they told him, was to take the next train back to Brussels, get off at Midi station, and pick up the THALYS service which would whisk them from one capital to the other in less than ninety minutes. So he bought a through ticket, and reported back to the bench where Carla was watching over his suitcase and the CD player.

She walked off to un-make with little further delay ('We'll meet up at a café near the station, Toni ...'), and left him to his thoughts during their brief and separate initial journeys. By half-past two they were back in Brussels, and a few minutes later they were on their very high-speed, parallel ways to Paris in the spring time ...

Paris, France

Carla considered joining Toni in his compartment, but he had made no effort to find a quiet spot, and she had little more to say. So she amused herself for a while by pretending to crash at great speed into the fabric of every bridge they passed under. Then she got bored, and sat back in her comfortable Handler's chair and read a good Doman novel.

Toni got on with his novel too, but he had managed very little sleep the night before. After half an hour, despite the pull of the compelling story, he nodded off, only to wake again abruptly a few moments later. That pattern continued for the rest of the journey, and when they arrived at the Gare du Nord at 1604 precisely, he was more exhausted than when he had departed.

Then he remembered he'd made no hotel plans. He guessed they'd be staying here for at least a couple of days, as usual. So he kept his eye out for a reservation bureau in the concourse, and soon spotted a large sign: *Accueil de Paris*.

'Ah,' he reasoned aloud in French, nearly awake now and applying his finest logic to the situation. 'If they're welcoming me here, maybe they can find me a room ...'

'*Mais oui, monsieur* — that is precisely why we are here! And it is good that you make the effort to speak our language. *Merci bien!* You will a need a street plan, of course ... *voici* ... and how much can you afford per night?'

Toni got the gist of the reply, and continued the conversation in his limited French — he knew it made sense. He wanted to be reasonably central, and he tried to pitch his budget somewhere between parsimonious and extravagant. This put him well below the average rate for a Paris room.

'Very well, sir, I have a nice little hotel in the Rue du Faubourg St Honoré ... a small room on the seventh floor. There is no lift, I am so sorry — but there are good views of the Paris rooftops ...'

'Ah, that sounds good! Which rooftops?'

'Just those of the neighbouring buildings, sir.'

'OK, I'll take it,' said Toni, quickly running out of steam and repartee, as usual.

* * *

The still-unseasoned traveller towed his suitcase rather wearily through one of the many front entrances to the station, turned to the right (it looked more promising) and plodded off in search of a café. He was very glad to have landed up in Paris. He had always wanted to visit this mecca of the visual arts (he had been here once before with his parents, but he was only ten at the time and he really could not remember much about it), so he was determined to exploit the opportunity to the hilt. But right now he could not shake off his malaise — yes, that was a good French word for it ... malaise ... he liked that ...

Straight ahead of him now, across a huge, busy junction, was an ideal-looking bar: Le Cheval Noir. Toni negotiated the early rush-hour traffic and sat down outside. He already had more than enough self-sympathy, and he didn't fancy a cup of tea, so he stuck with tradition, ordered a small beer, sat back and opened his eyes properly.

Without realising it, he was experiencing a classic first view of typical Parisian streets. The Boulevard de Magenta, the Rue de Maubeuge, the Rue de Dunkerque and another small street all converged here at the Place de Roubaix, and he was looking back down into Place Napoléon III and the imposing façade of the famous station through which he had just dozily passed.

He was still getting his bearings with his new street map, and enjoying his first Parisian beer, when Carla strolled up to the table.

'*Hola.*'

'Hello, Carla. Good trip?'

'Entertaining, thank you.'

'Right,' he said, polishing off his drink. 'I've booked a hotel. Let's go and find it now — I'd like to see some sights this evening!'

'I shall follow you discreetly to your room, Toni, then I would prefer to leave you alone. I shall join you when you wake up. Please set your alarm for eight o'clock.'

'Another early start?'

'We have a job to do. I'm sure there will be time for some touring together once we have set things in motion. Oh, by the way — don't forget our standing rendezvous arrangements, if we should lose each other ...'

She pursued Toni's taxi to his modest hotel, felt only mildly sympathetic as he lugged his suitcase up the ever-steepening flights of stairs, and noted the location of his room.

* * *

As the sky darkened and the sun set behind his unremarkable rooftop view, Toni left the room and set out on his evening tour. He had decided to stay north of the river, but he was willing to put in some legwork. And he was not going to allow Carla's strange behaviour, or his own thankfully diminishing malaise, to get in the way of his enjoyment of this wonderful city.

He started, because it was so close, at the beautiful church of the Madeleine. Then, determined not to rush things, with the whole night ahead of him, he strolled slowly up the boulevard on the right until he reached the neo-Baroque magnificence of the Opera House. He stood for a long time simply trying to absorb the immense amount of detail in its façade alone, and failed completely.

Then he set off to the north, up the Rue de Clichy, eventually reaching the square and turning into the broad boulevard which would take him eastwards back towards his goal for the evening, the incomparable Basilique du Sacré-Cœur.

He was getting hungry now, and was looking for a nice restaurant. But as he wandered down towards Pigalle, he realised that he was once again in a rather special part of town. But this was not the friendly calm of the Amsterdam alleyways. No, it was just a lot of run-down, seedy-looking frontages with unattractive men and women lounging outside and chasing down the street after him (*'Viens, viens, monsieur, c'est pas cher!'*) if he gave them even the tiniest of sideways glances ...

He reached the Anvers metro station entrance, and suddenly got his best view yet of the wonderful, floodlit Sacré-Cœur, still a long way up the steepest part of the hill of Montmartre.

'That can wait till after dinner,' his stomach and his legs insisted, all at once.

He walked a little further along Boulevard de Rochechouart, and soon found a pleasant enough café-restaurant. But he did not linger long over his meal, keen to get going again and take on the climb up to the basilica.

Several times on the way up he turned round to admire the panorama, and each time it blossomed more fully before him. 'Yes,' he said to himself, 'I do enjoy touring on my own. I can go wherever I want to, at exactly my own pace ...'

He reached the top and spent many minutes gazing back again at the huge city spread out beneath him. Then he wandered around the exterior of the Sacré-Cœur, captivated by its brilliance against the backdrop of the northern night sky.

He had done his research with the map while waiting for his dinner. He knew he was not far from the artists' quarter of Montmartre, and it took only a few minutes' stroll, along the railings and past the church of St-Pierre, to reach the famous Place du Tertre. There were not many artists left wooing the tourists at this time of the cooling evening, but, he persuaded himself, the spirit of place he was seeking was definitely there.

Then he set off on another short pilgrimage, without expecting much success: he wanted to find the site of the Moulin de la Galette, the subject of one of his very favourite paintings. He eventually spotted the old windmill, high up inside some private grounds; he found an alley that might have given access, but did not; and he skirted back, down and around the property, finally discovering an entrance gate which was locked and gave no indication of whether or when the shrine might be open to the public. He was rather sad that Renoir's special place seemed so "unacknowledged" — but then he thought again, and decided it was probably for the best. 'Anyway,' he reasoned, 'hopefully I'll be seeing the real thing in the gallery tomorrow ...'

He was too tired to pick up on the metaphysical contradictions of that idea. His legs had really had enough now. So he descended quickly and easily back onto Rochechouart, ignored the siren calls of Blanche and Pigalle, and took a taxi straight back to his hotel.

* * *

He was rudely woken by his wristwatch alarm, and found Carla sitting on the tiny chair at the end of his bed.

'Ready for the briefing, Toni?'

'You're a hard taskmistress! I'd rather have a cup of coffee first ...'

'It's seven flights down and seven up again, plus a walk to the corner and back.'

'Ready for the briefing, Carla.'

'Good. Now, I wish to make direct contact with our next subject myself. The information we have collected suggests this will be the most effective approach.'

'You mean you don't need my help?'

'That is not what I said, Toni. Listen — we are going to try and phone our politician at his office desk. Of course, if that fails, we shall need to plan the pursuit of more indirect routes. So when you are dressed and ready for action, you will please dial the number I dictate, but say nothing, and allow me to set the trap ...'

Toni prepared himself for a day which he hoped would be mainly devoted to more sightseeing. At some point, he realised as he looked in the mirror, he really would have to visit a barber and ask for advice on managing his new beard, which he'd now had for almost a week. Of course, before that, he'd need a good breakfast ...

But that would all have to wait a little longer. At nine o'clock, he picked up his mobile phone and, following Carla's dictation, dialled the direct extension, so thoughtfully provided by Josef Samek, of Junior Minister Delegate Nallier. He then held the phone up vaguely in front of Carla's face, and quite close to his own ear. When the call was answered, he found he could just make out what was being said at the other end ...

'*Allô?*'

'Hello,' said Carla, brightly. 'Is this Monsieur Nallier?'

'*Mais bien sûr! Qui est-ce qui appelle?*'

'Good morning, Minister. Please excuse my speaking English — I regret I have no French. I am a good friend of the lady you have recently been staying with in Cortina — I do not think I should mention her name ...'

Jean-Christophe Nallier swallowed hard. 'Yes ...?'

'It is clear to me, *monsieur*, that we can both gain much from a proposal I wish to make. It could ensure great benefit for you and the French government, in the matter of imminent decisions, of which you are well aware, on investment in certain expanding industries in the Czech Republic. As well as ensuring my silence on certain other matters ...'

'Those decisions should all have been finalised last Friday ...' growled the Minister, cautiously.

'Ah, yes — but there has been some last-minute thinking. There is still a good possibility of success for yourselves, if you care to pursue it with me ...'

'Go on ...'

'I do not wish to say any more on the telephone, *monsieur*. But time is of the essence. I wish to meet with you privately as soon as possible today, here in Paris. Particularly, may I add, since our mutual friend assures me that you are a gentleman of great discretion and charm, and extremely good company ...'

'You flatter me, *madame ... pardonnez-moi ... mademoiselle*. Very well. But I cannot get away until late morning — and I can spare half an hour at the very most. *Attendez* — I will meet you at eleven o'clock precisely, at the Concorde end of the Jardin des Tuileries. It is only a few minutes' walk for me across the bridge. My personal detective will be with me, but he will keep his distance.'

Carla noticed Toni's immediate physical reaction to this news.

'If he does not, *monsieur*, you will regret it in many ways, I promise you ...'

'I will ensure it. And, *mon Dieu* ... for the first time in my life, I have to ask this question — how will I recognise you?'

'I shall be wearing a light blue suit. I hope that you will be pleased with what you see. You should greet me as Carla; I will call you J-C. I hope that can set the tone for our *petites affaires* ...'

At Carla's signal, Toni cut the call.

'Hmm,' said Toni. 'That's almost exactly the same plan we made with Raymond two days ago!'

Carla observed dryly that the arrangements in Brussels had worked extremely well, just for once, so even if Toni found them a little unimaginative, she was very comfortable with them, thank you.

Toni thought about this for a moment and was forced to agree. 'But I don't like the idea of getting that close to the police again ...'

'Don't worry. We shall minimise the risk to you, I promise. You can just set up the Strauss music for me, then keep your head down while I wait for Jean-Christophe and get to know him. In fact, I'll be the one with the problem — standing out in the middle of a public park, with a detective watching! I shan't be able to disappear this time ...'

Then Carla explained her latest game plan, and issued Toni with his orders. He was hardly in the mood to give her the benefit of the doubt about the policeman, after suffering her own inexplicably icy mood over the past twenty-four hours. But she seemed to be very much back in the driving seat at the moment, and he did not feel he had the strength to stay and fight.

So he nodded, picked up his CD player, removed the Gershwin CD, and inserted the Strauss. Leaving Carla to follow him unseen, he took to the hotel stairs, with plenty of time to study his map while enjoying a leisurely breakfast on a typical Parisian street corner ...

He left the café before ten, and followed his carefully planned, indirect route to the rendezvous.

It led him along Avenue Matignon to the vast roundabout half-way down the Champs Élysées. The stunning vistas offered by that vantage point, both up past the Concorde Obelisk and though the Tuileries Garden to the Louvre, and down to the glorious Arc de Triomphe, were just as he remembered them from more than ten years before. That made him simply feel very happy.

Then he turned back towards the sun, as it rose over the Sun King's city, put on his sharp new shades, and set course for the Obelisk.

* * *

Just after ten-thirty, he strolled nonchalantly and convincingly into the Tuileries like a student with too much time on his hands and little inclination to study anyway. He tossed his denim jacket onto the closest corner of the lawn and flopped down onto it, facing safely away from the entrance but able to observe it out of the corner of his eye. He pulled out his paperback, and switched on the radio of his CD player. He found a station playing some light orchestral music, turned the volume up high enough to aggravate any near-neighbours or passers-by, then lay back in the shade of the trees and pretended to read his novel.

It was a good performance, and it was a pity that nobody had watched it.

At five to eleven, Carla materialised from behind some large bushes and breezed towards the entrance, passing not far from Toni but ignoring him completely. Then she stopped and waited, in clear view of the paths coming off the square, and with the sound of the radio still within clear virtual earshot.

Three minutes later, two men purposefully approached the Tuileries from the direction of the river. Even the inexperienced Toni could recognise a French politician and his bodyguard when he saw them. He surreptitiously pressed the CD button on the player, and the strains of the opening bars of *The Blue Danube* took over and wafted loudly across the grass.

Jean-Christophe Nallier was surprised and then delighted to hear his favourite music playing at the same moment as he spotted the undeniably attractive female smiling undeniably in his direction.

His detective's unspoken reaction to both the sound of the music and the sight of the woman was much simpler: 'Oh no, not again.'

'It's OK,' said the Junior Minister, and quickened his pace.

Maintaining a close eye on the now dozing student, whose tastes in music were suspiciously similar to the minister's, and deciding that the woman looked harmless enough — no handbag, nothing obviously extraneous beneath her clothes, hopefully not secreting a tiny knife or handgun — the bodyguard stopped walking and backed off as far away from that too-often-heard music as he could sensibly remain, while Nallier continued his passage towards Carla, readying to kiss her pretty little hand ...

'Carla?'

'Enchantée, J-C!'

Carla withheld her hand, and her pose encouraged Jean-Christophe to stay, for the time being, outside her personal space. He was happy, however, to take that as a little challenge for the future.

But such plans were temporarily forgotten, as Carla converted her welcoming smile into one far more powerful. Nallier's bodyguard was then surprised, and as usual reluctantly impressed, at what he calculated to be a new record for his protégé's speed of transition from the polite greeting of an apparent stranger to the receipt of her impassioned embrace ...

> Good morning, Minister. My name, should you wish to use one, is Quo.

'Bonjour, Quo. I detect that you are not French, but I am honoured that you appear to be talking to me in our beloved language.'

> I always make the effort to give of my best, Monsieur Nallier. Or may I perhaps call you Jean-Christophe?

'But of course!'

> Jean-Christophe, we have learned much about you in the past few minutes. We can see that you will prove invaluable to our objectives here. We hope that you too can now appreciate those aims, and the role which you can play ...

'It is already surprisingly clear to me, Quo.'

> That is excellent, *monsieur*. And, of course, you now recognise that you may completely forget the facile pretext of a business deal and that *soupçon* of blackmail which led you here today ...

> Jean-Christophe, you have revealed to us that there are apparently immense differences and disagreements between the so-called partners or allies of your European Union. Not just on the pressing subjects of Iraq, and the war on terror, and the euro, and enlargement, all of which

are now somewhat familiar to us; but in many, many other areas, such as policy on taxation, the handling of asylum seekers, relationships with America and China, relationships within the Union itself, agricultural policies, and so on.

Of course, it is no surprise to us that there are such significant differences of opinion amongst your many independent states. This is quite natural — and the airing of such differences is a keystone of what you call "democracy" and what we call something akin to your phrase "the only way".

But what has already stunned us, from our limited observations to date, is the true depth of these disagreements, and the degree to which those truths are disguised, or concealed, or denied by your leaders and the representatives of your peoples. In our homeland, such differences, on any and every subject, are open for all to see — it cannot be any other way — and the Consensus of a substantial majority then reigns, as a self-portraying truth. On Earth, or in Europe at least, power and influence appear instead to rest in the hands of the most convincing of the many persuaders ...

'You have summed up my views, Quo, and those of a regrettably small number of other public figures, in a most effective fashion. The ways of your homeland, as you describe them, present to my mind the image of a large and fully open book. By contrast, I see all around me a never-ending game of poker ...'

Merci, Jean-Christophe. Your own summary is most graphic and equally effective. And, I must add, I can see that you believe it absolutely. This confirms my hope that you may be an excellent servant in the furtherance of both of our causes. Indeed, I suspect that we might have been able to gain much from recruiting you personally to pursue this general subject for us in greater depth. But, as you will discover later, we have in mind for you a much more specific mission.

Fortunately, you have also revealed to us ... (Quo, ever-inclusive, ever-loquacious, was still conducting this unspoken briefing in French, and warming to the task, but was in consequence edging inexorably into and beyond increasingly grotesque and flowery hyperbole) ... you have also revealed to us the name of another politician, in England, who seems to be even more intensely frustrated than yourself by the vagaries of European politics, as you have just portrayed them for us in a style so redolent of your great city.

It appears that this like-minded acquaintance of yours, The Hon. Jeremy James Farant, established some time ago a small organisation known as CAMRUTH — *The Campaign for Real Truth*, of which you are a founder member. The aims and ideals of CAMRUTH would seem to bear an uncanny resemblance to the reality that we have achieved in our own political process.

Mr Farant will prove, I have little doubt, to be an extremely useful further contact for us. I should therefore be most grateful if you would procure, in time for our next engagement, which will take place this evening, that gentleman's London home and parliamentary office telephone numbers, which you do not appear to have committed to memory ...

'It will be my pleasure.'

Now, it is also clear, *monsieur*, that you are well aware of the political stance and the character of a more recent recruit to the ranks of CAMRUTH, one Mevr. Hilde van Wostraap of the Netherlands, but you have not had the pleasure of meeting the lady herself.

We are very interested in procuring an opportunity to make the acquaintance of this illustrious champion of honesty for ourselves. Therefore, Jean-Christophe, we should also greatly appreciate your conducting some further research into that lady's planned movements over the coming week, and also into the possible channels which we might pursue in order to effect that encounter.

'Quo, I will do all I can to assist you. And may I also compliment you on your excellent command of our language, and your obvious devotion to the classical style!'

> Ah, you are most kind. But, like every sensible student, I see the value of emulating quality whenever I observe it.

> Now, I require you please to rendezvous here this evening with your new friend Carla, having completed the two tasks which have been assigned to you.

'Quo, if I may make so bold, I feel that these gardens are not really the ideal situation for discussions of so delicate a nature. It would surely be more sensible for Mlle Carla to visit me in my town apartment, *n'est-ce pas?* — it is but fifteen minutes' walk from here ...'

> Very well, Jean-Christophe, we will accept your good judgement. I have already noted the details of your street address — and that your entry phone is labelled "Valéry". Carla looks forward with pleasure to meeting you again at eight-thirty tonight ...

Jean-Christophe Nallier was disengaged. He surprised himself by resisting the temptation to try once again to kiss Carla's hand, and strode back to his detective, reassuring him that everything was fine and that it had simply been, as he had advised him earlier, a small personal matter.

'When are you meeting him next, Carla?'
She was surprised at Toni's unaccustomed interest.
'Tonight — at his apartment.'
'Really? And you'll be going in alone?'
'I expect so. I think that is what J-C wishes.'
'I'm sure it is ...'
'Toni ...'
'All right, Carla. I suppose you know best. But I hope you were able to do the job properly just now, without disappearing! Right — can we take a proper look at this part of the city together?'

'Certainly. I know how much that will please you. But we must locate Nallier's apartment first — it's on Quai Voltaire.'

'Sure — wait, I'll check the map ... yes, it's quite close. No problem. Now, I suggest we look round Notre-Dame and the left bank area before lunch, and after that I must show you the wonderful paintings and sculptures in the Musée d'Orsay ...'

'You're in charge for now, Toni!'

They walked the full length of the Tuileries, then crossed the river at Pont Royal and found the apartments on the elegant Quai Voltaire, close to the Rue de Beaune, situated above several fine art galleries, and with excellent views of the river and the buildings of the right bank.

'Look, there's a special plaque on the wall,' said Toni, and he translated it aloud: '*In this building, Rudolf Nureyev lived for several years before his death in 1993.*'

'Who was Nureyev?'

'A wonderful Russian ballet dancer, Carla. The greatest. He was born on a train, you know ...'

'Well, you've been borne on lots of trains over the last few days, Toni. And I hope I shall not be expected to dance here tonight!'

'Ha ha ha! That's better — two jokes in the same breath! I'm glad you're feeling more cheerful! Now, I need a beer ...'

* * *

After the beer, they began their little tour, soon arriving at an impressive cluster of buildings set back from the embankment. Toni went over to study the inscription.

INSTITUT DE FRANCE

Académie Française
Académie des Inscriptions et Belles Lettres
Académie des Sciences
Académie des Beaux Arts
Académie des Sciences Morales et Politiques ...

'Aha!' he said. 'This is where they protect the French language!'

'From whom, Toni?'

'From the likes of us!'

They meandered up-river towards the Ile de la Cité, crossed the narrow channel at the Petit Pont, then took in the full splendour of the Cathedral of Notre-Dame.

'We must go inside, Carla. Come on!'

Carla was still content to be the passenger again for a while.

Toni had not, from his childhood visit, remembered the immensity of the building.

'It's not so much the length that's remarkable, Carla ...' (he was staring upwards and his rhapsody was addressed mainly to the ceiling and to himself) '... no, I don't think it's particularly longer than some of the other cathedrals I've been in. It's the height that's the amazing thing ... yes, it's just incredibly high, and every single wall is windowed, look, and all the windows are so ornate ... there's glorious stained glass everywhere ... it's just unbelievable ... how did they manage to build it ...?'

'It is indeed very beautiful, Toni — and I am deeply moved by your passion for it.'

Carla did not do sarcasm either, nor did Toni even suspect it.

'And look here — a sculpture of Saint Joan of Arc. I'll translate the text for you.'

'Joan of Arc, 1412-1431
Born in Lorraine, burned alive in Rouen
as a heretic and a witch.
The decision to re-establish her reputation
was made in this Cathedral.'

'She must have been a very special woman, Toni.'

'A very special girl, really, Carla. Younger than me, when she died. Just a girl. She was an infiltrator, too, in her way. But her motives were always good. She inspired her king to recover his throne, but later she bore the wounds and the humiliation of his defeats. She nearly won through. But in the end, another power triumphed. It took them five hundred years to decide to make her a saint ...'

Carla was again impressed by Toni's fervour, but did not push for more details, deciding to leave the normally irreligious young man alone with his thoughts, as they completed their tour of the inspirational Notre-Dame de Paris.

Toni's thoughts were, in fact, primarily focused on the impression Carla seemed to be giving of slowly, at last, getting back to her normal self ...

They retraced their steps down the river and turned into Boulevard St-Michel, stopping to admire the mighty, sombre fountain at the end of the square, with its memorial to another more recent and more successful campaign of liberation. Toni studied it in silence, and then they moved on and soon reached the entrance to the Jardin du Luxembourg.

'I've always wanted to come back here again, Carla — there's a lovely little round lily pond in the middle, right next to the palace, with children feeding the carp ...'

But the pond was not as small or as round or as romantic as Toni had remembered it, especially since the sun had just disappeared behind a cloud. It was quite plain, and octagonal, with a fountain in the middle held up by a statue, and a few seagulls and ducks floating idly around. There were no water lilies; and if there had once been carp cruising around, and delighted children laughing as they fed them, well, they were there no more. The pond was in the middle of the gardens, true enough — but the palace was some way off to the north.

Toni put a brave face on it.

'Pity about the lilies and the carp. Still, I think these are the most informal formal gardens I have ever been in! Really nice, now the sun's come out again, don't you think, Carla? — and the Palace looks so elegant up there, solid but smiling at us, with those confidently sloping grey roofs, and the domes, and that flag flying proudly on the top. Look at the colour of the stone, and the wonderful windows, and the balance of the whole thing! It's like having the Pitti Palace of Florence in the middle of Paris!'

Carla was now feeling rather proud of Toni, the son of the architect. She sensed he might be nearly ready for a little more personal development ...

Then he emerged from his raptures, remembered his stomach and proposed lunch.

'That's fine,' said Carla. 'I'll see you in the gallery afterwards. By the way, I like this place too! I think I'll invite J-C here for our final engagement at this time tomorrow ...'

She disappeared behind a tree and un-made, then followed Toni as he crossed over *Boul'Mich*. He strolled back towards the Seine, and soon spotted, in a narrow street leading off up to the Panthéon, a neat little Chinese restaurant where he enjoyed an excellent meal, a good house red wine, and very gracious service.

* * *

Junior Minister Delegate Nallier was regrettably skipping his own lunch that day.

Instead, he was first consulting the European Parliament's public web site.

This led him straight to the full list of Dutch MEPs, then to a profile of Hilde van Wostraap herself and the names of her two accredited assistants, then off to her own web site, and then, far more easily than he had anticipated or considered wise, to her agenda for the coming week:

Monday 7 - Thursday 10 April
Plenary Session of the European Parliament, Strasbourg

Next, he telephoned a Member of Congress in his own political party who, he remembered hearing recently, had on several occasions over the past few years visited the various European government institutions in Strasbourg, and had reputedly always been afforded some very special evening entertainment opportunities.

'And who, if you please, is the gentleman who makes all these interesting arrangements for you?' ... '*Non, mon ami*, I can assure you it would *not* be in your best interests to withhold this information.' ...

'Ah, that is better — and perhaps a telephone number?' ... '*Merci, mon camarade!* Consider it now forgotten!'

Finally, after consulting his address book and committing to memory the office number of The Hon. Jeremy Farant, MP, he had a quiet word with a close friend in the French Foreign Ministry's own intelligence unit, who additionally obtained for him without delay the ex-directory home number of the venerable West London politician.

* * *

Carla pursued Toni as he left the restaurant and strode off towards the Musée d'Orsay. It was nearly two o'clock, and he had suddenly had a revelation: there might be a bit of a queue!

His judgement was most definitely improving. As he approached the entrance, the wide file of bodies stretched off into apparent infinity.

Antonio Felipe Murano would, undoubtedly, have meekly and properly walked the full length of the line, taken up his rightful place, and, like all the other tourists in front of him, wasted at least two precious Parisian hours fretting about whether and when he would manage to get in, and how much time would be left, even if he did.

Rafael Luis Barola, however, had abandoned some of Toni's well-instilled principles. He held off, made a quick plan, then ambled very slowly up to the head of the queue and continued down it at the same gentle pace. It took him precisely twenty seconds to identify, at a manageable distance, his native Castilian being spoken energetically by a group of four teenage girls only a couple of years younger than himself.

He went for it. Smiled broadly in apparent recognition, he breezed up to the least pretty of the girls in the party, with a happy 'Ah, there you are!' followed by a perfect approach for a friendly kiss on the cheek which turned into a whispered 'Look, *chica*, the queue is absolutely huge ... can I join up with you? I'll happily pay your entrance fee. And my name's Toni — what's yours?'

He tolerated their company for the next few minutes, and he did indeed try to pay for his new friend, although she politely refused to let him. But once he had deposited his CD player, and the girls had handed in all their carrier bags and were noisily getting their bearings, he mumbled 'Please excuse me for a moment' and rushed off towards the toilet. Emerging though a different exit door, he hurried away from the main foyer ...

Carla followed him throughout this charade, feeling a strange combination of disapproval and admiration. Then, once he had clearly established his next plan of action after a quick word with a curator, she continued to pursue him as he pressed on up the side stairs to the upper level ...

Toni passed most of the next hour absorbed in the paintings of Pierre Auguste Renoir.

He spent at least half of that time in front of the magnificent *Dance at the Moulin de la Galette*. He kept shifting position, to take in the lighting effects of Renoir's paint from countless different angles, and to marvel at the artist's subtle perspectives on the joyful crowd of dancers and revellers. Carla found it quite exhausting just watching him — she could see, however, that he was totally captivated, and for a long while she did nothing to distract him. But after a decent interval, she appeared from the shadows of the staircase and strolled up to him.

'You're certainly enjoying this one, Toni!'

'Carla, don't you think it's just glorious? It's set up on the hill of Montmartre, where I went last night. Look at the colours and the light effects! Wouldn't you have loved to be there? Over a hundred years ago, of course — it's nothing like that now! All the men around the table or on the dance floor were really good friends of Renoir — and most of them were artists themselves! And the two women in the foreground, who look so much like each other, with wonderful inviting smiles like yours — well, they were sisters, neighbourhood girls making some extra money as the artist's models. And notice how there's only one couple who are actually absorbed in one another — all the other people are dreamily gazing at someone or something else ...'

'It is very beautiful, Toni. Yes, we are all observers, it seems ...'

'It's one of my two favourite paintings. The other one's also by Renoir, and it has a very similar feel — but it's not in Paris, I'm afraid ... it's in a private collection in Washington D.C! But there are lots more Renoirs here — and so many other wonderful artists.'

Toni stayed with his beloved impressionists for another hour. He paused for some time when he reached Manet's *Picnic on the Grass*. 'You know, Carla, this painting scandalised Paris when it was first exhibited ...'

He then had to speed up, as he tried to cover as much of the rest of the huge gallery as possible, with his legs rapidly wilting beneath him. By a quarter to five he was cultured out.

'I reckon we should call it a day now. I'm tired and thirsty, and I don't want to spoil things by overdoing it!'

'Good thinking, Toni.'

But as they passed through the gallery's shop, on their way to the exit, he spotted the section on the works of Renoir.

'Oh look, Carla — here's a whole book devoted to the other painting I mentioned ... *The Luncheon of the Boating Party*. I can never decide which of those two I love the most! This one is magnificent ... fourteen more of Renoir's friends, can you see? — dotted around the tables after their lunch, overlooking the Seine — but once again, only two of them are looking at each other! Everybody else is either fascinated by a different person in the party, who doesn't even seem to know they're there, or by something in the distance. All observers again, as you said! And the beautiful girl in the flowery hat, who's only interested in her lovely little dog ... she was one of Renoir's favourite models — her name was Aline Charigot — and they were married a few years later! What a brilliant composition! Just brilliant ...'

'Toni, you really are an artist at heart, you know!'

'Oh no, Carla. I told Quo on the day I met you — I can't draw to save my life!'

'I think you're wrong, Toni. We can all draw beautifully if we try. Look — we have some time to spare before we need to meet up with Nallier. Quo did suggest to you, right at the start, that we might be able to share some of our skills. Would you like me to show you what I mean?'

'Would you really, Carla?'

'Of course, *carísimo*. But we must do a bit of shopping first. We need to find a little compilation of simple pencil sketches and studies.' She set off on her search. 'Here, this one looks good ...'

Toni picked it up and turned the pages for her. It was full of drawings by Picasso, Durer, Degas and many other great artists. But the text was in French. Then he spotted a Spanish language version, and chose that instead.

'That's perfect, Toni. Now, get yourself a pad of drawing paper, some soft lead pencils and a large pack of coloured ones — and an eraser too. We'll buy a newspaper from the pavement kiosk outside — and don't forget to collect the CD player ...'

* * *

They strolled back across the river to another quiet bench in the Tuileries Garden, and Carla began her lesson.

'Your brain is not too different from mine in certain key respects, Toni. One half of it, the left side, is preoccupied with reason and precision, order and logic, mathematics and languages, timekeeping and efficiency, and so on. The right side is much more interested in music and art, in spatial concepts, in dreams and possibilities, in perception and invention. The left brain demands the dictionary and the musical score; the right brain prefers to hear the poetry and the symphony ...

'But the left side is stronger, more dominant. It needs to be, to allow you to do all your daily living safely and successfully! Most of the time, the right brain is crouching shyly in the background. Sometimes it takes over for very short periods, such as when you were waxing lyrical about the Cathedral, and Joan of Arc, and the Palace, and the Renoirs. But it is soon put back in its place again by the "let's get busy" left side!'

'This is all a bit abstruse, Carla ...'

'It doesn't matter if you don't accept the theory, Toni. You're going to prove it to yourself now, in practice ...'

She stood up and walked behind the bench, then asked Toni to open the book he had bought, and to slowly turn the pages again as she watched over his shoulder.

'Stop there! Now take an ordinary pencil and copy that simple Picasso caricature of a seated man, straight onto your pad of paper. Do it within ten minutes.'

'This won't take that long,' thought Toni, as he began to copy, watching precisely the poor results he was expecting as they materialised before his eyes. In less than six minutes he declared it finished.

'There,' he said. 'It's awful — I told you so!'

'I agree — it is not a good effort, Toni. Your left brain was in charge, and it was keen to beat the challenge of the clock, and anyway it felt the whole thing was a waste of time — it would have preferred you to be getting on with something much more productive. And the results have proved it correct. So it is sitting there very smugly at the moment — the decision it made for you, many years ago, that you simply cannot draw, has been reinforced once again!'

'So, Carla ...?'

'So, Toni — you have just drawn what you *thought* you could see. What your clever left brain thought a simple human figure should look like. As far as it is concerned, drawing's only good for scribbled street maps or formal engineering blueprints, and little else! Now your right brain is going to help you draw what you *actually* see ...

'Find a clean sheet of paper. Now turn the Picasso upside down.' ... 'Yes, upside down! Now put the paper alongside the Picasso, and take as long as you wish to reproduce exactly what you see. Try to make every single line the perfect length and shape and angle. Don't rush it — and if your left brain tries to tell you it's a waste of time, or it can't make sense of what it sees you producing, just tell it to shut up for a while ...'

Toni rather reluctantly agreed, and abandoned himself to his muse. This time it took several minutes for him to relax sufficiently to make even the first mark. Fifteen long minutes then passed before he was satisfied. He had paused at length on several occasions. He had used the eraser a lot. Finally he spoke.

'All right, Carla. I've done what you asked. It's just a bunch of linked lines — but I've tried hard to reproduce the original.'

'Turn the book the right way up again, Toni. Now turn your new drawing round as well ...'

Toni was stunned at the result. It did not have the passion or the fluidity of the original, but his own little "picasso" was a very fair, well-proportioned copy of it, and the subject was easily recognisable this time.

'Wow!'

'Impressed?'

'You bet!'

'It's your left brain that's impressed, Toni. It's the one that makes all those sorts of judgements for you. It cannot argue with the facts. It is very pleasantly surprised to see how well you did, and to acknowledge reluctantly that you did it without its own help, and to admit that it enjoyed that good long rest from its usual mundane responsibilities. And to agree that it might even be comfortable with the idea of letting you do it again, if you can produce results like that for it to be so proud of ...'

'I want to do another one straight away, Carla!!'

'Sure, Toni — but calm down! Turn the book upside down again. Start turning the pages slowly for me — OK, stop there. We'll use the drawing on the left. There are lots of curves in that one, as well as straight lines. Get a new sheet of paper, and position it close by, on the right, so that your observation can be as easy and accurate as possible. Try to make the copy the same size, and alongside the original.

'Now close your eyes and relax. Then tell your left brain that you are going to have another go. When it tries to argue, just remind it how much it will appreciate another restful break, and will enjoy the results at the end! Once it fully agrees, and gives in and goes off to sleep, open your eyes and begin. Take all the time you need. It's going to be beautiful, Toni ...'

When Toni emerged from his second reverie of creation, and his right brain momentarily admired the result, it was, indeed, quite beautiful. Then his left brain kicked in, and enthusiastically agreed — and now, at long last, it was back under its master's control ...

'Have we got time for one more, Carla?'

'Yes, Mr Left Brain! OK — pick up your newspaper and turn it upside down. Now look away, and slowly turn its pages while I study the captions of the photographs ... Stop! That one's perfect. You need to tear out the picture down at the bottom right, Toni, without trying to read the caption or the headlines — and don't turn it the right way up! Then fold it so that only the photo is showing — no text. That's it.

'Turn your drawing pad lengthways and put the upside-down photo on the left hand side. Now you're ready to copy it across onto the right-hand side of the pad. You've got nice soft pencils, so try to capture the different shades of grey rather than tracing any outlines. Copy exactly what you see, not what you expect. OK — close your eyes, dismiss the left brain, and then begin ...'

Half an hour later, having scarcely paused this time, Toni stopped and studied the image of monochrome contrasts which he had produced. The original photo was clearly a human face — he had known that from the start. But he had no idea who the mystery person was ...

Carla spoke up. 'Don't look at the photo yet — just turn your drawing up the right way ...'

Toni was speechless as he found himself admiring a superb likeness of the Prime Minister of Spain.

Then he suddenly realised how cold he was feeling. It was nearly half-past seven — with his right brain largely in control, over two hours had slipped by quite unnoticed, the sun had fully set, and a cool breeze had come up. But Carla had been watching the clock in her own particular way.

'Time for dinner, Toni!'

'You're right! Thank you so much for the lesson, Carla. I really enjoyed it — I'm so excited, and I love the results! But it's also made me feel quite strange inside ...'

'Nothing a good Parisian meal won't cure, I'm certain! Now — can I ask you to eat fairly close by, so that you can be back at Nallier's apartment block before eight-thirty? You can help me get in, and then I'd like you to wait outside for me until I've finished ...'

Toni left Carla to her own devices and wandered hungrily back towards Jean-Christophe's apartment. Only a few metres further along the embankment, on the corner of Rue de Beaune, he discovered Le Voltaire bar-restaurant.

'Yes,' he thought, 'I know just how Candide felt. This can be my revenge!'

He pushed open the door (*'Bonsoir, monsieur!'* came a call from the back), marched confidently up to the bar and, in his best French, asked for a Cunégonde baguette and a small Pangloss on ice. The young barman and waiter shook their uncomprehending heads. He chuckled to himself, and settled for a fillet steak and fries and the best of all possible beers.

* * *

Carla and Toni met up again at twenty past eight, outside Nallier's apartment block.

'Toni, please press the button marked "R. Valéry" for me ...'

The entry phone crackled. 'Carla?'

'Yes, J-C.'

The entrance door clicked open.

'Bonsoir, mademoiselle! Ah, you are a little early — I was in the bathroom, but it is no problem! Please come straight up. Third floor, second apartment on the right after you leave the elevator. I will leave my door unlocked ...'

There were many people walking around nearby, so Carla did not want to un-make just yet. Instead, Toni pushed the front door fully open. There was nobody in the lobby. Carla whispered 'See you later,' and walked inside. Toni pulled the door gently back, and it closed and locked itself. He then retreated, to wait across the road by the wall of the river bank.

Once safely inside, Carla un-made, passed up the lift shaft and down the corridor, and poked her head and nothing else through the second door, which was also labelled "R. Valéry".

She saw a large, dark living room, lit only by the last vestiges of the Parisian sunset, a weak street light, and a tiny lamp in the corner. Her target was clearly still occupied in the small room over to her left. She decided not to intrude further on his privacy, but simply completed her entrance, re-made, and sat down calmly on a small upright chair close to the door.

A few moments later, Jean-Christophe switched off the bathroom light, emerged in a splendid silk dressing gown, then spotted his seated guest. It was hard for her to see him in the poor light, which he was now blocking still further. But she smiled at once her captivating smile.

Nallier did not appear to have noticed it. 'Carla, welcome! You must have come in so quietly! I did not realise that you were here ...'

He began to walk towards her.

'J-C, please do not come too close, so quickly. And anyway, you know, I can hardly see you ...'

'Ah, the romance of the twilight, *ma chérie* ...'

Carla tried to turn up the intensity of her own sort of charm, but her smile was still not getting through. Jean-Christophe was holding back for now, thank goodness, but he was taking firm control of events ...

Quo communicated instantly to Carla, like a radio news producer to an interviewer, and told her not to panic, and to play along for a little while to avoid alienating their valuable subject.

'Carla,' Nallier persisted, 'I have gathered the information you and Quo requested. But I feel I deserve a small reward for all my efforts. You are a very beautiful woman, you know. I will be happy to divulge everything I have learned, if we may first ... together ... you know ...'

'*Non, J-C.*'

'Ah, Carla, you are playing with me. I am sure your little "*non*" is not what it seems, *hein*?'

'*Non, J-C.* It is out of the question. Believe me!'

But Nallier continued to insist, Carla held her less than solid ground, and there was temporary stalemate.

Quo and Carla were both quite confident that J-C was really only trying his luck, and that he would eventually provide them with their information, whatever happened (hopefully he *had* been properly and fully engaged earlier in the day!).

They knew too that Carla could at any time choose to insist on more light for her smile and then get on with her first collection, as planned.

But Quo still preferred not to aggravate the man unnecessarily. So the Handler was strongly encouraged by her management to think of something, and keep him very sweet.

Carla thought briefly, as instructed — and she could not ignore the logical conclusion that the offer of a modest little striptease ('but no touching!') might provide the necessary key to the deadlock. But she had some rather strange reservations about proceeding. And also, she suddenly thought, she had not formally studied and remembered an appropriate image — so she had no firm idea of what she should look like beneath her smart Italian suit!

Then Quo reminded her that she had observed lots of mannequins modelling underwear in the fashion stores, and plenty of sculptures and paintings of nudes in the gallery that afternoon, and in particular those girls in the Amsterdam windows. She could surely construct something convincing from all that informal input! 'Yes, that's true,' thought Carla; but she was still feeling curiously embarrassed by the prospect of what was to come, and was not at all certain she could generate any accurate images in that unaccustomed state of disquiet ...

She made her compromising offer.

And Nallier quickly decided to accept it as a pleasant step in the right direction. The night was still young ...

Then, in a final attempt to avoid this charade, Carla insisted, to J-C's mild disappointment, that she would need a screen for her performance — and, 'quel dommage,' there were none to be seen. But Nallier, carefully moving across the room to sit down in a particular armchair, at once declared that she should improvise with the already half-open door to the bedroom. So, having exhausted all her objections, she pressed bravely on.

She disappeared behind the bedroom door, un-made, re-made in a fetching crimson camisole and matching French knickers that she had secretly admired in a shop window only a few hours earlier, stepped back into view and, despite her natural inclinations, found herself doing a provocative little twirl.

Jean-Christophe grinned widely and nodded in lusty approval. 'Bravo! Encore! Continue, continue, ma petite ...'

She moved behind the door once more, and un-made again. This was it! At least he would barely be able to see her in this light. She took the equivalent of a deep breath, re-made, and re-emerged.

Her audience of one was amazed to discover that, despite her slim and delicate frame, his latest intended paramour, silhouetted beautifully in front of the weak light from the north-facing window, was endowed with astonishingly large examples of the primary features of the female, and a strangely undefined lower half, covered by an extremely real-looking fig leaf ...

His reaction was predictable. He leapt out of his chair and moved swiftly towards Carla, his arms opening for an embrace and his lips gushing further compliments.

She had one second in which to react, and in that second she decided to get away at once and handle the consequences later. So as Jean-Christophe reached his object of desire and threw his arms around her, she vanished completely, and all he succeeded in embracing was himself.

Carla re-made behind Toni, who was standing patiently by the wall of the river bank, clutching his precious drawing materials and creations, and gazing across at the floodlit Sacré-Cœur, high up on the hill of Montmartre.

'*Hola.*'

She briefly described her little adventure, and without waiting for any reaction, told Toni that they must ring the door-phone once again, and that he must speak this time, and introduce himself as her assistant, and pretend they had only just arrived ...

Of course, when Nallier answered, he insisted that Carla had been with him only minutes before, and demanded to know what was going on. Toni denied any knowledge of the incident, and apologised for their slightly late arrival, and joked with Jean-Christophe that he must surely have just been asleep and dreaming ...

The already shocked minister now had no idea what to say or to think. But they had at least managed to cool his ardour. He pressed the entry button, and this time he met them both at the apartment door. The lights were back on inside.

He looked first at Toni, and vaguely recognised him and the CD player from the gardens earlier that day. Then he turned to Carla.

'But you are even wearing the same clothes, *mademoiselle*!'

'I have been wearing them all day, *monsieur*. But I am flattered that you remembered me so vividly in your little fantasy ...'

Beaten at his own game for the first time in a long time, Nallier abandoned the idea of pressing Carla for any further favours and quickly ushered them both inside. As she walked past him, thankfully unaccosted, she smiled her special smile, moved to the centre of the room, and was at last back in full control. She motioned to Toni, and he turned his back on her performance once again.

Jean-Christophe closed the door and immediately succumbed to Carla's embrace. She disappeared (the *Mater* was taking no chances this time), and he quickly revealed the answers that Quo was initially seeking.

First, he provided the two requested London telephone numbers for The Hon. Jeremy Farant, MP.

He then confirmed that Ms Hilde van Wostraap would definitely be in Strasbourg from the Monday to the Thursday of the following week, with the historic final debate and voting on European enlargement scheduled for the Wednesday morning session.

Finally, he suggested that Quo might be interested in making contact, on the third phone number which he had easily memorised, with a certain Monsieur Bernard Lamargue, a senior member of the small section of the Parliament's Secretariat permanently based in Strasbourg. Monsieur Lamargue, he assured Quo, apparently knew just about everybody who was anybody in the government organisation, Europe-wide, and probably knew a lot more about many of them than they expected or realised.

And although the dapper Bernard, a lifetime bachelor, was acknowledged as a loyal, skilful and hard-working civil servant, he was also believed by one or two astute observers to have several significant but undisclosed business interests, for which he regularly organised strong and unattributable parliamentary lobbying.

More interesting still, he was understood to lead something of a double life in the Strasbourg nights. This almost certainly embroiled him in illicit gambling, the handling of minor drug dealers, and prostitution. He was suspected of moving around the city in many disguises, but was believed to have established one particularly strong second identity.

Last but not least, there were indications that many senior figures working in Strasbourg, or visiting the city regularly, were able to take advantage of Bernard's rich range of services — including provision of their own sophisticated disguises, if required.

However, Jean-Christophe was keen to point out, no official evidence was known to be held on any of this.

(How, Quo could not help wondering, does he then know so much about it all ...?)

And, Nallier insisted, there was no suggestion whatsoever that Ms van Wostraap was involved in any of these dubious activities. He nonetheless had no doubt that the silver-tongued and influential apparatchik Lamargue should be able to beat a path for Quo to the door of the lady herself.

So now Quo could make the action plan for the next few days. Toni and Carla would go to London for the weekend, then move on to Strasbourg in plenty of time to take some more soundings before the main event.

And Nallier could be given his next mission.

Jean-Christophe, that is all very satisfactory. I thank you. We shall now take things a little further.

Firstly, you will make personal contact by telephone, early tomorrow morning, with your kindred spirit Mr Jeremy Farant. You will encourage him to accept a call at his office desk, in the early afternoon, from a young Spaniard by the name of Esteban Leopoldo de Hernández y Victoria.

You will tell him that this talented graduate of Salamanca University, who happens to be the son of a celebrated Spanish film star and a darling of the Italian media, is presently engaged in the writing of a doctoral thesis entitled *Politics and Integrity in the Age of the Soundbite*; that you have today granted him an interview and been most favourably impressed with both his professional approach and the acuity of his insights into the issue about which you both share such concerns; and that you most strongly recommend that Mr Farant too should allow Sr. Hernández y Victoria an immediate audience, while he is still so close to London and before he departs to continue his research in the USA.

You will add that for reasons of personal security and privacy, the postgraduate student is naturally pursuing this research under an assumed name, and that there will be no record to be found of any individual with his family background in either the public or the private files of the University itself.

You will mention that Estebán always insists on presenting his interviewees with a small token of his gratitude. His preference is to give a compact disc of that individual's favourite music. So please invite Jeremy to suggest to you something appropriate.

You might perhaps also propose to The Hon. Mr Farant that the possibilities, at an appropriate time, for associated press releases and other publicity, in international publications of many shapes and colours, make this an almost irresistible opportunity to further your common cause ...

Secondly, you will proceed to procure written summaries of the European Parliament's main resolutions for EU enlargement, as well as documentation on the individuals who have developed and investigated those proposals.

You will report on your telephone call, and deliver the printed results of your research, to Carla tomorrow afternoon, at one-thirty precisely, beside the large pond in the Jardin du Luxembourg.

'It will be done,' agreed Nallier, very meekly.

Bravo, Jean-Christophe. Now, you will please escort your guests back to the lift ...

'Toni,' said Carla, now detached from J-C and back in full view. 'We're ready to leave.'

* * *

The front door of the apartment block closed quietly behind them. Then Carla found herself having to hurry to keep up with her escort's surprisingly rapid pace as he strode off down Quai Voltaire.

'Thank you for helping me, Toni. I'd buy you a drink if I could make my money last for more than a few metres!'

'I'll buy my own.'

They found a small pavement café nearby, and Toni sat straight down. Carla was obliged to squeeze herself into a chair that was rather too close to the table.

'Have you really told me everything that happened up there, Carla?'

'Yes!'

'Are you sure that's all he made you do?'

'Of course! Nothing else is possible!'

'You and Quo are very good at inventing truths, Carla.'

'Toni, stop being ridiculous!'

'Oh, it's me being ridiculous now, is it? Huh!'

And he stood up and stormed off, to the surprise of the waiter approaching the table.

'*Et pour mademoiselle?*'

Carla shook her head ('*Merci, rien!*'), squeezed back out of her tight position and pursued Toni across the road towards the river wall, with a new set of concerns now filling the Handler's mind and a definite damage limitation plan already being built in Quo's ...

'Toni — this is crazy. Will you please calm down?'

'No, Carla. I agree it's crazy — and I've had enough!'

He was staring across the river into the distance, and had still not turned round to look at her.

'Very well,' said Carla, responding to Quo's summary order and moving directly behind him. 'We must continue without you. I shall make contact again tomorrow ...'

She reached out her arms and took his head in her hands. Quo enabled the appropriate engagement sphere, reversed the circuit direction to cater for the couple's interesting deviation from the normal missioning position, and planted the simple instructions in their sherpa's mind that he must be back in his hotel room by two o'clock the following afternoon, and that he must then fulfil Carla's requirements to the letter.

When Toni, completely unaware of this latest violation, finally decided to turn round and look at his fickle companion, she had already evaporated into the leafy shadows.

Then, though the Paris night was still very young, he plodded slowly back to his hotel, climbed the long flights of stairs, dumped everything on the table without bothering to admire his beautiful artistic creations again, and went to bed feeling exhausted and most dispirited.

* * *

He slept in very late the next morning. By the time he dragged himself out of the hotel and into the street corner café, it was nearly half-past eleven. He was very hungry, so he turned breakfast into an early lunch, then wandered off down towards the Louvre. He picked up the never-ending Rue de Rivoli, followed it all the way to the Hôtel de Ville, then turned left and came upon Igor Stravinsky square and the immense Georges Pompidou Centre. He translated the top line of a mission statement sited in front of one of its buildings:

Institute of Research and Co-ordination in Acoustics and Music

'What on earth does that mean?' he wondered, rather unkindly. He translated all the sub-themes on the large notice, and understood a little better. But he decided he would stick with just playing and listening to the music he loved, for the time being at least. He had already learned quite enough new artistic theory the day before.

Then, as one o'clock approached, he found himself walking inexorably back down towards Notre-Dame and the left bank. As he reached the river, his impatience got the better of him still further, and he hailed a taxi ...

* * *

Carla was already strolling elegantly around the pond as Junior Minister Delegate Nallier walked down the steps to their meeting point in front of the Palais du Luxembourg. He tried to avoid her smiling gaze as he approached, but he was less successful at that than most of Renoir's characters, and he soon came back under her spell.

Then she led him over to a little clearing in the middle of a few bushes and small trees, out of view of prying eyes, and they sat down together on the grass — but not for Manet's picnic. She took his head in her hands once more, then vanished from his sight ...

How interesting, Jean-Christophe (concluded Quo, as the junior minister held up and the *Mater* read, one after the other, the documents detailing the ten recommendations on EU enlargement) — how very, very interesting. Thank you.

So we now have before us, printed out from information available to anybody on your public Internet, the names of the *rapporteurs* representing each of the investigations into the ten countries' separate applications for membership, as well as the names of every MEP who voted on the Committee's adoption of each set of recommendations.

'Precisely, Quo,' said Nallier, recognising he had little to add to this conclusion.

Jean-Christophe, you will travel this weekend to Strasbourg.

It is apparent, from everything we have learned, that most, if not all, of the good people listed in these documents will be in that city from next Monday onwards, in readiness for the historic enlargement votes to be taken on Wednesday.

You will therefore arrange, using your many contacts and your very good offices, to organise personal discussions throughout Monday and Tuesday with each of the ten *rapporteurs* named in these documents, or, in the absence of any of them, with a good alternative selected from the list of voting MEPs. You may invent whatever pretexts you choose for these meetings.

But your objective in every case will be to establish the real personal views of each interviewee, on the question of the admission into the Union of the particular country that he or she has been investigating.

You will be able to do this in a newly empowered way, by smiling a special smile, and then simply observing each person's true position on the issue, and the various factors contributing to that position. You will easily memorise your findings, and you may then continue and conclude each meeting in the normal way.

You will complete this mission by eight o'clock on Tuesday evening. You will then report back to Carla two hours later, at ten o'clock precisely. Kindly suggest a suitable location for this rendezvous ...

'Let us meet at the carousel on Place Gutenberg,' said Nallier.

So be it, Jean-Christophe.

You have clearly also succeeded in preparing Mr Farant to receive the telephone call from young Estebán — and you have established that Jeremy is a lover of the comic operas of Gilbert and Sullivan. Excellent! I thank you once again for your very thorough support.

Now, please return at once to your office, and begin your planning.

Nallier extracted himself from Carla's hold. Recognising that he was not permitted to deliver even a peck on the hand of his reconstituted anti-paramour, he satisfied himself by blowing her a big kiss, declaring '*Au revoir, mademoiselle* ... until Tuesday!' and striding off towards the steps.

It had been Toni's turn to observe, unnoticed. He had of course seen nothing very different from any of Carla's other performances in her previous public engagements. But it made him feel better, just for having tried. Now, with less than twenty minutes to spare before the start of his curfew, he sprinted back to the *Boul'Mich* and jumped into the waiting pumpkin that was still masquerading as a taxi with a very expensively ticking meter ...

Not worrying, as Toni was, about possible traffic delays, Carla returned immediately to his hotel room. So she too was awaiting him, when he reached the top of the stairs with one minute to spare and now as docile as a lamb.

'Good afternoon, Toni. It's time to phone London.'

'Yes, Carla.'

She briefed him thoroughly, then dictated Jeremy Farant's office number.

The long-in-the-tooth Member of Parliament answered the anticipated call at once, listened carefully to the research student's speech of introduction, and agreed to the interview.

'Tomorrow, at noon, you say? Very well. I suggest we meet at Piccadilly Circus, underneath the statue of Eros. Can you find that?' ... 'We can then seek out a quiet public house in the backstreets of Soho, where I will not necessarily be recognised. I shall wear a green fishing hat. And you?' ... 'A pink carnation! How very civilised! Until tomorrow, Sr. Hernández y Victoria ...'

'So, Toni — what's the best way to get to the centre of London?'

'Well, I fancy the Channel Tunnel. The train goes from Gare du Nord — I spotted that on Wednesday. It must be quicker than getting to and from the airports, for such a short distance ...'

'Then the Tunnel it is. Please phone and book it straight away — and a hotel. Then get yourself packed, and we can be off!'

'Yes, ma'am.'

'Oh, and if you see a CD of Gilbert and Sullivan on sale at the station, please buy it. If not, you'll need to pick one up when you get to London ...'

All the World's a Stooge

Considering the immensity of the challenge facing him, and the fact that it was still only forty-eight hours since he had placidly accepted his latest mission, Deputy Political Advisor Raymond Graves felt he had made substantial progress.

On the afternoon of his empowerment, he had returned directly to his office and had succeeded with consummate ease in gaining the approval of his boss to his unexpectedly needed grand tour. In passing, he had sneaked a quick insight, as instructed, into the Senior Political Advisor's own true thoughts on the enlargement of the European Union ...

He had then embarked on the huge task of personally organising his twelve meetings and constructing a feasible itinerary for them. With a combination of good luck, dogged persistence, the calling in of several favours, some very fortunate flight connections, and much juggling of provisional appointment times, he had managed to fix up five of them before close of play on that Wednesday afternoon.

Then, before rushing home to pack for his own whistle-stop tour of some of the centres and outposts of the European empire, he had held his latest team meeting. Unfortunately, only four of his seven team members were in Mons that day, but they had all agreed to remain in the office a little later than usual, intrigued by their colleague's sudden spate of privately-conducted phone calls, and very keen to learn more. Raymond, however, had left their meeting considerably better informed than any of them ...

He had flown out of Brussels on a mid-evening departure, and had completed three of his pre-arranged meetings the next day — one in the morning, one in the afternoon, and the last very late in the evening. The other two sessions which he had set up in advance would not be taking place until the Sunday morning and afternoon.

En-route, throughout that Thursday, he had placed several more phone calls, and had managed to book three further appointments — one for the Friday morning, one for the afternoon (he had just emerged from that one), and another for early the next day.

He was also reasonably hopeful that two more meetings could be organised in a single city on the coming Monday morning — this would be his next little challenge, as he travelled back to the latest airport. Even if he managed to arrange both of those sessions, he would still only have achieved ten out of the twelve that he had been tasked with. But he would have done his best. He knew that.

He would then return to Brussels on the Monday afternoon — and if he was very lucky, he might also get a little time with his other team colleagues, and even with some of his senior managers, as Quo had requested ...

Although the diplomat in him was hesitating to jump to any rash conclusions, Raymond Martin Graves could not avoid the depressing fact that, out of the total of ten absolutely true private opinions he had so far obtained, no less than seven had proved to be fundamentally different from their public versions ...

London, England

Toni checked out of his hotel soon after three, and took a taxi to the Gare du Nord. The Friday rush hour was building nicely, so Carla had un-made and was just tagging along behind. But they reached the station before three-thirty. He picked up his ticket, bought a baguette and a cola for later, exchanged a large handful of twenty-euro bills for ten-pound notes, and boarded the 1607 Eurostar departure for the three-hour trip to London Waterloo International.

He was still very unhappy, and he spent some time just staring out of the window and brooding: angry with Carla, but not able to justify his anger; annoyed with himself about many things, but again not able to put his finger on a single one ...

Carla joined him after a while, still un-made but keen to observe his behaviour following the previous evening's tantrum. She whispered gently in his ear, asking him if he would like to find a less crowded carriage, so that she could re-make and sit and talk with him. But he took no notice of her and stayed where he was. She concluded there was little change in his state of mind, and Quo agreed that it was certainly not sensible to re-admit him to their schemes for some time to come.

A little later (and he was not sure why), Toni did get up to investigate farther along the train. He found a quiet section where Carla would be able to re-make in private if she chose to. He went back and collected his suitcase, and then settled into his new seat, assuming she would get the message, but not really caring if she did or did not choose to appear.

She did so, with a vengeance. Quo had decided on some shock therapy. So for the first time since they had met, Carla re-made before Toni's very eyes. The effect was admirable.

'Aarrgghh!'

'Sshhhh, Toni!' hissed Carla; then, quick as a flash, she continued, loud enough for everyone in the carriage to hear and understand, 'Oh, you poor thing! You must have been having a really bad dream ...'

Normality settled all around them again, and Toni glared at her.

'You nearly gave me a heart attack! You shouldn't go re-making in front of people like that!'

'I'm sorry. We didn't think it would be that much of a surprise ...'

'Huh!'

The conversation petered out. Carla's conclusions on Toni's instability remained unchanged. But she wanted to stay with him for a little longer, to see if he would mellow as the journey progressed. So, especially after his reaction to her recent arrival, she needed to give him a little word of warning right away.

'Toni, you told me while you were packing that we'd be going into the Channel Tunnel about half-way through the trip — and that it is very long, and is under the seabed ...'

'Yes ...'

'Well — there's a good chance that I shall fade away when that happens.'

'That's nothing new ...'

'Toni! Behave! And listen to me! It's not the same as un-making. It will be because I have lost a lot of signal energy. Quo told you about that possibility, back in Bilbao — surely you remember?'

'Yes, I think I do ...'

'So, if it happens — don't panic! I should be able to track you and the train perfectly well, and see and hear everything, but I won't have enough power to speak to you. If something goes wrong, and I don't reappear when we come out of the Tunnel, please just wait for me at the exit from Waterloo Station. I can follow the tracks and work something out from our co-ordinates database, and then I can be there in a flash — well ahead of you. But I don't know the location of your hotel yet. So just don't move away from the exit, or get in a taxi, or we'll lose you for ever!'

'Would you really mind that, Carla?'

'Oh, for goodness' sake, Toni, when *are* you going to grow ....'

'To grow what, Carla?'

But Carla's voice, and then her image, had evanesced.

Toni spent the entire tunnel transit wondering just how many station exits there might actually be at Waterloo. Fortunately, Carla's precautions had been wise but unnecessary; twenty seconds before they emerged from the tunnel at Folkestone, she reappeared in her seat. Toni was now, of course, all keyed-up for this potential occurrence, so her materialisation caused no new shock to his system, just a substantial sense of relief. But he was not going to admit to that, today of all days — and he barely acknowledged her return.

'Right,' said Carla, her project manager's hat firmly back in place, and the decision now taken not to waste any more effort looking for an early change in Toni's mood. 'I'll be off again in a few moments, but I'll follow you when we arrive, and see you at the taxi rank, OK?'

'Sure, Carla — whatever you say ...'

* * *

They reached Waterloo exactly on time, and Toni had remembered the various reminders to set his watch back one hour — to 1813 precisely.

He made his way to the taxis, got into the queue, and waited. Two minutes later, Carla strolled up, and he felt he could relax again at last. He wished he could understand why ...

They climbed into a spacious black cab, which burrowed quickly underneath the station complex and emerged close to Westminster Bridge. As they drove west and approached the River Thames, with Big Ben and the Houses of Parliament rising proudly across to their left, the corridors of Whitehall power lurking more surreptitiously over to the right, and the great London parks awaiting them straight ahead, Toni enjoyed his first, glorious Waterloo Sunset.

But although it was a Friday night, he wasn't Terry, and she wasn't Julie, and they certainly weren't in Paradise at that moment. So Carla never learned the song that was filling his thoughts.

Instead, he simply described the sights as they drove alongside St James's Park, circled Buckingham Palace, skirted Green Park on their way up Constitution Hill, then rounded Hyde Park Corner and entered Park Lane.

'You've been here before, haven't you?' observed Carla.

'Yes, twice,' said Toni vacuously. 'The last time was only three years ago — on a school exchange visit. I like London — it's very big and very busy, but it's got so many peaceful places in the heart of the city ...'

'Well, Toni, you've got all day tomorrow to get to know it even better. I'll be meeting Jeremy Farant on my own. I'm sure I can follow the signs to Piccadilly Circus and the statue of Eros ...'

Toni was still feeling rather angry, and was now even angrier.

'Do you really think that's wise? You do seem to get yourself into scrapes when I'm not around, even for a few minutes! Look what happened at the jazz club in Prague! Then there was J-C's apartment ...'

'Toni, it is not up for discussion. I suggest we meet again after I have finished with Mr Farant. Let's make it one o'clock, also beneath Eros (I assume you'll be able to find it too!), and then we'll discuss what needs to be done next.'

He shook his head in dismay and incredulity, but Carla knew that he would be there as instructed.

'By the way, Toni — who is Eros?'

'Eros?' sighed Toni. 'Eros, Carla, is the god of Love.'

* * *

They arrived at an elegant-looking hotel on the Bayswater Road (Toni had insisted on something rather better than what he had accepted in Paris), and Carla quickly reminded him once again of their standard fallback plan. He held his tongue.

'OK, Toni. Give me five minutes before you leave the lobby to go upstairs.'

He opened the cab door. She slid out and walked off to the next corner, rounded it, found a quiet alcove and un-made, then returned to the front entrance and sailed though the un-revolving door. She whispered her presence to Toni as he was checking in, then followed him up to his room, logged its position, and gratefully handed over the watch to one of her juniors ...

It was still only seven o'clock, and Toni had slept late that morning, so he had plenty of energy left to take on Soho on a warm Friday night. He just needed to forget about Carla for a while, and then he could start to enjoy himself. And he very quickly managed to do both.

He took the Underground straight to Tottenham Court Road, then strolled down Charing Cross Road and into the little streets and squares of Chinatown. He meandered around that colourful neighbourhood for over an hour, absorbing the exciting variety of sights and sounds. He found himself ghoulishly fascinated by the rich displays of yet-to-be-cooked meats, poultry and seafood in the front windows of the countless restaurants. Eventually, one of those tableaux proved irresistible, and he dined lavishly at the grand, convincingly named "China China".

Remembering Carla's shopping instructions, as he paid the bill with his bank card to keep his cash intact, he sought out a large music store and bought a recording of Gilbert and Sullivan's *The Sorcerer*, performed in 1966 by the D'Oyly Carte Opera Company. Then he wandered off towards Covent Garden: not to the Royal Opera House, but to the now reincarnated site of the old fruit and vegetable market; he knew it was always good for some live entertainment. He was not disappointed. Jugglers, sword-swallowers, fire-eaters, streetlife serenaders, mime and statue artists — he saw them all. And on his way around and about the happy city scene, which made him momentarily think again of the Moulin de la Galette, he dropped into two separate pubs, just to keep his spirits up.

But when his legs had once more had enough, he took the easy option and grabbed a taxi back to his hotel.

* * *

After a hearty English breakfast, he picked up his CD player, swapped out Strauss in favour of Janis Ian (he wanted some reliable, friendly company this morning) and at nine o'clock put his best sightseeing foot forward once again.

'Day 12 of my travels,' he thought for no particular reason, as he crossed over into Hyde Park.

He spent the next three hours on a very pleasant walk, with a gentle musical accompaniment, through many of the tranquil London places of which he had such fond memories.

He covered the full length of Hyde Park and the Serpentine Lake, and almost decided to hire a rowing boat for himself — but something told him he didn't have the time to spare. And as he left through one of the exit gates at the southern end of Park Lane, he noticed a colourful advertisement for an open-air rock concert, in that very park, the following afternoon.

'What a great idea that would be ...' he thought, rather loosely.

He crossed Park Lane and strolled through the quiet streets of Shepherd Market, emerging on Piccadilly and stopping at Henry's for an early beer. He ambled through Green Park, and took a much better look at Buckingham Palace than he had been able to grab from his twilight taxi ride. Then, as he walked off down the Mall, he realised he was timing things nicely to be at Piccadilly Circus just before twelve noon. So he finally admitted to himself that he was once again planning to watch over Carla's next involvement.

He approached Eros with several minutes to spare, and hovered around near one of the Underground subway exits, desperate to avoid being noticed by Carla, and at the same time passionately intent on sighting either her or the English gentleman in a green fishing hat who was expecting to meet a Spaniard sporting a pink carnation.

* * *

Carla was the first to appear. Her plan of action had been formulated in detail, half an hour earlier, after she had successfully found her way to Eros with the help of a friendly London bobbie. She had even managed to conjure up a carnation.

She stood in clear public view at the foot of the statue, taking great care, for several good reasons, not to smile too directly at any passers-by. But when the fishing hat and its owner emerged from the southern section of Regent Street, gazed around in search of Esteban, and registered with mild surprise that today was a very good day for pink carnations, she put on her most captivating smile, and The Hon. Jeremy James Farant, proud holder of several trophies from his exclusive angling club, was himself well and truly hooked.

Carla had decided to play this big old fish in the way she had initially handled the smaller but very cute one in Bilbao, at the start of her mission. Hopefully they would encounter no hidden obstacles on this occasion. So she moved off quickly towards Haymarket, keeping Farant on a long tight line.

Toni, in his turn, stealthily pursued her catch like a hungry pike with the sniff of an easy meal ...

She crossed Haymarket and penetrated a quiet, much smaller street linking it with Leicester Square. She walked up three steps and along a short passage, then stopped at the front door of an office building that was obviously closed for the weekend. Then, out of view of everyone but the few people passing by, none of whom would in any case be looking her way, she hauled her capture in.

Toni, who was by now only yards behind Farant, was dismayed to see his quarry stride up the steps and disappear into the dim passage. He was forced to come to a halt just short of it, not daring to peep around the corner, and having to be satisfied with just listening intently ...

Inside the passage, Jeremy was holding off. Carla's smile was once again not achieving its usual result.

'Who are you, madam? I was expecting to meet a young man. But for some reason I am following you. This is not right. I can tell that you are deceiving me. I have a good nose for these things ...'

'Do not worry, Jeremy. I am a friend of Estebán. He is not well this morning, and he has asked me to come in his place.'

'No, I'm not having this. For one thing, it is not what I agreed. But more important, I can see that you are lying. I'm calling the police — don't try and move!'

But The Hon. Jeremy Farant could not bring himself to remove the phone from his pocket.

'Jeremy, you are clearly a man of immense integrity. I am delighted to have found you ...'

'Don't give me all that. Just stay there! If only I could get hold of my phone ...'

'Jeremy, please look at me properly.' Carla turned her smile up beyond the normal safe limit for a few seconds; she was sure this would cause no lasting damage.

'No, I will not!'

Farant continued to stand his ground — which was not surprising, since he was effectively glued to it. But he was not melting at all ...

Toni had heard all this, and recognised there was an obvious impasse. And now his fundamental missioning from Quo took over from his still-fermenting anger and jealousy. So he started thinking

again. The very honest Mr Farant obviously had a high level of
resistance, and Carla's smile was presumably just not strong enough
to overcome it in that low level of light. So she needed some music —
and he still had the brand-new CD of *The Sorcerer* in his jacket pocket!

It took him fifteen seconds to unwrap it and swap it into the
machine. Moments later, the strains of *Ring Forth, Ye Bells* filled the
downtown air. He waited another twenty seconds, then poked his nose
around the corner. Farant was now at the far end of the passage, facing
away from him and completely alone, his body language reflecting the
deep state of bliss that Toni knew he must now be in.

Any other passers-by who happened to look down the passage
might well have imagined, however, that the honourable gentleman
was in fact engaged in a far less inspirational activity ...

Good afternoon, Jeremy. It is a pleasure to make your
acquaintance, at last.

'And you are ...?'

You make call me Quo. It matters little. "A rose by any
other name ..."

'Ah — Romeo and Juliet!'

Indeed. Without the heart attack.

'I beg your pardon?'

A trifle! Forgive me. Now, honourable Jeremy, we have
chosen to unite our minds with yours because we see in
you a spirit most akin to ourselves.

'Speak in plain English, please! This is not a Shakespeare play!'

I am sorry. I have been long abroad. I shall try harder.

Jeremy, I must advise you at once that the young student
Estebán does not exist. He was simply a ruse, to allow us
to make contact with you. However, the subject which he
represented — honesty and integrity in politics — is
precisely what we do wish to discuss with you ...

'Go on ...'

We already have a general understanding, from your
French associate, Monsieur Nallier, of the aims of the
organisation you call CAMRUTH, the *Campaign for Real
Truth*. But we wish to gain a fuller appreciation of it.
Would you care to summarise your motivation for
founding it, in your own words?

'That's a very easy question! I have been adamant for a long time
(almost as long as I have been in politics) that it is intolerable to
believe one thing and to say something different. It is as simple as that!

'But whenever I discussed my convictions with anybody (good
people, mind you, well-motivated people — I am no moral snob), I
was almost universally pitied for my innocence and my idealism. And
all the obvious arguments against my belief — pragmatism and
practicality, getting things done, little white lies, keeping your powder
dry, political survival, holding on to your friends, and so on — were
then always rolled out, one by one.'

I empathise strongly with you, Jeremy.

'Thank you, Quo.

'But I never allowed that polite mockery to wear me down. I always
held my ground. Then, a few years ago, I decided I must do something
more active ...

'And I recalled that, throughout my twenties, the big breweries in
the United Kingdom had used the powerful new medium of television
advertising to persuade just about every man and boy in Britain that
the bland, mass-produced new chilled keg beer they were pouring
down their throats in all the modern pubs actually tasted as beer really
should ...

'Of course, the stuff *was* beer, in a legal definition, and its recipes
were not hidden or falsified — and plenty of people enjoyed it. Again,
I am no snob. But the methods by which it was made and kept and
served were just completely different from the traditional ways in
which cask-conditioned ales had been handled and enjoyed in Britain
for centuries past. And the flavour — well ...

'Eventually, when I was about thirty, a grass roots organisation
grew up, opposing this "untruth". It pressed, by honest and softly-
softly means, for more and more pubs to fight back against the tide of

the big breweries, and to support the smaller ones, many of which had been forced out of business. It encouraged pubs to learn once again how to handle and serve great British beers at natural temperatures — beers that *did not represent a distortion of truth*, aimed at the ill-informed or the gullible.

'That organisation was called CAMRA — the *Campaign for Real Ale*. It changed the face of British pubs once more, over a long period of time. Now, there is fine, well cared-for British beer available everywhere. There is still also the lesser stuff, of course — but the people know, and rejoice, that they have the real thing available to them once again.

'And when I remembered all that, Quo, I realised that what had been done for something as mundane as beer could and should be done for something as important as Truth. And there you have it!'

Well, Jeremy, I am seriously surprised. A humble drink is indeed not the "stuff" I would have anticipated as the inspiration for your great dreams! But the success of the CAMRA crusade which you have described is very clear — and your respectful exploitation of its popular name obviously means you have an ear for a good soundbite yourself!

'I am no fool, Quo. Honest, yes. Foolish? Never!'

So, Jeremy, let us raise our sights again, from the everyday to the sublime. A man with ideals as high as yours must have formed some fairly strong opinions about his own personality. What, in your view, are your own greatest strengths?

'Ah, that's the sort of directness I admire! Well, I think I have a very good feel for when people are, or are not, telling the whole truth. In fact, I think I almost always get it right. And I am proud to say I am outspoken on the subject of honesty in politics.'

A powerful and concise summary. Thank you. And your weaknesses ...?

'*Touché*, Quo ... *touché*. Well, to be brutally honest, I cannot forget that when I was much younger (before I had ever heard of CAMRA!),

I too was guilty of occasional mild dissimulation. This is the Achilles heel that I shall carry with me to my grave. But I have turned this failing into a crusade. I am constantly seeking to discover disciples of our cause who can indisputably claim to be "totally pure". That group of people can one day supply my natural successor as the figurehead of CAMRUTH.'

> Do you have any individuals presently in mind for that honour, Jeremy?

'Well, there are already several distinguished names on my special list. But most of them hold high office, and would probably not be in a position to accept the role, if invited. But there is one person in that group who probably *could* take on the challenge ...'

> Yes, Jeremy ...?

'Since the moment I became aware of her, Quo, and particularly since she applied to join our campaign and was naturally subjected to our deep but unannounced scrutiny, I have found nothing to reveal any flaw in the past or present integrity of Ms Hilde van Wostraap, a Dutch Member of the European Parliament. Have you perhaps heard report of her elsewhere?'

> We have indeed, Jeremy. We have indeed — and we intend to meet that fine lady ourselves, very soon. In fact, you will be able to smooth our path a little in this endeavour. We cannot ask you to organise a meeting for us; we do not yet have a firm plan for our own movements, beyond London. But I note that you employ a special campaign password for secure communication among your members — and I see that it changes each weekend. Perhaps you would like to decide, here and now, on the new password for the coming week?

'Certainly, Quo. Let me see ... ah yes ... may I suggest *Silence*?'

> Thank you, Jeremy. Will you please communicate this by e-mail to all your members, as soon as you return home today?

'I will.'

Now, would you kindly tell us a little about some of your other illustrious members? In this country, to begin with ...

'Well, Quo, I am proud to say they include a Senior Bishop of the Church of England, and also a high-ranking Government Minister ...'

How interesting. We shall return to this in a moment.

And others, from abroad? You might perhaps begin with our mutual friend ...

'Ah, Monsieur Nallier! The film actor turned politician! So well-meaning! So pure in future intent! Jean-Christophe is a fervent believer in political integrity. He has no qualms about "doing deals", but he always insists they must be totally open to scrutiny. In fact he is convinced that these days he is whiter-than-white — and he probably is! He disagrees absolutely with my position on the European Union and the euro, and he argues vociferously against me, all over Europe. But he never enters into false claims or dirty tricks — and he enthusiastically praises and financially supports our CAMRUTH work in many different ways!'

So he has no flaws?

'Of course he has! He is willing to lie through his teeth and employ absolutely any legitimate device to seduce each and every woman who catches his eye! But he does not consider this to be in any way incompatible with his political ideals — and he insists he has never encountered any practical conflicts between the two! So he now feels he is totally pure — "guilt-free", he calls it ...'

Why do you say "these days" and "now" about him, Jeremy?

'Well, he has of course conveniently forgotten the many *peccadillos* of his early years in politics. Whereas, as I said earlier, I am not able to forget mine ...'

That is fascinating, Jeremy. And I see you have some other powerful supporters ...

'Yes, Quo, our frontiers are steadily expanding. Our membership now includes two other senior European political leaders — including a head of government.'

I notice you recalling that each of those two well-known politicians is listed in your records under a false name, Jeremy. How do you feel about that?

'Ah, there is the pragmatism argument, in full relief. I do not conceal my own support for CAMRUTH. But I cannot insist on public exposure for those who do not wish it ...'

Do you detect any inconsistency of principles here, Jeremy?

'I do indeed, Quo — but not in my personal position. Any campaign benefits from powerful backing and a softly-softly approach, particularly in its early days. You need a sprat to catch a mackerel ...'

Very well. Let us now return to your British associates, Jeremy.

You are going to conduct a little experiment for us. It is a further test of a main hypothesis of our Mission: that there are, as a general rule, significant differences between what people really feel or believe, and what they actually say. This is fascinating to us because, on our own world, such differences no longer exist. Everything an individual feels or believes is patent to all around — unhideable, undisguisable, and undeniable.

'That is extremely interesting. But how can I help you with this ...?'

Simply, Jeremy, by establishing the whole truth. You are convinced of the integrity of your two most senior British members of CAMRUTH. You have a thorough understanding of their stated beliefs on many important aspects of modern life in your country. With a little help from ourselves — in fact, using a special little smile, which you have now been taught — you will be able to enquire within the minds of your associates, on any subjects you choose, and at last judge for yourself the purity of their truths.

'I am not convinced of the morality of such an undertaking, Quo. But I cannot deny that I am fascinated by the opportunities it affords ...'

Excellent, Jeremy. So be it. You will conduct your research over the next forty-eight hours (I appreciate it is a weekend, and you may require a little time to make personal appointments with the bishop and the cabinet minister), and you will report back to the lady with the pink carnation, at Eros, on Monday at noon.

* * *

Toni had quickly become bored with watching Farant talking to himself at the end of the passage. So after a while he had turned the CD player's volume down to a tolerable level (he reckoned that Gilbert and Sullivan must have done their job by now), and had simply sat down on the pavement, with his back to the wall of the office block, and immersed himself in a musical genre which until then had been completely unfamiliar to him.

But he hit the "Stop" button as soon as he heard the MP's footsteps. As Farant emerged and marched off down Haymarket on the lookout for a taxi, Toni scrambled to his feet, consulted his watch, and then peeped back down the passage. Carla was nowhere to be seen. So with plenty of time to spare before his one o'clock appointment, he sauntered back up towards Eros and took up a fine position from which to watch the girls go by.

Carla arrived on the hour precisely. She had been very grateful for the rescue mission which, unprompted, Toni had conducted so effectively, and she was now feeling suitably contrite. But she wasn't going to show it too soon. And although she and Quo were being forced once again to acknowledge Toni's true value to their operation, they had decided not to reinstate him just yet.

But she did proffer a brief 'Thank you, Toni,' and she did not argue with his suggestion that he needed some lunch. They walked off together down Coventry Street, and as they approached Leicester Square they found a café that had dared to take advantage of the mild spring weather and had placed a few weedy-looking tables and chairs on the pavement outside.

As he got stuck into a rather unappetising steak sandwich and a surprisingly good glass of real draught beer, Toni mentioned the rock concert he had seen advertised in Hyde Park.

'You know, Carla, I'd love to go to that, tomorrow afternoon, if I'm still not really needed. Will you be busy? Would you like to come too?'

Toni's fast-improving attitude, and this very personal invitation, prompted from Carla a surprisingly rapid response.

'Yes, Toni — I think I would!'

'Great! Now — what about this afternoon?'

'No plans! What do you suggest?'

'Well ... I've been to England, of course, twice before, but I've never had time to travel outside London. Seeing the publicity for the rock concert made me think of Woodstock — that was the most famous rock festival ever, in America, in the sixties — and then that made me think of the village named Woodstock here in England, which is where Winston Churchill was born ... at Blenheim Palace. It's in a beautiful area called the Cotswolds — and Stratford-upon-Avon and Oxford aren't far away. The weather's still good. We could hire a car and spend the whole afternoon out there ...'

'Now *you've* got it all worked out, Toni! It sounds perfect. Except — do you have a driving licence in the name of Rafael?'

'No, I don't. But I can't drive anyway! No, I meant we could use a private car tour service. I've got unlimited funds, so I'm sure we could organise one very quickly — everybody has their price!'

'Two lovely invitations in the space of one minute, Toni! You really are spoiling me. Let's do it ...'

Toni was inspired. He and his money worked hard for half an hour on the challenge he had set himself, and just before two o'clock a powerful car with a very nice driver picked them up on the corner of Regent Street and Piccadilly and cruised away to the west ...

* * *

They went to Woodstock first. Their driver waited in the car while they strolled around the grounds of Blenheim Palace. The passionate young student of history told Carla a little of the life and times of Churchill, and she listened with care and attention.

Then they sat back and enjoyed their Cotswold tour. The driver provided an expert commentary as he took them to Chipping Norton and on through the beautiful villages of Moreton-in-Marsh,

Broadway, Stow-on-the-Wold, Upper and Lower Slaughter, Bourton-on-the-Water and Burford.

Then they picked up the main road to Oxford.

They arrived soon after five. The sky was clear and it was still light, but dusk would be coming on quite soon. The driver handed Toni a simple plan of the streets and the colleges, and gave them a short tour around the city centre to let them get their bearings. Then, at Toni's request, he dropped them off at Carfax, the central cross-roads, and agreed to meet them back there exactly two hours later.

They strolled down the glorious High Street, branching off several times to discover one beautiful college or university building after another. The architecture and the stonework impressed Carla almost as much as they enthralled Toni.

As they approached the end of The High, they could see the elegant tower of Magdalen College rising above the river bridge. They reached the college entrance, and as they peered in through the gates, a voice behind them said quietly 'Would you like to have a quick look inside?'

'Oh yes, we would,' said Toni, turning and seeing a well-intentioned but obviously under-informed chap sitting on a bicycle. 'But the notice over there says that the college is closed to visitors now. Every college we've looked at seems to be closed by this time of day! I'm afraid we've left it all a bit late ...'

'Follow me,' said the cyclist, locking his bike to the gates. 'I'm an Old Member ...'

The gentleman nodded to the Head Porter as they passed through the lodge, and the Porter smiled back politely. And Toni and Carla were then given a personal, thirty-minute sunset tour of one of Oxford's greatest treasures. They saw the ancient and the modern quadrangles, and they admired the Chapel and the Cloisters. Finally they emerged onto the open lawns in front of the broad façade of the New Building.

'It's still called that to this day,' said their friend, who was obviously devoted to his *Alma Mater*. 'It was actually built in 1733. And beside it, over to the left — well, take a look ...'

Then Toni and Carla were delighted to see before them, in the twilight heart of the great university city, a large natural park populated with nearly forty head of beautiful deer.

There was no more time to spare. They thanked their guide profusely, and Toni offered him a small cash gift. 'No, no, no,' he said, 'it was my pleasure. But perhaps you can put it in the Appeal Fund box when we get back to the lodge. Then it will help to keep the college and its students going for another five hundred and fifty years!'

Toni dug deep, and his donation was three times the amount he had prepared as a tip. Then he and Carla hurried back up to Carfax, and made their rendezvous with only three minutes to spare.

* * *

'I really enjoyed this afternoon, Toni,' said Carla, as they sped back towards London. 'Thank you very much.' And she blew him a big kiss.

Toni blushed, of course.

'So did I, Carla. It was great to have your company. Now — how are your energy levels?'

'Still quite high!'

'OK — I really fancy a Saturday night on the town! I'd like to go down to Soho again, and have a great meal, and then find us a really good music bar — and I insist on staying with you all the time, this time.'

Carla laughed. 'It's a deal, Toni!'

Toni sat back and smiled. It had been days since Carla had seen such contentment on his face.

'And Toni ...'

'Yes?'

'Quo and I would both like to apologise to you. I should not have behaved as I did after what happened in Amsterdam — and we should have been more understanding and supportive of you after the incident in Paris. So, Toni, we are truly very sorry. We recognise how valuable you are to us, and we want you properly back in our team. And I am *so* happy to have seen Paris in your eyes ...'

Toni was lost for words, so he sat thinking for several minutes.

'Carla — how did you know about Amsterdam?'

'How did *you* know, Toni, that I needed help earlier today?'

* * *

As Toni and Carla were getting out of their car outside the Bayswater hotel ('... and don't forget the CD player, Toni!'), The Hon. Jeremy James Farant was greeting a very old friend at his London club.

Tomorrow was Sunday, so the bishop's diary was full for that entire day. But he had agreed to Jeremy's invitation, at short notice, to a little chat over an evening meal ('... mind you, I mustn't be late home — I've got a sermon to finish!'), and he was wondering with considerable interest what might have prompted the obvious urgency of this discreet *tête-à-tête*.

It was Jeremy Farant, however, who gained considerably more insight into the thinking of his equally venerable dinner partner that evening.

* * *

Toni got showered and changed, and at nine he met up with Carla outside the hotel. The Tube would be too risky for her at that hour on a Saturday night. So they grabbed a taxi. 'Covent Garden,' said Toni to the cabby, without a second thought.

They got out by the Underground station on Long Acre, and walked down James Street. The place was heaving.

'We might have some problems here,' shouted Toni, above the general background noise.

'I'll manage,' Carla shouted back. 'If they don't like what they bump into, they'll just have to cope with it!'

Toni grinned. Then he spent a few minutes searching for a good place to eat. Finally he plumped for the Crusting Pipe, down in the lower courtyard of the old market, with a string quartet playing lovely classical pieces ... a really relaxing environment. He found an empty table, asked Carla to mind it for him, then went inside and ordered his meal and a glass — 'actually, two large glasses, please ...' — of fine red wine.

'Isn't this just perfect, Carla?'

'Well, I won't say "yes", Toni, because that would mean it couldn't get any better!'

* * *

Toni's stomach was full, and the alcohol had done its work.

'Right, lover — it's my twelfth night! Let's go where the music plays on!'

They walked off down King Street, turned into Garrick Street, and then Toni followed his nose. They reached Leicester Square station, and he turned right into Charing Cross Road. When they got to Shaftesbury Avenue, he automatically turned left — his sensors must have been stuck on Piccadilly Circus. But he soon recovered his drift, and after a while he turned right again into a side street. And there he found just the sort of music bar he was looking for — with a live jazz-funk band due to start their set in only ten minutes' time!

Toni breezed up to the door. 'For two, please ...'

'Hey, man, you're jokin', right? Place is sold out!'

Toni sighed deeply, took out his wallet, and started again.

'All right — how much?' ... 'OK, but you don't frisk the lady!'

They were then shown to the very best table in the club, and they had the night of their lives together.

Toni was particularly impressed by the band's keyboard player. It was obvious he was completely blind, but he had the finest "feel" and sense of rhythm that Toni had ever heard.

And at an early point, in a break between their pieces, the singer, who was no novice himself and very versatile, but normally confined himself to the latest cool sounds and rhythms, spotted Carla sitting at the celebrity table close to the small stage, and was unwittingly entranced by her happy smile. He turned round and mouthed two words to the rest of the band. Then, as the simple but irresistible bass guitar line kicked in, he went down on one knee in front of Carla and broke into a perfect rendition of the first verse of Cliff Richard's *Living Doll*.

Toni and Carla alone were able to enjoy the perfect, wonderful, unintended joke.

* * *

They took a cab back to the hotel, arriving well after one o'clock. But they were both still in excellent spirits ...

'See you in the morning, Toni?'

'Oh, no ...' he groaned. 'Surely not that early — please!'

'OK.' Carla was in the mood to compromise. 'Twelve, then? At the pub next door?'

'Make it a bit later!'

* * *

So they lunched at half-past noon. As Toni got stuck in to his burger, and Carla enjoyed the spring sunshine, he remembered their discussion on the train to Villach.

'Carla, you never did tell me about your other hobbies — apart from your music. Indulge me, while I'm busy eating!'

'There are many things that you simply would not be able to conceive, Toni. But — well, I have noticed that here on Earth, the game of Chess seems to be popular and widespread. We have a very similar game on Dome, and I have developed fair skill at it.'

'Tell me more ...' munched Toni.

'Well, Doman Chess is played by virtually *being* all sixteen pieces at once, and experiencing in your mind all the agonies and the ecstasies of the battle, absolutely.'

'Wow! That sounds very painful! But wait a minute — you Domans can read each other's minds, can't you? So how can you possibly keep your tactics secret?'

'Yes, we can hear each other's thoughts, when we choose to, Toni ... but only in direct "line of sight" — although we do not need to actually look at one another to do so. And by the way, our leaders cannot hide themselves away and plot in secret. No Doman can hold any position of power without being regularly and literally in the public eye.'

'So do the two players at Doman Chess need to be located in separate places?'

'Yes — or at least separated by a special barrier screen.'

'That's fascinating.' Toni was really enjoying his burger. 'But are the rules the same as ours?'

'Well, I haven't made a thorough study of the differences! I really only know what you have revealed to us about your own version. It seems very similar to ours. The aim is the same — to protect your Queen against all comers, and to try and stifle your opponent's Queen ...'

'Hang on, Carla — in our game it's your King who needs to be protected, and the other King who must be defeated!'

'On Dome, Toni, it is most definitely the Queen.'

'Oh! Right ... so, you're quite good at it, eh?'

'I have had my successes. But I am no great champion. We do have one on board the *Mater*, though! Quo is an Inter-regional Grandmistress.'

'Ah, Carla, excuse me — the word is actually Grandmaster.'

'No, Toni, I do mean Grandmistress ...'

'You mean Quo is a woman?'

Carla paused, trying to gauge her Illuminator's likely reaction to what she had to say next.

'Toni — look, I suggest you swallow that mouthful straight away ... that's better — Toni, all Domans are female.'

His physical reaction was predictable, but he was naturally speechless yet again.

'But there's no need to let it worry you, *carísimo*,' said Carla, who was clearly an Inter-regional champion of understatement. 'Let's go and enjoy the concert. We'll talk more about it another time ...'

* * *

The Hon. Jeremy James Farant was eating only a few miles away, at the country house of his colleague the Cabinet Minister. Not a colleague in government, of course — Jeremy most definitely batted for the opposition. But a brother-in-moral-arms, who had been delighted with Jeremy's unexpected call suggesting a swift gin and tonic at their golf club, but had insisted on converting it into a light lunch at home ('... I've already started making it ... it's smoked salmon, if that's all right — there's far too much here for me to manage on my own!').

After the very surprising revelations, the previous evening, of the bishop's true thinking on several topics, Jeremy was not relishing this second assignment. So he had decided in advance not to smile too sweetly until the salmon and the fine salad accompanying it had been enjoyed and washed down with a very pleasant white Burgundy.

Then he switched on his new-found super-charm, and was soon even more astounded than he had been the night before.

* * *

The concert had just begun as Toni and Carla walked into Hyde Park.

It was not one of the big-name, sell-out "park parties" which had become so popular again in recent years. Many of those would be held in cities across Britain later in the summer, when there would be a fair chance of good weather to make things enjoyable for the crowd and tenable for the technicians. By comparison, today's event, dubbed the "Spring Rock Revival", was more of a warm-up for the real thing — and it was all for charity.

Very few of the acts on the bill were well-known, and many were basically "tribute bands" dedicated to the music of one or other famous rock group of the sixties, seventies or eighties. But they would all be decent musicians, and although they were not being paid any fee, they would be having fun and getting free exposure. There would also be bucket collections and raffle draws going on all day for the officially nominated charities, to boost any profit from the modest ticket price.

The event had been finalised at quite short notice, after the organisers had studied the medium-range weather forecasts and decided to take a chance. Their bet had paid off — the day was warm and dry with little breeze.

'Perfect!' smiled Toni, as they strolled across the grass towards the distant stage. He had already managed to put Carla's stunning revelation to the back of his mind for the rest of the day.

They picked up something for him to eat and drink later, and found a nice little space to sit down — not too near the stage, where it was very crowded. Then they relaxed and enjoyed the music for the whole afternoon.

At one point, some ageing hippies appeared and arranged themselves in a rough circle nearby. They were dressed for the occasion in very well-preserved old gear, and were smoking something to match. After a while, one of them looked across at Toni and Carla, smiled serenely, and intoned: 'You don't know what you missed, man ...'

'Well, I think I can imagine,' said Toni, nodding contentedly.

'No ...' said the happy hippie, frowning and shaking his spaced-out head violently in profound sympathy for the bad timing of Toni's birth. 'No, you had to be there ...'

The seating plan of the group of hippies was the exception. Almost everybody near them in the crowd was, just like Toni, facing forwards to watch the performances, and taking little notice of people beside or behind them.

But Carla was an observer by nature and profession, and she had amused herself from time to time by having a good look all around, even though the eyes of her human image were still trained on either Toni or the stage ahead. And during the third of these virtual excursions she suddenly spotted, not far behind them, a face she immediately recognised.

'Excuse me, Toni. I'm just going for a little walk on my own. Don't go away!'

'I'm not going anywhere, Carla! But don't get lost yourself!'

'I shan't!'

Carla stood up and walked carefully back between several little clumps of people. She stopped beside a woman who was sitting cross-legged on her own, wearing a wide-brimmed straw hat pulled down low over her forehead, and clearly immersed in the sounds of the music of her youth. With no human inhibitions to restrain her, Carla crouched down, smiling quite naturally, and whispered 'Hello! It's good to see you here!'

'Sshhhh ...' was the equally smiling and whispered reply. 'Thank you! But it's my afternoon off! My few hours of rest and anonymity!'

'Of course! It's just that ... well, I have a friend — you met him the other day — but he was so nervous and shy ...'

'Is he here today?'

'Yes, just over there, look ...'

'Oh yes, I do remember! OK, tell him he can come over for a little chat if he likes — but, please, very discreetly ...'

* * *

Carla and Toni finally left the park at eight o'clock, as the last band was playing and the evening spring time chill was taking hold. Toni was flying high up in the clouds, but filled with a beautiful warmth from his head to his toes. Carla was feeling pretty good, too. She wished she could kiss Toni goodnight.

Instead, she had to settle for joining him in his room at nine the next morning. He was clearly readying himself for some more touring.

'*Hola.*'

'Hi, Carla. Another nice day. Coming for a walk?'

'Yes, please. It's about time I saw a bit of tourist London with you! But you'd better do your packing first, and get a good breakfast. We'll be meeting up again with our friend Jeremy at twelve (but I won't need any music, and I won't be disappearing!) — and we'll probably have to move on very quickly after that ...'

Toni bought a pocket guide from a pavement kiosk, and they took a cab towards Westminster. He decided they should get out at St James's Park station.

'Right,' he said, still consulting his guidebook. 'That immense edifice opposite is the main Home Office building. But it says here it's not big enough for them — so they're having an even larger place built, just down the road! Now *that's* what I call moving home!'

They sauntered down towards the park and along Birdcage Walk, then up the steps into King Charles Street. Toni was still reading as he walked.

'Those are the old Cabinet War Rooms, Carla. This huge complex is the Foreign and Commonwealth Office. Now, straight ahead is Whitehall ... we'll turn left ... there's the Cenotaph war memorial ... and here's Downing Street, where the Prime Minister works and the Cabinet makes its decisions. Then opposite, there's the Department for Work and Pensions, and then the Department of Health ... and just beyond them, the Ministry of Defence. Wow — everything is so close together!'

'I wonder where Jeremy Farant is right now, Toni ...?'

'Hmm. Anyway — see over there, Carla ... from 10 Downing Street they can look across Whitehall, through the gap between those ministry buildings, and get a perfect view of the people high up in the new London Eye observation wheel!'

'But can the people in the London Eye get a perfect look down into the corridors of power?'

'Ha ha ha — you're doing it again! Brilliant!'

They still had plenty of time left. They strolled down Bridge Street to the river, and marvelled at the proud beauty of the Houses of Parliament, and in particular, Big Ben.

'That's actually the name of the biggest of its famous bells, Carla — the whole thing is officially called The Clock Tower of the Palace of Westminster.'

'I prefer Big Ben, Toni.'

'So does everybody else.'

They crossed Parliament Square ('... remember Friday's sunset, Carla?'), and took a long walk around the vibrant glory of Westminster Abbey.

Then there was time for Toni to have a quick cup of coffee before they hailed another taxi.

'Piccadilly Circus, please!'

* * *

Jeremy Farant MP arrived on time, returned Carla's smile, and nodded politely to her companion, whom he had not spotted at all during Saturday's proceedings. His well-concealed anger was not directed at them — and he knew anyway that it would be fruitless to waste his energy on mere go-betweens ...

'Mr Farant,' said Carla, 'I feel we need the privacy of our office entrance once again, but I am certain it will be in use today. May we take up your original suggestion of a local pub where you will not be recognised ...?'

'Of course, madam. Follow me, please ...'

They trooped off down Coventry Street, then turned left as they approached Leicester Square, and penetrated into Chinatown. They walked in convoy into The King's Head (the barman gave them a polite but non-committal nod of welcome), and they all sat down at the table in the farthest corner from the door. Then Toni remembered that he was in England, and after establishing that the Hon. Mr Farant would also like 'a small glass of draught beer, thank you very much,' he stood up again and went over to the bar.

Carla, however, was not keen to be a lady-in-waiting, and she quickly got on with her own job. When Toni returned with the beers two minutes later, she had already begun her second, and this time public, close encounter with the member for the leafy constituency in West London.

The barman, having seen it all over the past thirty years, took no notice of their antics whatsoever, and returned to reading his newspaper ...

Good afternoon, Jeremy. I am sorry to observe that you appear mildly distraught.

'Distraught, Quo? That's a good word for it! Mildly? No! Extremely!'

Perhaps you will explain why — in your own words ...

'There is not much to explain. It is very simple. On every subject I investigated, I found that both of my good friends were concealing their true beliefs and opinions behind a front of either watered-down or beefed-up positions. I could not find a single issue, for either of them, in which the line they have taken in public was in full accord with their real feelings! Distraught? No, that's *not* strong enough! I'm mortified!'

Jeremy, please be calm. I regret that I have caused you such distress. Of course, it is not of my making — I am merely the agent of your improved insight. I think the parallel with your free press is a fair one — and like its reporters, I can bear no responsibility for the effects of the revelations which I enable ...

'Don't be so pompous and hypocritical! You're *worse* than the press! You gave me the key to Pandora's box, knowing I could not resist it. That is just downright immoral!'

Jeremy, listen to me ... (Quo turned up the strength of the outbound transferral circuit) ... Jeremy, you have merely learned the truth. The real truth. You have seen that, with its current make-up, the human species simply cannot achieve the heights of integrity to which you personally aspire.

'Quo, I really do not feel happy about this ...'

Jeremy ... (the power went up another few points) ... Jeremy, you must concentrate on what I am saying to you. Your aims are immaculate. Your cause is the most worthy. Your purity of intent matches that of Joan of Arc. You must continue, to the best of your great and inspirational ability, to pursue everything that you believe in — for it is the way of the future. **The only way**.

But ... it *is* of the *future*.

Your peoples will never be able to achieve the integrity you seek until each and every individual has been taught — as we Domans were taught, long ago and far away, and as you yourself were taught, only hours ago — to know each other's minds. But here and now, Jeremy, is not quite the time for that great lesson to be taught on Earth.

'I feel, Quo, that I understand you at last.'

That is good. So, Jeremy — fine, honest Jeremy — you will now resume your great crusade. You will recall nothing of the extraordinary events of the past two days. In particular, your insights into the thinking of your illustrious colleagues will be exactly as they were before you began to assist us. Your faith will be completely renewed — and you will have totally lost the special powers which we lent to you.

However, if you should be asked over the next three days about the young man and woman who have twice provided us with our service of introduction, you will confirm that they are trusted freelance journalists, and *bona fide* new members of CAMRUTH.

Until the next time, Jeremy ...

The fully-restored politician blinked, and spotted the beer in front of him.

'Ah, how good of you,' he said graciously to Toni, and drained his glass in one go. 'Well, it has been a great pleasure to bump into two very contented constituents. Thank you again for paying for the beer (very fine beer, didn't you think?) — at least I can't be accused of trying to corrupt my voters! And I do hope I can count on your continued support at the next election!'

He rose, nodded politely, and walked smartly out of the bar.

'OK, Toni,' said Carla, without pausing for breath. 'Can you get straight on the phone and organise a flight to Strasbourg as soon as possible? You'll need to arrange a hotel at the same time ...'

Toni eventually completed his latest tasking.

'That was interesting,' he said, as they stood up to leave the pub.

'What was?'

'Well, considering Strasbourg is the centre of European government, it's awfully difficult to get there from this particular outpost of the empire! There's only one more direct flight today — and that's not until half-past seven. There's no meal provided. It doesn't arrive until ten o'clock local time, after we've adjusted for the European zone again — and we'll need to go out deep into the English countryside to catch it!'

'Every picture tells a story, Toni. And it *is* a pity — it means we can't do anything useful in Strasbourg tonight. I was hoping we could make contact with Monsieur Lamargue. Never mind — it should just about give me time to see you to your new hotel room, before I nip back to Belgium to meet up with Raymond again. Let's hope the flight arrives on time!'

'What happens if it doesn't, Carla?'

'We panic. But there's no rush for now. You can get yourself a good lunch after all, and perhaps have a gentle stroll back to Bayswater — and then pick up your luggage and make your way to the airport. I'll be right behind you all the way, and I'll see you first thing in the morning — we're going to have a busy day tomorrow!'

Toni would rather have spent some more quiet time with Carla straight away, to pursue her own recently-revealed, astonishing truth. But she was already hurrying off towards the nearest side alley ...

* * *

The walk back to his hotel and the journey out to Stansted Airport by tube and train were uneventful, and, fortunately, the flight to

Strasbourg did depart on time. So, well before eleven-thirty that evening, Carla was able to ensure that Toni was safely ensconced in his latest hotel room on the Place de la Cathédrale. She then made her ultra-rapid return to the bench outside Mons railway station.

Mons, Belgium

Carla was already sitting and waiting demurely when Raymond Graves arrived ten minutes ahead of schedule, at a quarter to midnight. He came like a lamb to the engagement, with no need for her to worry about supporting sound or invisibility.

I see you have produced significant results, Raymond.

'I have done my utmost for you, Quo.'

That is very clear. We are most grateful for all your labours. Would you care to sum up your achievements in your own words?

'Well, I have seen the true thoughts of many great people this week. Specifically, I have observed my immediate boss; five of my seven team colleagues; ten out of our identified group of twelve senior politicians and heads of agencies and academic bodies; and two of my three higher superiors in SHAPE.'

Raymond, that is excellent. If I include yourself (for your own true thoughts are already well known to me), I calculate that we have gained a total of nineteen full insights out of a possible twenty-four. An extremely good effort!

And the findings are fascinating, Raymond. I can see that you too are intrigued and a little concerned by them. Let me reward all your hard work by showing you how we can now proceed to draw some conclusions ...

We use a little technique known as "Truth Delta Analysis".

We take an Issue — in this case, the enlargement of the European Union — and we break that issue down into its component issues ... in this case, ten of them: one for each country applying to join the Union.

For each of these, we separately establish a particular Individual's true view: what he or she really believes, or would prefer to see as an outcome. We assign to each of those true views a starting value of 100.

Then for each one, Raymond, we look at the Pressure Points. There will always be factors working against a person's basic moral instincts on any issue.

For example, let us suppose that our individual is an elected representative of a national parliament or assembly. And that, for specific reasons associated with military stability and cash aid programmes, and being in possession of some unpublished supporting evidence, he or she feels strongly opposed to the admission of one particular country to the EU.

The following examples of pressure points might then work against that initially strong position:

- Claims by the applying country, that its relatively poor standards of healthcare and education will be dramatically improved after joining, have captured all the headlines and public opinion throughout the continent.

- The Arms Industry in the individual's home state (with factories in his or her own constituency) stands to gain major new business from the admission of the applying country.

- The members of our individual's own political party naturally hold a broad range of opinions on this issue, but the party itself has publicly come out in favour of the admission of that particular country.

- Our individual is keen to run for high office in the party in the near future.

- There have been clear hints from "friends" that if his or her true views are publicly expressed, they will be ridiculed in the press.

- And he or she has received an ill-disguised threat that much worse will happen if any of the supporting "evidence" is ever revealed ...

We can then look at the relative potency of each of these pressure points, Raymond, and give them each their own value, ensuring however that they add up to a total of precisely 100.

Then we can consider the individual's resistance to each pressure point.

If, in fact, he or she can and will resist any of them completely, then the value of those resistance factors will equal the value of the corresponding pressure points, which will then effectively be wiped out.

If the individual is however being swayed to some extent by a pressure point, its resistance factor value will be between zero and the pressure point's value.

But if he or she has in fact been completely malpersuaded by a particular pressure point, the value of the resistance to it will be zero.

Then we add up each resistance factor value and obtain a total, and we take that away from the maximum pressure points total of 100.

Now at last we have our Truth Delta — the extent to which the individual's real position is about to be swayed by the actual net effect of all the pressure points.

And, Raymond, if an individual is being heavily persuaded, that truth delta might be as much as 75 or higher ...

We then subtract the truth delta from the Real Truth value of 100 — and we see the New Truth.

But if that New Truth value is less than 50, we have an Inversion! The new truth is in fact an Untruth. And our individual comes out in favour of that country's application for membership!

'That is amazing, Quo. With a technique like that, everyone could analyse their own personal level of integrity, on any subject!'

Indeed they could, Raymond. Given sufficient honesty ...

But let us return to your findings. We have recorded nineteen full observations, including that of yourself. We have already computed, for each of those nineteen people, the pressure points and the truth deltas for each of the sub-issues. And we have summed it all up, to observe the overall extent of Untruth.

In every individual, there were inversions. In some, there were very many. Since we are discussing here the main, over-arching Issue, we are watching carefully for a predominance of sub-issue inversions in each person.

The concerns you have been feeling, Raymond, as your research progressed, turn out of course to be very well founded. We have simply applied some science to the raw data, and we agree with your own instinctive conclusions.

Inversions are, in fact, rife.

On the overall issue of enlargement of the European Union, fourteen of our nineteen subjects — almost 75%, Raymond — have been denying their heartfelt position and have been publicly presenting an Untruth.

'I really do not know what to say, Quo.'

Say nothing, Raymond. Return to your home and your work, and pursue your goals with the great integrity you have always possessed.

And please do not over-analyse yourself — for nobody is perfect. Be true to your most important beliefs. Ensure it is only the less important ones which are ever compromised.

You will now lose all your newly-learned skills of empowered collection. You will forget all the private thoughts of the distinguished people you have observed. Those people may be flawed, but they too, remember, are only human. They too are doing their very best in this most difficult world.

You will, of course, provide your honourable colleagues with a balanced and honest conclusion from your "special policy tour" — using only the information you have gathered naturally.

And finally, Raymond — we have noted with great interest that you hope to return to the USA later this year, at the expiry of your present contract ...

'Yes, indeed, Quo. I have a mind to enter politics ...'

You have a mind that may turn out to be very well equipped for that challenge, Raymond. We wish you luck and success. And, who knows, perhaps one day we may encounter you again ...

Strasbourg, France

Toni slept soundly until Carla woke him at seven.

'*Hola.*'

'Oh ... hello, Carla.'

'Good morning, Toni. Can you get ready quickly, please? We have a lot to do!'

He groaned, but dragged himself out of bed as requested. When he was dressed and alert, Carla continued.

'We must make contact with Bernard Lamargue as soon as possible. We need to persuade him to co-operate with us. I want you to phone him on the number J-C gave us, and pretend to be an investigative journalist who has gained a thorough insight into Bernard's double life. You must tell him that you are intending to publish everything you know, but you will look sympathetically on removing some of the worst evidence if he is willing to give you a little information.'

'Do I really have to, Carla?'

'I'm afraid so. Then you must instruct him to find out Hilde van Wostraap's precise planned movements for the rest of the day — and her mobile phone number, and her musical preferences. Warn him that he must do all this without alerting the lady herself, or anybody else — otherwise your revelations will be completely ruthless! And insist that you will phone back to collect this information at half-past nine precisely.'

Toni placed the call just after eight.

Lamargue's initial reaction was predictable, but Toni kept his silence, waiting for the man to agree to his demands.

And after some thought, Bernard decided to conform. It would be no great trouble to gather the information being requested, and if that reduced the impact of any revelations, all well and good. The thing to do right now was to keep this damned journalist sweet for a little while. He could try and negotiate some further concessions once he was ready to deliver something ...

'Very well — I'll have what you want by nine-thirty. But I am admitting nothing!'

Toni ended the call.

'It's done, Carla.'

'Bravo! I think you deserve some breakfast now.'

* * *

Back in his room, Toni placed his second call.

'I hope you are ready for me, *monsieur*.'

'Yes,' the bureaucrat answered. 'I have obtained what you requested. But may we discuss things a little further? After all, you cannot expect me to simply hand this information over without any proof that you *do* have the evidence you claim to have about me. Even then, how could I be sure that you *would* remove some of it from this article you are threatening to publish?'

'Monsieur Lamargue,' said Toni very coolly, 'I have obviously not made myself sufficiently clear. You will provide all three pieces of information to me, unconditionally, at once. In return, I promise to remove from my draft a number of references to long blonde wigs, particularly interesting items of clothing, and French politicians. There will be no bargaining. Now, the information, please ...'

Bernard knew he had no more cards left to play. His earlier, hurried attempt to trace the owner of the journalist's phone had revealed a false name and address in the south of Italy, so he was reluctant to pursue the caller's identity any further, or to argue any harder. He would need to do some pre-emptive damage limitation as soon as he put the phone down — and then just hope and pray the man was bluffing, and was really only seeking access to van Wostraap. If that *was* the case, Bernard might never hear of him again ...

'All right. But I am still admitting nothing. And I trust you to keep your promise.'

'Of course I shall. I am a journalist. Now, please continue, *monsieur* ...'

So Bernard Lamargue revealed to Toni that Hilde's schedule would keep her in the European Parliament building throughout that day and well into the early evening. The plenary session's agenda did however include, between one and three in the afternoon, the usual two-hour break for lunch and personal business.

Then he supplied the number of Hilde's personal mobile phone — and he understood, from a friend of her personal assistant, that in her twenties the lady had particularly enjoyed the songs of Abba ...

'Thank you, Monsieur Lamargue. If this information proves correct in every detail, you may expect considerable relief from your concerns over my plans to publish. But it will be wise for you to remain on your guard ...'

Toni switched off the phone. Carla was enthusiastically but silently applauding the undiscovered actor in him. He was simply perspiring a lot.

'Bravo, Toni. Right — let's go for a nice long walk! Wherever you like, as long as it takes us past the Carousel and the Parliament Building ... and a music shop!'

* * *

They left the hotel, and straight away Toni spotted the Tourist Information Office, just around the corner. He popped in for a street plan of the city.

First they visited the Cathedral, and he enjoyed a good look at the intricacies of another venerable astronomical clock. Then they strolled down to the bank of the River Ill, and sat together for a few minutes on a bench in the Fishmarket Square while Carla issued her briefing on the plan for a lunch-time phone call to Hilde. When Toni was comfortable with his role and his script, they wandered back towards the shops, and he stopped to pick up an early version of *Abba's Greatest Hits*.

'Now ...' he said, consulting his map, 'Place Gutenberg is just over there ...'

And they discovered the huge, beautiful Carousel which dominated the square and was to be the spot for Carla's rendezvous with Jean-Christophe that evening.

It was now definitely time for a beer, and they stopped for a while at the Pilier des Anges. Then they made a more purposeful move towards the north-east.

They passed the Hôtel de Ville, and Toni took a look round the courtyard and was fascinated to see dozens of current, hand-typed notices of Marriage Banns, pinned up inside tired old display cases. He was convinced nobody else ever came to read them.

'Look, Carla — this is how we begin the formal process of continuing our species!'

She smiled and held her virtual tongue.

They moved on, past the impressive Opera building, across the Place de la République, and up the long, leafy Avenue of Peace. Then they came to the lavish and modern Centre for Music and Conferences. Toni had a quick look round and was very impressed.

'I'd love to perform here one day!'

'I really hope you will, Toni,' said Carla, 'Now, it's nearly one o'clock — I suggest you pick up a sandwich at the cafeteria. But don't eat it yet — we have a phone call to make!'

Toni followed the path of least resistance, bought his future lunch, and then followed Carla's instructions to move back out into the grounds and sit down on yet another bench.

* * *

'OK, Toni, it's one-fifteen. Time to contact Hilde. And by the way — you'll need to quote a password straight away. It's *Silence*. We are hoping that's not a coded message telling Hilde to say nothing. There's not much we can do about it, if it is ...'

Toni held the phone up close to Carla, so that she could hear, and dialled Hilde's number.

'Hello? Mevr. van Wostraap? Good afternoon, and ... *Silence*.'

'My goodness!' Her English was perfect. 'You are not Jeremy. But you must be one of our group! What is your name please?'

'My name, madam, is unimportant. You may call me Toni if you wish. My colleague, who is with me, is known only as Carla. We have very recently joined the group — and we have some information which we believe you will be very interested in receiving ...'

'One moment — I need to make my excuses — please hold on while I move to a more private corner.' ... 'Hello? ... Yes, I can talk now — and I do understand there are some new members. But first I need to confirm that this call is *bona fide*. Please tell me precisely what type of headgear our friend was wearing when he gave you the new password ...'

Very clever, thought Toni to himself. Fortunately, he could remember the answer. 'It was a green fishing hat, madam!'

Hilde's sigh of relief was clearly audible. Then her caution returned.

'But he would not have given you my phone number!'

'No, madam,' said Toni. 'Let me explain ...'

And he told the redoubtable Hilde that he and Carla (who spoke up at one point to introduce herself) were both freelance journalists, were very sympathetic to her cause, had both been recently accepted into CAMRUTH, and had obtained her phone number by putting pressure on a certain gentleman who was aware of a conspiracy developing against her.

'What do you mean — a conspiracy?'

'We should not discuss details over the phone, Mevr. van Wostraap. We must see you in person — today. The timing is critical for our publication deadline. There are two very important topics we need to cover.

'Firstly, in our investigations we have discovered that certain people are planning to fabricate evidence which would destroy your reputation, unless you bow to pressure which they are about to bring to bear upon you — pressure to keep your silence on a particular subject. We can help you prepare to fight them.

'Secondly, we have just finished researching and drafting an exclusive set of articles (a real "scoop", believe me!) on that same subject, which we know is very dear to your heart. Our findings should give you great encouragement and ammunition for your cause. We want to share that information with you, and ask you to corroborate it.'

Fear, outrage and temptation wormed their separate ways into Hilde's honest heart.

'Very well. I must obviously meet you. But I shall have to ask for a police guard to authenticate you when you arrive ...'

'Oh no, madam — that would compromise us all, as well as our exposé! In fact, neither of us is carrying a journalist's ID — that would be far too risky. We must meet with you in secret. You must trust us — surely our CAMRUTH password and our personal acquaintance with its founder are enough?'

'I'm afraid they are not! I must check with Jeremy straight away. Call me back in ten minutes ...'

The line went dead. Carla smiled and said 'Good job, Toni — fingers crossed!'

Then they both waited rather less than patiently. At last he hit "Redial".

'Is that Toni? Very well — I am satisfied. But our meeting will have to be very late this evening. We have parliamentary debates scheduled through until midnight, although I am not planning to stay until the end. I will expect you at my apartment at eleven o'clock. Here is the address ...'

Toni looked up the street name on his map ('It's on our way back into town later, Carla'), and was finally free to devour his sandwich.

Then they walked across to the striking building of the European Parliament. Another of Carla's meeting places could now be fixed. And once Toni was satisfied that he had seen the amazing structure from all possible angles of the vast interior courtyard, they moved off and sauntered down the canal behind it, enjoying even better views of the edifice across the wide basin formed by the convergence of two waterways.

Then they came upon the Court of Human Rights.

'What an uninspiring façade for a building of such importance!' Toni exclaimed.

Carla was forced to agree.

And when they arrived at the Palace of the Council of Europe, Toni was even more vehement. 'Now that *is* what I call a façade!'

Carla was still struggling with her ability to distinguish between honest sentiment and irony. So in this particular case, she would never be quite sure of Toni's true intent.

Soon afterwards, they located Hilde van Wostraap's apartment building on the Allée de la Robertsau. Now Carla could relax — she was, at last, all set for her several imminent engagements ...

They strolled slowly back towards the city centre, as the sun and the temperature both went steadily down. They crossed the Faux Rempart canal and wandered along the bank of the central island, then began to wind left and right along the small streets hiding behind the mass of the Cathedral and the Seminary.

Just after five, Toni stopped for a beer in the Place du Marché Gayot.

When it had arrived, and they were both sitting comfortably amidst the busy outdoor tables, he plucked up his courage again.

'Carla — you did promise you would explain what you meant the other day when you said "All Domans are female" ...'

'Yes, I did. But are you sure you want me to?'

'Yes, Carla. I really do.'

'All right, Toni, I'll try — but this may not be easy for you ...'

'Our scientists know a great deal about the biological history of Dome.

'Long ago, our world was populated, as yours is today, with males and females of many different species.

'But over countless millions of your years, the critical features in the make-up of the males — the things that defined their very maleness — slowly began to deteriorate. Eventually, for many species, those features decayed away completely — and with them went the males themselves. Of course, those entire species then simply died out.

'The controlling species (we have been calling ourselves Domans for you, Toni), became fully aware that this was happening, of course, long before those traumatic final millennia for the majority of life forms. So they researched and discovered a number of possible solutions: ways to adjust the nature of the male, so as to avoid dependence on the critical, slowly failing element. And they were able to rescue many species from extinction.

'But the political and moral implications of implementing such a change across the whole of our *own* species were enormous. So the issue was repeatedly avoided and shelved — and things just got progressively worse.

'However, as the outlook darkened for the male, the Doman female began to appreciate and relish her increasing confidence and power, and to reconsider her true need for the male. This led, of course, to huge and lengthy further debate.

'To cut a very long story very short, Toni, it was finally decided, once the males had lost the will to object and any ability to implement a solution themselves, to allow them to softly fade away.

'The techniques for artificially administered fertilisation of female egg by female egg were then perfected, and were made not only more convenient and pain-free, but positively pleasurable! And the new order, of course, was now two female parents, and female children ... every time.

'And we must not forget the positive side effects. I have made no mention of the terrible combats, local and inter-regional, that had raged on Dome for most of its history. But what had always instigated and sustained all that suffering and waste? The answer, of course, was Doman maleness, the driving force of the never-ending spiral of lust and bravado, greed and war.

'In the new order, physical war itself died away quickly — although there was plenty of simple female pride and self-improving greed around to keep the New Domans gossiping and bickering, and sometimes even resorting to mild slaps! But with less and less of the energy of the species directed towards real battles, immense leaps were then made in the social and technological civilising of our world.

'One other thing happened soon after this (in terms of the time spans involved!), although we do not believe it was causally related. By a chance of fortune which you alone can understand, Toni, we were taught to know each other's minds, and to communicate in thought alone. So, like the Doman male a little earlier, the Domans' use of speech soon died out as well. Now there could be no double-talking.

'Ever since, our disputes have always resolved themselves through total openness and a simple world constitution, based on majority Consensus and the funds and flexibility needed to adapt to regular desires for change. It does not always work perfectly, of course — small power bases arise from time to time, usually associated with some hankering after a little more of a particular Doman resource — but this is once again driven by simple selfishness and greed, Toni, not futile *machismo*.

'And we adapt to those occasional events as we need to, and we thrive.'

Toni, as usual, needed to think about all of this for some time. Finally he sighed and offered a reaction.

'Well, I am surprised you have often seemed so interested in me ...'

'Are you really, Toni? Are you really? Put yourself in my shoes. Does the opportunity for a little private investigation into another way of life not seem at all attractive? If it is any consolation, I have very much enjoyed getting to know a few men — and one in particular ...'

Carla waited for a couple of minutes, but Toni said nothing more, so she stood up and left him to rest and digest.

'See you at eleven, Toni. Don't be late — and don't forget the music!'

He smiled ruefully, and waved to her as she walked away. Then he ordered another beer, and had a little snooze.

* * *

At seven o'clock he was vaguely alert again. So he went in search of dinner, and found himself back at the Carousel. Then he spotted Le Gutenberg restaurant, liked what he saw, and went inside.

An hour later he began to hunt for a music bar. He was delighted when he immediately found one, Le Bistro Jazz Club, literally just around the corner. Then he was downhearted to discover that it only had live bands on Fridays and Saturdays. But wait ... "Jam Sessions every Wednesday". Ah, no — today was a Tuesday! But if he was still in Strasbourg tomorrow evening, he knew where he would end up ...

He resumed his search, but it was either too early in the evening or Strasbourg was not the place for music bars. He suspected it was the latter. At nine-thirty he gave up and stopped off for another beer ...

* * *

At ten o'clock a rather less than dapper Jean-Christophe Nallier walked up to the Carousel on Place Gutenberg and spotted once again the charming lady with the endearing smile.

'*Bonsoir, mademoiselle.*'

'Good evening, J-C. I trust you are well.'

'I am well enough, *merci*. But I must admit to being very tired, after the exertions of the past two days. And I wish to apologise for my appearance. I have come straight from my final ... ah ... rendezvous, and I have not had the opportunity to ... well, to make myself as presentable as you deserve.'

'Oh, Jean-Christophe, you are addicted to flattery! But I will graciously accept your apology, which anyway was not necessary. Now — enough of such flirting! Let us take a little ride together on this delightful entertainment ...'

Then, once the carousel was moving round, Carla embraced her Frenchman for the last time, and disappeared. No-one was watching closely enough to notice ...

We meet once more, Jean-Christophe.

'*Ah ... bonsoir*, Quo.'

I see you have worked quite hard for us again, *monsieur*.
Please tell me what you feel you have achieved ...

'Well, I was already otherwise engaged in Paris on the nights of Friday and Saturday. So I did not arrive in Strasbourg until Sunday evening. This did not matter — I had not tried to make advance plans. I was not acquainted with any of the ten *rapporteurs* at that time, and I simply could not have found good reasons to telephone them and just ask for a meeting.'

A reasonable argument, I suppose. Pray continue ...

'So, on Monday morning I obtained a weekly pass to the Parliament building, and for the last two days I have simply been wandering the corridors and seizing my moments. It has not been easy, and I was not able to reach all the *rapporteurs*. In fact, I only managed to meet up with four of them. But I was also able to get some time with three other good alternatives, including one on each evening. I have just come from the last of those. So, in all, I have seven rather surprising results for you.'

Thank you, Jean-Christophe. A fair effort. As it happens, the results do not surprise us quite so much. But then we do have the advantage over you! Yes — as you have observed at first hand, there is a significant truth delta across the full set of results, and several occurrences of inversions.

'Do you mean there is considerable dissimulation, Quo?'

An elegant summary, Jean-Christophe. An elegant summary.

You may now relax, *monsieur*, and return to your normal affairs. You will forget everything that happened in Paris, and all that you have discovered in such a privileged way here in Strasbourg, and you will lose the power to gain such insights in the future.

May you maintain your new-found political integrity, Don Juan — excuse me, Jean-Christophe — and may your soul remain forever calm in the face of its own moral dilemmas.

Carla left Nallier to dismount from the carousel on his own. With plenty of time to spare, she took a little break before moving on towards Hilde's apartment block and her eleven o'clock rendezvous with her colleague investigative journalist.

* * *

As Carla was taking her final leave of Jean-Christophe, Toni was deciding to climb down from his barstool, which he could have sworn was beginning to revolve a little like the carousel. He walked rather nonchalantly back to his hotel to collect the CD player, then grabbed a taxi, got out at the John F. Kennedy Bridge, and made his way along to Hilde's apartment block. The fresh air had sharpened him up — a little.

He prepared the Abba CD, and waited.

'*Hola.*'

'Hiya, Carla baby! So — another good session with sweet lovin' man J-C?'

'Just a useful meeting, Toni. We obtained some more results — that's what matters.'

'Cool! Hey, I had a really great time too — let me tell you all about it ...'

'No thanks, Toni. Is the music ready? Right — sober up, and ring the bell!'

Hilde could be heard approaching the door, so Toni started the CD player.

The incongruities of a Swedish group performing *Waterloo* on that particular evening, in that particular city, and for that particular audience escaped his normally keen historical mind. And Hilde had no opportunity to enjoy the ironies. Ignoring Toni completely, she caught Carla's dazzling smile and was putty in the Finder's hands ...

Carla pointed Toni firmly at the kitchen, while she and Hilde moved into the living room and sat down together on the sofa, like two long-lost school friends suddenly reunited and with an abundance of news to exchange.

'You may turn down the volume, Toni!' called Carla. Then she reached out to their latest candidate for empowerment ...

Hilde, I am honoured to know you at last.

'You have the advantage over me!'

I apologise. Please call me Quo. I wish at once to reassure you, Hilde, that there exist, in fact, absolutely no conspiracies against you — at least, none of which we are aware! That story was a necessary pretext, to allow us to make your acquaintance with minimal delay.

'I am very relieved to hear it, Quo. But I do hope your other promise was not also false!'

I regret that indeed it was, madam. We bring no specific insights into the subjects which most concern you. On the contrary — we are here precisely to establish what those subjects are. So, would you be kind enough to explain for me the essence of your renowned political motivation ...

'The essence? You're asking me to make a very short speech, aren't you? That won't be easy. Long ones are much simpler! But all right, I'll have a go — we Dutch will try anything once!

'I am a recently elected Member of the European Parliament. I am a well-educated, well-respected, professional woman with very high ideals. I try to be a woman of equally high integrity.

'I am extremely dismayed at the overall state of affairs in the European Union. I am frustrated that I cannot personally improve anything very quickly. I am incensed by the partisan pressures that try to prevent me from freely publicising all my concerns.

'I have spoken out in general terms about many things — inefficiencies, restrictive practices, social injustices, and so on ... often against the general line of my party — but I have to admit that I have not, as yet, chosen to attack any specific major issues directly. I am awaiting my moments ...'

Will you be more specific with me, please Hilde?

'Yes, Quo, I certainly will.

'I have serious concerns across a whole range of subjects.

'I am frightened by the excessive and growing active power of certain States in the Union. I equally abhor the spoiling tactics adopted by certain States on international issues.

'I feel personally affronted by the vagaries of policy which I observe across the Union; for example, in areas such as agriculture, budgetary deficits and monetary union, to name just three!

'I am convinced that the over-rapid enlargement project which is currently underway, aiming to adopt into the Union many new Eastern European and other states, will cause huge organisational and financial problems for the Union, and will not bring benefits to any single state or to the whole for a very, very long time, and will instead reduce its cohesion still further.

'I observe great human weaknesses in the making and changing of policy. I already have my suspicions of corruption in several specific areas, and I am amassing some good evidence, which needs to be watertight before it can be exposed. I was truly hoping you would be offering me something in this area ...

'I believe that party politics are far too prevalent at the European level. This should be the stuff of the national parliaments (as it always was and is!). Decision-takers such as myself in the European Parliament should be far more independent — much more able to reflect what their constituents want and need, and to do it more dynamically, without all the extra baggage of one or other party to hold them back.

'I feel intimidated and almost powerless in the face of the increasingly dominant influences that masquerade as Corporate Public Relations. The continent is run by the corporations! Maybe that's the way it always has been, for centuries even — but it is not the way it should be. If this is allowed to continue, the power of a few technologically superior, ruthless, and arbitrarily fortunate commercial institutions will one day be insurmountable!

'And finally (you asked for the essence, Quo, and that is what I have given you), I deplore the increasingly "presidential" style of the political leaders of the most powerful European States. Politics and government here is being turned into a channel-hopping pastime, a scramble for the best-rated soundbites, a "Reality TV" game of survival, a subject for humorous on-the-spot *reportage* slotted in before the football footage. Do you think I'm joking? Try to imagine what further varieties of dumbing-down media might evolve from TV, the Internet, and the picture phone! I dare not think how our great national publics will actually select (and flippantly discard) their leaders in fifteen years' time, let alone fifty!'

> Thank you, Hilde. A most compelling speech! I conclude that you are indeed a woman of great integrity, for I am able to observe that there is a near-perfect match between what you truly feel and believe, and anything you have ever stated in public.
>
> However, your equally great morality, as you have said, still awaits its day. It is strikingly clear to me that, on the many subjects which you have just enumerated, and on which you feel so very strongly, you have not yet committed yourself publicly in any way.
>
> I suspect that on most of these issues you will sooner or later have to speak out, or burst. But up till now, you have not broken silence ...

'You are quite correct, Quo. But do you hold me in some way guilty for this?'

> I do not know, Hilde. I really do not know ...
>
> What I do know, however, is that our anticipation of finding a politician who may one day qualify also as a saint has been rather over-encouraged by the reputation that has preceded you. You have done harm to nobody, Hilde; you possess the strength of character to speak out when you dare; and your instincts are purer than most others'. You rate very highly in our Truth Delta Analysis — you have rarely, if ever, actively presented even a minor Untruth. But there are so many issues of note on which you have chosen simply to present no public position at all ...

'I need time, Quo.'

> Do not let that monster slow you down, Hilde. Be brave, and be brave soon. And take no prisoners.
>
> Now, madam, to our second reason for engaging you tonight.
>
> We are fully aware that, tomorrow morning, the European Parliament will conduct its formal debates on the applications of ten countries to be admitted to the Union.
>
> We note that you will not only be attending the full debate, but that you are expecting to have the floor, albeit very briefly, during the final hour, which is allotted to individual Party Members' speeches.
>
> Perhaps you have a mind to speak out strongly on this issue for the first time. But that is not our concern. We require from you a different contribution, as I shall now explain ...

As soon as Hilde had been released from Quo's intellectual hold and Carla's electronic grasp, she jumped up, hurried into the kitchen, and apologised profusely to Toni for having left him sitting in there.

'I don't know what came over me!' she said. 'But quite honestly, I really can't remember much of what we've been talking about. I must be very tired. It's a hard life, governing a whole continent!'

Toni laughed politely at her joke, picked up the CD player, and ushered his companion towards the door. Hilde van Wostraap shook his hand, then turned to Carla — but the Finder's hand was already safely stored in her coat pocket. So Hilde merely smiled and nodded, and Carla said 'Goodnight, my friend. Thank you for all your help — and I wish you luck for tomorrow ...'

* * *

As nine o'clock approached on the morning of Wednesday 9 April 2003, an uninvited and unobserved guest pursued the stream of MEPs proceeding into the chamber of the European Parliament. And Carla then took up a ringside seat for the entire debate that followed.

First, the overall report on enlargement was presented.

Next, one after the other, the ten nominated *rapporteurs* summarised the owning committee's recommendations on the application of each candidate new entrant to the European Union.

Then, after various formalities, came the turn of the Members to speak. Carla waited with a radimote's equivalent of some trepidation.

When her moment arrived, Mevr. Hilde van Wostraap of the Netherlands rose to her feet.

Her speech was short, but impassioned, and she did indeed dare to go a little further than ever before in her criticism of certain EU institutions and procedures. But on this very special occasion she would have little time or opportunity to expand her arguments. As her own allotted deadline approached, she turned to embrace the entire assembly in her gaze.

'So, my dear colleagues, as we proceed towards these momentous decisions, I ask you simply to look into your hearts, in silence, for just a few short moments ...'

In the extended and highly pregnant pause that followed, as all eyes were fixed upon her, Hilde smiled a most reassuring smile. And she then rapidly recorded in her own mind the true views, on the issue of enlargement of the European Union, of every one of the five hundred and forty-three other MEPs seated in the parliament's chamber on that historic morning.

At twelve noon, the debate was concluded and the formal votes were counted. The results were very different from those of the Doman straw poll taken only minutes earlier ...

* * *

Toni had slept in very late that morning. He had finally emerged for a light breakfast in a nearby café just before eleven o'clock, and then strolled aimlessly and quite happily around the city centre for two hours. Then he had discovered the special business lunch menu at the Au Dauphin restaurant, and enjoyed, for the first time in his life, a wonderful fillet of zander fish, followed by a superb apricot tart.

Then he had followed the instructions issued by Carla the night before, and taken a taxi back out to the north-east.

By two o'clock he was standing beneath the serried flags outside the Parliament building, alongside the many other people who had come there to recognise, in one way or another, the huge significance of this day for the whole of the European continent ...

* * *

Quo had allowed Hilde an uninterrupted lunch this time. So the MEP waited until precisely two o'clock before again making her excuses to the colleagues at her table and hurrying off to the ladies' room. Carla pursued her closely and unseen.

Just as Quo had instructed at the end of her previous engagement, Hilde went straight to the basins and washed her hands. Then she turned around. Carla was sitting, smiling, inside one of the cubicles. Hilde stifled a laugh, walked across in silence, and closed the door behind her ...

> Thank you, Hilde. Your performance in the debate was admirable, and your mission for us was completely successful.

'I am rather surprised at what I appear to have discovered, Quo ...'

> The understatement of a cautious politician, Hilde! I would expect most people to find the results quite chilling. However, they have not surprised us. In terms of Truth Deltas and Inversions, they are closely in keeping with all of our previous findings ...

> But I do not wish to burden you with this knowledge any longer than is necessary. So it will now be removed completely from your mind. You will return to your lunch with no greater insight than any other fellow MEP into the true feelings of this parliament on the issue of enlargement.

> We thank you sincerely, Hilde, and we humbly encourage you to continue your saintly ways.

'Saintly? My goodness, Quo, I am no saint. I simply try to take guidance from my own heart, and inspiration from those whose integrity I most admire ...'

> Oh? May I be so bold as to ask you to reveal the source of your greatest inspiration?

'But you are teasing me, Quo! You have of course already observed this, have you not? Although I have never met or even corresponded with the gentleman in question, I have, for a long time, held the Prime Minister of Spain in extremely high regard ...'

> Yes, I can indeed see that — and it is a fascinating insight.
> I thank you once again, Hilde. Go now ... and may you
> find your peace with the world before it is too late.

* * *

Carla joined Toni under the fluttering flags.

'Right, Toni. I have a short meeting to attend. Can you get a taxi straight back to the hotel and wait for me in your room? I shan't be long — and I suspect I might bring back some rather special news for you!'

Handler's Studio, *Mater*

The Captain, for her own good reasons, had called for the latest progress meeting to be held in the Handler's Studio.

The first item on the agenda was a review by Quo of the full set of Insights gained to date.

'Over to you, Number Two.'

'Thank you, Captain,' Quo reflected. 'Let me start by reminding you all that we have addressed three separate topics during this initial major exercise.

'The first could be described as our relatively informal observation of a small set of individuals, which has provided us with a good range of insights into their overall levels of integrity. As you know, the ten people we investigated directly from the *Mater* were Antonio, Giuseppe, Salvatore, Eva, Josef, Mireille, Raymond, Jean-Christophe, Jeremy, and last, but not least, Hilde.'

The Captain interrupted Quo's train of thought with her own. 'Yes, Number Two — we did indeed know this. Please move along ...'

'Certainly. Our broad conclusion on the general integrity of these ten subjects, using the multi-issue variation of Truth Delta Analysis, is that, with one or two notable exceptions, they demonstrate surprising high resistances $[R]$ to pressure points in general $[P]$, and correspondingly low truth deltas $[P-R=D]$. There are only occasional inversions, where $[T-D=N<50]$, and in nearly every case we therefore observe a human individual for whom Untruth is a rare characteristic indeed.'

'Do you mean,' deduced the Captain, 'that most of those people are basically very honest?'

'I do, ma'am.'

'Then kindly say so. Please go on ...'

'The second topic,' Quo continued, 'was our brief observation, through secondary engagement, of the general integrity of two senior public figures who expressly purport to maintain extremely high standards. The results indicated that there may be major levels of subconscious truth inversion occurring across a wide spectrum of persons in positions of high power and influence.'

'You mean that many leaders may be deceiving themselves and others, often without always realising it?'

'Another excellent summary, Captain.'

'It comes with practice. And the results of the third investigation, please ...'

'The final topic, ma'am, has been our study of the specific issue of the proposed enlargement of the European Union. For this we have gathered two types of data.

'The first set comes from the three individuals we observed directly on this particular issue: Raymond, Jean-Christophe and Hilde.

'The remaining information derives from the empowered observations conducted by those recruits. Raymond achieved a total of eighteen insights from a group with a wide range of interests in this issue; Jean-Christophe produced seven from a group focused tightly upon it; and Hilde's triumphal observation of no less than five-hundred and forty-three souls, each one having only a slightly less sharp focus on the issue, may prove enough to allow us to complete the exercise.'

'But are there not some overlaps in this data, Number Two?'

'There are indeed, Captain. We must remove from Hilde's results the duplicated views of the seven subjects already questioned in greater depth by Jean-Christophe.

'Summing it all up, then, and including the views of the three empowered agents themselves, we have a total of precisely five hundred and sixty-four separate true opinions on enlargement, which we may then contrast with the same number of publicly stated positions.'

'And the conclusions which you therefore draw, on the question of Truth ...?'

'I recognise, ma'am, that you wish me to be succinct. Therefore I shall be. There are huge variations between three quite separate sets of measurements: the views which, over time, our individual subjects have publicly expressed; the true private views of each one of them, as gathered through our focused observations; and the specific formal voting patterns of the vast majority of our subjects, at the end of today's enlargement debate ...'

'Succinct, I believe you suggested, Number Two ...'

'... and we find ...' (Quo had almost ignored the Captain's interjection) '... we find that, applying the generalised formula $[T-(P-R)=N]$ ...'

'Number Two!'

'... we find that inversions are prevalent across the whole picture, and the overall measured level of Untruth is ... approximately ... sixty-two percent!'

'Meaning that nearly two-thirds of all the stated positions or opinions of our subjects are actually the opposite of what those subjects truly believe?'

'Yes!'

'You appear to have reached the end of your conclusions at last, Number Two.

'I shall now consider for myself the validity of our sample.

'As you are well aware, any survey with about one thousand subjects usually gives a result that is within three percentage points of the findings which would have been obtained even if many hundreds of thousands of samples had been taken.

'I would ideally have preferred us to achieve at least a thousand subjects — particularly as we have hardly been selecting them at random!'

A polite smile crossed the faces of all present.

'However, we have other pressures on us, as you are all well aware. Our actual sample of less than six hundred reduces the accuracy of any conclusions we might draw. The likely variation from the true picture will be closer to plus or minus 10%.

'Our unadjusted findings indicate an overall level of Untruth of some 60%. I believe we must be conservative — or generous to our subjects, if you wish —' (another set of smiles filled the studio) 'and must reduce this value by some 10%, to allow for this potential sampling error.

'So, Number Two, are you willing to agree that we may consider the overall level of observed Untruth to be, rather intriguingly, at least 50%?'

'I cannot question your logic, Captain!'

'In that case, we may at last take our attention away from the rather uninspiring topic of EU enlargement! I consider the "hearts and minds" element of our Insight Gaining Aim to have been adequately addressed. Number Two, you will formally document all relevant data, findings and conclusions and present them for approval.'

'Ma'am.'

Attention turned to the Chief Surveyor.

'Chief, you will now finalise the excellent provisional action plans that you have been developing. We shall proceed, at a time in the very near future, to a much-increased intensity of detailed Fact Gathering. We shall also, at that time, implement our controllers' instructions on a revised focus for Insight Gaining, targeting geophysicists and other such specialists in Earth Sciences. Needless to say, Chief, you will personally mistressmind this next phase.'

'Of, course, ma'am,' reflected the Surveyor, a real smile on her face at last. 'I am relishing the challenge!'

The Captain addressed Quo once again. 'Which brings me to offer my formal thanks, Number Two, for your fine work in the management of our first major phase of discovery.'

Quo nodded, almost modestly.

Then, with a rascally smile on her face, the Captain turned to Carla.

'We shall of course be deploying a different Handler for the next phase — one who is a little less of an "artist" and slightly more of a "scientist" ...'

Carla smiled politely — she knew this compliment was honestly given and also very accurate.

'... and we shall recruit a similarly specialised new Illuminator to assist her. I think a certain young man in Venice could prove very suitable ...'

Carla knew this change would also be essential, but it still came as something of a shock.

The Captain continued.

'I have held this meeting in your studio, Handler, to recognise your invaluable role in our work to date. You will receive an exceptional achievement award, for your highly effective management of Toni, and for your sustained devotion to duty (and to your sherpa and Illuminator!). You will soon be able to enjoy an extended period of rest and recuperation ...'

'I am most grateful, ma'am.'

'And we shall now allow Toni to return home, with an irrefutable cover story.'

As Carla pondered her several reactions to the Captain's inevitable announcements, the applause of her colleagues rang out loud and completely sincere.

'Now — is there any other business?'

'Yes,' thought Carla. 'I should very much like to be able to offer Toni an award, as well. But I realise how difficult that would be, in practice ...'

'An excellent idea, Handler. I suggest that you simply follow your own fine instincts.'

'Thank you, Captain.'

'So — is there any further business?'

'Yes,' mused Quo. 'There is one more informal opportunity for Insight Gaining which I cannot resist proposing ...'

After a little careful consideration, the Captain and Carla both agreed to their colleague's polite and compelling suggestion ...

Changing Landscapes

Toni had just arrived back in his hotel room. Carla was already waiting for him.

'*Hola.* Time to get packed again, Toni — you're going home!'

'What, to Bilbao? Right now?'

'No — we're going via Madrid. Quo has one last special job for you there ...'

He got on the phone once more, and soon had a reservation on the direct flight departing at 1845.

'Ah, yes — hold on, please ... Carla, will I need a hotel too?'

'Yes, you will — and please choose a top class one, in the city centre! You deserve some luxury, and you won't have all that free money for much longer — and we'll need to use its business services tonight.'

The hotel room was booked at once, along with a taxi to the airport at four-thirty.

* * *

By three-fifteen, Toni, who had been very quiet since finishing the call, was nearly ready and was about to re-pack the drawing materials from Paris at the top of his case.

'Toni ...'

'Yes, Carla?'

'We have a whole hour to spare. I'd like to give you something back for all you have done for us ...'

He blushed as usual.

'No, Toni, be sensible! Some things can never be. I was going to ask if you would like me to help you draw a vision of Arunura.'

'Oh! ... oh, yes, Carla, I can't think of anything I'd like better at this moment ...'

'Shut the window, Toni — there's far too much traffic noise!

'That's better. Now set up your favourite CD, but turn the volume down very low.

'Close the curtains. Dim the lights.

'Take your coloured pencils and your sketch pad, and sit comfortably in your chair.

'Be tranquil, Toni. There is no rush. I will tell you when you need to finish.

'Start your special music.

'Now close your eyes a moment or two, and float in a silky sea ...'

When Toni opened his eyes again, Carla had disappeared. In her place she had revealed a glorious, vibrant perspective on the warm lagoons and the sunset skies of her mysterious homeland. Toni's coloured pencils at once set to work ...

* * *

When the songs of his muse had come full circle, and when only twenty minutes remained before the arrival of the taxi, Toni's exquisitely-disguised model whispered 'It's time to finish off now. When it's done, just close your eyes once more ...'

Then Carla un-made from her image of Arunura, and re-made again in the image that Toni so loved.

'*Hola.*'

Toni emerged from his long trance, looked down at his sketch pad, and smiled a very happy smile.

'Please may I see it, Toni? Oh, that's absolutely perfect! You really are becoming an inspired artist ...'

'I like it too, Carla!'

'This is my gift to you. *Gracias*, Toni — with all my heart!'

* * *

The taxi was already waiting as they left the hotel. A little over an hour later, Toni was fully checked in for his flight — he had decided on an upgrade from economy class, just for once — and was walking through to the departure lounge with his unseen companion.

At Carla's special whispered request, he went over to the bookshop and bought several Spanish newspapers, and a street plan of Madrid. Then he noticed a wide-screen TV running a non-stop news programme.

The story being featured, as he sat down to watch, was that afternoon's overwhelming vote of acceptance of all ten new candidate countries into the European Union.

'In each of the ten separate votes on enlargement,' the reporter was saying, against a backdrop of the very flags beneath which Toni had been standing only hours before, 'a small number of individual votes were cast against the admission of the applying nation. Some states suffered only very minor levels of such "rejection". There was stronger opposition to the applications of certain other countries, mainly on specific long-running issues of human rights. But even in those cases, the European Parliament's voting in favour of acceptance dramatically outweighed any dissent ...'

The anchorman took over and began to introduce the next item. Before Toni even knew what the subject matter would be, he could tell that the presenter felt much more comfortable with the "interest level" of what was to come. No doubt, he thought, it will be a trivial video feature on the private life of some cheap sports "celebrity" ...

He was wrong. The picture changed to a clip of his own Prime Minister emerging from his car in front of the Spanish Parliament building. He was surrounded by banner-wielding journalists and photographers. They had all downed their notebooks and cameras in protest against the deaths "in action" of two of their colleagues, who had been reporting on the invasion of Baghdad when a shell burst into their hotel ...

Toni suddenly realised he was a little out of touch. He had been on the road for over two weeks, and had not read a single paper or watched any TV news throughout that time. He checked his watch. Still ten minutes before boarding. He waited to see what else was going on ...

The anchorman was back, looking mildly flustered but exhilarated.

'And we have just received these startling images — there is no commentary yet, I'm afraid ...'

The screen was suddenly and silently filled with dramatic footage of the coalition forces' invasion of central Baghdad, followed by a long and loosely edited sequence showing the progressive toppling of a huge statue of the ousted Iraqi leader.

Toni boarded his aeroplane on schedule at six-fifteen.

Madrid, Spain

Toni travelled back to his own homeland in warm business class comfort, and started work on his final task for Quo by carefully scanning each of his newspapers and taking occasional notes. Meanwhile, Carla had a cold but visually stimulating night flight. They both arrived at Madrid Barajas at ten to nine, and they both separately passed through Spanish customs without incident. By ten-thirty they were safely installed in Toni's luxury hotel.

He still had plenty of energy left, after his late start that morning and a little doze near the end of the flight, so he did not complain about Carla's request for him to spend a further hour at work in the hotel's Business Centre, using the Internet, the TV and the latest evening newspapers.

By the time he had finished, he had established a quite accurate picture of the likely movements of the Spanish Prime Minister for the whole of the following day ...

Carla had left Toni to concentrate on his task, and had been very impressed with what she had observed. But just before midnight, once the only other businessman using the Centre had gone off to bed, and Toni was gathering together all his notes and printouts, she turned up behind him once again.

Then, using their street plan of Madrid, they methodically discussed the best locations for possibly catching sight of the Prime Minister the next day, as he moved from one engagement to another. And finally they built their shortlist of three opportunities: one in the early morning, one mid-afternoon, and the other late in the evening ...

'Excellent,' said Carla. 'We could not have wished for a better situation, Toni. Thank you once again.'

Then, before he realised what was happening, she reached over towards him and, for the first time since their enforced engagement on the bank of the River Seine, she once again took his head in her lovely hands. And now it would be his turn to become fully empowered by Quo ...

* * *

The next morning, with Carla in unseen tow, Toni arrived ahead of time at the first location they had selected, and managed to find a position not too far from where he expected the Prime Minister to emerge from his initial meeting. And they had judged it well. But the politician was obviously running rather late, for he hurried out of the building and straight into his waiting car without even acknowledging the small groups of people standing some distance away.

Toni shrugged his shoulders and took a taxi to the second location they had chosen. With much more time to spare, he was able to make a better plan. On this occasion, he reckoned, he should be able to get within about fifty metres, if he was lucky — but he would need to be there well ahead of their predicted moment. Fortunately, however, he still had plenty of time for a nice lunch ...

* * *

It was two o'clock, and Toni had installed himself at his new personal observation post, his eyes glued to the main entrance of the building housing the ongoing meeting. Carla was watching from a different vantage point, with similar anticipation.

Almost an hour later, the Prime Minister finally emerged from the front door and walked slowly, in the middle of a tightly-knit group, towards his waiting limousine. Apart from one or two individuals who were booing noisily and shouting various protests, the crowd was very supportive and was cheering and applauding him. He reached his car, then stopped to look directly towards them, smiling and waving cheerfully. And the humble citizen Rafael Luis Barola returned his leader's smile with a supremely irresistible one ...

Toni caught a fleeting glimpse of some honest opinions of four or five of the politician's close aides and bodyguards, before the Prime Minister himself fell captive to his temporary new charm. Then, in no time at all, the newly-empowered observer gained a complete insight into the purest thoughts of the Spanish leader on the question of enlargement of the European Union.

* * *

Carla was once again waiting for him in his room.

'You have a result, I assume, Toni!'

'Yes, Carla ... I really think I've learned the truth — on Day 17!'

'Well done, my friend. I am very proud of you. And ... ah, I think Quo would like a few more words now ...'

Carla walked over to him, reached out to him, then paused for a moment and smiled a sadder smile than he had ever seen before. It brought a lump to his throat and moisture to his eyes, and he knew at once that he would not see her again ...

> That was excellent work, Toni. You have, as usual, affirmed our great faith in you.

'Thank you, Quo. So, if I'm going home soon, have you finished your work too?'

> Only the initial phase. We feel we have now learned enough about your leaders and their integrity. We are ready to move on to other areas of discovery ...

'But you've only been here just over two weeks — and you've only met up with a dozen people at most!'

> We have learned the thoughts of many others, Toni. Enough to satisfy us.

'I told you I was not a statistician, Quo. But I am a historian of sorts! I still don't accept that your conclusions can possibly be valid. You just haven't studied things broadly enough, or for long enough!'

> You must trust me on the statistics. But let us look for a moment at your thoughts about History. You place a lot of faith in History, don't you, Toni?

'Yes, I do. It is our reference book for civilisation. We must turn to it at all times, to remind ourselves of what can go wrong if bad or selfish decisions are made by our leaders ...'

How much trust do you place in the "stories" part of your "Histories"?

'What do you mean, Quo?'

You know precisely what I mean, Toni. I mean Varieties of Truth. I mean the documenting of events as people wish them to be remembered, not as they necessarily were. I mean the pure invention of a story which becomes a history. I mean the errors always introduced by translation from ancient to modern languages, or even between current ones. I mean the purposeful re-writing of history by historians or zealots with their own world views or aims. I mean the unintended corruption of individual memory over time ...

'I think you are being very unfair.'

Am I really? Did you never give your parents a less than perfect explanation of your behaviour? Did you never make a wrong translation of language at school? Did you simply write boring chronologies in your history essays, or were you not encouraged (and happier) to analyse and interpret events as you understood them? And have you already forgotten your own romantic and false recollections of the Jardin du Luxembourg, last week? That was after a gap of only ten years ...

'What are you trying to do to me, Quo?'

I am certainly not trying to destroy your faith, Toni. I am only encouraging you to constantly question it. Our own experience on Dome, the account of which has been handed down by pure memory, incorruptible by false reports, is that before we learned to know each other's minds, anarchy ruled in the land of History, and Truth was always potential victim to any lie that could be invented.

Be careful with the truth, Toni. It is rarely what it seems. As I must now dramatically demonstrate ...

You have already lost your new and special powers of observation. And by the end of the day, you will have steadily forgotten everything that has happened since you returned to your apartment on that special Monday.

In its place, you will remember a very different course of events, triggered by the actions of the police at the café that afternoon. You were very wise to ignore your great-uncle's advice and keep all your personal documents safely, even without our encouragement.

You will find you know exactly what to do next, to retrieve your old self. And when that is done, Toni, your new story will then be, for you, the absolute, immutable truth. This will be your immaculate defence, when you surrender yourself to the authorities back in Bilbao.

We shall watch over you, to ensure that you emerge from their investigations completely innocent and free. If there are any problems, we shall help you to resolve them. So you must have no fear. Just tell the story we shall now teach you. It is, of course, just another variety of truth. But it must always be your true story.

And Carla promises to speak to you again before she leaves.

Goodbye now, Toni. May you maintain, in your life, the stability you relish so much ...

He was back in his hotel room, all alone. And he knew without any doubt that he was, once again, none other than Antonio Felipe Murano.

It was four o'clock. He phoned the concierge and asked for information on train services to Bilbao. There were only two real options — to take a night train and be there at seven-thirty in the morning, or to wait until the next day and arrive in Bilbao at half-past four in the afternoon. He decided to get on with his final tasks, and aim to catch the ten forty-five departure that evening ...

Then he began the process of systematically erasing the story of Rafael Luis Barola.

* * *

He went back down to the hotel's Business Centre, collected a large quantity of unmarked envelopes of various sizes, and bought a small pair of scissors, some elastic bands, and a good supply of postage stamps.

He pulled the rucksack out of his suitcase, and changed into the cleanest of the old shirts, pullovers, trousers, underwear, socks and shoes that had been kept in it since his last day in Venice. He left all the other old clothes inside the rucksack, along with his shaver. Then he threw in his toilet bag.

He rolled up his five precious drawings inside the rest of the blank sheets from the sketch pad, and secured them with elastic bands. The roll also went into the rucksack, along with his Spanish-language art book.

He picked up his own precious CD and saw Janis' personal note on the front cover. 'That'll be all right,' he said to himself. 'She often signs CDs ordered through her web site, if you ask her to.' It went into the rucksack.

He cut Rafael's passport into tiny shreds, and distributed them across several individual small envelopes, which he then sealed and screwed up. But he kept back the photograph and placed it carefully on the table next to his wallet.

He removed the SIM cards from both of his mobile phones, placed each one on the floor in a large envelope, and crushed them underfoot. Bits from each set of remains went into several more envelopes, which were all then stuck down and screwed up.

He took both of the phones themselves, wiped them clean of fingerprints, sealed each one in its own large envelope, and crushed them as well.

He pulled the street plan of Rome out from the back of his pocket guide, and tore off the part where his great-uncle had written his address. That scrap of paper, and then the map itself, went into two further sealed envelopes.

He stuffed all the envelopes he had prepared into a hotel laundry bag. Then the music magazine and all the newspapers were put into a second bag, along with the old brown envelope, the cover of the sketch pad (the text was in French), the envelopes used to destroy the phone cards, and the printouts from the previous evening's Internet research. Both laundry bags were then stored at the top of his rucksack.

He kept back a large quantity of euro notes, totalling a little less than the amount he'd already had in his wallet when he left Bilbao after making his two big withdrawals. This was far more than he would need for the rest of the day and his train fare home.

He wondered for a moment just what he should do with all the other cash — and then he had the answer. The rest of the euro notes, and the remaining sterling and Czech bills, were placed in a large envelope, which he addressed to his favourite singer's favourite charity, and endowed with more than enough postage stamps.

He put his few euro coins into his trouser pocket. His Czech and British coins were left for the hotel maid.

The sheet of paper recording Rafael's web ID and password went into his trouser pocket, along with the scissors and elastic bands, the pages on which he had written the co-ordinates of all the position fixes, his notes on the Prime Minister's anticipated movements that day, and the scraps of paper recording the address of the Prague jazz club and the various phone numbers of Giuseppe Terleone, the son of his friend in Prague, and Mlle Mireille Daurant.

His wallet, now containing only his own cash and plastic cards, his other personal papers, the postage stamps and, temporarily, Rafael's passport photograph, went into the inside pocket of his old jacket. In the other pockets he stored the stamped envelope full of cash, his bunch of keys, his old pen and pencil, his comb, his own passport and identity card, plenty of spare envelopes, and Rafael's doomed shades and bank card.

He then placed all of Rafael's new clothes, plus the hated cagoule and baseball cap, into the wheeled suitcase. He picked up the GPS unit, erased all the stored "marks", and did a full system reset. Then he did his best to wipe his fingerprints off the GPS itself, the mobile phone charger, the marker pen, the drawing pencils and the eraser (they all had French writing on them), all the other city street plans and guidebooks, his British-published paperback, the outrageous cheap sunglasses, the CD player and all the CDs that he had purchased, and the various spare batteries that he had acquired. All of these were added to the suitcase, which he carefully wiped clean.

Then he put on his old jacket, and with his rucksack on his back, his case rolling behind him, and Rafael's glasses still on his nose, he left his room and checked out of the hotel, using his alter ego's bank card and signature for the very last time.

* * *

He took a taxi straight to the address of a Third World charity shop which he had obtained from the concierge. He wiped the handle of his suitcase with a handkerchief, left it wrapped around the handle, trundled the case inside, let them open it for inspection, and then discreetly pocketed his handkerchief and left without saying a word.

Then he sat down on a pavement bench. He cut Rafael's bank card into a dozen pieces, each of which he put into a different envelope. These were then screwed up tightly and stored in the laundry bag along with all the others.

He then strolled around the city streets at random, making the acquaintance of a very large number of Madrid's roadside litterbins. At every second or third one, he stopped and discarded a single screwed-up envelope from the bag. When this was finally empty and thrown away, along with the wiped-clean scissors and the elastic bands, he sought out a larger bin, and dumped the other big bag full of newspapers and general rubbish.

Next, he went to a kiosk and bought a box of matches. In a quiet side street, he took the photograph from his wallet and the various sheets of hand-written notes from his trouser pocket. He set fire to each of them in turn, letting the ashes fall into further spare envelopes. He then screwed up all of those and found yet more litterbins for them. The box of matches was dumped as well. Finally he threw away the few remaining hotel envelopes.

He stopped outside an optician's shop, and removed Rafael's glasses from his nose and the matching shades from his pocket. He wiped both pairs clean, then dropped them into the shop's charity collection box.

He found a post-box and sent off his anonymous donation to Janis Ian's charity.

Then he checked and re-checked his rucksack and all his pockets. All clear. All just Antonio. Now he felt he could have a little break, and the glass of beer he had been looking forward to all afternoon.

Once he was refreshed, he found a hairdresser's. He had a wash and trim, and another application of a matching dye. Then he asked them to shave his beard and moustache off completely.

He was certain he had completed his chores in Madrid. He took the metro to Chamartin station, ate a good meal, drank a couple more very nice beers, paid cash for his train ticket, and boarded the 2245 departure for Miranda de Ebro and onward to Abando station, Bilbao.

Communication II

CP8, third-born of the latest set of quins from Dome, had come at last within range of the *Mater* and sent, without hesitation, the message carried by each identical sister:

TimePoint/Ref: 336.657.7754.35 / SC-IME-MI-R2

To: Star-craft Captains, Initial Missions of Exploration

Subject: Mission Instructions — Revision II

BACKGROUND

1. Most recent Council of Regions debated new proposals.

2. Reduced-scope proposal for extension to objectives of Initial Missions, now entitled "Limited Unharmful Exploitation Imperative" (LUEI), presented and accepted. See Orders following, including new explicit Imperative Priorities. Principal features of LUEI:

- Identification of deposits of certain minerals for which specific need exists in one or more Regions

- Identification of any resources critical to New World and in under-supply or over-supply (as basis of potential future negotiations)

- Preparation for limited exploitation experiments

- Optional conducting of limited exploitation experiments (Captain's discretion to commence)

3. Proposals for associated changes to existing Imperatives presented and accepted. See Orders following, including new explicit Imperative Priorities.

ORDERS

4. Further revisions to Observation Imperative, immediate effect. Imperative Priority = 1.

- Mapping and Modelling Aim merged with Fact Gathering Aim. Combined Aim to be even more strongly focused on physical resources of each New World: in particular, on gathering full details of any known deposits of mineral groups A72RW, C98RR and Y58PL, and on continuing to identify New World resources which are observed to be both highly important to that world, and either in very short supply (now or in near future) or in abundant supply.

- Insight Gaining Aim re-prioritised to Very High. Engagements still to be restricted to experts in geophysics, as per previous revision. This Aim now key to establishing true, as against openly-published, information to support research under Combined Aim above.

5. Limited Unharmful Exploitation Imperative (see Background) to be included in Mission Objectives, immediate effect. Imperative Priority = 2.

6. Passive Moral Imperative ("specific assistance or improvement") unchanged. Continues to apply to all Missions. Imperative Priority = 3.

7. Individual Captains to conduct ongoing situation analyses, take regular decisions on potential value of continuing observations into all candidate minerals, and make provisional plans for exploitation experiments, as per basic Mission training scenarios. If and when decision taken to suspend or terminate observations, limited exploitation experiments may be commenced, pending receipt of further specific Mission Instructions by Special Communication.

END

The carrier pigeon, its value spent but its inertia unchanged, then calmly continued on its course for infinity.

Captain's Office, *Mater*

The Captain was determined to run this meeting smoothly and speedily.

'I did not expect to have to draw you all together again, so soon after our recent, very effective progress review.

'However, it is essential to do so. I have received another Special Communication.'

Carla and the Chief Surveyor looked pointedly in Quo's direction. She parried with a perfectly executed glare that said, unmistakably, 'Don't look at me!'

The Captain ignored their antics.

'The Council has added a new Imperative to our objectives. It has been named "Limited Unharmful Exploitation" — a fascinating choice of words!

'This change obliges us to place absolute focus on the mineral resources of the Earth. It confirms that we must move at once to the implementation of the plans which the Chief has now fully prepared. It not only requires us to build, as originally missioned, a comprehensive model of the Earth's natural resources (an exercise which, for practical reasons that we all understand and accept, we have scarcely begun) — it also requires me to stand ready to implement some basic exploitation experiments on which, as you are well aware, the Chief and I have been briefed as part of our mission training.

'You will all soon become familiar, as before, with the full text of the latest Special Communication. Meanwhile, are there any immediate questions?'

There were none.

'In that case, Phase One of our Mission will be considered officially complete when, but only when, Antonio Murano has returned safe and free to his home environment. Our support of that outcome remains paramount.'

Quo and Carla both nodded their unreserved acceptance of the Captain's crystal-clear mandate, and the Chief Surveyor smiled her acknowledgement of the implied order to commence Phase Two as soon as that goal was achieved.

'Now, my friends,' winked the Captain, opening her desk drawer and removing a bottle and four sparkling glasses. 'I have a few opinions of my own to share with you, before allowing you to return to your duties.'

When their glasses were fully charged, the Captain continued her rather less formal thinking.

'I realise that we have not yet spread the net of our general Insight Gaining very widely. We are situated over Africa, so we have been limited to the territories in that section of the Earth's circumference. From that base we chose, arbitrarily but with sensible intent, to operate initially on the continent of Europe.

'But I have no doubt, from the limited but already useful content of our General Facts Model, that we could have much more to learn, in terms of the totality of human mores, from a similar level of observation of the Americas, or of China, or possibly of several other major regions of population and power.

'We are all aware of the potential duration of our full Mission. In that context, the amount of time we have spent in Europe — less than three Earth weeks — is very small.

'For the time being, we must abandon our gaining of insights into the general integrity of the Earth's peoples and their leaders. I am already resigned to such peremptory changes of direction. But I have little doubt that our leaders will re-prioritise that aspect of our Mission at some stage. Everything comes around ...'

Quo was clearly keen to participate, and appeared a little frustrated.

'Are you suggesting, ma'am, that we do not, even now, have a complete Mission policy and a stable set of Imperatives and Aims?'

'But of course we do not, Number Two! Have you perhaps lost your famed abilities at Chess? We are little more than pawns in the grand game of empire — and, in truth, you know that as well as I do, my friend!'

Quo nodded, rather abashed, and resolved to keep her mental silence for the rest of the meeting.

The Captain, acute observer and fine manager that she was, immediately refilled the glasses of her trusted team-mates and changed the subject.

'You will all, I hope, recall the rarely mentioned "Passive Moral Imperative". So rarely mentioned that, as you will later notice, the Council felt the need to remind us of its main features in the latest Special Communication!'

As her colleagues all smiled their polite smiles, she turned to look Quo straight in the eyes.

'In my considered opinion, Number Two, you have implemented that Imperative with great flair and passion, in your sustained and hopefully successful efforts to encourage those true-hearted individuals, with whom you have engaged on Earth, to persevere on their paths of immaculate intent. You are the very embodiment of the Moral Imperative. I raise my glass to you!'

Quo — wise, unassailable old Quo — who only moments earlier had been teased and silenced, smiled a smile almost as broad as Carla the Finder's, and happily acknowledged her Captain's honest praise and the toasts of her highly respected colleagues.

Then the Captain looked hard at Carla.

'Your gift to Toni was inspired and wonderful. Return now to your post, take back your personal watch, and safeguard him until he is home.'

'I will.'

Off the Road Again

Toni's journey home through the Spanish night, back under Carla's own watchful eye, was not a relaxing one. It was two hours before he got properly off to sleep, and after that he woke up many times in a very confused state of mind. At last, after he had endured the hour-long wait at Miranda del Ebro, his second train pulled in to Bilbao just before seven-thirty.

He had done his homework thoroughly at Madrid station the previous evening. He stayed on his own platform for fifteen minutes, then went onto the concourse, threw his ticket into a waste bin, and studied the board for the platform number of the 0757 overnight arrival from Barcelona.

When that other train pulled in, he merged into the stream of people leaving it, and walked out of the station into the early morning sunshine of his hometown.

He wandered around the nearby streets for half an hour or more, then went for a quick café breakfast, plucking up his courage for what was to come. Finally, when he was ready, he marched confidently down the Gran Vía, across the square where he had picked up that taxi, and then past the café where he had spotted that elegant young woman with the crimson scarf ...

'Yes,' he thought. 'I believe I'm myself again.'

He continued alongside the park, then turned left towards the headquarters of the Bilbao police forces. As he approached the doors, a voice whispered gently in his ear.

'Be brave, *mi amigo* ...'

He heard it, but he did not understand ...

* * *

'*Buenos días*. My name is Antonio Felipe Murano.'

'Yes?'

'I was kidnapped ... and I've been released ... and I wish to make a statement.'

The young officer on the front desk had not encountered this particular situation in his training, and a detective sergeant was immediately summoned and given a whispered briefing.

The sergeant ushered Toni rather uncertainly into an interview room.

'Please just tell me just a little more, sir — and then I will be able to decide who else needs to join our discussion.'

'Well,' said Toni, ready to tell everything if only he were allowed to, 'I live here — in the centre of Bilbao. I was last here two and a half weeks ago, when I got caught up in a police raid on a café just up the road. But you released me after a while — and then ... well ... then I was sort of ... kidnapped.'

'Are you hurt at all, sir? Do you need a doctor?'

'No — I'm fine!'

'In that case, do you mind waiting a few moments? I must talk to a special branch inspector. Can I get someone to bring you a cup of coffee ...?'

* * *

Toni vaguely recognised the faces of the two people who walked into the room three minutes later. Despite his shorter hair, the woman certainly recognised him.

'Antonio Murano! So you have come to give yourself up!'

'No! I've told the other officers already! I was kidnapped!'

The inspector was efficient by nature, and usually single-minded, but she was no fool. She looked into Toni's eyes, and already had a strong suspicion that he was telling the truth. But she would keep her options open for a while, and see how he responded to a little pressure. So she noisily ordered a special guard on the door, agreed reluctantly that Toni could have the cup of coffee which had just arrived, demanded one for herself, and motioned her own sergeant to sit down.

'Talk to me, Antonio. You're not under arrest. But I'd like to tape-record this — is that OK with you?'

Toni nodded, and the sergeant moved over to the machine.

'You were there, weren't you?' said Toni to the inspector. 'Waiting in the wings while the other men were questioning me ...'

'Yes, I was — and I have been involved ever since. So tell me what happened after you were released ...'

The tape recording began.

'Well, the police car took me home from the café. I sat down and tried to understand what had been happening to me. I'd only been there about half an hour when the door buzzer rang.

'I though it must be the police again. I opened the door. There was a big man standing there, with a mask over his whole face. He put his hand over my mouth and pushed me back inside, and closed the door, and told me to keep quiet or he would make sure I did ...

'He made me sit on the sofa. I was very scared. Then he asked me what I'd said to the police. I told him exactly what I'd told them — that I'd seen that woman ... and then I'd decided to follow her ... and that was all.

'But he didn't believe me. He asked me, over and over again, who else I had seen at the café. I kept saying "I can't remember!" And he kept asking me what else I had told the police. I kept saying "Nothing!" Eventually he gave up. Then he went quiet for a very long time.

'Finally he took out his phone, and made a call, and said some things I didn't understand at all — about how he "couldn't take the risk of letting it drop", and that he could "try to put them off the scent", and that I'd have to "be there for the next test" ...

'Then he told me I was going to have to help them. He asked me who lived at our apartment. I told him. He asked if I had a girlfriend. I said "Yes". Then he said ...' (Toni's voice was wavering very convincingly) '... he said if I co-operated, and didn't go to the police or anyone else, then everything would be fine. But if I didn't do what they wanted — then my mother and Paula would also be kidnapped ...

'Then we just waited for ages. The house phone kept ringing, and later the door buzzer, and Paula was calling out for me. Each time, he warned me to ignore it. Finally his own phone rang again.

'After that I just did everything he told me to. I had to pack my rucksack and book a flight to Rome the next morning. Then he made me sit down and try to relax with a glass of beer and some music. Then he got me to write two little notes, to Paula and my parents.

'He gave me the address of a café in Rome, and told me to be there at two-fifteen the next afternoon, and to wait for a further contact.

'Then he said I must go straight out and get plenty of cash to take with me, and buy a GPS unit, and take some fixes at both cafés. "That will confuse them, too," he said to himself.

'Then he left, telling me not to talk to anybody for any reason, and warning me again what would happen if I disobeyed him.

'I did exactly what he'd told me to do. I didn't answer the phone, even though it kept ringing, or the door-buzzer — even when Paula came back and called out for me. I was just too scared for her sake, and my mother's ...

'In the morning I took the fix in Bilbao, and I caught the planes to Madrid and Rome.

'I went to the café just before two-fifteen, and I took the other GPS fix. Then I waited. But five minutes later I heard police sirens coming closer and closer, and I panicked. I got up from the table and hurried away as the police cars stopped outside.

'But I had only gone two hundred metres down the road and around the corner when someone came up behind me and said "Keep walking — and don't make a sound or try to run ... you know what will happen if you do". And then he seemed to be speaking on a mobile phone ...

'A couple of minutes later, a car with very dark windows drew up alongside me, and the voice told me to get in. So I did. The driver had a big hat on and I couldn't see his face at all. As I sat down in the back seat, the other man pulled a hood over my head, and everything went dark. Then he got in next to me, and we drove away ...

'The man said their plan had misfired because I had walked out twenty seconds too soon. I was worried about what they would do to punish me ...

'We drove around for hours. The man kept making short phone calls, in an Italian dialect I didn't understand. Sometimes we were moving slowly in the city. Then we were obviously out on a motorway. Then in the country. Then back in the city. We stopped at one point, and the man made me give him my wallet. He told me he was taking my plastic cards. Then I think the driver got out, and came back five minutes later. They gave me back my wallet — I could feel that both cards were in their place. Then we drove off again, out into the country ...

'Eventually we stopped and they let me out and took me indoors, and put me in a room and locked the door behind me. Then they called out that I could take off the hood and relax — but that I must make no sound. I was in a little bedroom in some sort of farmhouse in the middle of fields and woods. Nothing else in sight. And there were solid lumps of timber screwed onto the little window frame.

'I think only one of them stayed behind when the car drove off. He brought food for me regularly, and took me to the toilet when I needed it. I always had to put the hood on before any contact with him. So I never saw his face.

'They kept me there for over two weeks. At least I had my watch to keep track of time and dates! I got very bored and very angry. They'd taken my mobile phone, of course — and the GPS unit. I did have a book with me, and there were some old newspapers in my room — and I read them over and over again! But I never argued. I just kept hoping it would soon all be over ...

'Then last Wednesday evening, just after dark, I heard the sound of a car arriving. They told me to pack my bag and put the hood on. They took me out to the car (it smelt like the same one). Then we just drove and drove, very fast, only pausing for petrol. They gave me food and drink when I wanted it, and a few times they left the main road and stopped in a deserted spot, and we took turns to ... you know. On three of those stops they let me take off the hood. The light was so bright the third time! But all I could see was trees, and they ordered me not to turn round, of course ...

'At one point they pulled the car over, stuck a piece of tape over my mouth, and gave me the same old warnings about keeping perfectly quiet. Then they made me get in the boot (it was a very big boot, I think), and drove off again. They let me out ten minutes later, and we carried on. They did the same thing once again, many hours later. That's when I guessed it must have been for border crossings ...

'At last I could tell we had arrived in a big city, and eventually we stopped.

'And the man in the back seat spoke to me. "You're in Barcelona. Here's your rucksack. We don't need you any more. You'll have to talk to the police. That's all right, now. We won't hurt anyone if you do. You'll need a shave and a hairwash first. We're parked right outside a barber's shop. When I take the hood off, get out and go straight through the door and keep walking inside. Don't turn around. If you do, I will come in and get you and everyone will be in big trouble." I did just what he said. The daylight was so dazzling! And I never saw the car again.

'I decided I didn't just want a hairwash. I wanted to try and get the whole thing out of my head. So I told them to cut it quite short. And I certainly needed a shave. I felt a bit better after that.

'It was early evening again. I had no idea where I was in the city, and I didn't care. I just wanted to go home. So I grabbed a taxi, went to the station, had something to eat, and got on the night train.

'And here I am. And now I want to see my parents, please ... and Paula!'

The inspector asked him lots of questions: rather harshly to begin with, more sympathetically as time passed. Every answer Toni gave matched closely with his first full account, and he never added a single further detail, simply saying "I don't know" when he simply did not know.

* * *

They left him to drink another cup of coffee, while they searched his rucksack in the inspector's office.

She had not uttered a word since they had left the interview room. But the sergeant offered an opinion.

'What a story! Straight out of a B-movie. Load of nonsense, every word of it!'

The inspector disagreed.

'Murano? That shrinking violet? He couldn't even invent a story like that, let alone stick to it under questioning! Look at him. He's a tired, dispirited student who's almost certainly been abducted. Poor kid. But he hasn't been physically harmed, and he seems to have coped with it all right. I'm not going to let him waste any more of our time than necessary. We still have no evidence against him. We know he went to Rome. There's no law against that. That police sighting of him near the café, and the cash machine alerts, and everything in his rucksack — they all corroborate his story perfectly! And he *is* our citizen — but the physical kidnapping is not our crime, it's the Italians'! So we'll give them our news, just like they gave us theirs, and let them get on with it. I've got my own suspicions anyway, about whether we're really dealing with criminals here, or some other clandestine agency ...'

The sergeant wisely decided not to argue. The inspector continued.

'We'll get the doctor to examine him right now, of course. We'll ask for his unofficial opinion on the boy's state of mind. Then we'll get Murano to volunteer to come back for a lie detector test as soon as it can be set up over the weekend. He'll agree to that, of course. Then he can go home — I've got nothing to charge him with, so we don't have to worry about bail. We'll watch the apartment until he's taken the test. But he'll pass it! Believe me, he's telling the whole truth ...'

And the inspector did not wish for another tangle with Toni's father just yet. She knew the strong-willed preacher would give her plenty of his attention in the hours and days to come. So she decided not to alert the parents to their son's return. When the medical examination was completed, she just ordered a patrol car to drive him straight home.

* * *

As Toni inserted his key into the door of his parents' apartment, a voice whispered gently in his ear once more.

'*Hasta la vista, Toni. Hasta la vista ...*'

He paused, turned around, shook his head in mild puzzlement, and opened the door.

There was nobody at home. Friday afternoon, of course — both out at work. But they would be back soon. He was safe now.

He went straight to his bedroom and dumped the rucksack on his bed. Then he saw a small pile of unopened envelopes sitting neatly on his desk. He flicked through them and stopped as soon as he recognised Paula's handwriting ...

Friday 28 March

Dearest Toni ...

I'm really sorry you did not try to talk with me before you left so suddenly the other day. It took us all greatly by surprise! I know your mother is very unhappy — and your father too, though he won't be showing it. I hope you'll be particularly kind to them now that you're back.

I had a very special reason for asking you to meet me at our bar on Monday afternoon. But I never got a chance to tell you my news, or to hear your reaction to my plans. Believe me, I've tried to phone you many times. But I could never get through. So I had to carry on and make my decision without you.

And now I feel I must tell you about it, even though it has to be in a letter. There's no other way, is there?

Toni, I've learned a lot about myself in the past few months — but I really don't think you've noticed anything different, have you?

I know now that it is time for us to part. I truly hope this will not hurt you too badly. You've been a good and faithful friend to me. Thank you.

But I've had a new friend for many weeks now. She lives here, in Bilbao. Her name is Lisa.

She's wonderful, Toni. We're very happy together. She's a few years older than me — and she's married. But, like me, she has now learned her own truth, and has taken her own decision ... and she will change things as soon as she can.

Toni, I do hope you'll get to know Lisa one day. I'm certain you'll like her immediately — there's something very special about her, something indescribable. She's beautiful ... so beautiful ... long dark hair, and a gorgeous smile ...

And you'll never guess how I met her — it's really ironic! Do you remember the gift voucher you gave me last Christmas? For the new beauty salon ...

Well, I'd only been there five minutes when she walked in and sat down right opposite me. She was wearing a lovely red silk scarf ...

Printed in the United Kingdom
by Lightning Source UK Ltd.
134689UK00002B/253-258/A